BEYOND
A BROKEN SKY

Also by Suzanne Fortin

All That We Have Lost
The Forgotten Life of Arthur Pettinger

BEYOND A BROKEN SKY

Suzanne Fortin

An Aria Book

This edition first published in the UK in 2022 by Head of Zeus Ltd,
part of Bloomsbury Publishing Plc

9 7 5 3 1 2 4 6 8

A catalogue record for this book is available from the British Library.

ISBN (PB): 9781800243804
ISBN (E): 9781800243798

Cover design: Rory Kee

Typeset by Siliconchips Services Ltd UK

Printed and bound in Great Britain by
CPI Group (UK) Ltd, Croydon CR0 4YY

Head of Zeus Ltd
First Floor East
5–8 Hardwick Street
London EC1R 4RG

WWW.HEADOFZEUS.COM

Dedicated to the English village of East Chinnock and
Anton Günther

'We must accept finite disappointment
but never lose infinite hope.'
Martin Luther King, Jr

1
Rhoda

2022

She liked to come out here when the first craggy fingers of dawn were breaking across the horizon. When she could hear nothing but the lap of the water against her ears as she floated on her back, turned away from the shore and gazing out as the morning sun broke cover. When the world rotated and another day tempted her with promises of good times and better things to come, and when she hoped that by the time the earth had turned on its axis, those promises would be fulfilled.

Rhoda had already looked at her social media accounts that day. The hope that one morning she would wake up to the news she longed for never left her, because if she didn't have hope, what did she have?

The crunch of feet on the stony West Sussex beach broke through the stillness and Rhoda rolled onto her front, casting a casual glance towards the sound. It was Shani – another early morning swimmer. A veteran compared to Rhoda's five years of open water swimming, Shani had been taking a dip in the sea every day since she was in her late teens. Rhoda had never asked Shani how old she was, but she had to be in her seventies. The salt water clearly hadn't done her any harm. Shani waved as she slipped off her towel and, bare-footed, trotted across the pebbles and shingle as if she was walking on a deep pile carpet, unlike Rhoda, who still picked her way gingerly across the painful terrain.

They exchanged good mornings as Shani dipped her shoulders under the water and swam out towards Rhoda.

'Rather fresh this morning,' said Shani.

'Roll on the summer.'

It was April and, although the air temperature was warming up, the sea was still cold.

'So, what's on the agenda this week?'

Shani always took an interest in Rhoda's work and posed the same question every Monday morning.

'I'm going to look at a chapel in Somerset today. It's on a privately owned farm.'

'Somerset? That's a bit of a way.'

'Yes, but it will be worth it. The chapel has a rather special stained-glass window that needs looking at. Apparently, it was made by an Italian prisoner of war. Looks like the chapel is being relocated to the museum,' Rhoda explained, swimming breaststroke alongside her friend.

The local museum at Singlewood, where Rhoda rented a workshop and undertook some freelance work for them from time to time, was located on fifty acres of Sussex countryside, with over sixty historic buildings on site, together with gardens, walks and a millpond. First opened in the early 1970s, when the local village rallied together to save a medieval banquet hall due for demolition to make way for a new bypass, the museum had grown from there, and now the charitable trust was hoping the chapel would be its latest addition.

'I've got to go down and make an assessment of the glass window.'

'A POW, you say? It's easy to forget we had plenty of POW camps in England during the war.'

'It is fascinating, really,' said Rhoda. 'I'm interested to see what the workmanship was like. I've been sent pictures of the window but I'm looking forward to seeing it in real life.'

They spent another five minutes in the sea before Rhoda needed to leave. She had a stained-glass commission she wanted to deliver on her way to Somerset that morning.

'I'll see you later in the week!' she called as she picked up her towel and wrapped it around her wet hair. She pulled her other towel around her shoulders and slipped her feet into her flip-flops.

Shani waved from the water and Rhoda headed back to the flat where she had lived for over five years now; although it was tiny, she wouldn't swap it for the world. She'd worked two jobs and saved every penny she had in order to get together enough for a deposit, and despite tying herself into a mortgage for what was probably the rest of her working life, to Rhoda, it was worth every single penny. It was hers and no one could take that away from her. She had a home and the security that went along with that. She could have afforded something bigger and more modern, had she been willing to compromise on location, but she'd hated the thought of not being able to wake up to the sound of the sea crashing on the shoreline and the seagulls squawking overhead. It gave her a sense of freedom, something which had been lacking during the years she'd spent growing up in care of the local authority.

Back in her apartment, Rhoda showered and dressed for the day ahead, but before she set off on her drive to Somerset, she sat down with a cup of tea and opened the social media apps on her phone for the second time that day.

First, she opened the Facebook page 'Dean Sullivan – Missing Person' and scrolled down for any new comments or messages. She had the alerts on, but she still liked to check, just in case something slipped through the notifications.

There was nothing.

No comments.

No messages.

No new information.

And one unfollow.

That hurt the most. Someone had lost interest in her brother's disappearance. Someone had given up on him ever being found. Someone no longer cared. Rhoda took a sip of her tea. There were still 209 members – 209 people who still cared about Dean.

Rhoda uploaded a picture she'd taken that morning down on the beach. She'd caught the sun just as it had tipped the horizon. She added the caption. 'Another day passes and we are still thinking of you Dean. Please get in touch if you see this. We miss you.'

She tried to post every week to keep the page active, in the hope it would jog someone's memory. There were 209 people out there who would be reminded that her brother was still missing; 209 people who might otherwise forget as the years rolled on.

Next, she checked the UK Missing Persons page. It had been updated overnight with a picture of a muddy trainer, placed next to a tape measure. Scottish police had found the footwear and human remains washed up on the west coast.

Rhoda looked at the picture. Was it the sort of trainer Dean would wear? Was he even in Scotland, or had he ever gone to Scotland? She had no idea. A lot could happen in ten years. She peered closely at the trainer: Nike, size 8, according to the information. Dean was a size 9. She sighed and hoped a family would be able to identify the shoe; at least they would have some sort of closure, even if it was the worst possible outcome.

The drive down to Somerset was stress-free, with only a little traffic congestion as Rhoda went through the New Forest, making a detour to New Milton, where she dropped off the commissioned piece of glass she'd been working on for the past month. It was for a feature stairwell of a converted barn, and the owners had sought Rhoda out through her website. Rhoda had been particularly pleased with this job as it was a substantial amount of money and meant it covered the majority of her bills for the next two months, with enough to reinvest into the business and cover her living expenses. Meeting her bills was a constant source of pressure, but Rhoda couldn't ever imagine herself working for anyone. She liked being her own boss; she liked the autonomy which came with it and, for her, that balanced – and, in some cases, outweighed – the burden and loneliness of independence.

The Somerset farm, Telton Hall, where the chapel was situated, was part of a compulsory purchase order; it stood on the outskirts of a small village where a sea of green hills rolled out beyond. The views were stunning, and Rhoda couldn't help mourning a little for the loss of the environment once the ground workers came in and flattened everything to make way for over three thousand new homes.

Telton Hall was situated on the edge of the village, behind a creamy-coloured stone wall. Two piers heralded the entrance to the farm. Rhoda came to an abrupt halt in the road. Blocking her way, preventing her from swinging into the drive, was a tractor – a blue Massey Ferguson, to be precise – and sitting in the cab was an elderly man. Rhoda reversed a little to allow the tractor through. She flashed her lights and put up her hand to the farmer. He glared back at her but made no effort to move.

It wasn't until Rhoda switched off the car radio and buzzed down her window that she realised the tractor's engine wasn't even running. Had it broken down?

Rhoda drummed her fingers on the steering wheel for a moment, waiting to see if anything was going to happen, but the farmer didn't look to be in any hurry to move the vehicle or even to get out of his cab. She decided to go over and speak to him.

'Morning!' she called up to the cab. 'I have an appointment at Telton Hall. Would you be able to let me in, please?'

Now she was closer, Rhoda estimated the farmer to be in his mid-seventies, and it struck her that he might actually be the owner of the farm.

'Mr Hartwell?'

He looked down at her.

'Yes. You from the museum?'

'Yes, that's right. Rhoda Sullivan.' She smiled up at him, pleased with the breakthrough. 'I've come to have a look at the stained-glass window.'

'I know.'

He sat back in his seat and looked straight ahead.

Well, this wasn't quite going to plan.

'Could you let me in, please?' She paused, waiting for a response, but there was none. 'Or shall I park here on the road and walk in?'

'No one is coming in.' Mr Hartwell remained staring ahead of him.

'But I need to assess the window. Did the museum not explain that to you?'

'Yes. And, as I said, no one is coming in.' He moved his gaze to look at her again. 'Not you. Not the council. Not the developers. Not anyone.'

Rhoda recognised the steely look of determination in his eyes. Jack Hartwell was deadly serious.

'I'm sorry,' she said, 'there's obviously an issue I don't know about. Is it something I could help with at all?'

He gave a snort. 'Ask your boss at the museum. I told him what the score was.'

Rhoda took out her phone. She had no idea what Mr Hartwell was referring to, and she was sure the museum hadn't passed any message on to her about a problem. She scrolled through her emails and text messages but there was nothing from the museum. She'd have to ring them.

'There's been some misunderstanding somewhere,

Mr Hartwell. If you give me a moment, I'm just going to make a phone call.'

The farmer shrugged. 'Do what you like, but I'm not moving.'

Rhoda went back to her car and called the museum office. Eventually, the call was picked up by Eric, one of the managers. Rhoda quickly explained the situation.

'So, I'm currently sitting in my car in some sort of stand-off with Mr Hartwell and his tractor.'

'Oh, bloody hell, just what we need,' said Eric. 'I didn't think he was serious. I thought he was just being difficult. Can't you sweet-talk him?'

Rhoda raised her eyebrows. 'Sweet-talk?'

'OK, maybe that's asking a bit much of you.' Eric let out a sigh.

'What exactly is the problem?' Rhoda asked.

'He doesn't want to sell. That's why there's a compulsory purchase order on the farm. Even so, I didn't think Hartwell would be that much of a problem.'

'Ah, so you're not buying the chapel directly from Mr Hartwell?'

Rhoda wasn't privy to how the charity obtained their buildings; that was all dealt with by the committee. She had simply been asked to assess the stained-glass window and the work involved, whether that be carried out back at the museum or in situ.

'No. We're negotiating with the council, who I believe are negotiating with Mr Hartwell. It's all a bit convoluted. The developers are pushing for a completion date as they want to get started, so that doesn't help either.'

'What do you want me to do?'

'Sit tight for now. I'll see if I can speak to him myself.'

Rhoda ended the call and sat back in her seat, looking at Jack Hartwell perched in the cab of the tractor. She couldn't help admiring his defiance. She felt a wave of empathy for the man who was being forced, by the council, to move out of his home. It brought back unwelcome memories of her time spent in care and being moved from one place to another without any autonomy or say in the matter. It brought with it a feeling of complete helplessness, the stripping of any power or control over her life. She'd hated that feeling then, and she hated it just as much now. Her heart really did go out to Mr Hartwell's plight, and she felt guilty for being there.

2
Alice

1945

It had been a long day working in Rice's Department Store and Alice Renshaw was relieved it was finally over. She made her way down the rear staircase to the ground floor, where her friend Jess was waiting for her.

'Sorry I'm late,' she said. 'Bloody Mrs Travers made me take an inventory of all the knitting wool.'

'I'm glad I don't have to work in haberdashery,' said Jess.

'Yeah, menswear is much more exciting than fabric and yarn,' agreed Alice.

'You wouldn't have thought that today,' said Jess. 'I had to serve a man in his eighties, looking for a new shirt. It took ages, he was so fussy. Now, had it been a nice young man or a soldier, that would have been a different matter. But eighty! Come on, how is that fair?'

Alice laughed as they went out of the rear door of the department store.

'Maybe you'll find yourself a nice rich older man – one who has a particular penchant for ties or socks or vests.'

Jess pulled a face. 'It's all right for you to joke about it. At least you've got lover boy.'

'Lover boy? If you mean US Airman Brett Cunningham, then yes,' replied Alice with a grin. She slipped her arm through Jess's. 'There's a dance on the base tomorrow night – you're going to come, aren't you? Brett's friend Howard will be there.'

Jess shrugged. 'I don't know. Howard's got a girlfriend back home in America.'

'Still come, though,' said Alice. 'He likes you. As a friend. I don't want to go on my own.'

'Aha, so that's why you want me to go.'

'No! It's not. We always do things together. Come on, please, Jess. I've got a spare pair of stockings you can wear.'

'That's bribery.'

'But worth it. Sheer nylon with a seam up the back.'

Alice raised her eyebrows at her friend. One of the benefits of an American boyfriend was the luxury items that they just couldn't get in England anymore.

Jess sighed. 'Oh. All right. But can't you see if Brett's got another friend, preferably one that's single?'

'I'll see what I can do.'

They caught the bus home and spent the fifteen-minute journey to their Suffolk village talking about what they were going to wear for the dance. Alice had exhausted every item in her meagre wardrobe since she'd started dating Brett.

'I thought I might have a look at my mum's clothes,' she said, tamping down the sadness that accompanied the thought.

'Ah, that will be nice,' said Jess. 'She'd have loved that.'

'They're in a suitcase at the back of my wardrobe. Dad wanted to throw them out, but I wouldn't let him.'

Alice had actually got into a huge row with her dad about the clothes. He'd been all for throwing them on the fire, but Alice hadn't been able to bear the thought. For the same reasons it pained her father to keep any of her mother's possessions, it pained Alice to even contemplate letting them go. In the end, she'd persuaded her dad to let her hold on to them if she promised to keep them tucked away where he wouldn't have to face looking at them on a daily basis.

The bus pulled up outside the village shop and the girls hopped off, before walking home. They lived just a few doors apart in a row of terraced cottages, and as they reached Alice's house, she could see the glow of the standard lamp in the living room. Her father worked as a gardener at the 'big house' in the village and got home around the same time as she did.

'Have fun tonight and don't do anything I wouldn't do.' Jess gave a snigger and nudged Alice with her elbow.

Alice rolled her eyes and smiled good-humouredly.

'That doesn't leave a lot!'

She waved at her friend as they parted company.

Alice's father was in the kitchen already, peeling the carrots.

'You're late,' he said, not looking up.

'Stocktake,' replied Alice, quickly shrugging off her jacket and hanging it on the back of the door. 'Here, I'll do that, Dad.'

She washed her hands at the kitchen sink and took over

from her father. She could murder a cuppa but that would have to wait until she'd sorted tea out.

That evening they were having cauliflower cheese with carrots and bacon. Fortunately, Alice's father was given a small quantity of vegetables each week from Mrs Armitage up at the big house to supplement their rations. It wasn't long before they were sitting down at the kitchen table, eating their evening meal. The cauliflower cheese was much blander these days, with no cheese going into the actual dish. The small amount of cheese they were allowed each week was grated and sprinkled on the top to give the sauce some sort of flavour.

There was a slice of apple pie left over from yesterday's meal, and Alice happily let her father have that. Brett nearly always brought along chocolate of some description with him when they met, so she'd be able to satisfy her sweet tooth later.

Once she'd cleared the table and done the dishes, Alice sprinted up the stairs to get herself washed and changed. She'd wear one of her everyday dresses for seeing Brett that evening. They weren't going anywhere special, just for a walk along the riverbank. Now and again, Brett took her to the village pub, but it invariably drew some sort of complaint from her father once the village gossips had got to work. It wasn't that the villagers minded Brett; in fact, they were very welcoming of the American servicemen, who were always polite and respectful. For some reason, though, her dad wasn't so impressed. Alice wasn't even convinced his disapproval was because Brett was American; she was pretty sure her father wouldn't like any man she saw, because then he'd have to admit she was a grown woman and might just marry and leave him. Then who would be there to do all the cooking and cleaning?

Alice let out a sigh as she brushed her hair. It was a mean-spirited thought, and as her gaze fell on the photograph of her mother resting against the mirror, Alice immediately felt guilty. She turned her thoughts back to Brett and the excitement of seeing him – it was a sure-fire way to bolster her mood.

As she came downstairs, ready to go, her father looked up at her.

'I take it you're off out tonight.'

'Yes. I'm meeting Brett,' said Alice, trying to sound casual.

'You're still seeing him, then?'

'Of course.'

Her father gave a snort. 'Don't go getting yourself too attached. You know what those Yanks are like. Anyway, he'll be off before you know it. Might not even come back.'

Alice held in the sigh that threatened to escape. She was sure somewhere deep inside, her father was only looking out for her, but sometimes she'd just wished he would be a bit happier for her.

'Brett's a nice bloke, Dad,' she said. 'He's not like that.'

Her father put down the paper he was reading.

'You can't say that until it's put to the test. You mark my words. Half of them have got a girlfriend or a wife back home.'

'Half of them are young men who haven't got anything of the sort,' retorted Alice. She didn't really know why she was arguing with her father; he was a stubborn old sod at times. 'Anyway, let's not fall out about it. I'll see you later.'

It was often a fine line they trod with each other these

days, neither wanting to give way to the other but equally, neither wanting to get into a full-blown argument. Going head-to-head with each other without her mother to reason with them and defuse the tension was not a good idea. Alice pulled her coat around her. She missed her mother so much. She had always been optimistic and happy. She had brought a sense of joy wherever she went. Since her death two years earlier, Alice wasn't sure her father had laughed once, let alone smiled.

Alice hurried through the village towards the bridge which was her and Brett's usual meeting place. She felt particularly tired that evening and put it down to the long day at work. Ideally, she'd like to be tucked up in bed right now with a good book, but she didn't want to give up the opportunity of seeing Brett. The American servicemen got a lot of free time while they were here, but Alice was aware it was borrowed time and Brett could be called up at any moment to go on a bombing mission. She couldn't bear the notion of him not coming back and shrugged away the gloomy thoughts.

As she turned the corner from the High Street, she could see the tall frame of Brett Cunningham standing on the bridge, leaning rather laconically against the wooden railing, smoking a cigarette. He looked like the lead actor in a Hollywood movie. Alice's breath caught in her throat as he saw her and smiled, flicking his cigarette into the water and pushing himself away from the bridge.

'Hi,' he said as she reached him.

He pulled her in towards him and kissed her on the mouth.

Alice felt the thrill of excitement and wrapped her arms

around his neck. She didn't care if anyone saw them. As they pulled out of their embrace, Brett produced two bars of chocolate from his pocket.

'Here – thought you might like these.'

'Oh, thank you!'

Alice popped them into her bag. She'd quite like to scoff at least one bar right now, but she really should show some restraint.

'And I have these for you.' Brett presented two packets of silk stockings. 'You said your friend Jess needed some.'

'Oh, you're ace,' declared Alice. 'Thanks so much.'

After she put the stockings in her bag along with the chocolate bars, they began to walk along the river path. Brett took her hand and Alice felt an overwhelming surge of love for him. It didn't surprise her. She'd known she was falling in love with him soon after they started dating. If she was honest, she was already in love with him.

They reached the spot on the riverbank where they liked to sit. It was a few minutes' walk out of the village, where a large willow tree bowed over the riverbank; its hanging branches provided a curtain of privacy on one side, and a wall of bulrushes stood proud in the water on the other side of them, effectively hiding them from view.

They made themselves comfortable on the grass bank and Brett trailed a finger up her arm, across her shoulder, brushing her neck and jawline.

'You're so beautiful,' he said softly, his fingers now finding her hair and gently teasing some strands free from the pins.

Alice gave an embarrassed laugh. She pulled up her legs and rested her hands and face on her knees, looking sideways at him.

'You're not so bad yourself.'

'Why is it you British girls can't take a compliment?'

'Us British girls? Have you tried that line on lots of others, then?' Alice noted the unexpected prickle in her voice.

'Only you,' replied Brett. 'I'm just going by what the other guys have said.'

'You talk about me, do you?' Again, Alice was more annoyed than she wanted to be.

'Hey, don't take offence. That's exactly what I mean. I talk about you because I can't believe how lucky I am. I want everyone to know what a beautiful girl I have.' He smiled at her and any annoyance Alice felt was swept away. Brett moved in and kissed her shoulder. 'Good job I don't take offence. I'm not like the others – I value what I have.'

Alice couldn't help smiling. She'd never known anyone like Brett before – certainly none of the lads in the village. They wouldn't dream of talking so openly or tenderly to a woman. Christ, they'd more likely talk lovingly to their bloody cows before they would their girlfriend.

'I ... I love you.'

She'd said it before she had time to think about it. She swallowed as Brett froze in his caressing of her. His face turned serious, all the humour disappearing in an instant. Oh God, she shouldn't have said anything. She should have just kept that thought to herself. She shook her head and looked away, trying to blink back the tears of humiliation.

'Ignore me,' she muttered. 'I was just being silly.'

His hand found hers. 'You're not being silly at all. And I have no intention of ignoring you.'

Alice turned back to him. He was so handsome and so different from any man she'd ever come across before. His dark hair, deep brown eyes and smooth flawless skin set him apart from all the others. He was exotic by comparison to all the boys she had grown up with. Brett leaned closer and kissed her, his hands finding her hairpins, discarding them so her hair cascaded over her shoulders.

'So beautiful,' he murmured.

Alice closed her eyes. She didn't care they were on the riverbank; she didn't care there was a war raging in Europe; she didn't care what her dad would think if he knew, or what her mum would think if she could have known. She didn't care about anything, only being in that moment with Brett – the man she loved.

3
Nate

2022

Nate Hartwell had got the call half an hour before, telling him that his father was staging some sort of protest in his driveway. The call had come from his Aunt Aggie, who lived across the road in Telton Cottage.

'I don't know what your father's up to now, but he's got the bloody tractor parked across the driveway and refusing to allow anyone in,' she'd reported to him.

Nate could imagine Aggie peering through the net curtain of her living room window from her wing back chair as she observed the comings and goings of the village of Telton.

He was just seconds from the village, perhaps going a little faster than he should when he rounded the bend, and he had to steer sharply to avoid an estate car parked on the side of the road. Nate swore under his breath at the near miss, but his attention was distracted at the sight of his father sitting in the cab of the tractor. He pulled up at the gateway and got out of his car.

It was a warm day for April and Nate rolled up his shirtsleeves, leaving his jacket on the passenger seat.

'All right, Dad?' he called up to the cab, lifting his sunglasses to his forehead so he could make eye contact.

'Nate,' Jack replied in acknowledgement. 'Don't tell me, Aggie phoned you.'

Nate gave a sigh and replaced his glasses. 'What are you up to?'

'Just passing the time of day. Got nothing better to do.'

Nate checked his watch. 'Haven't you got an appointment about now?'

Jack shrugged. 'What if I have?'

'You're going to have to let them in.'

'Who says?'

'Come on, Dad. You can't stop people doing their job.' Nate rested his hands on his hips. It was a conversation he'd had plenty of times with his father. Much as no one liked it, the purchase order had been pushed through and Telton Hall was going to be developed. They'd done everything they could to stop it, and Nate thought his father had accepted his fate. 'Why are you doing all this now, Dad?'

'Because I want to and because I can. I don't want anyone here.' He gave a nod down the road and as Nate turned to follow his gaze, he noticed someone sitting in the driver's seat of the car he'd nearly run into.

'Is that the council?' asked Nate.

'Museum.'

'Ah. The chapel.' Nate recalled details of the last email that his father had shown him. 'Look, Dad, you need to let them see the chapel. The museum has nothing to do with the purchase order. They're going to be preserving a part of the farm. They're kind of on our side.'

'Our side?' questioned Jack. 'Didn't think we were on the same side. You're all for letting them take the farm without a fight.'

That wasn't strictly true, and it was disingenuous of his father to suggest otherwise, but Nate didn't feel now was the time to argue over petty details. He'd done everything he could to help his father fight the compulsory purchase order – everything legal, that is. He wasn't about to condone his father's actions. Obstructing the valuation might not technically be illegal, but it certainly wasn't acceptable.

Nate glanced back again at the estate car and then at his father.

'Look, Dad, you've made your point. You've caused a bit of inconvenience but it's pointless. You're not going to stop it going ahead.'

Nate tried again with a more sympathetic approach. To his own ears, he sounded like he was talking to his ten-year-old son, Isaac – gently trying to coax him to do something, like when Isaac wouldn't come out of his room last weekend when he didn't want to go back to his mum's.

'Why don't you take the tractor back to the barn and let them have a look at the chapel? It's not achieving anything sitting here, plus it will save a load of grief from the council.'

Nate turned around at the sound of a car door closing and footsteps approaching. It was the occupant of the car – a woman in her mid to late twenties, not looking particularly official in her jeans, T-shirt and hoody. Her dark hair was tied up in a ponytail; she looked more like she was off on a casual hike.

'Hi,' she said with a smile. 'I'm Rhoda Sullivan from Singlewood Museum in West Sussex.'

'Hi. Nate Hartwell. Jack Hartwell's son,' he said and then added, 'Sorry about this. He's not taking the sale of the farm too well.'

'So, I understand.'

'I won't bore you with the details, but it's a CPO – compulsory purchase order. New housing and all that.' Nate gave a pleading look in his father's direction.

'Which is why he's not happy to see me,' replied the woman.

'Yeah, you could say that. No offence.'

'None taken.' She hesitated but then spoke again. 'I'd be the same if someone wanted to take my home away from me.'

She looked in the direction of Telton Hall.

Nate wasn't certain, but he thought he could detect Rhoda's underlying sense of disapproval that he wasn't sympathetic to his father's plight.

'There's more than one reason why he can't keep the farm on,' Nate found himself replying.

'Telton Hall is a beautiful house. Not quite what I was expecting when I was told it was a farm,' said Rhoda, looking back at Nate.

'It was turned into more of a working farm during the First World War,' explained Nate. 'And has been ever since then – through the Second World War, right up until today.'

'Are they going to develop Telton Hall or pull it down?'

'Apartments, I believe.'

'How long before your father has to be out?'

She asked a lot of questions. Nate replied politely, 'Twelve weeks.'

'Not that long, then. Has he got somewhere else to go? Moving in with you?'

Nate wasn't quite sure how any of it was this woman's business, and again there was that slight edge to her voice, as if she didn't really approve of what was happening. He could do without any judgement on her part. The past two years had been a nightmare, between trying to negotiate with the council and placate his father.

'Look, I'm sorry, but you may be wasting your day waiting for him. He can be very stubborn when he wants to be.'

Rhoda pursed her lips and made a clicking noise with her tongue.

'I'm really sorry, but I need to look at the chapel today. My boss is pressing me for a report. If we leave it too late, we might not have enough time to make all the arrangements to move it.'

'I'm doing my best,' said Nate, feeling irritated. He knew she was just doing her job, but she really had no idea how obstinate his father could be.

He wasn't sure if it was the frustration at his father perched up in the cab of the tractor that was stressing him, or Rhoda Sullivan's tone of disapproval towards him.

Nate was glad when her phone began ringing and she excused herself to take the call. He went over to the tractor, hoisted himself up onto the side steps and opened the cab door so he was level with his dad.

'Honestly, Dad, you need to back this up now and let the

woman in to view the chapel. You know they are perfectly within their rights to call the police,' he continued. 'Imagine all the fuss of you being forcibly removed and carted off down the police station. All this is pointless.'

Nate felt sorry for his dad. He knew how much it would hurt his dad's pride to give in.

'Mr Hartwell!'

It was the woman from the museum calling up to them.

Nate and his father both looked down at her.

'Mr Hartwell,' she said. 'That was my boss on the phone. He wants me to call the police.'

'Told you so,' muttered Nate.

'But I don't really want to do that,' Rhoda continued. 'I am perfectly within my rights as a representative of the museum to view the chapel. I could just climb over the wall and it wouldn't be trespass.'

'Are you listening?' Nate asked his father. He looked down the road and could see some of the locals were gathering to watch with intrigue and, no doubt, amusement.

'But I don't really want to climb over the wall, as that would be a rather undignified way for me to gain access and it would also be embarrassing for you.' She gave a sympathetic smile. 'You could get us both out of an awkward predicament.'

Nate was impressed with her approach. Somehow, she was managing to make it sound like she was on his father's side.

'What do you say, Dad?'

Jack Hartwell blew out a long breath, his brow furrowing like one of his perfectly ploughed fields. Finally, he spoke.

'Do you want to get off while I park this thing up?' His

voice was gruff, but Nate knew his father was covering up his wounded pride.

Nate jumped down from the side of the tractor and went over to Rhoda.

'He's going to let you in. Thanks. Appreciate what you did there. You can tell your boss he doesn't have to get the police involved now.'

'I was never going to let that happen,' said Rhoda. 'I would have been quite happy to hop over the wall, but your father deserves a bit of respect and understanding.'

She turned and went back to her car.

Nate wasn't sure if he'd just been subtly admonished or not. He didn't know what to make of this Rhoda Sullivan woman at all. On one hand, she was kind and empathetic to his father, but on the other, starchy and disapproving towards him.

He drove his car in through the gates of Telton Hall and over the bridge which straddled the stream, parking up near the front of the farmhouse. He could do with getting back to the office but wasn't sure exactly how co-operative his father would be. Using his mobile, he rang his assistant.

'Hey, Marcus, I'm going to be held up here at the farm for another hour or so, but I'll be back in time for my 2.30 appointment. Can you field any calls for me while I'm out?'

Rhoda Sullivan had now pulled up next to him and didn't hesitate as she got out of her car and went over to meet Nate's father, who had parked the tractor in the far corner of the yard.

'Yes, of course,' replied Marcus. 'Anything else you need doing?'

'No, that's all.' Nate watched as Rhoda spoke to his father. 'Thanks a lot, Marcus.'

Marcus was a good lad, and in the six months since Nate had taken on an assistant, the role had been a godsend. It freed Nate up to come out on emergency dashes like this one, and gave him more flexibility with co-parenting.

Nate got out of the car and was rather surprised to see his father smile at Rhoda. That was a quick turnaround. She was like some sort of horse whisperer but with grumpy old farmers instead.

4
Rhoda

2022

Rhoda took a deep breath, genuinely glad Jack Hartwell had agreed to let her into the farm. She knew her boss was on the verge of calling the police, and that was the last thing she wanted. Jack didn't deserve that sort of humiliation when all he was trying to do was hold on to his home.

From the corner of her eye, she could see Jack's son heading over to them. She quickly spoke to Mr Hartwell Senior.

'Let's get up to the chapel and I'll see what I can do.'

Jack nodded and gave a small smile. 'Right you are.'

'I'll just get my boots on,' said Rhoda.

Quickly she changed into the wellingtons she'd brought with her and shrugged on her jacket, before hooking her Singlewood Museum lanyard over her head. Glancing up, she could see Jack's son talking earnestly to his father –

probably wondering what she'd said. Well, he could wonder all he liked. All she'd said to Jack was that when she assessed the stained-glass window, it might be that she recommended the repairs took place in situ, before the chapel was taken down. This, of course, would mean a delay in the sale. She'd given him a knowing look. Although it wouldn't stop the farm being sold in the long run, it would afford Jack Hartwell a little more time in his beloved home.

Telton Hall was built in the same Bath stone as the boundary wall. A driveway swept around to the left, with a meadow on one side and a field on the other. Outside the house itself was a turning circle, laid to lawn, with a pond and water fountain in the centre. Telton Hall wasn't looking its finest, with the stonework grubby and the flower bed, which ran under the windows on the ground floor, looking untended. A rambling vine, possibly ivy, ran along the facework. An oak door occupied the centre of the building, with two sash windows each side and repeated again on the first floor, with an additional window above the front door. Two small dormer windows rested in the roof, overlooking the grounds like beady eyes.

A small terrier scampered around the corner of the house and, with an excited yap, ran right up to Rhoda. A little taken aback at the speed the animal moved, she gave a squeal.

Jack laughed out loud. 'She won't hurt you. She's just happy to make a new friend. Useless as a bloody guard dog.'

Rhoda reached down to give the dog a stroke. It was a dear little thing. 'What's her name?'

'That's Tink,' said Jack. 'She was the runt of the litter, that's why she's so small, even for a Jack Russell. Right, shall we get up to the chapel?' He turned to his son, who was hovering in the background. 'You going back to work?'

'Er ... No. I hadn't planned to. Thought I'd tag along.'

Jack gave a tut. 'Suit yourself.'

Rhoda looked away, slightly embarrassed on Nate Hartwell's part that his father wasn't exactly bowled over at the prospect of Nate accompanying them, but if he wasn't being very supportive towards his father over the forced house move, then perhaps he deserved it. Rhoda hated the idea of any sort of bullying, whether it was outright obvious or subtle and small-scale. The sale was being imposed on Jack, who was clearly hostile to the decision, and the fact that his son didn't appear to hold the same sentiment irked her. She'd always fought for the underdog, even when it had got her in trouble when she was younger.

'Glad to see you brought your boots. There's been a lot of rain this past week,' said Jack as they made their way across the yard. 'The developers, Redridge Housing, are keen to get on with the groundwork. In fact, they wanted to start before the sale had been completed, but I said no.'

'Before you'd even moved out?' asked Rhoda. 'Honestly, they are terrible.'

'It's not unusual,' put in Nate Hartwell. 'Especially in cases like this where it's a dead cert, what with it being a compulsory purchase order.'

'Well, I think it's wrong,' retorted Rhoda, trying not to sound like a petulant child. She turned back to Jack. 'How have the developers been in general? I know some of them use bully-boy tactics to get their own way.'

'I might be an old farmer who's barely been out of

Somerset, but I'm nobody's fool. Don't worry, I have the measure of them. They don't intimidate me.'

'I'm pleased to hear it.'

They walked around the farmhouse and through a gate which opened onto a footpath. The chapel was situated at the top of a small hill.

'Glad it's not raining today,' said Rhoda as they waded through a particularly large puddle that stretched across the track.

A few minutes later, with Tink scampering along after them, they reached the top of the hill.

'I haven't been up here for a while.' Jack was puffing hard, and his cheeks were flushed.

'Are you all right, Dad?' asked Nate, coming to stand beside his father. He rested his hand lightly on Jack's back.

'Don't mind me. I'll be OK in a minute,' said Jack, taking a moment to lean on the stick, carved out of blackthorn, he'd brought with him. 'Don't be fussing now.'

Rhoda exchanged a look with Nate, who gave a small shrug.

'Whoever decided to build the chapel up here must have been dedicated,' remarked Rhoda.

She took the opportunity to take in the view around her, of far-reaching hills and countryside against the backdrop of the Mendip Hills.

'They took their religion seriously, that's for sure,' replied Jack. He appeared to have regained his breath now, much to Rhoda's relief.

It was a small family chapel, not much more than the footprint of a tennis court. It was built from the local Bath stone, a sandy colour which, like Telton Hall, was now a dirty brown after years of being exposed to the elements.

Rhoda walked around the exterior of the building, coming to a halt at the large stained-glass window she'd come to assess. From her viewpoint, she could see the quality of the work involved and the detail of the scene, which depicted animals boarding Noah's Ark with a white dove flying above, holding an olive branch in its beak. From her own research, Rhoda was aware the stained-glass window dated back to the mid-1940s.

'It's beautiful,' she said softly. 'Whoever did this certainly knew their craft.'

Her gaze travelled the length of the window from top to bottom, coming to rest on the huge crack running through the centre of the tracery arch, which, in turn, had caused another crack to make its way through several panes of glass.

'The damage doesn't look too bad,' said Nate, coming to stand next to her.

'Maybe not to the untrained eye,' replied Rhoda. 'Do you know how long it's been like this?'

'It's been repaired once after a storm, back in the forties, but this latest damage is from subsidence.'

'You think you'll be able to save the window?' Jack gave her a sideways look.

Rhoda knew now was the time to deploy her perfectly honed poker face. Years of being in the care system had taught her how to hide her feelings and emotions, so no one knew what she was really thinking. Enigmatic, her foster mother had once described her. That was exactly how Rhoda liked it.

Rhoda looked up at the window again and scrutinised the glass before jotting a few notes down on her iPad and taking several photographs.

'I'll need to see the inside,' she said. 'Do you have an exact date the window was made?'

'Sometime between 1945 and 1947,' replied Jack. 'End of the war.'

'Before your time,' said Rhoda with a smile.

'I wish,' said Jack. 'No. I was a kid during the war.'

'I don't believe you. You're just a spring chicken,' said Rhoda, enjoying the joke with the older man.

'Ha! Are you flirting with me?'

Rhoda couldn't help laughing. 'Just don't tell my boss.' She looked back at the window. 'Do you know anything about the POW who made it?'

'Not much. He and his whole platoon were captured in Tripoli. They spent time in a POW camp in Egypt, then Johannesburg, before they were dispersed between America, Canada and England. Some of the Italian POWs agreed to work on the farms. What with all the able-bodied men being away fighting, folk needed help on the land.'

'Do you know his name? Did he go back to Italy after the war?'

'Not sure about his name.'

'How come he made this window?' asked Rhoda, intrigued by the backstory to such a fabulous piece of craftsmanship.

'The POW was some sort of glazier. It just happened to be his job back home in Italy, so he offered to fix it.'

Rhoda stepped back to get a better view of the gable end of the chapel. From where she was now standing, she could see the whole west side of the building had dipped several inches, causing the crack to weave its way down the stonework.

She was no architect, but from her limited knowledge, the chapel looked to be in relatively good condition. Of course, one of the big hurdles wasn't just dismantling the structure so it could be rebuilt at the museum; it was the practical issue of getting the stone down to the farm.

'Is there any other access up here? Just wondering how we will transport the windows down. What about a tractor? Could you supply us with one?'

Jack picked up Tink and rubbed the dog's ears. 'I'm sure we can come to some agreement.'

Well, he was absolutely right when he said he was nobody's fool. Rhoda was in no doubt that payment would be needed.

'I'm sure we can,' she replied. 'So, shall we have a look inside now?'

'I haven't been in here for a long time,' said Jack.

'Not when the developers or the museum came to survey it?'

'I dealt with that,' said Nate. 'Dad wasn't very well at the time.'

'A touch of bronchitis, that's all,' said Jack.

'When I came up, that's when we realised the building had moved,' explained Nate. 'Prior to that, I don't think anyone's been in there for years. We used to play up here as kids, but the chapel was always locked up.'

'I don't need to see too much,' said Rhoda. 'Just the main window and the smaller side ones. I need to work out how long it will take to remove them. It's usually relatively straightforward as long as the glass isn't too fragile.

'And if it's too fragile?' asked Nate.

'I will just take a bit longer, that's all.'

'How long?' Nate pressed. 'Dad hasn't got an indefinite amount of time left here.'

'As long as it takes,' replied Rhoda, trying – and failing – to keep the edge from her voice. 'I will have a better idea once I've been inside. Oh, there was something I've been asked to check – was the ground consecrated and, if so, has it been deconsecrated?'

'Yes, I had all that done as part of the sale agreement of the land,' said Jack. 'All costs met by Redridge, of course.'

'Of course,' replied Rhoda.

'Right, let's go inside,' said Jack, pushing the key into the lock.

Without too much resistance, the door opened. Tink was in first, nose down, sniffing all around the place.

The smell of the cold and damp was the first thing Rhoda noted as she stepped across the threshold. The interior was thick with a mustiness and a stillness which made the air feel heavy. Their footsteps echoed around the stone walls and ceiling.

Shafts of light shone through the windows, highlighting dust motes in the air and illuminating the inside of the building as the sun managed to cut through the layers of dirt and grime of the main stained-glass window and the three windows on either side of the chapel.

There were several rows of pews, with a central aisle leading to a stone altar. Two tall candelabras made from wrought iron stood either side. Halfway along the east wall was a stone bowl on a plinth.

'Is that a baptism font?' Rhoda asked.

'That's right,' replied Nate. 'Dad was baptised there.'

'Oh wow! That's wonderful,' said Rhoda.

'I was the last one to be done,' said Jack.

'Why was that?' She looked at Nate.

'For some reason, I was baptised down at the village church.'

Rhoda looked towards Jack, expecting an answer. He frowned and gave a shrug. 'His mother wanted it that way.'

Tink was whining and running back and forth from the side of the chapel to Jack.

'What's up with him?' asked Rhoda.

'Probably the mice,' said Jack. With that, Tink scampered off to the side again and started scratching at the ground, stopping every now and again to bark. 'Come on, Tink. Over here. Leave those mice alone.'

The little dog obviously wasn't in the mood for obeying her owner, and continued to scurry around, whining and yapping.

'I'll get her,' said Rhoda.

'No, you get on with what you need to. I'll get her,' said Jack, heading across the chapel towards the side.

'Let me,' said Nate, following his father. 'You sit down there, Dad.'

'Stop fussing,' puffed Jack, waving Nate away with his hand.

Rhoda recognised the pride in the older man's voice. He wasn't the sort to take kindly to old age catching him up, and she could see Nate was conflicted whether to respect his father's wishes or override them and help him.

Rhoda took the decision away from Nate and followed them over. 'What's all the fuss about, Tink?' she said, skirting around the Hartwells to see what the dog had found so fascinating.

She took her torch from her pocket and directed the beam to the ground, ignoring the huff of annoyance from Jack. As she cast the light around the flagstone flooring, she saw that a large stone had once been repointed and one corner had started to sink into the ground, leaving a gap.

'Is there an underground chamber? A crypt? Or anything like that?'

She walked around the flagstone, keeping the torchlight focused on the hole, which was the size of a shoebox. There was a certain amount of light coming in through the windows and the open doors at the end of the chapel, but not enough to see clearly into the recesses.

'Not that I know of,' replied Jack. 'This was just a place of worship, not burial. The family are all nicely settled in the village graveyard, and I dare say I'll be joining them in the not too distant future.'

'Oh, don't,' scolded Rhoda. 'I can't see you going anywhere like that soon.'

'He's far too stubborn for that,' said Nate with a wry smile.

Rhoda shot Nate a look. 'Must be a bit inconvenient for you.'

'What?' Nate glared at her.

Rhoda inwardly winced, realising she'd overstepped the mark. She really ought to keep thoughts like that to herself.

She knew she should apologise but couldn't quite bring herself to do so.

More excited yapping from Tink brought their attention back to the flagstone. The little dog now had her nose in the hole.

'Come on, Tink. Out of there now,' said Jack, moving towards the dog, but before he could reach her, Tink dived down through the gap. 'Tink! Tink! Come here!'

Rhoda looked on with a growing apprehension that the dog wasn't going to come back – either that, or she couldn't.

'Here, let me shine my torch in there,' she said, crouching down beside Jack. 'How long has the flagstone been like this?'

'Must have happened recently. Subsidence, I guess,' replied Nate as he crouched down beside his father. 'Dad, let me do that.'

'No. No, it's OK. I can do it.'

Jack's breathing was laboured as he leaned on his hands and knees.

The last thing Rhoda wanted was for Jack to have some sort of medical episode up here on the hill.

'Let me look,' she said.

'Don't worry, the dog will be out in a minute,' insisted Jack.

Rhoda wasn't so sure. Whatever had enticed the dog down there was far more exciting than being above ground.

Jack got back on his feet, refusing the helping hand his son offered, opting to use his blackthorn stick as leverage, and then sat heavily down on the end of the wooden pew. Rhoda hesitated for a second as she considered the state her new trousers were about to get into. The sound of Tink whining excitedly tipped her judgement and she got down on her hands and knees, ignoring the Hartwells' protests, and shone the torch into the hole. She couldn't see the little dog, but she was sure she wasn't that far away. She didn't fancy putting her hand in and having a feel around; she wasn't quite sure what sort of furry creature she might end up yanking out.

'Any history of rats?' she asked, trying to keep her tone light.

'Pah! Rats. Who knows? I doubt it, there's nothing here for them to live on.'

Jack took a hanky from his pocket and coughed into it.

Rhoda had accepted she was going to have to sacrifice her whole outfit for the dog and was now lying on her stomach to get a better view of where the canine might be. Pressing her face down on the cold flagstone to get a better view, she shone the torch right in.

Two little eyes reflected back in the torch beam.

'Tink! Come on, girl.'

The dog just barked at her. Remembering she had a cereal bar in her bag, Rhoda decided she'd have to resort to bribery. As she resumed her position flat on the floor and peered into the hole once again, she held out the treat. It was enough to tempt the dog towards her; Rhoda made a grab for the scruff of her neck and rather unceremoniously yanked her out of the hole.

'Ah, well done!' said Jack gratefully. 'Come here, you stupid dog.' It was said with much affection and Rhoda was glad to reunite dog and owner.

'Now what was all that fuss down there for?' asked Nate, giving the dog's head a ruffle.

'Don't be worrying about that now,' said Jack, his breathing still on the fast side.

'Come on, Dad. Let's get you outside for some fresh air,' said Nate, helping his father to his feet.

Rhoda saw the hesitation in Jack's face.

'I won't be long. I'll just quickly take a few notes and photos of the window and I'll be right out.'

She held her notebook up as reassurance and smiled before heading over to the main window. She waited until she heard the chapel door close behind Jack and Nate and then quickly made her way back to the flagstone.

Rhoda's interest was piqued now and, seeing as her clothes were already dirty, she had nothing to lose. For the third time, she was back on the floor of the chapel. Without the dog obstructing her view, she shone the light in to see what Tink had been so fascinated with.

At first, she wasn't sure what she was looking at. It looked like some rags and rubble, but as she swept the torchlight around the cavity, she realised exactly what it was. She let out a scream and rolled away from the entrance of the hole.

At that moment, Nate Hartwell came back into the chapel. He hurried over to where Rhoda was now sitting up. 'Whatever's wrong? Are you OK? Did you fall?'

'I'm fine.' Rhoda closed her eyes and took a deep breath. 'I need to have another look down that hole, just to make sure it is what I think it is.'

She was rather more prepared this time.

Nate was now on the flagstones next to her. Rhoda took one last look, just to confirm what she was seeing, before rising to a sitting position. She passed Nate the torch.

'You might want to have a look.'

Nate shone the light into the hole. Swore. Shook his head. Took another look and swore again. He, too, sat back up on his knees. 'There's a bloody skeleton down there.'

'Ten out of ten for observation,' said Rhoda.

Nate got to his feet and strode towards the door of the church. 'I need to speak to Dad.'

Rhoda followed him, concerned how Jack might take the news. She caught up with Nate at the door. 'Just take it easy with him, yeah?'

Nate gave her what could only be described as an old-fashioned look. 'I'm not about to torture him.'

Jack, who'd been perched on the edge of a buttress, pushed himself to his feet as they came out of the chapel. 'All done?'

'Not quite,' said Nate. 'There's something you should know.'

'Maybe we should discuss this back at the house?' suggested Rhoda.

'You might as well tell me now,' replied Jack, his eyes darting back and forth between his son and Rhoda.

Nate nodded. 'OK. Erm ... the reason why Tink was so interested in the broken flagstones was because there's something down there. Underneath them.'

'Is that right?' said Jack.

Rhoda tried to read the expression on the older man's face, but it was indecipherable. She exchanged a look with Nate. 'You need to tell him,' she said.

'There are skeletal remains down there, Dad,' said Nate. 'Not a body but human bones.'

Jack made a scoffing sound. 'Bones? You sure it's not a dog or something?'

'Positive,' said Rhoda. 'There's a skull.'

'Must have been buried there in that case,' said Jack.

'But I thought you said there were no burials here,' persisted Rhoda.

Jack gave a huff. 'I must have got it wrong.'

'It doesn't look like it's been buried there,' continued Rhoda. 'I'm not an expert, but I didn't see any sign of a coffin.'

'You don't remember anyone ever mentioning it before?' asked Nate. 'Could there be others?'

'No. I don't remember,' said Jack, his agitation showing in his voice.

'We'll need to let the police know,' said Rhoda gently. 'Let's go back to the house. It's a shock for everyone. We should have a cup of tea.' She looked at Nate who nodded in agreement.

'Good idea,' he said.

'The police,' muttered Jack. 'That's all we need.'

5
Alice

1945

Alice pulled out the suitcase from the back of her wardrobe and placed it on her bed. She felt surprisingly nervous as she slid the locks to one side, releasing the clasps. Was nervous the right word? Apprehension maybe? She wasn't sure, but the thought of wearing one of her mother's dresses that night filled her with trepidation.

She took a deep breath and lifted the lid of the brown leather suitcase. She took another breath as a faint smell of her mother's perfume was released into the room. Alice carefully lifted the dresses out and laid them out on the bed, discarding the case on the floor so there was enough room to see the beautiful fabrics in all their glory.

Her mother, Emily Louise Renshaw, née Brice-Baker, prior to meeting and marrying Alice's father, had been a seamstress in London. She had often been allowed to take home pieces from sample collections for some of the wealthier clients.

Alice remembered Emily coming home with evening gowns which she had nowhere to wear, but she would let her daughter dress up in them. Sometimes Emily would cut them up and recreate a smaller version for Alice to wear and indulge in make-believe games of cocktail parties and gala dinners.

Oh, how she missed her mother. Alice picked up the white trouser suit Emily had proudly worn to a wedding: a cropped jacket with puffed three-quarter length sleeves, and trousers that were high-waisted and wide-legged. Emily had worn a multicoloured blouse underneath, with a flouncy necktie. Alice remembered her father staring in disbelief as her mother had come down the stairs. She had taken his breath away. He had made a deep bow before kissing her hand. It was hard to believe he was the same man who was now sitting at the kitchen table.

Alice felt a wave of sadness wash over her that caused her heart to ache and tears to spring to her eyes.

Beautiful as it was, the trouser suit wasn't the right thing to wear to the dance with Brett. Alice looked at the three other outfits. One was a long pale blue evening gown, with hand-sewn sequins and embroidered flowers. It had a low-cut back and, although undeniably stunning, it was probably too grand to wear to the American base.

That left the floral A-line dress with capped sleeves, or the closely fitted emerald green cocktail dress of silk and lace.

Alice tried on both. Goodness, her mother had been slim.

The cocktail dress was beautiful, but too tight. Alice had to force the zip and was sure she wouldn't be able to sit down in it. What a shame, she could have really wowed Brett in that. Fortunately, the floral A-line dress was rather more forgiving and fitted well, showing off her curvy figure. She wasn't quite sure how she'd managed to put on weight, seeing as she ate like a sparrow due to the rationing, but she filled the dress nicely and hoped Brett would appreciate her fuller-looking bust.

Once she'd done her make-up and hair, Alice gave herself one final inspection in the full-length mirror and was very pleased with what she saw. She checked her watch. She was meeting Jess at the end of the road in five minutes, and then they were going to meet Brett and Howard at the church.

Brett had on more than one occasion offered to meet Alice at her home, but she'd always declined. She wasn't sure her father would be very welcoming, and she could do without any trouble between the two men.

'I'm off now, Dad!' she called from the hallway, slipping her arms into her coat and tying the belt around her.

'What time will you be back?'

Her father appeared in the doorway of the sitting room.

'Not sure. There's a dance at the mess. I'll be with Jess.'

She gave him a quick smile and went to open the front door.

'Wait!'

Alice paused, her hand on the lock.

'What?'

'Turn around.'

'I'll be late, Dad.'

'What are you wearing?'

Alice swallowed. 'Just a dress.' She tried to sound casual and turned to meet her father's gaze.

There was a mix of anger and pain in his eyes. 'Who said you could wear that?'

'No one said I couldn't,' Alice replied evenly. 'Besides, Mum would be pleased to know I was wearing it.'

'Put something else on.' His voice was harsh.

'I haven't got anything else and I'm going to be late.' Alice reached for the lock again.

'Do as you're told!' her father snapped.

'Dad, I'm eighteen years old. I'm an adult. I can wear this dress if I want.'

'Don't argue with me. If you're that much of an adult, what are you still doing living under my roof?'

'Living under your roof but paying my way,' retorted Alice. 'Cooking and cleaning for you. Doing the shopping. Doing the washing. It's not exactly for free, is it?'

She didn't know who was more surprised by her outburst. Alice didn't usually flare up so easily at her father, but she hadn't been able to stop herself.

'Don't you be so bloody cheeky, young lady!' Her father raised his voice.

'I'm wearing this dress and I'm going out.'

With that, Alice was out of the door, slamming it behind her before her father could say another word. She marched down the path and out into the street, her anger pushing her on as her heels struck the pavement. She could see Jess waiting at the end and by the time she reached her, the anger had morphed into hot tears.

'Alice! Whatever's the matter?' cried Jess, giving her friend a hug.

'I'm fine. Honest,' said Alice, fishing her hanky from her bag. She dabbed at her eyes. 'I'm going to end up looking like a panda.'

'Here, you've missed a bit,' said Jess, taking the hanky from her and wiping under her left eyelid. 'What happened? Argument with your dad?'

'Yes. He got all funny about me wearing Mum's dress and wanted me to change. Then he started on about living under his roof and all that usual stuff.' Alice sighed. 'I just couldn't help myself and told him I could do what I like.'

'You're brave.' Jess handed her back the handkerchief.

'Stupid, more like. And I don't even know why I'm crying. I'm angry, really.'

'Come on. You don't want Brett to see you all red-eyed and blotchy. Forget about your dad. It will blow over, like it usually does.'

Alice suddenly felt weary and really wasn't in the mood for going out now. Not even the thought of seeing Brett was lifting her spirits. What was wrong with her? She needed to forget about her dad and concentrate on having a nice evening. Despite still feeling unusually emotional, Alice forced a smile and fell into step alongside Jess.

Jess linked arms with her. 'That's better.'

Their heels click-clacked down the street.

'Oh, did you hear about Betsy Grainger?'

'No, what's that?'

Alice remembered Betsy from school – she had been a couple of years above her and Jess. Studious type of girl, if she remembered rightly.

'She's only gone and got herself pregnant.'

Alice stopped walking and turned to Jess.

'I don't think girls go and get themselves pregnant. I'm pretty sure there's a bloke involved in it, too.'

Jess laughed. 'Oh, Alice, you are funny. Anyway, what do you reckon to that?'

'She's probably one of the last people to get caught out,' said Alice as they began walking again. 'Who's the father?'

'Some lad from town. She's been seeing him for about a year.' They turned the corner into the High Street. 'Shotgun wedding coming up. What a silly cow, though, you know, to let that happen. She's over three months pregnant apparently, so the wedding is going to be as soon as possible. My mum was talking to her aunt yesterday and she said ...'

Jess's voice trailed off as Alice's mind began to churn her own dates over. When did she last have her period? She did the mental calculations. Six weeks ago? Or was it seven? She swallowed as her throat dried. Seven weeks, maybe even eight. She couldn't get her brain to work properly. It was the day after Brett's birthday, that's right. Back in February. She gulped again. Eight weeks! Was that right? Definitely right. Her hand went to her stomach, and she thought of the tight waistband of the dress, the fit of the fabric across her bust – her bigger than usual bust. And there was the tiredness. The extreme emotions. She hadn't been sick, but she knew well enough not every woman suffered with morning sickness. Oh, bloody hell. She felt light-headed and had to hold tighter on to Jess's arm.

'Jess,' she whispered. She was still trying to process it all but there was no denying it. 'Jess.'

'I don't know where they're going to live,' Jess was saying, still talking about Betsy Grainger. 'Probably with her mum. They've got enough room at their house.'

'Jess ...'

'It's not like she hasn't got the room.'

'Jess. I think I'm pregnant.'

'What's that?' Jess clearly hadn't heard Alice.

'I said, I think I'm pregnant.'

The words sounded foreign on her lips. How could she even be saying this? They'd taken precautions. They hadn't even done it that many times and yet ...

'Pregnant!' Jess's voice was high-pitched. 'You're bloody joking. Please tell me you're joking?'

Alice turned and looked at her friend. She shook her head.

'Not joking.'

'Oh, my God, Alice. Are you sure?'

'As sure as I can be. Eight weeks late. Thicker waistline. Bigger bust. Tired. Irritable. Emotional.'

'Sick?'

'No, but that doesn't mean anything.'

'True.' Jess looked long and hard at her. 'What are you going to do? Your dad will kill you. And then kill Brett.'

'I know.'

'Have you told Brett?'

'Not yet. I've only just realised myself.'

They stood in a stunned silence for a moment, before Jess spoke.

'You know, there are options.'

Alice looked at her friend, taking a moment to understand what Jess was saying. She shook her head.

'I don't think I can do that ... you know, get rid of it.' She contemplated the idea some more. 'No. I can't. I couldn't do that.'

'In that case, you need to tell Brett,' said Jess. 'You're

going to start showing and if he does want to marry you, you'll need to get that sorted.' She let out a long sigh. 'Bloody hell, there's me prattling on about Betsy Grainger and you're …' She waved her hand in the direction of Alice's belly. 'You're …'

'Going to have a baby,' finished Alice, holding her chin high.

They walked on in silence down the road, the church coming into view as they rounded the bend.

'Tell him tonight, Alice,' said Jess. 'You've got to tell him straight away, so you know what you're going to do.'

'I will,' replied Alice, breaking into a smile as Brett stepped out from the shadow of the lychgate. 'Don't say anything to anyone until I've spoken to him. Promise?'

'Promise.'

'Hey there, beautiful,' said Brett as they reached them.

He took Alice in his arms and kissed her.

Alice relaxed at the warmth of his embrace. She was nervous as anything – there were no two ways about it – but his kiss was reassuring and gave her confidence. They would be all right.

'You're what?' Brett looked at Alice, horror and disbelief all over his face.

This was not how Alice had imagined the conversation was going to go. They were outside the mess hall, taking the opportunity to have some time alone. In reality, that meant making out in the now darkened grounds of the base, the trees and bushes surrounding the recreation area giving them privacy.

Brett was now pacing back and forth between a hydrangea bush and a laurel hedge, his hand running agitatedly through his thick brown hair.

'How?'

Alice raised her eyebrows. 'That's a stupid question.'

'You know what I mean,' he snapped. 'How? We used a rubber.'

'Well, I hate to be the one to break the news to you, but they don't always work.'

Alice could feel the fear rising in her, which she was channelling as anger. She'd known he'd be surprised, but not hostile.

'And it's mine? Damn it. I didn't mean that.'

Now the anger was real and pure.

'How dare you?' Alice demanded, striding over to him, the urge to slap him hard across the face only just contained.

'I'm sorry. Sorry,' bleated Brett. 'I don't know why I said that. I'm just ... just shocked. Shit. I'm only twenty-one.'

'I'm only eighteen.'

'What are we going to do?'

Alice gave a shrug. 'What do you want to do?'

Much as she'd had a rosy image of Brett dropping to one knee and proposing to her, she wasn't naive enough to think it was going to happen. Not after his reaction, anyway. Her mind was racing ahead. Maybe he wasn't going to ask her at all. Then she would be in a predicament.

'I don't know. I need time to think about it.'

'Well, that's a luxury we don't have.'

Brett ran his hand down his face and then stood with his hands on his hips, staring down at the ground. After a few moments, he seemed to have come to a decision. He looked up. Took a breath and strode over to her.

'It will be OK. I can speak to my sergeant. He'll know someone who can help. I'm not the first to be in this situation. I'll pay for it, of course. It will be done properly.'

'Wait. Stop right there,' said Alice, stepping back. 'I'm not getting an abortion, if that's what you're thinking. No way. Absolutely not.'

'You want to keep it?' Brett looked startled by this revelation. 'You want to saddle us with a kid?'

'I wasn't thinking "saddling" was the right word, but yes. I want to keep it.' She looked him dead in the eye. 'I thought you loved me.'

'Whoa, there. I don't think I said anything about love.'

Alice wanted to cry. His words were like a knife twisting in her heart. If she was honest, he'd never mentioned love. Sure, she'd told him she loved him, but now she thought about it, he'd never told her.

'I just need to know if you're going to stand by me,' she said, trying to keep control of the tremble that had taken hold of her voice.

There was a heavy silence. Despite being out in the fresh April air, Alice was suddenly struggling for breath. It was like a hot summer's day when a storm was brewing. Heavy. Sticky. Close. Muggy.

'I'm in the air force,' said Brett. 'We're in the middle of a goddamn war. I'm in a foreign country. I need time to think this through. It's not just how it affects us – it's how it affects everything else. My career. My family. Your family. Our future. Just give me a couple of days when I'm not trying to think through several beers and the shock of it all.'

'All right. That's fair enough.' Alice didn't have a lot of choice. 'You need to let me know by Wednesday. It's my half-day. We'll meet at the bridge. One o'clock.'

'Yeah. Sure.'

'I'm going home now.'

'Wait, I'll walk you.'

'No, you don't have to.'

She wasn't sure she could bear the closeness of him, knowing he was having to think about whether he could commit to her and his baby. Their baby.

'I insist. I'm not that much of a schmuck, that I'll leave you to walk home alone.' He caught her hand. 'Thank you,' he said softly.

Alice looked at him, not knowing how to reply.

'Can you get my coat,' she said, slipping her hand from his and looking in her clutch purse for her cloakroom ticket. She passed it over to him. 'Will you tell Jess and make sure Howard walks her home?'

'Yeah. Sure.'

Brett seemed to take ages before he reappeared with Alice's coat.

'I thought you'd abandoned me already,' said Alice, trying to make a joke, but judging by the look on Brett's face, failing miserably. He held her coat up for her and she slipped her arms in. With her back to him, it was then she felt his lips kiss the back of her neck.

'Alice,' he said softly, turning her around to look at him. 'I'm sorry about how I reacted. I promise I won't let you down.'

As they walked home together, Alice felt such relief. She wasn't quite sure what Brett meant by that – he hadn't proposed to her, but she could only assume he would do so in better circumstances. Maybe he wanted to speak to her father or buy her a ring first. She didn't know, but as she kissed him goodnight, she felt a happiness she hadn't experienced all night. And as she walked up the path to her house, there was a relief, too. Soon she wouldn't have to live under the same roof as her father.

14 July 1944

Carissime Mamma e Sofia – Dearest Mother and Sofia

I hope you are both well.

Thank you for your letter, which I received last week. It was good to hear from you. The post has been slow, and I received your second letter at the same time! So it was doubly nice for me that day. I hope this letter doesn't take so long to get to you, though.

I am now in a prison camp in South Africa. Who would have thought I'd end up seeing so much of the world as a prisoner? I'm in a prison hospital while my leg heals. The doctor is hopeful of a full recovery, but I shall be in plaster for many weeks. It comes right up to the top of my leg. It is hot and itchy. But still, I am alive and that is the important thing.

What good news your letter brought, though, that Sofia, you are now a mother and your baby arrived safely last month. I have been thinking about you and wondering if I was now an uncle. I may only be eighteen, but I will be such a good uncle to little Luca and I can't wait to hold him in my arms. I will very much look forward to taking him to the park, teaching him to climb trees and fish in the lake near our house, just like Father used to take me.

Have you heard from Franco? I expect he will be delighted to learn of the safe arrival of his son. We shall have such a party to celebrate when we are all together again.

I am glad you are in the country and away from the big towns and cities, so you are safe from the bombing raids I have been hearing about. We are not officially told much, but word from home has spread among the men and it is an anxious time for us all as we think of our families and loved ones.

Take care of each other.

Il vostro amorevole figlio e fratello – your loving son and brother

Paolo

6
Nate

2022

'I'm no expert but I think it's fair to say those are human remains,' said Detective Sergeant Shepherd as he exited the chapel.

Under instruction from the DS, Nate was waiting outside the chapel with both his father and Rhoda Sullivan. Nate had tried to persuade his father to wait back at the farmhouse, but he was being particularly stubborn about it – that, of course, wasn't anything new. Rhoda Sullivan had been asked to wait by Shepherd as he would need to question her.

Rhoda was on the phone to someone – Nate assumed it was her boss – giving the museum an update. She ended the call when she saw the DS come out, and made her way over.

'And you're the one who found the body?' Shepherd asked her.

'If you mean was I the first to see it, then yes. Technically, the dog found it,' she replied. 'Are you likely to need me to stay to give a statement, only I've got quite a long drive back to Sussex?'

'I can take an initial statement,' replied Shepherd, 'but I'd like forensics to have a look first.' He turned to Jack. 'Is there a crypt or a burial chamber?'

Nate's father shrugged. 'Not that I know of. I suppose there could be.'

'Are there any historical records for the chapel? Something that might tell us if anyone's been buried here? Or any records of work being done here? Might give us some clue when the floor was last dug up. The body must have been buried at that time or after.'

'Not that I know of.' Jack gave the same answer as before.

Nate flicked his father a look. He was being particularly obtuse.

'Isn't there a family Bible with all the births, marriages and deaths listed inside the cover? And what about the farm ledgers?' He turned to Shepherd. 'My grandmother kept meticulous records of all the income and expenses relating to the farm, including maintenance work.'

His father frowned at him. 'I've no idea where that Bible is, and as for the ledgers, they're all packed away somewhere.'

Nate let out a sigh and gave the DS an apologetic look.

'If there is something like a Bible with all the names, it might prove very useful,' said Shepherd. 'Perhaps you could have a look round. Is it likely to be in the chapel?'

'No. Nothing like that in there,' said Nate. 'It will be in the house, if anywhere. I'll have a look for you.'

'Thank you, Mr Hartwell.' Shepherd's phone buzzed and he looked at the screen. 'Ah, that's good. Forensics have just pulled up.' He took out his pocketbook and made a note of something. 'How long has the crack in the flagstones been there?'

'Hard to say,' replied Jack. 'No one comes up here regularly.'

'It could be from the subsidence,' said Rhoda.

'Are you an architect?' asked Shepherd.

'No. That's way above my pay grade. I specialise in glasswork – restoration, in particular – but the subsidence is indirectly why I'm here,' explained Rhoda. 'I've come up here to assess the damage to the stained-glass window. The damage has been caused by movement in the building. It's on the same side as the building is pitching. It seems the logical explanation.'

Shepherd looked back through the open chapel door. 'It's a big window. Impressive. You're going to restore that?'

'Yes. I am.'

Nate picked up on the tone in Rhoda's voice, as if she was challenging Shepherd to think otherwise.

'You sound very confident.' Shepherd gave her a sceptical look.

'It won't be the first one I've done,' Rhoda said tersely.

Shepherd nodded. 'I see. What's so special about this one?'

'It was made by an Italian prisoner of war,' interjected Nate. 'He worked on the farm from 1944 to 1946.'

'He was still here after the war?' queried Shepherd.

'Took a bit of time for them all to be repatriated,' said Rhoda. 'They didn't all just pack their bags on 8 May

1945 and wave goodbye as they caught the bus to the train station.'

Nate managed to choke down the burst of laughter that tried to escape his throat. Rhoda Sullivan wasn't one for holding back – and with no apologies for her outspokenness.

Shepherd's face reddened a little. 'Well, no. Of course.' He looked down at his notebook and cleared his throat. 'There is some pointing around the flagstones which looks a different colour to the others. More recent. Do you know anything about that, Mr Hartwell?'

He looked at both Nate and his father.

'Not that I know of,' replied Jack.

'If there's any record of any work being carried out on the building, I'd like to see that,' said Shepherd.

'My mother ran this farm up until I took over in the sixties,' supplied Jack. 'I would have been just a nipper, so I can't help you there. We'd have to look through the farm records. That's if it's even recorded.'

'And is your mother still around to talk to?'

'She's in the village,' said Jack, and before Nate could say anything, he quickly added, 'In the graveyard.'

'Ah, I see. She's passed away?'

Jack gave a snort. 'You're quick to catch on. No wonder you're a detective sergeant.'

Nate gave a sigh and caught Rhoda's eye; she looked away, clearly trying to smother a smile. His father was a cantankerous old sod at times.

'And has any work been done here since then? In your time?' the DS continued, either oblivious to Jack's comment or choosing to ignore it.

'A bit of maintenance, but not in recent years.' Jack looked uninterested. 'Maybe someone did redo the flagstones at some point.'

'Is there anyone in your family I could talk to who would know a bit more about what happened here during the war?'

'Nope,' said Jack, at the same time that Nate said 'Yes.'

The DS looked confused. 'There is or there isn't?'

'There's Aunt Aggie,' said Nate. 'She's Dad's cousin. She lives across the road in Telton Cottage. She would have been about—'

'She won't know anything,' cut in Jack.

'I will probably need to speak to your cousin,' said Shepherd. 'Just to make sure I've covered all bases. Routine, as they say.'

At that point the forensic team arrived and, after a bit of persuasion, Nate managed to convince his father to wait in the house while the police did what they needed to.

'Is all this going to hold up the sale?' asked Jack as they went down the hill.

'Depends on what they find,' said Nate.

'Also depends on when I can repair the window,' put in Rhoda. 'From my initial inspection, I'm going to recommend the repair work is carried out before anything else.'

'The council and the developers won't be very happy about that,' said Nate. He saw Rhoda wink at his father.

'Oh well,' she said. 'They'll just have to wait, won't they?'

They were outside the house now.

'You're going to come in for a cup of tea, aren't you?' asked Jack.

'I won't intrude,' said Rhoda. 'I need to write up my

report, which I can do in my car. Save me having to do it when I get home tonight.'

'Are you sure?' asked Nate. 'At least let me bring you out a cup of tea.'

'I'm absolutely fine but thank you.'

'Don't be daft,' said Jack. 'You can sit in the dining room and work there.'

Rhoda went to apologise but realised it would be futile and agreed to Jack's request. The trio trooped inside.

Nate showed her into the dining room. 'Sorry about this.'

'About what?'

'Being forced to come into the house. Seems Dad has taken a shine to you.'

'It's mutual.'

Nate gave a smile. 'Not sure how you did it. One minute he's blocking you from coming in, the next he's got you sitting in the dining room to do your work.'

Rhoda looked around the room, her gaze coming to rest on the bank of photographs displayed on the sideboard.

'Your father has a lot of memories here.'

'Yes. Lived here all his life.'

'Must be frightening for him, having to move at his age.'

'Yeah. It's pretty tough. We've done everything we can to oppose the CPO, but they've rejected every suggestion,' explained Nate. 'We asked to keep the house and allow all the development to go on around it, but they said no to that. We even suggested Dad gets one of the apartments, but they're just not interested.'

'Bastards. They don't take the individual's feelings into account. They just ride roughshod over people. I hate the system.'

Nate could see the resentment on her face, but when she saw him watching, she quickly shifted it to a more neutral expression.

'Anyway, I'd better get this report done.'

'Yes, of course. I'll make a cup of tea. I'd better also warn my aunt about the police wanting to talk to her. Not that I think she'll be any more help than Dad was. She knows even less.'

Nate left the room and went out into the hall. He poked his head into the living room. His father had nodded off in the armchair by the fireside. Nate crept in, took the blanket from the back of the chair and placed it over his father's lap.

After making Rhoda a drink, he popped over to Telton Cottage to see Aggie.

Nate let himself into the cottage through the back door, which Aggie always kept unlocked, despite his efforts to persuade her otherwise. He called out to her so as not to startle her and went into the living room.

'Seems rather a to-do going on over there,' said his aunt.

'Yeah, you could say that.'

Nate went and stood at the window, where he could see down the driveway of Telton Hall on the opposite side of the road.

'Now, don't be alarmed ...' he began, and quickly, with minimal detail, he told his aunt about the skeleton in the chapel.

'A skeleton! Human remains?' she repeated.

'That's right. Forensics are up there now. I expect they're trying to get an idea of how long it's been there.' He paused as he waited for his aunt to take in the information. 'You don't know if anyone has ever been buried up there, do you?'

His aunt looked quite pale. 'No. At least I don't think so. If there was, it must be from when it was first built.'

'I've asked Dad, but he doesn't know either, and he didn't think there was any underground crypt or anything. Do you remember Gran ever saying anything about it?'

His aunt shook her head. 'No. Goodness, this is a shock.'

'The police said they will need to speak to you. Don't worry, it's just a formality,' reassured Nate, wondering if there was any way he could persuade the DS not to come over. His aunt looked particularly upset by the news. 'You don't know anything, so it won't take long. I'll be here when they come, though.'

'Thank you, dear,' replied Aggie. She gave a shudder. 'Oh, what horrible business.'

'They're keen to know if any building works have been carried out at the chapel. Do you remember anything?'

His aunt shook her head. 'No. No, I don't. To be honest, I've never liked that place. Used to give me goose bumps. I've not been up there since I was a child. I hope the police aren't going to question me too much.'

'Don't worry. It's just routine.' The clock on the mantelpiece chimed the hour. Nate double-checked his watch. 'I'd better go. I didn't realise that was the time. Got to pick Isaac up from school.'

'Okey-dokey, dear. See you later.'

Nate nipped back across the road and up the drive to Telton Hall, to explain to his father and Rhoda that he would be back in just under an hour.

'He lives with his mum, but we co-parent,' Nate found himself explaining to their guest.

Rhoda raised her eyebrows. 'Lucky boy.'

Nate assessed her for a moment, unsure how to read her comment. 'Yeah, well, I like to think I'm the lucky one,' he found himself saying. 'Me and his mum get on reasonably well. There's never been any animosity between us.'

He stopped himself from talking, unsure why he felt the need to explain his and his ex's personal arrangements with a stranger.

Rhoda smiled. 'Lucky you as well, then.'

She turned her attention back to her screen and, feeling as if he had been dismissed, Nate left the room.

The thought that Rhoda disapproved of him, for whatever reason, niggled him. He wanted to shrug off the thought, but as he drove away from Telton Hall, he found himself stewing about it. He couldn't work out why he got that vibe from her, or what he'd done to deserve it.

7
Rhoda

2022

Rhoda stood at the dining room window, watching Nate Hartwell's car disappear out of the drive. She'd been a bit harsh with him, she knew that, and she was annoyed with herself for it. After all, what happened in the Hartwell family was none of her business. She couldn't make up her mind if he was on his dad's side or not. She also couldn't make up her mind why it bothered her.

She returned to her report, rather than ponder the complexities of the Hartwell family.

An hour later, Rhoda had just finished her second cup of tea and was debating whether she should go up to the guy from CID and ask how long she would need to wait, when she heard a car pull up outside. From her position, she could see it was Nate Hartwell, together with his young son. The timing couldn't have been better, as DS Shepherd came into her line of sight. The two men exchanged a few words and then came into the house.

Rhoda saved her document and went out to the hallway to meet them. Nate's son had already disappeared into the living room, and she could hear him talking to his grandfather.

'Sorry to keep you,' said Shepherd. 'I've got an initial assessment from forensics that I need to discuss with you all.'

'Of course,' said Nate. 'Please, this way.' He opened the living room door and Rhoda followed on behind the DS. 'Hey, Isaac, why don't you come with me to the kitchen? I'll sort you out something to eat and drink. You can watch something on the tablet, if you want.' He coaxed his son out of the room. 'Won't be a moment.'

Nate was back within a few minutes and sat in the armchair on the other side of the fireplace to his father; Rhoda had already seated herself on the sofa, while DS Shepherd remained standing. She had to withhold a smile at the thought they looked as if they were on the set of an Agatha Christie mystery, and the policeman was just about to reveal the name of the killer. They only needed a gardener, a maid and an eccentric aunt to complete the cast.

'Are you OK, Miss Sullivan?'

It was Shepherd. Rhoda looked up, startled to realise Shepherd and the Hartwells were looking at her.

'Sorry, was a bit distracted.' She sat forward on the sofa to signal he had her full attention, and pushed any thoughts of Christie from her mind.

'So, forensics have been able to establish a few things,' began Shepherd. 'Obviously, this all needs confirming back at the lab, but from what they can tell, the remains are those of a young adult male, judging by the bones.'

Rhoda felt her stomach instantly turn at the description, although she knew it was irrational to associate this unnamed body with her disappeared brother. 'How long has he been there?' she asked.

That would be the simplest way to rule out whether it was Dean. She hated the way she thought in terms of finding his body, rather than him. *When had that started to happen?* She blinked away the thought, concentrating on Shepherd's answer.

'Can't say at this point. Bone can survive in good condition for a long time, depending on the soil.' Shepherd paused for a moment before continuing. 'Have you any idea who this might be? Was there a family member, or a farm worker possibly, who went missing? Did your family ever talk about a missing person when you were a boy?' He looked at Jack.

Jack gave a perplexed look. 'I can't remember anyone ever talking about a man going missing.'

'But if it was foul play, then they probably wouldn't,' Rhoda piped up. 'Was it suspicious circumstances, because I guess if the body was hidden, never meant to be found, then the chances are it wasn't a natural death.'

Shepherd raised his eyebrows. 'I'm supposed to be the detective around here.'

'So, was it natural causes? Or can't you tell?'

'At this early stage it looks like the victim was struck on the head with a blunt instrument and that was the cause of death.'

'Could he have tripped and hit his head on something?' asked Nate.

'Apparently, with a fall, they would expect to see a different pattern of injury, like a fracture spreading out, but the injury was caused by an object of about two centimetres in diameter.'

'Like a hammer?' asked Nate.

'Yes. Like a hammer.'

Rhoda appreciated the tact the DS was using – gradually revealing the evidence that was clearly pointing towards murder.

'So, we can say murder?' she said.

'Unofficially,' confirmed Shepherd.

'People don't usually go around doing that to themselves or by accident,' replied Rhoda.

'No, not in my experience,' replied Shepherd.

Rhoda couldn't make out if he was annoyed or amused at her – either one wasn't appealing.

'So, a murder investigation?'

'Possibly.' Shepherd pulled out a clear plastic bag from his pocket and held it out to Jack. 'Do you recognise this at all?'

Rhoda watched as Jack peered closely at the bag.

'No. What is it? A ring?'

'Yes. Probably a home-made one, as it doesn't join up. You'd just squeeze this to fit.'

'May I?' asked Rhoda, intrigued at the find. Shepherd passed her the bag. 'I'm not an expert, but I've come across these things before. It looks like it's made out of an old coin, possibly bronze. If that's the case, then it's from the late 1800s onwards. I don't know if you'll be able to get any detail from it once it's cleaned up, like a date or something, but you might be able to see if it's an English coin or a foreign one.'

'What makes you think it might be foreign?' asked Shepherd. There was genuine interest in his voice.

'It was only a suggestion,' said Rhoda. 'But I'm here to look at a stained-glass window that was made by a prisoner of war at the end of the war. What's to say it's not an Italian coin?'

'No, it wouldn't be that,' said Jack. 'The POWs wouldn't have had their own currency on them. They got paid, all right, but they were paid with cigarettes or tokens to use in the camps. They had a mobile shop that came around where they could buy things with their tokens.'

'A lucky coin, perhaps?' suggested Rhoda.

'Only not so lucky if it belongs to the skeleton.' Shepherd gave a laugh, which no one joined in with. Clearly realising the bad taste of the joke, he tried to turn it into a cough.

'An Italian POW wouldn't have need for an English coin either,' said Jack. 'Was the ring on the body?'

'No, alongside,' replied Shepherd. Every effort to regain his position of authority oozed from him, as he adjusted his tie and stood a little taller.

'So, it might not even belong to the body,' said Jack.

'True, but it might belong to whoever buried the body.'

'Say you find the date,' said Rhoda. 'Unless it's recent, it's not really going to reveal very much.'

'That's for me to worry about,' said Shepherd.

'How long do you think the body has been there for?' asked Nate.

'Could be as far back as the war,' replied Shepherd.

'Forensics might be able to give a more precise date once they've got the bones back at the lab.'

'And you'd investigate an eighty-year-old crime?' asked Jack.

'There's no statute of limitations on murder,' replied Shepherd. 'Having said that, we'd have to weigh up the chances of finding out what happened, the perpetrator still being alive – or indeed, anyone being alive and the costs and resources involved.'

Rhoda felt her blood pump a little harder through her veins at his reply. 'You're saying you wouldn't investigate it?'

'Not if it wasn't in the interest of the public.'

'But that's someone's son up there,' protested Rhoda. 'Someone out there might still be wondering what happened to their loved one.'

'Son?' said Shepherd. 'The parents are most likely dead.'

'Or brother – or he might be someone's father.' Rhoda rose from her seat, so she was facing the DS. 'You can't just ignore the fact that there is quite possibly someone directly related to that man – and he was a man. Just because it's a skeleton now, you can't lose sight of the fact that he was a man. He had a life that was taken away from him, and the chances are no one knows and has spent all these years wondering what happened to him. You have the opportunity to help put someone out of their misery.'

She stopped as the words choked in her throat. She hadn't meant to say all that, but she hadn't been able to stop herself – it was all too raw and close to home. Rhoda managed to compose herself and sat back down, aware that all eyes in the room were fixed firmly on her.

Nate's gaze seemed to penetrate the most, and Rhoda knew she'd perhaps given too much of herself away.

'There may be no statute of limitations on murder,' replied Shepherd, 'but there is a limitation to the effectiveness of investigating a crime which could be eighty or even a hundred years old.'

'But surely you can't do that? Surely you owe it to the person who has been murdered to at least try to bring their killer to justice.' Rhoda really couldn't believe what she was hearing, but her tone was much more under control now. She looked to Jack. 'Don't you want to know who has been killed and buried on your property?'

Jack looked decidedly uncomfortable. 'Of course, but like the sergeant said, it's hard to find anything out when there are probably no witnesses still alive.'

'Is this likely to hold up the sale?' asked Nate.

The turn of question seemed to throw everyone off for a moment. Shepherd recovered first.

'We will try to deal with this as quickly as possible. It all depends on what we find out and whether we open a murder investigation. I'm sorry I can't tell you anything more at this point.'

Nate frowned. 'We could do without this, to be honest.'

Rhoda couldn't bite her tongue. 'I'm sure the family of the murder victim will be pleased to hear that.'

'OK, I think we're probably done here for today.' Shepherd looked at Rhoda. 'If I can take some contact details, I can let you get on your way. You've got a bit of a drive ahead of you.'

Rhoda dug out a business card from her bag and handed it to Shepherd.

'All my details are on there.' She got up from the sofa and hooked her bag over her arm. 'Please don't just dismiss the investigation. It's important that any family of the victim has closure.' Her heart tightened and she found herself having to take several deep steadying breaths as she picked up her jacket and the rucksack she used for work. 'I'll be in touch again soon, Jack,' she said, finding her voice and feeling grateful it was under control. 'Goodbye, Nate. Nice to meet you. Sergeant.'

'Safe journey,' replied Shepherd.

'You'll get caught in all the rush hour traffic,' said Nate.

Rhoda looked at her watch and was surprised to see it was almost 4.30. 'What's the local pub like for food?'

'Nothing fancy, I'm afraid,' said Nate. 'You'll probably find something more refined in town.'

'Good old pub grub is fine by me. Right, I'll be off.' She smiled at Jack. 'I'll keep you in the loop with what's happening with the window. Obviously, I can't do anything until the police have finished with the chapel. Call me if you need to talk about anything.'

Jack returned the smile. 'Thank you. Appreciate that.'

Getting into her car, Rhoda was quite happy to leave Telton Hall. Her earlier feelings of admiration for the property had morphed into one of apprehension and disquiet. There was something about it she didn't like. She hadn't felt it when she'd first arrived that morning, but the discovery of the body – and trying to persuade Shepherd that he should investigate the death, however old the case might be – had triggered all sorts of deep-rooted emotions. She felt the anxious churning in her stomach as she thought of her own circumstances: the years of being taken into care; the fear of the unknown and of the known; but most of all, being separated from her brother, and the subsequent events which had unfolded.

Rhoda closed her eyes for a moment as the familiar but unwelcome bubble of distress rolled around inside her, churning her stomach and squeezing her heart. From the inside pocket of her bag, she slipped out an old photograph, faded with age and crumpled with use. The smiling face of her then eighteen-year-old twin brother looked back at her. She ran her finger over the image – a gesture she did most times she looked at Dean – and asked the same question.

'Where are you, Deano? I'm still looking for you. Please come home.'

From the corner of her eye, she noticed Nate coming out of the house and walking over towards her. She fumbled to get the key in the ignition so she could buzz down the window, and only just managed to as he reached her.

'Erm ... Sorry, this may sound weird ... but are you OK? You seemed a bit upset in there?'

'Did I?' Rhoda started the engine. 'I just like to see fair play, that's all.'

'Fighting for the underdog, eh?'

'Something like that.'

Nate rested his hand on the roof and dipped his head so it was level with hers. She saw his gaze travel to the passenger seat, and the photograph she had discarded in her fluster to get the key in the ignition. She snatched up the photograph, wanting to shove it into her bag out of the way but something made her stop. A knot of agitation fought its way up to her throat and her reply came out as a strangled noise. She coughed. 'It's my brother. Dean. He went missing just before our eighteenth birthday.'

'I'm sorry. That must be tough.'

Rhoda nodded. 'We have no idea what happened to him. You're right. It is tough. Some days are very tough. He's my twin brother.'

'I'm sorry,' Nate repeated. 'That must be especially difficult.'

Rhoda shrugged. 'I guess so. Look, we are twins, but we didn't have any of that twin telepathy going on. We hadn't even lived under the same roof since we were twelve but, you know, he's still my brother.'

'Of course. I don't have any siblings.'

'Only child?'

'That's the definition of having no siblings.' He gave a laugh and somehow Rhoda sensed he was having a bit of sport with her.

She couldn't help a small smile escaping. 'I deserved that.' She put her car into reverse.

Nate didn't move away. 'Actually, Dad asked me to invite you in for fish and chips. He said we shouldn't subject you to Harry's pub grub and I'm inclined to agree.'

'Oh, that's really kind,' said Rhoda, preparing herself to politely decline – a reflex action that was her modus operandi as she shied away from spontaneous decisions with people she didn't know – OK, make that trust – but for some reason, she found herself hesitating. Despite the cold and insidious atmosphere of Telton Hall, there was also an unrelenting draw to the place. She wanted to find out more about the remains of the man in the chapel. It was such a strong desire, she found herself agreeing.

'I don't want to intrude, but I must admit I don't think I can turn down the offer of fish and chips.'

'Excellent. It will stop me getting earache from Dad about not making you stay for supper.'

Rhoda switched off the engine and got out. As she walked back up towards Telton Hall, something made her look up to the first floor of the building. The shadows cast across the individual windowpanes of the sash meant she couldn't see clearly, but she was sure someone was standing at the window at the end, looking down at them. The sun chose that moment to pop out from behind a cloud, causing her to squint.

'Ah, you're staying for supper. That's good.' Jack was standing in the doorway.

'Couldn't refuse such an offer.'

Rhoda gave another glance up to the window, her eyes now adjusted to the evening sun. The window was empty. It must have been Nate's son, Isaac.

Stepping into the house again, Rhoda gave a shudder as goosebumps inexplicably pricked her skin.

8
Alice

1945

'Oh, you look so beautiful,' said Jess as she fixed Alice's hair with a pear-drop tiara. It was one Alice's mother had worn on her wedding day and, by luck, her mother had given it to her about six months before she had died.

'You need to keep this safe,' she'd said. 'I don't suppose you'll want my wedding dress. It's not fashionable, but the tiara was my mother's, and it will never go out of fashion.'

As Alice looked at herself in the mirror, she couldn't help thinking that neither she nor her mother had envisaged a wedding day like today. They'd both had much more romantic ideas, but with the war still going on in Europe – and, more importantly, with Alice's ever-increasing waistline – they couldn't afford to wait indefinitely for world peace.

She smoothed down the dress over her stomach.

'Your mum was so kind to make this for me,' she said to Jess.

'She's not up to your mum's standards, but she doesn't do a bad job,' replied Jess.

The dress was fitted at the bust, but the waist was gathered and full-bodied in an attempt to hide the pregnancy. Not that it was particularly a secret, but it seemed the decent thing to do.

'Well, she's done a good job and my mum would definitely approve.'

'How's your dad been?'

'He's barely spoken to me the last few weeks,' admitted Alice. 'Not that I'm bothered. He was so blunt with Brett, it was embarrassing.'

'I thought he might be better once he'd got used to the idea.'

'I was hoping he'd come around, too. Especially as I'm going to have to live here for a while.'

'It's a shame you have to stay here until the war is over.'

'I know. I thought Brett would be all for us getting a place in the village, but he says he has to stay on base. Besides, if we're going to move to America eventually, what's the point? Brett reckons the war is going to be over in the next eighteen months.'

'I hope so. Please God.' Jess picked up the bouquet of purple and yellow freesias. 'These are beautiful. I can't remember the last time I saw flowers. It's all spuds and carrots now.' She raised them to her nose and breathed in their delicate scent. Most people had turned their gardens over to growing fruit and veg in line with the government's 'dig for victory' campaign. 'Where did these come from?'

'Actually, they were from Mrs Armitage up at the big house. She gave them to Dad this morning.'

Mrs Armitage was well known for her generosity to the community. Despite coming from a wealthy family, she and her sister, Louise Hartwell, had followed in the spirit of their parents' philanthropic ethos, believing their privileged position could be used to benefit those less fortunate.

'Ah, that's so lovely.' Jess grinned at Alice. 'I know it's not the perfect circumstances, but it is so exciting. You're going to be Mrs Brett Cunningham and you're going to move to America! I'm going to bloody miss you and I don't mind admitting I'm so jealous – you get to escape from this place.'

'I know! It is exciting. Scary, too. Brett said his family were surprised, but they are happy he's happy. Apparently, they are looking forward to meeting me. I hope I can get on all right with Mrs Cunningham, especially as I haven't got my own mum anymore.'

She blinked back the tears. If she could have one wish in the whole world, it would be to have her mum with her today.

Jess gave her a comforting smile and another hug, before pulling away. 'Now, isn't it time we got you to the church?'

'I'd better make sure Dad's ready,' said Alice.

She'd heard him in the bathroom earlier, and then moving around in his bedroom. She went across the landing, knocking on his door.

'Dad? You all right?' There was no answer. Alice tapped again. 'Dad?'

This time, she opened the door slowly and poked her head into the room. He was sitting on the edge of the bed, his head bowed. In his hands was a photograph. Alice recognised it instantly. It was a photo of her parents' wedding day. She went into the room and sat down on the bed beside him.

'That's such a lovely photograph,' she said softly. 'You both look so happy.'

'We were,' he said after a pause. 'Your mother never looked so beautiful.'

'She was always beautiful.'

Alice swallowed hard, trying not to let the bubble of emotion get the better of her. This was one of the few times she and her father had spoken about her mother.

Her father looked up at her. 'You look beautiful, too.'

'Thanks, Dad.'

It wasn't much. There were no displays of affection, no hugging, no apologies or declarations of love and acceptance, but Alice appreciated the truce they appeared to have settled on. He replaced the photograph on the bedside table.

'Right, I know it's the bride's prerogative to be late, but all the same, you can't keep a man waiting too long.'

As they stepped out of the cottage, Alice gave a gasp when she saw the car. It was Mrs Armitage's Armstrong Siddeley convertible. White ribbons were tied in a bow on the sidelights and door handles. Mrs Armitage's driver, Ted Palmer, was standing alongside the vehicle, looking especially smart in his uniform. He nodded towards Alice and opened the rear door.

'Compliments of Mrs Armitage,' said her father. 'There's enough room in there for Jess, too.'

A small group of villagers had gathered on the path and clapped as Alice, holding on to her father's arm, walked proudly down the path and climbed into the back of the maroon and black car.

'Thank you, Dad.' Alice exchanged a smile with her father.

Ted Palmer dropped Jess at the church and then, as instructed by his employer, took a circuitous route around the village and back again, so Alice could enjoy the moment and arrive at the church in style a few minutes later.

'There, just three minutes late,' said her father as the car pulled up outside the church.

Before they could climb out, Jess was at the door. 'Can you go around the block again?' she said to the driver.

She glanced over at Alice and gave her a quick smile.

'What's the matter?' asked Alice.

'Nothing. We just need a few more minutes.'

Jess shut the door and, much as she'd tried to give her a confident smile, Alice could tell something was wrong.

Ted had the subtlety not to drive Alice through the village again, and this time he headed out towards the town at a rather slower speed than he might have otherwise travelled. It was another seven minutes before they arrived back at the church.

Alice could see Jess on the pavement outside in deep conversation with Howard – Brett's elected best man. The expressions on their faces as they looked at her told Alice everything she needed to know. Brett wasn't there.

'Just wait here,' said her father.

'No. I need to speak to Howard,' said Alice. 'Maybe Brett's been called up for something. A mission. You don't know. It could be some vital top-secret mission he's got to go on.'

She wasn't sure who she was trying to kid, but if she

could delay the moment of truth for just a few seconds more, it was better than having to deal with what really was happening.

'Alice,' said Jess, putting her arm around Alice's shoulders.

'What's happened?' asked Alice, looking directly at Howard. She couldn't help feeling sorry for him; whatever he was about to tell her was clearly terribly awkward for him.

He exchanged a furtive glance with Jess.

'I'm sorry, Alice, I really am ...' he began.

'Just spit it out, lad,' said Alice's father.

Howard swallowed hard. Cleared his throat.

'Brett's not coming.'

'Not coming?' repeated Alice. 'As in, not coming now? Today? Ever?'

Howard looked down at his feet. 'Ever.'

'Bastard.' It was Jess. 'Sorry, Mr Renshaw.'

Alice's father shook his head. 'No need to apologise. You're absolutely right.' He brought himself up to his full height. 'Where is he now?'

'I don't know,' replied Howard. 'He's been transferred out to another base.'

Alice could feel the tears building in the back of her eyes, but the last thing she wanted to do was to cry. There was a small crowd gathering outside the church, all waiting to see the bride, but this was turning into something more spectacular for all the wrong reasons. The humiliation was fierce.

'When did he go?' she asked.

'This morning.'

'And did he put in for this transfer?' she pressed.

Poor Howard, having to clear up the mess Brett had left behind him.

'I think his father has connections,' Howard admitted. 'Look. I don't agree with what he's done at all.'

'He must have asked his dad to step in,' said Jess. 'What a coward!'

'I can think of worse to call him,' said Alice's father.

'Did he want to be transferred?' Alice's voice sounded small and broken.

Howard awkwardly looked down at the ground again and then back at Alice. 'He didn't object.'

It was Alice's turn to avoid eye contact. 'That's a yes, then.'

At that moment, a military vehicle from the US air base pulled up and an officer stepped out. He looked at Howard. 'Airman Jeffers, you're dismissed. Wait in the car.'

Howard saluted his superior. 'Sir.' He paused, took an envelope from his pocket and passed it to Alice. 'He left this for you … I'm sorry.'

Alice managed to nod. She couldn't quite bring herself to speak.

'Off you go,' the officer instructed Howard.

'I take it you know all about what one of your men has done?' said Alice's father, glaring at the American. 'What a bloody shambles you lot are.'

'I'm Captain Mitchell, and I was in charge of Airman Cunningham, but as of 0800 hours this morning, he was transferred out and I'm not at liberty to divulge any further information. Now, I understand this is a difficult situation—'

'Difficult? It's bloody disgraceful,' snapped Alice's father.

'Dad, just leave it,' said Alice quietly. She tugged at her father's arm. 'Let's go home.'

Alice's father shrugged off her hand. 'I haven't started yet,' he said, going nose to nose with the American captain. 'You get that excuse for a man back here so he can fulfil his obligation to my daughter.'

'I'm sorry, that's not possible,' replied Mitchell. 'And as far as I'm aware, he has no obligation.'

'What are you talking about?' demanded Alice's father.

The captain raised his eyebrows. 'The obligation is not his. Impossible, actually. You know some British girls have been taking advantage of American servicemen. They think there's a better life waiting for them across the water. They haven't always been ... how shall I say? ... honest about the apparent obligations for our airmen and the origin of such obligations.'

Alice could see her father's face turn a bright red. The anger was just seconds away from bursting out of him. She stepped between her father and Mitchell.

'I'm not even going to give you the satisfaction of an answer. I suggest you go before you say anything else you regret.'

Mitchell turned on his heel and strode back to his car. Alice watched as it sped away from the church.

'You go home now,' said Jess. 'We're causing quite a scene. I'll go and tell the vicar.'

Alice nodded; the build-up of tears was perilously close to tumbling from her eyes. She pulled her dad by the sleeve and silently they climbed back into the car.

As soon as they arrived home, Alice raced upstairs to her bedroom, dumping the bouquet of flowers onto the floor. It was then she allowed the hot, angry tears to cascade freely down her face as she yanked off her wedding dress. Tears of anger, humiliation, disbelief and hurt. How could he do this to her? How could he just leave without telling her?

In just her petticoat, she climbed into bed, pulling the covers up over her head. She wanted to be left alone. It was then the thought struck her and pulled her up sharp. She wasn't alone, was she? Her hand went to her stomach. She had her baby inside her. It wasn't just her who Brett abandoned; he'd abandoned their child as well. Now it was just her and the baby. No one else.

This made her cry all over again, but for different reasons. What on earth was she going to do? How was she going to look after a baby by herself?

She ignored the knock at the door the first time, but the second time, she raised her head from under the blanket. 'Go away, please.'

She couldn't face talking to her dad – not right now. He'd be full of 'I told you so' and she would have to admit that he was right and she was wrong.

The door opened a fraction.

'Alice. It's me. Jess.'

Alice hid her head under the blanket again. 'I just want to be on my own.'

The door closed but Jess's footsteps clipped across the floorboards. Alice felt the bed dip as Jess sat on the edge of the mattress. She pulled the blanket down from Alice's face. 'Want a hug?'

Alice nodded and Jess leaned over, her arms around Alicc's shoulders and her head resting against Alice's.

'I didn't think he'd do that to me,' sniffed Alice after a while.

Jess sat up. 'He didn't say anything to Howard either. Apparently, Brett carried on as normal.'

'He's obviously a good liar. He had everyone fooled. I'm the biggest idiot there is. I actually believed him.'

'What did he say in his letter?'

Alice had forgotten all about the letter Howard had given her. She'd stuffed it inside the bouquet of flowers. She got out of bed and retrieved the envelope.

Dear Alice,

I'm sorry. I can't go through with this. My parents are against it, too. I'm too young to be tied down to family, especially with a child that my family might not accept as a Cunningham. I wouldn't be able to take you back home, and neither could I stay in England once the war is over. It's best this way. I've enclosed some money for you. I'm sorry it's not more but I hope it will help.

From Brett

'The cheek!' said Jess. 'A baby his family might not believe is a Cunningham. You know what he's saying, don't you?'

Alice nodded grimly. She didn't need it spelled out by Jess. It was perfectly clear what Brett was implying. 'I don't know what I'm going to do.'

'Don't think about that right now,' said Jess. 'Give yourself a couple of days.'

She hugged Alice again and they sat back against the iron bedstead, Alice resting her head on Jess's shoulder. She knew Jess was trying to be helpful, but didn't really know what to say, because what was there to say?

14 September 1944

Carissime Mamma e Sofia

There's talk of us being transferred to England. They have camps there for German and Italian soldiers. Apparently, some of us will be sent to work on the surrounding farms and I hope I am chosen to do so. The British people are grateful for the help on the land as, like Italy, all their fit young men are away fighting. This war seems so senseless. Please pray it will end soon.

My leg is feeling a lot stronger now. It is still weaker than the other one, but I am doing exercises to strengthen it and am hopeful for a full recovery.

How is baby Luca? I expect he is growing up and changing so fast. I wish you were able to send a photograph of him, rather than just these flimsy letters. Does he sleep well at night? I can't wait to meet him.

I hope this letter doesn't take too long to reach you. I think it's usually about a month, but I know some are taking longer. Just as well there is no limit on the amount we can send, as I find it very comforting writing to you both. It's the next best thing to actually talking to you. Our letters are censored before they are sealed and sent via Switzerland and the Red Cross, who then send them on to you. We don't have to pay for them either, thanks to the Red Cross.

I will write again as soon as I can.

Until we meet again, take care of each other.

Il vostro amorevole figlio e fratello

Paolo

9
Nate

2022

Nate had sensed Rhoda's hesitancy at staying for supper, so he was surprised when she said yes. He wasn't entirely sure why his father wanted her there and wondered if he was perhaps a little lonely.

After collecting the fish and chips and dropping some around to his aunt, who had declined the offer to join them over at Telton Hall because she wanted to 'watch her TV programme in peace', Nate and Isaac returned to the house. From the hallway, he could hear Rhoda and his father discussing her work. It was nice to hear him talking about something other than the sale of the house for once.

'Where do you want to eat?' Nate asked, poking his head around the door to the living room.

'The kitchen will be fine for a fish and chip supper,' said Jack, rising from his chair and gesturing for Rhoda to go ahead of him.

Nate led the way down the hall to the kitchen at the rear of the property.

'Oh, you've got lots of photos,' Rhoda commented, pausing at the vast array of photographs hanging in the hallway. 'Some of them are quite old.'

'They've been there for years,' said Jack. 'My mother put some up and then Nate's mother added to them.'

'Bit of a rogues' gallery, as they say,' said Nate.

'So, you grew up here, too?' asked Rhoda as they entered the kitchen.

Nate put the bag of food on the table and went to the dresser to fetch some plates.

'Yes, that's right. I went to uni but never really came back to live at the house. I worked in London for a while and then relocated back to the area about ten years ago.' He laid the plates out on the table and took the food from the bag. 'There you go, Isaac.'

'Shame, really,' said Jack. 'I always hoped I'd be able to pass this place on to the next generation of Hartwells. I did ask Nate to move in when he got married but he didn't want to. Preferred a fancy new house in town.'

Nate mouthed an apology towards Rhoda, but before he could head the conversation off in a different direction, Isaac decided to pipe up.

'Mum didn't like it here. She said it was creepy.'

'I don't remember her saying it was creepy,' said Nate. 'Just not her style.'

'She definitely said creepy. She also said it was cold, draughty and smelly.' Isaac poked a chip into his mouth, keeping his gaze fixed on his plate.

'Out of the mouth of babes,' muttered Jack.

'Isaac tends to speak his mind,' said Nate. He looked over at his son, who was systematically moving his chips as far away from his piece of fish as the plate would allow.

'There's nothing wrong with speaking your mind,' Rhoda said, and this time without the spike Nate had expected to hear in her voice. 'Did you grow up here alone?' she asked Jack, and Nate was grateful for the steer in conversation.

'I had an older sort of stepbrother – William, everyone called him Billy. He was my mother's stepson from her first marriage – so no blood relation to me or Mum. His father, my mother's first husband, died. Billy didn't have any other family, so when he was injured in the war, my mother took him in. He was quite a bit older than me,' said Jack. 'Of course, I had my cousin, Aggie, who lives across the road. She's been more like a sister.'

'Is the cottage part of the Telton Hall estate?' asked Rhoda.

'No. It's privately owned. My aunt's a tenant. She's allowed to live there for the rest of her time,' explained Nate. 'It's on an old-fashioned type of agreement, and unfortunately Dad can't move in there as Aggie's not allowed to sublet, which is technically what she'd be doing. Basically, the agreement is watertight so no one else can continue to live there after Aggie dies. They don't want another sitting tenant.'

'Ah, I see. That's a shame. Where's Billy now?' asked Rhoda. 'Is he still alive?'

Nate took a sip of his drink. Rhoda didn't beat around the bush when it came to asking questions. Very direct. He looked at Isaac and felt a pang of sadness for his son. Isaac was direct and honest. Nate hoped he'd somehow be able to develop the communication skills to allow himself to fit comfortably into social situations.

'He's dead,' said Jack. 'Well, we assume he is.'

'Assume?'

'Yes. He moved on just after the war. He was always going on about wanting to travel and see a bit more of the world. He just had to wait until the war was over. Had fancy ideas about America or Canada. We weren't very close and didn't keep in touch.'

'Git,' said Isaac. 'G-I-T. Noun. An unpleasant person. Grandad said Billy was a git.'

'Isaac!' Nate put down his cutlery. 'You're not to say that.'

'Grandad said it.'

'It doesn't mean you should,' said Nate patiently.

He wanted to apologise to Rhoda again, but it almost felt like a betrayal of Isaac. Whenever Isaac said anything like this, Nate always had to quickly evaluate the situation and invoke damage limitation measures. Today, though, he didn't feel he needed to do that. Rhoda had suppressed a smile and carried on as if it was perfectly normal.

'Anyway, it's the truth,' said Jack. 'He was horrible. He came back from the war with a dodgy leg. Had sepsis. I'm sure that poison stayed in his blood. Made him very bitter and nasty. A proper git.'

'Dad!' Nate shook his head at his father.

'Proper git,' repeated Isaac.

'Sorry about them two,' said Nate.

'I didn't hear a thing.' Rhoda threw Jack a conspiratorial wink.

After they'd eaten their supper, Nate cleared the table, refusing to let Rhoda help, and then made them all a drink.

'I should be getting off soon,' she said, as they made their way out of the kitchen. 'I don't want to hold you up either.'

Nate checked his watch, surprised at how quickly the past hour had gone. 'You're not holding us up. We'll probably head off in about an hour.'

Rhoda paused in the hallway. 'I love looking at old photos.' She peered closer. 'Is this Telton Hall?'

'Yes, that was the turn of the nineteenth century, I believe,' said Nate, stepping closer to look at the photo.

'And this one – is more recent? Are these people your family?' She was looking at the next photo along.

'That was taken during the war,' said Nate.

'April 1945,' said Isaac.

Rhoda looked down at him. 'Do you know who the people are?'

'Don't be worrying about all that now,' said Jack. He had stopped further up the hall at the door to the living room.

'Louise Hartwell,' said Isaac, pointing at the photograph. He moved his finger along each of the people. 'Billy. Aggie. Alice. Lily. Granddad.'

'That's impressive,' said Rhoda.

'I didn't know you knew their names,' said Nate.

Isaac had a knack for retaining information.

'Aunt Aggie told me,' said Isaac.

'Is that you in this picture, Jack?' asked Rhoda.

'Yes. I was about ten, I think,' replied Jack.

'And the girls – are they related?'

'The younger girl, that's Aunt Aggie,' replied Nate. 'She's my dad's cousin. The other two were just staying here.'

'It's interesting to see how the landscape changed during the war. You can see all the home produce being grown at the front of the house.'

'Yes,' said Nate. 'They had to farm every bit of spare land to help feed the country.'

Rhoda was moving along the hallway, looking at the other photographs. 'And who are these men?'

Nate stepped closer to her and peered at the photo. 'You know, I must have passed these pictures a thousand times but never really paid much attention to them. Let's see ... Ah, yes, they are the prisoners of war who worked on the farm.'

'Paolo. Carlo,' said Isaac from behind them.

Nate turned to look at his son. 'And how do you know that? I'm not sure I even knew their names.'

'Aunt Aggie told me.'

'Aunt Aggie knows everything,' said Nate.

'I'm so impressed by your memory,' said Rhoda to Isaac. 'You're amazing.'

'Amazing,' repeated Isaac. 'A-M-A-Z-I-N-G. Adjective. Causing great surprise or wonder.'

With that, he walked off down the hall to the living room.

'He likes facts and figures,' said Nate. 'Spelling and reciting the meaning is his new thing.'

Rhoda nodded. 'Well, he is even more amazing in that case.'

Nate hesitated. He didn't like to highlight Isaac's

differences from what society regarded as 'normal', but at the same time, he wanted to tell Rhoda.

Rhoda saved him the dilemma. 'I take it Isaac's on the spectrum.'

Nate met her gaze. There was no pity in her expression, just a straightforwardness. 'Yes. He is, but he's also so much more than that.'

'Goes without saying.'

Nate wasn't sure if he'd been gently reprimanded by Rhoda or not, but he appreciated the way she didn't offer sympathetic platitudes which often followed the realisation that Isaac was on the spectrum, well-meaning comments as they were. Nate hated the way his son stopped being Isaac to people who couldn't see past his autism.

'He is the constant joy in my life,' said Nate.

'Again, goes without saying.' Rhoda returned her gaze to the wall of photographs. 'So, these POWs, they worked on the farm?'

'Actually, I think a couple of them lived on the farm. It wasn't uncommon, especially for the Italians, who opted to co-operate after Italy surrendered. Some of them went back to the POW camp in the evenings, but from what I've heard about my grandmother, Louise Hartwell, she was a very forward-thinking, liberal woman.'

'Sounds like it,' said Rhoda. 'Do you think it was one of these men who made the stained-glass window?'

'I think it was, actually. I don't know a great deal about it. Dad's not very good on the details. I could ask Aggie.'

'Would she know about the family Bible and the ledgers?'

'Quite possibly. I'll have a chat with her tomorrow.' Nate moved along the hall with Rhoda as she looked at more photographs. 'You should be investigating this case, not the police.'

'I don't think Shepherd seemed very interested in pursuing it,' said Rhoda. 'Aren't you interested? Concerned? Curious, even?'

There she was again, doing that thing where she spoke her mind and made him feel he was being told off. Like he'd got the answer to a question wrong, and she was giving him the chance to correct himself before it was too late.

'I am, as it happens,' he said. 'I don't think I'd be offering to find out more information if I wasn't.'

'True,' she said simply. 'Ah, this is your father, isn't it?' Rhoda tapped a photograph halfway along the wall.

'Yep. He's about twelve in that photo. And along here, you can see when my mother started adding to the wall. There's their wedding photo. And this one here is when I was born. I was a surprise baby, apparently. My mother's not about anymore. My parents separated after I finished uni. They were just waiting for me to leave home. She lives up in Scotland now.'

'Sorry to hear that.'

Nate gave a shrug. 'It happens. It hasn't scarred me or anything.' He lowered his voice. 'In fact, it was a relief. I used to hate coming home as there was always an atmosphere. That's why I went off to London.'

'It must be so nice to have all this family history right here, even if your parents have split,' said Rhoda, turning back to the wall pictures. 'All these photographs to look at whenever you want.'

Nate gave a shrug. 'I guess so. I've never really thought about it, to be honest. They've just always been there.'

'Lucky you,' Rhoda said softly.

10
Alice

1945

Alice stepped off the train, her battered brown suitcase in hand, and looked for the exit. She took the slip of paper from her pocket and checked the address and directions. Mrs Armitage had stepped in to help when she heard that Brett had abandoned her. After speaking with Alice's father, it was agreed that Alice should go and stay in Somerset with Mrs Armitage's sister, Louise Hartwell, for the duration of her confinement and the six weeks that would follow the birth of the baby. During this time, Mrs Hartwell would arrange for the adoption of the child.

Mrs Armitage had been the one to talk to Alice and convince her this was the best course of action, not just for Alice herself but for the baby. Alice had been too numb to argue. And what was the point? Everything Mrs Armitage said was true. What future could Alice offer a baby? An eighteen-year-old mother, no more than a child herself, with no husband, no home and no income, as she wouldn't be able to work once the child was born. Rice's Department Store certainly wouldn't employ an unmarried mother.

And so, the arrangements were made, and within two weeks of being stood up at the altar, Alice was now in Somerset.

She left the station and turned left, where, according to the instructions, she was to walk along the road heading out of the village until she came to a sign which marked the way to Telton Hall.

It didn't take too long before Alice found herself at the gates to Telton Hall.

The farmhouse was built in a creamy-coloured stone, different from that back home, with sash windows symmetrically placed across the face of the building. Two dormer windows looked out from the rooftop. Smoke plumed from the chimney pot and, although the paint was peeling from the gate, there was a homely feel to the place.

The grassed areas which ran alongside the driveway and the garden at the front of Telton Hall had all been given over to growing fruit and vegetables. The whole of the right-hand side looked like it had been dedicated to potatoes, and the other side to other types of root vegetables, some of which were just beginning to poke their way through the soil.

The rumble of an engine from behind took her by surprise. She turned around to see an army truck trundling up the driveway. As it passed, she could see half a dozen men sitting in the back, wearing some sort of uniform that she didn't recognise. A couple of them waved and called out to her.

'Hello, pretty girl!'

Alice was shocked. She could tell by their accent they weren't British, but German, and maybe Italian. What on earth were enemy soldiers doing driving around the place?

The door to the house opened and a woman in her mid-forties, with her hair pulled back, wearing a long white apron over a blue floral dress, called to her.

'Are you Alice Renshaw?'

'Yes. Yes, I am.' Alice looked to where the truck had now parked up and several men were disembarking. She turned back to the woman. 'Who are they?'

The woman laughed. 'Oh, don't worry, we're not being invaded. They're the prisoners of war. They work here on the farm.'

Alice knew her mouth had gaped open again. 'Prisoners of war? Working here on the farm?'

'We need all the help we can get with most of the men off fighting,' said the woman. 'For the most part, they're polite young men who seem only too glad to be out of the war. Anyway, I'm Louise Hartwell.'

'Pleased to meet you,' replied Alice automatically, while still trying to take in what Mrs Hartwell had just explained. She wasn't quite sure how she felt about enemy soldiers on the farm. It certainly wasn't what she had expected.

'You'd better come inside,' said Mrs Hartwell.

Alice followed the older woman into the terracotta-tiled hallway. The door on the right was ajar and Alice could see it was the sitting room. The door on the left was closed. Mrs Hartwell led her down the hallway to the back of the house and into a large kitchen – well, certainly larger than the one Alice had grown up with in their two-bedroom terraced house in Suffolk. A black range occupied the side wall, with a big mantel around it and shelving for various pots and pans. Above that was a drying rack, tied up out of the way with some laundry draped over the wooden rungs. On the opposite wall was a pine dresser, displaying mismatched crockery and various storage jars. On the other wall was the window, with a sink below and a wooden drainer. A blue and white checked curtain was strung below the sink, the tautness in the wire long since expired so the hem of the fabric touched the orange terracotta tiles.

Another woman, older than Mrs Hartwell, was standing at the pine kitchen table in the centre of the room, kneading dough. Standing next to her, peeling potatoes, was a young dark-haired girl, who looked about twelve or thirteen.

'This is Cook,' said Mrs Hartwell. And then to her employee, 'This is Alice Renshaw. She's come to stay with us.'

'Nice to meet you,' said Cook, smiling at Alice.

'And this here is my niece, Agatha,' said Mrs Hartwell. 'She lives across the road in Telton Cottage with my sister-in-law. Agatha's and Jack's fathers were brothers, but sadly neither are no longer with us.'

'Hello, Agatha,' said Alice.

'Hello,' said the young girl. 'Everyone calls me Aggie, except my aunt.' She gave an exaggerated sigh and rolled her eyes.

Mrs Hartwell chuckled. 'You'll have to excuse my niece, she's rather dramatic.'

The warmth between Aggie and Mrs Hartwell was clear – something that reassured Alice. She could imagine her mother being just like Mrs Hartwell.

'I'll make you a drink and something to eat once I've finished here,' said Cook.

'It's all right. I'll do it.' Mrs Hartwell busied herself with putting the kettle on the range to boil and ladling a bowl of soup out for Alice. 'Sit yourself down.'

'Thank you,' said Alice; the smell of the soup was making her stomach rumble.

'Once you've eaten, I'll show you to your room and introduce you to Lily. You'll be sharing with her. Nice young girl who will show you around,' said Mrs Hartwell, placing the bowl of soup on the table. 'I'll be back in a minute. If you need anything, Cook or Agatha will help you.'

'Don't look so scared,' said Cook after her employer had left the room. 'Mrs Hartwell's a good woman and she'll look after you. And Lily's a good girl, too. She came here last year and liked it so much, she didn't want to leave. Now eat up before it goes cold.'

A short time later, Mrs Hartwell returned to collect Alice and led her back out into the hall and up the staircase, which was at least twice as wide as the staircase at home. It looked more like it belonged in Rice's Department Store.

'It's a lovely house,' said Alice as they reached the first floor.

'It's not quite as grand as my sister's house and we don't have all the staff, so apologies if it's not quite what you were expecting. We do have running water and an inside toilet, so not too far behind the Suffolk contingent in terms of luxury.' There was a touch of humour to her voice and she smiled at Alice, underlining there was no sibling rivalry between the households. 'Now this floor is where me and my two sons, Billy and Jack, have a room each. Billy is actually my stepson from my first marriage. He lives here since being discharged from the army on medical grounds as he hasn't got any family. Jack is my son with Mr Hartwell. Anyway, you're along here. You'll be with Lily.' She paused at a door on the landing. 'This door leads up to the attic. We have a couple of Italian prisoners who live up there, so don't be alarmed if you see them in the house. You shouldn't need to go up there. They bring their own bedding down and keep it clean themselves. Besides, the stairs are very steep and I wouldn't want you slipping.'

'Yeah, we don't want any accidents,' came a male voice from the foot of the main stairs. 'We can't afford to have you laid up in bed with a twisted ankle or carted off to the hospital for something more serious.'

Alice and Mrs Hartwell looked around.

'Don't be saying things like that, Billy.' Mrs Hartwell turned to Alice. 'That's my stepson.'

Alice felt strangely unsure of herself as she gave a polite smile towards the man.

'Hello.'

He was leaning against the newel post, with one hand on the top of the post and the other holding on to a walking stick. His dark hair was cut short at the back and sides, with a fringe that had fallen over his left eye. His grey shirt was rolled up at the sleeves.

'You must be Alice,' he said, his gaze momentarily flitting to her stomach and then back to her eyes.

'That's right. Pleased to meet you.'

'Pleased to meet you, too. Louise has told me all about you.'

Alice felt an uneasy sensation roll around in her stomach and she pulled her cardigan across her body. She wasn't quite sure she liked the tone to his voice, but not knowing the first thing about him, she gave him the benefit of the doubt and bit down a smart reply that was threatening to burst from her mouth. Her father had always said her smart mouth would get her into trouble. Now wasn't the time for that to happen – not when she'd been inside the house for barely an hour.

'Let's go along to your room.' Mrs Hartwell headed off down the hall.

Alice followed, taking a glance back over her shoulder at Billy, whose slow smile and wink had her scampering after her hostess.

The room had three wrought-iron single beds. Two were made up with heavy blankets and eiderdowns, while the third was unmade.

'Is it just the two of us?' asked Alice.

'Yes, but I've room for one more if needs be. This bed is yours – Lily's got the one over here.' Mrs Hartwell crossed the room and pulled the curtains apart, then opened the window. 'I'm always telling her to let some fresh air in. Right, I'll leave you to unpack. The bathroom is back along the hall. There's a jug and bowl on the dresser here that you can fill up with water. Dinner is at six o'clock sharp. If you're late and it's all gone, then you'll be going hungry. Breakfast at 6.30.'

Alice nodded. She walked over to the window, taking in the glorious view before her.

'It's so beautiful here,' she said softly.

'Have you never been out of Suffolk?'

Alice shook her head. 'No. Not really. My mum took me to London once to visit a relation, but I was only young and I don't really remember much about it.'

'Well, I've never been to London, so you've done more than me now.'

Alice smiled as she continued to look out of the window. It was then she noticed a stone building on top of the hill.

'What's that up there?'

Mrs Hartwell followed Alice's gaze.

'Oh, that's the family chapel.'

Alice inwardly winced. She wasn't the religious kind at all – least not since her mother had died. She hoped she hadn't now stepped into an ultra-religious household.

'It looks …' She struggled for a word other than *bleak* but failed.

'Uninviting?' supplied Mrs Hartwell. 'Don't worry, I hate the bloody place. Up there on the hill, catching all the bad weather. It's as draughty as anything. You won't ever see me up there. I made that perfectly clear to Mr Hartwell when I married him.'

Alice smiled in relief. 'You didn't get married up there, then?'

'No, I didn't! Local village church. Right, well, I've got things to do. Have the afternoon to yourself and I'll see you for dinner at six.'

'Thank you, Mrs Hartwell, I really appreciate you taking me in,' said Alice sincerely.

The older woman paused in the doorway. Her face softened for a moment before she gave a small nod and bustled out of the room, calling over her shoulder as she went, 'Six o'clock sharp.'

Alice turned back to the window, her gaze inexplicably drawn towards the chapel. Her first impression of it remained: a bleak and unwelcoming building.

3 January 1945

Carissime Mamma e Sofia

Buon anno! – Happy New Year

If you have been praying for me, asking God to look over me, then I am happy to say your prayers have been answered.

I have been moved to a camp in the west of England. I am in a lovely part of the country. It reminds me of home. There are rolling hills all the different shades of green and there are wooded areas, too.

The camp is on the outskirts of a small village and there is a farm where I am working. I have been working there for a week, helping with the animals and with the crops they are growing.

There is a large kitchen garden that I know you would love, Mother. You could make some wonderful dishes with the vegetables and fruit which are grown there.

The owner, Mrs Hartwell, is kind to us. She has two sons, and there are some young women who work here, too. They help on the farm and in the kitchen. One of them is a fine mechanic and repaired the old tractor they have when not one of us could work out what was wrong.

There is a chapel on the farm. It is a strange building. It sits high up on a hill all on its own. It is a private chapel just for the family, but I don't think anyone uses it much. They go to the local village church. I have asked if I can attend church on a Sunday and am waiting to find out. As you know, I don't much believe in God, but being so far from home and feeling so helpless, it's the only thing I can think to do that might be of any use.

We are taken from the camp every day by truck under guard of British soldiers, and we are dropped off at the different farms each morning and then picked up again in the evening. Some of the prisoners have been given accommodation on the farms and live there. I am told that they are the most trusted prisoners, and you have to earn the right to stay at the farms. There is already an Italian prisoner living where I am working.

I am going to try to see if they will eventually let me live on the farm, it will be so much nicer than having to go back to the camp each night and be locked up. Every night, before we have to black out the windows, I lie in my bunk and look up at the sky through the window and I pray that you and Sofia and baby Luca are looking up at the same sky, the same moon. It makes me feel closer to home and to you both. I wouldn't admit it to any of the men here, but I have felt homesick. I'm desperate for the time when this war is over and I can come home. I will never complain about being bored or having nothing to do. It will make me happy just to spend time with my family.

I must sign off now as there is no more space on this paper to write.

Until we meet again, take care of each other.

Il vostro amorevole figlio e fratello

Paolo

11
Rhoda

2022

Two days had passed since Rhoda's fish and chip supper with the Hartwells, and she still hadn't heard anything from DS Shepherd as to whether the chapel had been released as a crime scene – and, more importantly, whether they were going to conduct a murder investigation, or at least try to find out who the victim was. It had been constantly on her mind and the previous night she'd even begun searching the internet, trying to find out a bit more of the history of Telton Hall in the hope that she herself might find some sort of clue to the identity of the body.

So far, she hadn't found out anything more than Nate had told her already. Telton Hall had always been a farm and had always been in the Hartwell family. It had moved from dairy to arable after the First World War, and during the Second World War had taken on German and Italian POWs as farm labour. Louise Hartwell had a philanthropic approach and was known for taking those less fortunate than herself under her wing. Rhoda had gleaned that last snippet from an online parish publication aimed at tourists. The stained-glass window also got a mention, but the name of the craftsman wasn't given. None of this helped her in identifying the body in the church, though.

She rinsed her cup out and left it on the drainer, then gathered up her bag and keys, ready to head over to the workshop at the museum. The drive over to Singlewood Museum was always a pleasure, especially when the South Downs came into sight, and that morning was no exception. Rhoda reached the crest of the hill where the valley rolled out beyond in a mix of fields and woodland. The museum was situated at the foot of the hill, and soon she was pulling into the staff car park.

After parking her car, Rhoda headed for the main entrance, stopping to have a quick chat with the ladies in the gift shop and a passing exchange of pleasantries with Stuart, the head groundsman.

She liked coming to Singlewood. It was a place where she felt comfortable, and she absolutely loved the location. The structures the museum had gathered over the years were at the foot of the hill, forming a town centre; spreading out beyond that were the residential homes and a schoolhouse.

Rhoda's workshop was set back off the main street, in a large 1920s barn which had been rescued from a local farm. She shared the studio with two other crafters: Harry, who was a potter, and Helen, who spun the wool from the sheep on the site and then knitted or crocheted items for the gift shop.

Today Rhoda had the studio to herself. She switched

on the radio, poured a cup of tea from her flask, and sat down to start working on a small private commission that had come in the day before – a suncatcher to celebrate a wedding anniversary. Before she could begin her work, the phone rang.

It was DS Shepherd.

'Just wanted to let you know that the chapel has been released now,' he said. 'You're free to go back in there.'

'OK. Thanks. I was wondering about that last night.' Rhoda moved a piece of glass from the workbench to the cutting table. 'Did you find anything else out about the man?'

'Only that he was probably in his early twenties, five feet ten, slight build.'

'How long has he been there?'

'Hard to say, but forensics estimate anywhere from eighty to ninety years.'

'And cause of death?'

'You ask a lot of questions.'

'That's how you find things out,' replied Rhoda.

'Well, seeing as you've asked … blunt force trauma, as we suspected.'

'Murdered, then.'

'Probably. Can't say for certain.'

Rhoda got the feeling Shepherd wasn't telling her everything. 'Are you going to investigate the murder?'

Shepherd cleared his throat. 'It's been decided it wouldn't be in the public interest to investigate such a historic incident. We've spoken with the Hartwells again, but they can't provide any further information and, in all probability, anyone connected with the deceased are probably dead themselves.'

'*What?* Are you serious?'

'I'm sorry. I know that's not what you wanted to hear, but the decision was taken by my superiors. It's out of my hands.'

'Taken by your superiors with your recommendation.' Rhoda stood up straighter. 'What about the man's family? He might have children. Surely they deserve to know what's happened to their father?'

'I hear you,' said Shepherd. 'But without being able to identify him, there's no way of tracing any family. He might not even be local. Telton Hall was a bit of a halfway home. People came and went quite regularly, and as it wasn't an official establishment like a care home or a poorhouse or anything like that, there are no reliable records.'

'Have you looked at missing persons?'

'Of course. Records are a bit sketchy that far back, but even in those we do have, no one has been reported fitting that description,' explained Shepherd. 'And it's not just that, but I'm sure you know how stretched the police force is – there just aren't the resources or the spend to investigate something like this. If the man was murdered, then the killer is more than likely to be dead, too.'

'That's what it's down to, really, isn't it?' said Rhoda. 'Funding.'

'It's a consideration, of course.'

'Have you told the Hartwells? What was Jack's response?'

'I've just got off the phone to Nate Hartwell and he's in agreement with me, and apparently so is his father.'

Rhoda made a huffing noise. She had dealt with the authorities enough in her lifetime to know when she was banging her head against a brick wall; pursuing this any further with Shepherd was one such occasion. As for Nate Hartwell – that pissed her off. She'd told him about Dean – for some unknown reason – and she thought he had understood and was in her corner on this. She'd certainly got that one wrong. Jack, she could understand to some degree. He had enough on his plate at his time of life.

'OK. Well, thanks for the call.'

Rhoda felt both deflated and angry after speaking to Shepherd. She could only imagine the torture that man's family must have endured in the weeks, months and years after his death. Even if it was at least eighty years ago, Rhoda felt such a sense of awareness. She knew it was because of her own agony, but it felt amplified today.

She looked down at the piece of glass she needed to cut, and even the usual joy and comfort she felt from her creative work was vanished. With little enthusiasm, she picked up the glass and placed it over the paper design pattern, taped down on the workbench. Using the glass cutter tool, she rolled the blade over the glass, scoring the shape of the piece. The creak of the glass and the squeak of the cutting wheel as she applied pressure sounded louder than usual. She pushed harder as she tried to relegate thoughts of the phone call with Shepherd from her mind.

A crack snapped her from those thoughts.

'Shit.'

She'd used too much force and broken the glass. Rhoda let out a long, frustrated sigh, put the broken piece to one side in case she could use it on a smaller section, and brushed the flakes of glass into the bucket she kept at the side of the workbench. With a fresh piece of glass, she started again, only to do exactly the same thing.

'What is wrong with me?'

It was a rhetorical question to no one – not even herself. She knew exactly what was wrong with her. Was she the only one who cared about the remains they'd found at the chapel? Why was she the only one who was bothered?

She picked up her mobile phone and, despite already having looked at it first thing that morning, she went to the 'Dean Sullivan – Missing Person' Facebook page. She clicked on the notification.

Dean Sullivan – Missing Person has 1 new like.

That was unusual these days. It tended to be the other way around, where people were dropping off, having lost interest. She clicked further into the page management settings to see who had 'liked' the page. She raised her eyebrows at the information.

Nate Hartwell

That was interesting, and she felt inexplicably grateful. There was also a notification that Nate Hartwell had shared her post. It was the one she had pinned to the top, that everyone saw when they clicked on the page, with a picture of Dean smiling at the camera, standing at the top of the Trundle of the South Downs National Park, overlooking the city of Chichester and the South Coast beyond. The sun was shining and it was one of Rhoda's favourite pictures of her brother. They'd met up on their eighteenth birthday and instead of hitting the pubs and legally drinking for the first time, they'd gone for a hike. Dean had turned up at Rhoda's foster home and her foster mum had driven them up to the vantage spot. It had been a glorious day, not just because of the weather, but because they had celebrated the freedom that lay before them, even though Dean's future wasn't as secure as her own.

Rhoda clicked on Nate's profile. She wasn't sure why. She knew a lot about him from just spending the day at Telton Hall, but she was curious to get more of an insight into his private life. She hadn't quite been able to weigh him up the other day. Initially, she wasn't that impressed with him, but as the afternoon had progressed, she'd found herself re-evaluating her opinion.

Unsurprisingly, his privacy was set to the max, and apart from his profile photo and banner, there was nothing for Rhoda to see. His profile picture was of him and Isaac on holiday in the sun somewhere. A sparkling blue swimming pool was behind them; their hair was wet, and droplets of water were sitting on Nate's bare and bronzed shoulders. The header picture was another picture of him and Isaac, but this time standing on a cliff with Durdle Door in the background.

Rhoda navigated back to Dean's page and underneath the main post, she tagged Nate, thanking him for liking and sharing. It was something she did every time there was any interaction on the page; it helped keep the page active and that, in turn, helped remind people about Dean.

Rhoda felt a sense of gratitude at this small gesture of support from Nate; her earlier anger, directed at Shepherd, eased.

Picking up a fresh piece of glass, she set about cutting it, this time in a calmer and more controlled manner – and, more importantly, successfully.

Later that evening, when she was back in her flat, there was a ping from her phone. A Facebook alert. It was a message on Dean's page. Rhoda quickly looked at the notification.

Nate Hartwell has replied to your comment.

'Any time.'

That was all he'd said. Rhoda didn't know why she had hoped for more, but she 'liked' his comment. She toyed with the idea of sending him a Friend Request, but ultimately decided against it. She wasn't in the habit of friending someone she didn't really know and, besides, Nate might think it was a bit weird. She put her phone to one side, together with any notion of making any further contact with Nate Hartwell.

That night Rhoda didn't sleep well at all. She'd spent the day working in her studio, but she'd found it hard concentrating, and when she'd gone to bed, her mind had flitted from thinking about the body in the chapel, to Nate, and then to her brother. She'd thought her nights of staring at the ceiling and imagining all sorts of scenarios concerning Dean's disappearance had long since gone, but they had come back that night with a vengeance.

She was awake by six the following morning. Her head felt groggy, as if she had a hangover, and even her body protested at being forced to move. There was, of course, a remedy for this sense of weight both in her mind and body – the sea. It was one of the reasons she'd started swimming in the sea in the first place. She used to just come down to the beach early in the mornings for a walk, to clear her head and try to have some thinking space. It was on one of those days she'd met Shani, who had waded out of the water and spotted Rhoda sitting up against a breakwater. Later, Shani had told Rhoda that she had sensed her sadness immediately, and had likened Rhoda to a frightened, abandoned puppy. Shani couldn't leave the beach without checking she was OK. And thus, their friendship had begun, gently on Shani's part and tentatively on Rhoda's. The open water swimming had proved a lifeline for Rhoda and was a staple part of her daily routine.

Shani was already in the water when Rhoda got down to the beach. The sea was flat, and the gentle lap of the high tide waves was inviting as the hazy early morning sun shimmered on the surface. Seagulls lined up on the breakwater and one or two were bobbing on the tranquil waters.

Rhoda left her towel on the beach and made her way into the water. She gave a small gasp as the cold took her by surprise, but she knew from experience that getting her shoulders under the water and swimming straight away would help her adjust to the temperature.

'Ah, I'm glad I've seen you today,' said Shani.

'Why's that?' asked Rhoda as they floated on their backs, drifting with the rhythmic rise and fall of the waves.

'You haven't seemed yourself the last couple of days, and last night I couldn't stop thinking about you.'

'Have you been fiddling with those crystals of yours again?' Rhoda asked good-humouredly. She closed her eyes and tilted her head back further, spreading her arms and legs out like a starfish. Shani was a spiritual soul and, although Rhoda teased her, she had to admit Shani was intuitive and had this ability to see through the facade that Rhoda sometimes needed to throw up around herself. 'You don't have to worry about me.'

'I know I don't have to, but I like to. Want to tell me what's bothering you?'

Rhoda didn't answer immediately. Normally when people asked if she was OK, she was quick to reassure them, because if she didn't, she'd be in danger of letting them see her vulnerable side – the side where she was fully aware she had trust issues, but at the same time, she didn't care. It was easier not to trust people; that way they didn't let you down. But Shani was different. She was someone who was genuinely concerned.

'I can't stop thinking about the remains found at the chapel. I don't know whether to be angry or sad.'

'Too close to home?'

'Yes, I guess so. It's kicked up a lot of feelings I have about Dean's disappearance.'

'Feelings you're not ready to deal with, or would sooner not?'

'Something like that.' Rhoda rolled back over onto her front and began to tread water. 'I feel so helpless with Dean. The last year it's been like hitting a brick wall. I feel I've let him down. And, yes, I do know he might not actually want to be found, but what if he does? I can't stop until I have some answers. And then this body at the chapel ... What if there's a family out there having the exact same feelings as I am? What if they have been crippled all this time, not knowing. Maybe I can help them instead.'

Shani looked out of the corner of her eye at Rhoda. 'You can't save everyone.'

'But I can try.'

'So, what is your exact dilemma? What's troubling you?' There was no challenge in Shani's voice; she had this way of simply posing questions.

Rhoda was silent again for a moment. 'That the police aren't looking into it.'

'And that's what's causing the negativity?'

'Yes, I suppose it is.'

There was, of course, no *suppose* about it. Rhoda knew without a doubt that it was making her feel fed up and frustrated.

'How about channelling that negativity in another direction – into something positive? Don't worry about what you can't change, only what you can.'

Rhoda considered what her friend was saying. 'You mean, I could try to find out who the body in the chapel is, and find his family?'

'If that's what you think will help.' Shani flipped onto her front and began swimming parallel to the shoreline.

Rhoda swam after her. 'But what if I can't find out who he is, or who his family are? That will be two people I've failed.'

'But what if you succeed?' Shani stopped swimming and stood up in the waist-high water. 'What if you put someone else's family out of their misery? Besides, you're going to be at Telton Hall for a while, sorting out that window. Use the opportunity to see if you can solve the mystery. You've got until the sale completes.'

Rhoda nodded. 'You're right,' she said, looking out at the horizon where the faint outline of a row of wind turbines shimmered in the morning haze. 'Just because I can't help myself, it doesn't mean I can't help someone else.' She smiled at her friend. 'I simply need to convince the Hartwells to get on board. Despite what they say, I'm sure the key to the man's identity lies within Telton Hall.'

12
Alice

1945

Alice stood looking out of the bedroom window at Telton Hall for a long while. From her position, she could also see the fields beyond, where some men, whom she presumed were POWs, were standing on a trailer drawn by a tractor and cutting back the hedges. Alice's gaze travelled down to the walled back garden of the farm. If it had ever been used for pleasure, there was no sign of that now. The garden had been sectioned off into four areas and although Alice was no gardener, she could take an educated guess that two of those sections were vegetables, one was fruit, and the other maybe a herb garden. She wasn't sure and made a note to ask about it – maybe she could learn how to grow vegetables and fruit. It might be something she could do when she was further along her pregnancy.

As she pondered this idea, she saw the gate in the back wall open and a young man walk through, carrying a trough. He was wearing a heavy knitted jumper and a pair of grey trousers that had a red circle on the front of one of the legs.

The sound of footsteps in the hallway distracted her. The bedroom door opened and in came a young woman about Alice's own age, maybe a little younger. She was wearing the same kind of clothes as the man in the garden, but minus the red circle patch. A headscarf was wrapped around her head, fighting to keep the blonde curls at bay.

'Hello! I'm Lily.' She walked over and held out her hand. 'You must be Alice.'

'That's right. Nice to meet you,' said Alice, shaking hands with her room-mate. 'I was just looking out of the window,' she added, worried Lily would think she was nosing around her belongings.

Lily moved next to her and looked down on the garden.

'Eyeing up the prisoners, eh?' Her Midlands accent coated her words.

'What? No!'

Alice took a step back from the window, as if to reinforce the notion. Lily remained in place.

'There's two of them here,' said Lily. She slid the window closed. 'They're Italians and sleep upstairs in the attic.'

'Yes, Mrs Hartwell said. So, they don't go back to ...' Alice wasn't quite sure where they'd go back to and left the sentence unfinished.

'There is a camp, but some of them stay here on the farm. The ones that can be trusted. The others come in on a daily basis, and there's an armed guard with them.'

'Are they trouble?'

'No, they're all very polite and do as they're told. Not

that I speak to them much, but you have to sometimes, out in the fields or with the animals.'

'Seems strange them being here. Why's he got a red patch on his trousers?' asked Alice.

'So if they try to escape, it's easy to see they're POWs.'

'Have many escaped?'

'Not in all the time I've been here.' Lily turned away from the window, as if bored now.

'How long is that?' asked Alice. She sneaked another look at the prisoner as he stopped at the vegetable plot and began to dig up some onions with a small trowel.

'Nearly two years. Mrs Hartwell took me in for six months and I ended up staying. Not that I had anywhere to go.'

'Why did you come here?' Alice looked around at Lily, who was sitting at the dressing table, having untied her headscarf, and was now brushing her hair.

'Same reason as you, I'm guessing.' Lily paused and looked over at Alice. 'Bun in the oven, as they say.'

Alice's hand automatically went to her stomach. She swallowed. 'That's right. I'm having a baby.' It sounded strange to be speaking the words out loud and actually admitting – no, not admitting; that sounded like she'd done something wrong and she refused to see it like that – no, she was telling people she was pregnant now. All this time, she'd had to talk in a whisper about the pregnancy in case anyone heard – well, no longer. 'It's due in October.'

Lily resumed her hair brushing. 'Mrs Hartwell is very good. She knows people who will find the baby a good home.'

'Hmm. I suppose so.'

Lily stopped brushing her hair. 'You don't sound very convinced.'

'I'm not sure I am. It wasn't my decision to come here.'

Lily turned around on the stool. 'How are you going to keep a baby? A single woman? No man's going to want to take you and another man's child on. When this war is over, and I've heard it will be soon, think of all those young men who are coming home. They're going to want to get themselves a woman. They'll be spoilt for choice. They're not going to want a woman with a baby.'

It was a conversation Alice was familiar with, and although she knew it made sense, she still couldn't fully commit to it. She returned to looking out of the window.

The prisoner had filled the trug he had been carrying with onions and stood up, hands on his hips. He arched his back and rolled his shoulder blades, and then his neck. Whether he sensed her watching, or had simply looked up at the window, Alice didn't know, but his gaze met hers momentarily. Alice looked away. She wanted to dip out of sight but at the same time didn't want to face Lily, who was telling her about the lovely couple who had adopted her baby, and how her child was going to have a life Lily could only ever dream of giving her. Alice looked back towards the Italian. He was still looking her way. Then, he suddenly looked towards the house and his whole demeanour changed. He picked up the trug in one hand and gripped the trowel in the other.

Alice could hear someone shouting but she couldn't make out the words. She craned her neck to see who it was and saw Billy limping down the path towards the Italian. He stopped in front of him, his face only inches away, their stares locked on each other.

'What's going on down there?' Lily got up and scrambled over the bed to look out of the window. 'Oh, that's Billy. Mrs Hartwell's step-son. No one likes him but then he doesn't like anyone either. He's always getting on at someone, especially the POWs we have here – Paolo and Carlo.'

'I met him briefly earlier,' said Alice, careful not to say too much just yet. She liked Lily but she didn't know if she could trust her.

'That was nice for you,' said Lily. 'He's an angry git. Came back from the war all messed up. It's made him angry at everyone and everything. Doesn't help that there are POWs here. He takes it out on them, as if they're personally responsible for what happened to him.'

'Must be hard for him.'

The altercation appeared to be over, as Billy did his best to march off down the path towards the end of the garden. The Italian gave a glance up at the window and then headed in the opposite direction towards the kitchen.

'Don't be wasting your time with any sympathy for him. Take it from me, he's plain nasty. Mrs Hartwell doesn't even like him and she likes *everyone*. You'll be best keeping away from him.' Lily went back to fussing with her hair. 'Hopefully, one day he'll clear off, like he keeps threatening to do. Always moaning about how he hates it here.'

Alice spent some time unpacking. It didn't take too long as she didn't have much.

'I think I'll go for a walk around the farm,' she said as she closed the drawer to the dressing table.

'I'll come with you, if you want. I can show you around.'

They made their way downstairs to the kitchen where the young girl, Aggie, was now chopping up cabbage and Cook was putting the dough in the oven.

'Ah, all settled in?' asked Cook.

'Yes, thank you,' replied Alice. 'Lily is just going to show me around.'

'Righty-o. Don't be late for dinner. It's rabbit tonight.'

Once out of the house, Lily pulled a face. 'I really don't like rabbit and we have it a lot here.'

'I don't think I've ever had it.'

'Lucky you. It's all right if they manage to catch a nice one but sometimes, they come back with some really old rangy things.'

'Who catches the rabbits?'

Lily slipped her arm through Alice's as they walked down the brick path of the kitchen garden towards the gate. 'Billy and Jack. Jack is Mrs Hartwell's son.'

'What's Jack like?'

'Much nicer than Billy. Jack's just a boy. I reckon he was a surprise for Mrs Hartwell, if you get what I mean.' Lily gave Alice a nudge in the ribs with her elbow.

It occurred to Alice that maybe that's why Mrs Hartwell had sympathy for unmarried women who found themselves pregnant; maybe it was because she knew that these things happened. Alice was reminded of her father calling it 'a mistake' when talking to Mrs Armitage, but to Alice's mind it could never be a mistake. It had just happened.

'Jack's too young to be called up, then?'

Lily gave a laugh. 'Yes, he's only ten.'

'What about Mr Hartwell?'

'Oh, he's been dead quite a few years. That's when Mrs Hartwell started taking women in. I suppose she needed the money. I take it you had to pay her?'

Alice wasn't quite sure if it was right to talk money to Lily; she had the feeling that Mrs Hartwell wouldn't like it. She opted for a vague answer. 'My dad sorted it out with her. He works for her sister, Mrs Armitage. About the only good thing he's done for me, and that wasn't for my benefit. He just wanted me out of the way. What about you? Have you got any parents?'

'Yes, but I haven't seen them for nearly a year. I haven't had the money and they're busy with my brothers and sisters. I'm the eldest of seven.'

'Wow! Don't you miss them?'

Lily gave a shrug. 'Not really – not my parents, anyway. I miss my brothers and sisters sometimes, but not that much. I was always being asked to look after them while my mum and dad went to work – or in my dad's case, went to the pub, and my mum went looking for him.'

'Does Mrs Hartwell ever ask you to look after Jack?'

'No, she doesn't really go anywhere much and if she does, there's always Cook to keep an eye on him,' explained Lily. 'He's no trouble, though. Nice kid. And Aggie, she's nice, too. I don't mind them hanging around, it's different when they're not actually related to you. It's easier to put up with them.'

'I sometimes wish I had a younger brother or sister,' said Alice.

They had reached the gate to the hill now and Lily swung it open, letting Alice through first.

'It's not all sweetness and light. Sometimes, having

siblings is a complete pain. That's why I wasn't ready to have a kid of my own. I had been playing mum for long enough. Besides, what have I got to offer to a child?'

Alice didn't answer. She thought Lily was directing the question towards her as much as explaining her own reasons. And Lily was right, Alice didn't have a lot to offer – not in the material sense – but she did have love. Just as her mum had loved her, Alice had an abundance of love, and she was saving it all for her baby.

5 March 1944

Carissime Mamma e Sofia

I received your letter, and I cannot say how sad I was to hear about Franco. I have been hoping all this time for good news about him. I even went to church last month and prayed for him. My dearest sister, I am so sorry you have lost such a wonderful husband and Luca a father. It is tragic and I am heartbroken for you.

All the usual things I would write to you about seem trivial now. I wish I could be there with you to look after you and comfort you.

I cannot believe I have been here six months now – in some ways the time has gone quickly, and in other ways, it has gone so slowly it is like being tortured every day. It is times like this when I know I should be home to look after you, that being here is pure hell.

Stay strong for your son, Sofia, and I know Mamma will be looking after you. Look up at the sky when you receive this letter. Look for the brightest star and know that I, too, shall be looking at it.

Il vostro amorevole figlio e fratello

Paolo

13
Nate

2022

Nate looked at the bag DS Shepherd had given him, with the ring inside. As there was not going to be an investigation, the police no longer needed to hold on to any potential evidence they had gathered.

'What do you want to do with this?' Nate asked his father, holding the bag between his finger and thumb.

Jack shrugged. 'Throw it away. Not exactly buried treasure.'

Nate weighed the bag in his hand before popping it into his pocket. 'You're not bothered about the bones found up at the chapel, then?'

'Why should I be?' His father unfolded his newspaper and flicked it open. 'That young woman from the museum phoned earlier.'

'Rhoda?'

'That's the one. Talking about organising the scaffolding for the windows. It's not going to be a five-minute job.'

'I don't doubt it,' said Nate. 'When did she say she was coming?'

'In a couple of weeks.'

'Oh.' Nate pursed his lips.

'Is that a problem?'

'No. Not at all. I thought she'd be back sooner.' Nate gathered up his phone and briefcase. 'Right, I need to collect Isaac from Siobhan. I'll see you in a while.'

Nate had Isaac every other weekend, as well as seeing him during the week. On those weekends, he tended to stay at Telton Hall; there were far more things for Isaac to do than when he was cooped up in Nate's little one-bedroom flat in town.

Nate and Siobhan had somehow managed to navigate their divorce amicably, despite Siobhan ending up married to Nate's former best mate, Harrison. It had stung at the time, and both had promised nothing had been going on prior to the marriage breakdown, but it had been the death knell for his friendship as well as his marriage.

Nate pulled up outside the gates of the modern architectural statement property Siobhan and Harrison had had built for them the previous year. He reached over and pressed the buzzer.

'Hi. It's me.'

'Come on in, Nate.' Siobhan's voice came back.

The gate mechanism kicked in and the wrought ironwork slid back, allowing Nate to pull up on the driveway. He got out of the car but didn't approach the door. Siobhan often invited him in, but Nate always politely refused. The one time he had accepted the invitation at Isaac's insistence, Nate and Harrison had stood awkwardly in the kitchen – the high-tech, high-gloss, high-end kitchen with double bi-fold doors – where they tried to make small talk as if there was no water under the bridge for them. Nate had often wondered if he should have just punched Harrison on the jaw at the time he'd found out about their relationship and that would have cleared the air; three years down the line, he was a bit too old for rolling around on the floor in a display of misplaced and immature machoism.

Nate preferred to wait by the car for Isaac to come out, accompanied by Siobhan, only today, there was no Isaac.

'Hi, Nate.'

Siobhan was looking as immaculate as ever, even in her casual dress-down fit-wear like she was today. Nate was certain she had not purchased the outfit from the local supermarket.

'Siobhan. Everything OK?' He looked beyond her to see if Isaac was on his way.

'Yes. I wanted a quick word.' She glanced back at the house briefly. 'I heard about the body up at the chapel.'

'Grapevine's working well.'

'Actually, it wasn't the grapevine. Isaac told me all about it.' She sounded a little bit annoyed. 'I thought you might have said something.'

'Sorry, I didn't realise he'd taken it all in.'

'You know what he's like, Nate. He misses nothing.'

'He was in the other room.'

'That doesn't mean a thing.' She folded her arms and frowned at him. 'You still should have told me.'

'OK. Sorry. Again.'

'He's non-stop looking up murders and cold cases on the computer. I've had to threaten to take his tablet away.'

'I'll speak to him.'

'Do. But as I said, I'd sooner you spoke to me first in future, so Harrison and I can manage it at home.'

Nate let out a sigh. 'Message received.'

She paused for a moment, giving him one of her reproachful looks. 'Right, I'll go and get him.' Her face softened as she added, 'I'll warn you now, he's going to bend your ear reciting all the facts and figures of the unsolved cases since 1940.'

'Thanks for the heads-up.'

Nate exchanged a wry smile with Siobhan. It was much better these days, when they both veered away from confrontation. Besides, it would upset Siobhan's newly found karma, and she'd be off to her hand-crafted willow meditation dome at the bottom of the garden for the next week, drinking mint tea and eating her organically grown avocado on locally produced wholemeal multi-seeded bread, or whatever it was she ate these days.

Isaac came trundling out a short while later, with his rucksack on his back and Siobhan carrying his weekend bag.

'Hi, matey,' said Nate, ruffling his son's hair. 'All set?'

'Hello, Dad.' Isaac shrugged off his rucksack and climbed into the rear of Nate's car.

Siobhan passed the bag she was carrying to Nate. 'His uniform is all in there, and his book bag. He needs to read to the end of the book before Monday. Make sure you fill out the reading log. There's also a homework sheet about a project they need to do. I've written down some ideas so that you can go through them with him. I thought—'

Nate cut her off. 'It's OK, Siobhan, I think I'll be able to cope with Year 6 homework.'

Siobhan looked as if she wanted to argue, but instead she pressed her mouth closed and ducked down to say goodbye to Isaac.

Siobhan hadn't been wrong about Isaac memorising facts and figures. It began as they turned out onto the road.

'Did you know in England and Wales there were 695 homicide victims in the year ending March 2020?'

'No, I didn't,' replied Nate. 'How was school today?'

'Boring. The homicide rate in England and Wales for the year ending March 2020 was eleven point seven per million population, with male homicides nearly three times as many as female homicides.'

'Why was school boring?'

'Literacy. Maths. PE. Reading. Same as yesterday. There were 142 homicide victims aged between sixteen to twenty-four years old.'

'Shall we talk about something else other than murder?' suggested Nate.

'Are the police going to investigate the body at Granddad's chapel?'

Well, it was a slight improvement on the conversation.

'No. It happened too long ago.'

'Is the chapel going to be knocked down still? Is Rhoda Sullivan – S-U-L-L-I-V-A-N – coming back to fix the window?'

'They're not knocking it down, they are just going to

move it,' explained Nate. 'And, yes, I imagine that Rhoda Sullivan will have to come back.'

'I looked up where she worked,' said Isaac.

Nate raised his eyebrows. 'Did you? What did you find out?'

'The Singlewood Museum has over 150 historic buildings. Some of them date back to the Middle Ages. Rhoda Sullivan works there as a conservationist and specialises in artefacts and stained glass.'

'Good research. Would you like to go there one day?'

Nate wasn't sure why he'd suggested it, but the offer had left his mouth before he had time to consider the reasoning.

'Yes, please. Today?'

'Not today. There's not enough time.'

'Tomorrow?'

'Erm ...'

Was there a reason why they couldn't go tomorrow? Was there a reason for them to go, other than that Isaac wanted to go? Did there need to be a reason?

'I want to write about it for my project.'

'Well, that's settled, then. We shall go tomorrow.'

There, he'd said it, and he couldn't go back on his word to Isaac.

By the time they'd had their supper at Telton Hall, Isaac had provided his grandfather with a few more homicide facts and figures but since then had moved on to talking about Singlewood Museum.

When Nate came back from doing the dishes, Isaac was sitting with his grandfather and showing him pictures of the different buildings that had been relocated to the museum.

'And here's a picture of Rhoda Sullivan.'

'So it is,' said Jack.

Nate looked over his son's shoulder.

'Can I see? Oh, you're right. She's working on a stained-glass window, by the look of it.'

Rhoda was leaning over her workbench with a soldering iron in her hand. Her dark hair was tied up in a ponytail and, although she wasn't looking at the camera, there was just something about her body language and the intense but somehow enthusiastic look on her face as she carried out her work. It was the same expression he'd noticed when she was working at her laptop in the dining room.

He scanned the caption that accompanied the photograph.

'Says that she runs a workshop twice a year at the museum.'

'She certainly knows her stuff,' said Jack.

'Yeah. I think I'll take the ring with me and get her to have another look at it,' said Nate. 'There might even be someone at the museum who can shed more light on it.'

'I honestly don't know why you're bothering with an old worthless trinket,' said Jack, getting up from his chair. 'Come on, Tink. I'm going to take the dog out.'

The little terrier hopped up from beside the fireplace, ready for her usual early evening walk across the fields with her master. Nate watched his father head out. It was good he still took gentle exercise; he was a little more stooped these days and not as agile on his feet. Although the farming life had perhaps taken its toll on him earlier than had he not had a manual job, his father was a tough old sod, and his tenacity and stubbornness were good opponents for his advancing years.

Nate sat down on the sofa and absent-mindedly took the

ring from his pocket to have another look at it. He supposed it really was just a trinket, as his father had said. He wasn't even sure anyone at the museum would be interested in it.

Isaac came and sat down next to him. 'What's that?'

'That's a ring which was found up at the chapel.' He avoided mentioning the remains.

'Can I look?'

Nate shook it from the little plastic bag into the palm of his son's hand. 'It's been made from an old coin.'

Isaac examined the ring and tried it on his finger, before slipping it off and giving it back to Nate. He picked up the remote control. 'Can I watch my programmes?'

'Yeah, sure.'

'Aunt Aggie has a ring like that,' said Isaac as he flicked through the channels.

'Has she?' Nate stopped as he registered what Isaac had said. 'Wait. Aunt Aggie has a ring like this?'

'Yes. Exactly the same. Oh, cool. *Doctor Who*.'

Isaac's attention was now fully on the TV screen.

'Isaac.' Nate picked up the remote control and paused the TV. 'Sorry, mate. Quick question, then you can put it back on. How do you know Aunt Aggie has a ring like this one?'

'I've seen it. In her sewing tin.'

'When did you see it?'

'When it was her birthday and we had cake.'

Isaac swiped back the remote control and restarted his programme.

Nate knew he would be hard-pressed to get much more out of his son. He frowned as he looked at the ring. He had no reason to doubt Isaac's recollection; he was pretty good when it came to remembering stuff. As for Aggie's sewing tin, it was an old sweet tin she kept in her cupboard. She'd had it for years – or, at least, for as long as Nate could remember. But what was an old ring doing in her sewing tin, and why hadn't she mentioned it before, when he told her what the police had found? Maybe she didn't know the ring was there?

It felt significant and Nate didn't know why. He got up from the sofa and, with his hands in his pockets, looked out of the living room window, down the driveway to Telton Cottage. He needed an excuse to look in the sewing tin without raising suspicion, and he really wanted to find that ring before he went to see Rhoda the next day.

By the time his dad got back from his walk around the lower field with Tink, Nate had made up his mind to quickly see Aggie.

'Won't be long,' he called from the doorway. 'Just need to pop over to the cottage.'

He purposely didn't wait for his father to ask why.

'Hello, Nathan,' Aggie greeted him as he came into the cottage. She was probably the only person who called him by his full name.

'I thought you'd have locked up by now,' said Nate, giving Aggie a peck on the cheek. 'It's one thing leaving your door unlocked during the day, but honestly, Aggie, you really should lock it by teatime.'

She waved his comments away with her hand. 'Yes. Yes. I just forgot.'

Nate gave her his best 'did you really?' look but decided not to get on the wrong side of her, seeing as he needed her help. 'I just wanted to ask you something,' he began. 'I was showing Isaac the ring that was found up at the chapel, and he was adamant he'd seen one just like it in your sewing tin. Can I have a quick look?'

Aggie's face stiffened. 'A ring? In the sewing tin? I don't think so. Why would I have a ring like the one found?'

'I'm not sure. It's quite a coincidence.' Nate took the ring from his pocket. 'It looks like this, apparently.'

Aggie put her glasses on and took a closer look at the handmade jewellery. 'Oh, a ring like that.' She dropped it back into Nate's hand. 'The POWs used to make them all the time. I may well have one in the tin, although goodness knows what it's doing in there.'

'Can I look?'

'If you must.'

Nate didn't miss the hint of irritation in his aunt's voice but, undeterred, he went to the cupboard in the dining room and from the shelf he took the tin, placing it on the table. He prised off the lid and was confronted with a selection of threads and needles, a tiny pair of scissors, a coiled-up tape measure and other odds and sods, all on a bed of buttons.

'It's like stepping back in time,' said Nate. 'When did you last use the tin?'

'Oh, I can't remember. Never liked sewing.'

Nate took out the sewing items, so he could rummage around in the sea of buttons – wooden toggles, leather ones, some more fancy ones shaped like flowers or with gold embellishments, and plenty of white plastic buttons in various sizes. It was at the bottom of the tin he spotted the ring, easily overlooked among the contents. Nate picked it out.

'Here it is. Isaac was right.' He showed the ring to his aunt.

'Well, there's a turn up.' Aggie donned a surprised look. 'The POWs were always giving these out to the locals. I think they thought it would impress us.'

'Did one of them give it to you?'

Aggie shrugged. 'I can't remember. Probably. Or maybe one of the girls at Telton Hall gave it to me or left it behind. It was all a long time ago.'

'Can I borrow it to show Rhoda Sullivan from the museum?'

'I suppose so.'

'Just one more thing. Do you know where the family Bible is?'

'What do you want that for?' A frown creased Aggie's brow.

'We thought it might give us some clue to who was here at the farm, and who the remains might be.'

Aggie gave a disapproving scoff. 'I've no clue where the family Bible is. If anyone knows, it will be your father.'

As Nate walked back over to Telton Hall, he tried to work out whether this was important or not. Was another ring significant? The POWs made them. One was found with the remains. Was it a coincidence? Ultimately, did it make any difference to the police's decision not to investigate? Probably not but, all the same, something about it all was beginning to bother him. By the time he'd reached Telton Hall, he'd given himself a talking-to. He was trying to make a connection because that's what Rhoda wanted to hear. He needed to get a grip of his usual pragmatic no-nonsense self and stop trying to satisfy Rhoda's need to solve a mystery that didn't exist.

14
Rhoda

2022

Rhoda had been surprised to receive a call from Nate Hartwell the previous evening, explaining that he was bringing his son over to the museum and he wanted to show her the ring found at the chapel.

'I spoke to your dad earlier, just to keep him up to date with the schedule of works. I didn't think I'd be back down for a couple of weeks, but on reflection, there are a few things I need to double-check before work can start to remove the window. I'm a bit pushed for time this coming week, so was hoping I could pay a weekend visit.'

'There's no reason why you can't,' Nate had replied. 'I was planning on bringing Isaac up to the museum tomorrow. He's keen to have a look around. You could drive back down with us in the afternoon. I mean, in your own car.'

'Naturally.'

'Yes. Naturally. So ... erm ... well ... it's up to you.'

Rhoda had smiled to herself at his awkwardness. 'So, I'll see you in the morning.'

'Yes. Look forward to it. Isaac will look forward to it. I will as well,' he had hurried to qualify.

Nate and Isaac arrived just after ten, which had given Rhoda time to have a cup of tea and set out a small glass project she used when the local primary school kids came. She wasn't sure if Isaac would want to participate in anything hands-on, but at least the opportunity would be there.

A small tap at the door had Rhoda looking up. She could see Nate's face through the glass and waved him in. 'You made it. Did you have a good journey?'

'Yes, all very straightforward, thanks to the satnav.' Nate smiled at her.

Rhoda said hello to Isaac, who was slowly undertaking a full 360° examination of the workshop.

'Isaac, say hello to Rhoda,' encouraged Nate.

'Oh, don't worry,' said Rhoda, smiling to reassure Nate she wasn't at all offended. 'Do you want a drink? Tea? Coffee? I have water, or I think there's some squash over in the corner. It's Helen's, who does the spinning, but she won't mind.'

For some reason, the first five or ten minutes felt a little awkward. Rhoda wasn't sure if that was coming from her or from the Hartwells, but by the time they'd finished their drinks and talked about the traffic, the weather and how nice the setting of Singlewood was, they all appeared to relax a little.

'Did you want to have a go at making a stained-glass

window light?' Rhoda asked Isaac as she gathered up the empty cups.

Isaac looked at the workbench where Rhoda had laid out the pieces of glass which, when put together, would be the Superman logo. Isaac shook his head. 'No, thank you.'

'You might enjoy it,' said Nate. He looked apologetically at Rhoda.

'No. Thank you,' repeated the ten-year-old.

'That's absolutely fine,' said Rhoda. 'I like honesty.'

'Yeah, so, that ring,' said Nate, pulling a small zip-sealed bag from his pocket as if he was about to do a drugs deal. He placed it on the workbench. 'The police gave it back to me. I asked Dad what he wanted to do with it, but he didn't seem bothered so I thought you might like to have a look at it.'

'It's the same as Aunt Aggie's ring,' said Isaac.

Rhoda looked questioningly at Nate.

'I was just about to come to that,' said Nate. 'Isaac said he'd seen one over at my aunt's house. In her sewing tin, of all places. Anyway, sure enough, there was.' He produced another ring from his pocket and placed it next to the first. 'They look identical to me.'

'Wow. Your aunt had this?' Rhoda picked them both up and inspected them closely. 'Did she say where she got hers from?'

'She couldn't remember. Said the POWs used to make them and give them out all the time.'

'So, the …' Rhoda glanced at Isaac. 'The chapel business – that can probably be pinpointed to around the time there were POWs at Telton Hall.'

'That's what I concluded.'

'Shame your aunt doesn't remember how she got it,' mused Rhoda. 'Do you mind if I take a couple of photos of these? It might be nice as an anecdote to add to the display when the chapel is moved here.'

'Be my guest.'

'I can show you where they are going to site the chapel, if you like.' Rhoda went over to her desk to get her camera. 'I'll take you both on a personal tour of the houses.'

'That would be good, thanks. You'd like that, wouldn't you, Isaac?'

'Yes. I want to see the building that has a toilet over the garden.'

Nate looked confused and Rhoda laughed.

'That's perfectly correct, and all the kids want to see that. Upstairs at one of the houses, there's a little closet with a hole cut out as a toilet seat. It overhangs the house, and everything collects in a heap in the garden below. Obviously, long before mains drains.'

Nate pulled a grim expression which made Rhoda laugh again.

As Isaac didn't seem particularly interested in any practical stained glass session, Rhoda was only too happy to take them around the site. The weather was being kind to them, despite it having rained during the night. The sky was clear, and the sun was warming on their faces.

'It's a bigger site than I imagined,' said Nate as they walked around to the main square. 'And these houses are brilliant. It's like stepping back in time.'

'Exactly what they are trying to achieve,' replied Rhoda. 'Obviously, the houses and buildings are all from various centuries, but this area is supposed to represent the main market square where people would come to buy and sell things. They often have days where the volunteers dress up in old-fashioned clothing and you can buy some of their traditionally made crafts. There's also a big summer fair, and another in the autumn, where they have dog shows, food stalls, pony rides, heavy horse shows, ploughing competitions ... loads of different stuff. You should come to one.'

They explored inside some of the buildings, which Isaac seemed to be enjoying as he led the way with the map Rhoda had given him.

'This is an old Victorian school,' said Rhoda, as they approached a small flint-built structure. They stepped inside, where from behind a barrier they could see the wooden benches and blackboard set up, with slates and chalk laid out. 'Bit different to what your classroom looks like, I expect.'

'Victorian. V-I-C-T-O-R-I-A-N. It is a descriptive term for the time when Victoria was queen of England from 1837 to 1901,' announced Isaac.

Rhoda exchanged a look with Nate. 'Correct.'

'We are doing about the Victorians at school,' said Isaac. 'I've got to do a project on it.'

'Do you want to take some photographs of the classroom?' asked Rhoda.

'Good idea,' said Nate, taking his phone from his pocket. 'I forgot all about the project.'

'Mum said I had to remind you.'

'Yes, I've no doubt she did.'

Nate may have tried to hide the weariness from his voice when he replied to his son, but Rhoda hadn't missed it. Years of micro-analysing adult conversations while she was in care and foster homes, to try to get some idea of where her unstable childhood might take a turn next, being able to mentally prepare herself for the unforeseen, had proved a hard habit to break going into adulthood.

She stood back as Nate took some pictures, and then she offered to take one of Nate and Isaac together.

'Making memories, as they say.' She passed the phone back, realising she hadn't been able to hide the cynicism from her voice. She attempted a rather more light-hearted pitch. 'You can never have enough photos.' An unexpected feeling of sadness swept over her. She physically shrugged to rid herself of the emotion. Photos of her childhood had been few and far between, and most of the ones she did have weren't always attached to happy times. 'Right, let's go and find that toilet!'

They spent the next hour and a half wandering around the houses and buildings. They visited the house with the toilet in the bedroom which overhung the building. Isaac found it hilarious, and Nate had to apologise for his son's toilet humour.

'Sorry. Anything to do with toilets and bottoms is highly amusing for a ten-year-old.'

They carried on exploring some more of the outlying buildings, which were spread further out and more secluded.

'It's supposed to represent how rural England would have been structured,' explained Rhoda. 'Outside the main village, there is the odd house here and there.'

The walk took them up the hill and through the wooded area, passing by the stables where the two shire horses were, and on beyond the pigsty. It was another forty-five minutes before they had completed their circuit.

'That was great,' said Nate. 'I really enjoyed it. What did you think, Isaac?'

'I liked the toilet.'

Rhoda laughed along with Nate. 'What did you think of the Victorian school?'

'Didn't like that. It was boring.'

'Isaac! Don't be rude.' Nate turned to Rhoda. 'Sorry.'

'Hey, don't apologise. As I said, I like honesty.'

'Hmm. Well, Isaac can be a little too honest sometimes.' Nate gave an apologetic smile.

'He's just a typical schoolkid.' She noticed Nate's smile falter.

'Yeah. Typical schoolkid.'

'I'm hungry,' said Isaac. 'H-U-N-G-R-Y. Feeling or showing the need for food.'

'In that case,' said Rhoda, 'I'll show you where the cafe is. Perhaps you and your dad can have some lunch while I pack away a few things in my studio. Then we can head down to Telton Hall. How does that sound?'

'Are you having lunch with us?' asked Isaac, looking at the leaflet in his hand.

'No. I've got a few things to do.'

'You're more than welcome to join us,' said Nate. 'My treat. To say thank you for giving up your time this morning to show us around.'

'That's very kind, but, honestly, I've got a sandwich back at the studio.'

'What sort of sandwich?' asked Isaac.

'Ham. Yummy.'

'A ham sandwich?' said Nate. 'That doesn't sound very exciting.'

'Nothing wrong with ham.'

Nate raised his eyebrows. 'I'm sure the cafe has something a bit more exciting.'

If Rhoda was honest, the ham sandwich had been there since the previous day and was not at its best after a night in the fridge. Before she could think of an excuse, she found herself relenting and agreeing to go to lunch with them.

They arrived at Telton Hall later that afternoon. The traffic had been a bit heavy around Salisbury, adding extra time, but it was a pleasant drive and Rhoda had followed behind Nate and Isaac's car.

'Ah, it's nice to see you again,' said Jack, greeting her on the driveway. 'I'll put the kettle on.'

Rhoda trailed Jack into the house, walking alongside Nate while Isaac ran on ahead.

'So, what have you got to do this afternoon?' asked Nate.

'Just take a few more photographs and check the fixings around the windows. They're cemented straight into the walls so it can be more problematic removing them than had they been in wooden frames.'

She also wanted to have a poke around in the library of Telton Hall to see if she could find the Bible that had been mentioned, and ask Isaac to recite the names of the people in the photograph again, but she wasn't sure how she was going to do that yet.

However, the opportunity presented itself as soon as she walked in the door. The hallway looked different, and immediately Rhoda noticed the bank of photographs had been taken down.

Nate must have noticed her gaze. 'Ah ... For some unknown reason, Dad has decided he needs to start packing. I came downstairs this morning to find he'd taken all the pictures off the wall and was stacking them in the study.'

'Really? He's had a quick change of heart, then.'

'Surprisingly so.'

'I'll come up to the chapel with you,' said Jack, after they'd finished their drinks.

'You don't have to do that,' replied Rhoda. 'I can nip up there on my own. It will be pretty boring just watching me take a few photographs.'

'Nate will go with you, then.' He looked towards his son. 'Take the quad, it will be quicker.'

A few minutes later Rhoda found herself climbing on the back of the quad bike Nate had brought out from one of the sheds.

'You are honoured,' said Nate. 'Not many people get the offer of the quad. Hold on tight.'

Rhoda wasn't entirely sure what she was supposed to hold on tight to. There didn't appear to be any grips or handles. Nate twisted around to look over his shoulder.

'Sorry, that means holding on to me.' Rhoda tentatively put her hands on Nate's hips, whereupon he moved them up to his waist. 'I don't want you falling off. Ready?'

'Ready.'

Rhoda didn't want to admit that she was slightly apprehensive about being on the back of the quad bike, and she was grateful that Nate took it slowly as he eased away and headed towards the gateway.

Instead of taking the footpath up the side of the field directly in front of them, Nate steered the bike around the edge of the field and took a route up the west side of the hill, which was considerably less steep. All the same, she had to lean into him and was very conscious of the closeness of their bodies.

Nate unlocked the chapel for her and wandered around while Rhoda took the photographs she needed and made some extra notes. 'It's going to take a bit longer to get the windows out as they are fixed straight into the plaster,' she said.

'How do you get the window out?' asked Nate, coming to stand beside her.

'We take it out in sections. See those bars running across the windows? They keep the glass in place. There are wires soldered on to the lead, which are then wrapped around the poles. Each window is done in sections, so it's a case of taking one section out at a time.'

'Sounds tricky.'

'Yes, it's probably the trickiest part – especially when dealing with fixings like this one, which aren't in a frame. At least with a wooden frame we can take it out in one piece and then deal with each section once it's safely on a workbench.'

'Rather you than me.'

Rhoda's attention was caught by one of the glass panels in the bottom right-hand corner. She zoomed in on it with her camera. 'Oh, wow,' she muttered to herself.

Completely lost in what she was doing, she moved closer, taking several more photographs.

'What is it?' Nate came to stand beside her. 'What's "wow"?'

'The glass,' said Rhoda, lowering her camera. 'It's

engraved in the corner with the name Paolo Sartori. That's our glazier.' She brought the digital image up on the camera screen and showed it to Nate. 'I assume your dad never paid much attention to the glass. Although, to be fair, it can't really be seen from down here.'

'I guess a lot of people have missed it,' said Nate, examining the image. 'It's not mentioned online.'

'Perhaps you should arrange for that to be rectified.' Rhoda fixed Nate with her gaze.

He nodded. 'Yeah, maybe I should.'

'Right, well, I'm done here,' said Rhoda, breaking the moment.

She put her camera in her bag, looking over to where the slabs had been dug up by the forensics team.

'It's still bothering you, isn't it?' said Nate.

'Yes. It is.' She walked over to the side of the chapel, where the paving slabs had been stacked against the wall, revealing the shallow grave below. 'Aren't you at all bothered? Or even just curious?'

'You probably won't believe me when I say it's been playing on my mind, but there's nothing that can be done.' Nate checked his watch. 'Better head back and make sure Dad and Isaac are OK.'

The quad bike ride down to Telton Hall was uneventful and soon they were back outside the building. The sun was lower in the sky now, dipping behind the tall silver birch trees to the west and casting long shadows across the front of Telton Hall. The air felt cooler, and a chill breeze curled around Rhoda's neck.

There was a strange silence in the air. A sudden flapping of wings and a squawk, as a bird flew out from the branches of the nearby trees, had Rhoda spinning around to see a magpie disappear out of sight.

'One for sorrow,' said Nate, nodding in the direction of the trees. 'We have quite a few magpies around here.'

'Isn't it at this point I'm supposed to look around for a second one? Two for joy, and all that.'

'If you're that way inclined.'

'I'm not,' replied Rhoda, as she walked into Telton Hall. 'I don't believe in luck. You make your own luck.'

'Maybe so,' replied Nate. 'But I think there are different types of luck. The luck you make yourself, and the luck that you have from other people. I'm lucky in business because I've worked hard – that's the luck I've made myself. I'm also lucky to have Isaac in my life. He makes me feel lucky. Haven't you got someone in your life who makes you feel like that?'

Rhoda stopped inside the hallway and looked directly at Nate. 'I don't, as it happens.'

Nate eyed her for a moment, not breaking contact. 'Maybe you just haven't met them yet.'

'That sounds like a line from a cheesy love song.' Rhoda found herself breaking eye contact – not something she was given to doing, but Nate was digging too deep for her liking. 'I need to use the bathroom.'

'Yeah. Of course. Use the one on the first floor. Up the stairs, turn left and it's the first door on your right. I'll put the kettle on. Would you like to stay for supper? I'm asking you this now before my dad pulls me up for not inviting you. Anyway, no pressure. Let me know in a minute.'

Nate strode off down the hallway, his footsteps echoing around the sweeping staircase of Telton Hall as Rhoda made her way up the red-carpeted stairs. The fabric was a little threadbare in places, and she wondered how many feet had tramped this way over the years. Had the man found at the chapel walked up here?

She reached the landing and located the bathroom. It was larger than her bedroom at her flat, with a roll-top Victorian bath and high-level toilet cistern. There were two china sinks, with painted flowers around the edge. It reminded Rhoda of a plush ladies' restroom at a top London restaurant.

When she stepped back out onto the landing a couple of minutes later, she noticed the door on the other side of the hallway was open. It looked like a library, or perhaps a study. She could see a bank of bookcases lining the far wall. There was a large oval table in the centre and several stacks of what looked like picture frames. No. Wait. They were photo frames. She recognised them from last week. They must be the ones Jack had taken down.

She gave a quick glance up and down the hallway to make sure no one was about, before slipping through the open door and into the room.

There was a desk in front of a large window which overlooked the driveway. An old-fashioned rotary-dial telephone was on the corner of the desk, and a diary and a fountain pen were laid out. There was a leather Chesterfield sofa to one side, with a rectangular coffee table in front of it. Another bank of bookcases stood against the wall behind the sofa.

Rhoda went over to the table. These were definitely the photographs from downstairs. Trying not to clatter the frames against one another or on the table, she sifted through until she found the one she was looking for. It was of

Mrs Hartwell – Jack's mother – and the children standing in front of Telton Hall.

Rhoda took her phone from her bag and snapped a couple of pictures. She turned the frame over and was pleased to see it hadn't been sealed with brown tape, as a lot of old photographs often were. Her hands were shaking, but she prised open the clips which kept the backing card in place and opened it up. She wanted to see the reverse of the photo, to see if anyone had written on the back.

Bingo! They had.

In traditional cursive writing, the names had been listed. Rhoda didn't have time to study it, but quickly took a photo of it with her phone. Then she spotted the picture of the POWs. She felt it was important and wondered if that, too, had been written on the back. She was delighted to see it had been and took another photograph before replacing the backing card.

Her pulse was racing. She really should get back, but she desperately wanted to search the bookcases for the family Bible. She took a deep breath. She could make another excuse to visit the bathroom.

'What do you think you're doing in here?' Nate's voice was clipped and ice-cold as he stood in the doorway, staring at her.

Rhoda fumbled the photo frame she was trying to put back together, and it clattered onto the table. She silently swore to herself. How was she going to explain this?

Nate strode across the room and picked up the photograph, silently replacing it in the frame.

'I'm sorry …' began Rhoda, still not sure how to explain herself.

'You only had to ask,' said Nate.

At that point Isaac came into the room. 'You found her. We've been looking for you,' he said to Rhoda. 'We're going to have spaghetti Bolognese. Dad said he'd asked you to stay for tea. You are staying, aren't you?'

'Erm … I don't think—' began Rhoda, before Nate cut in.

'No. She's not. Rhoda was just telling me how she had to get back to Sussex and was about to leave.'

Rhoda wanted to shrivel up and die, right there on the spot like the Wicked Witch from *The Wizard of Oz*.

'Sorry,' she said to Isaac. She glanced at Nate. 'Sorry. I'll just say bye to your dad.'

'Don't bother. I'll tell him you had to leave suddenly,' came the terse reply.

'OK. Sure.' Rhoda shuffled past Nate. She could feel her face burning with embarrassment. 'I'll see myself out. Bye, Isaac.'

She slunk away down the stairs, cursing herself for trying to be so sneaky. She should have just asked Nate in the first place.

As she reached her car, something made her look up towards the study window. Nate was standing there, looking down at her. Crikey, those eyes bore heavily into her. In fact, the whole building felt like a weight of oppression on her, and she was glad to be accelerating down the driveway a few moments later and away from Telton Hall.

15
Alice

1945

Alice had been at Telton Hall for a week and was gradually getting into a routine.

Mrs Hartwell liked everyone up early to feed the small assortment of farm animals. Alice's job was to collect the eggs, Lily had to feed the animals with the help of two of the Italian POWs, while Billy saw to the two heavy horses. It was only then they could all sit down for breakfast before the rest of the working day continued.

'Come on, out of the way, you silly old chickens,' said Alice, as she shooed the hens from the roosting boxes.

The eggs were warm in her hand as she placed them into the basket. She was getting used to the smell of the poultry, although this morning it was particularly strong.

She shooed another hen out of the way and as she did so, the smell hit her hard. Turning her head away, she groped around for the eggs, only to feel something warm and runny on her fingers – chicken poo.

Alice gagged and rushed out of the chicken shed, gasping for fresh air and choking at the same time.

The sound of laughter made Alice look up. Across the yard, leaning against the wall to the pigsty, was Billy. So far, Alice had managed to avoid having any contact with him other than at the breakfast table. Even then, she didn't like the way he looked at her over his mug of tea but tried hard not to let him realise her discomfort.

'You want to try working with these two,' he called. 'Chicken shit is like smelling roses compared to pig shit.'

Alice nodded and gave a brief smile. She took another deep lungful of air and went back into the shed, wiping the muck from her hand with some straw. A moment later, the door opened and Billy stood in the doorway, silhouetted by the breaking dawn.

'Need some help?' he asked.

'No. I'm fine. Thank you, anyway.'

Alice opened the wire inside door into the main chicken pen, closing it behind her.

'I expect in your condition, it's not very nice being in here.'

Alice stiffened at his comment. So far, no one at Telton Hall had spoken directly to her about her pregnancy, and Billy was the last person she wanted to discuss it with. She regained her composure and moved on to the next nesting box.

'I don't mind it,' she said, focusing on collecting the eggs.

'I could get you doing something nicer,' said Billy. 'Like in the kitchen or in the garden. Wouldn't you prefer that?' He moved into the shed now, standing at the internal door.

'As I said, I don't mind this. I'll do whatever Mrs Hartwell tells me to.'

'Whereabouts are you from?'

'Suffolk,' replied Alice cautiously.

'Not much happening there, I don't imagine.'

Alice felt unnecessarily irritated by the comment. 'Plenty to do, actually.'

Billy gave a smirk and once again his eyes flicked to her stomach. 'I stand corrected.'

'To be honest, there doesn't seem much to do here either. Just another English village.'

'You're right, and I can't wait to get away from here.' Billy gave a sigh. 'As soon as this war is over, I'm off.'

'Where are you going? Don't tell me – London. Isn't that where everyone goes?' She was aware she was mocking him slightly, but she got the distinct impression he was just bragging and trying to impress her.

'As a matter of fact, I want to go to America.'

'What's so good about America, then?' Alice thought of Brett, and the life she had imagined for herself when they were married. Part of that fantasy was living in America, but that wasn't going to happen now.

'Everything is better over there. More opportunities. More money. More of everything. I'm not going to sit around here and waste my life feeding pigs.' Billy opened the door to let Alice out. 'Here, let me take that for you.'

'I can manage. Thank you, though.' Alice kept the basket between herself and Billy as she slipped through and hurried out of the shed.

The bright sunshine blinded her momentarily and she

paused to squint and adjust to the light. It was then she noticed one of the POWs watching her.

He was standing at the manure pile, pitchfork in one hand and the wheelbarrow by the side. He didn't say anything, just looked at her, then flicked his gaze to the shed and back to her again.

Alice looked away, unsure what to make of the POW. More than once over breakfast the past week, Billy had made his feelings known about the Germans and Italians. He didn't just hate them; he detested them with a passion, and never missed an opportunity to say so.

Twice she'd heard him shouting at the POWs, telling them what they'd done wrong on the farm and threatening to have them sent back to the prison camp.

Alice hurried on through the garden gate and down the path towards the kitchen. She wished she didn't have to be there, but she had no choice.

'Hello, Alice.' It was Jack, Mrs Hartwell's son.

'Hello, Jack,' said Alice. 'You're up early. Did you wet the bed?'

'No!' cried Jack. 'I don't do anything like that. I'm not a baby.'

Alice laughed and ruffled Jack's hair. 'I'm only joking. That's what my dad used to say if I ever got up early. Here, help me put these eggs in the pantry.'

Alice liked Jack. She quite often found him hanging around, with not much to do. He wanted to help out in the fields, but Billy was adamant he was too young, despite Mrs Hartwell thinking otherwise.

'I'm not having him on the tractor with me,' Billy had

said the previous morning. 'There's nothing for him to do. He'll just be in the way.'

Alice couldn't help feeling sorry for the boy, and they had struck up an unlikely alliance.

Breakfast passed without incident, or comment from Billy, for which Alice was grateful. She cleared away the plates as the kitchen gradually emptied and everyone went about their way, until it was just her, Mrs Hartwell and Jack left.

'Jack, would you bring some logs in from the shed and fill up the baskets in the dining room and living room, please?' asked Mrs Hartwell.

'I've done that already,' replied Jack.

'Just bring a few extra up anyway,' said Mrs Hartwell.

'Mind you don't bring any spiders in, though, won't you?' said Alice, flicking the tea towel in Jack's direction as he nipped out through the kitchen door.

'Alice, I wanted to have a quick word with you,' said Mrs Hartwell.

'Of course,' replied Alice, racking her brains to think what she might have done wrong.

'It's all right, don't look so worried. It's good news, in fact.' Mrs Hartwell smiled encouragingly. 'I've been put in touch with a young couple from Bath, Mr and Mrs Eggars, who are looking to adopt a baby.'

Alice's hand automatically went to her stomach. 'Already?'

'Yes. I was surprised, but it's wonderful that we may have found a couple so soon.' There was the reassuring smile again. 'They would like to meet you.'

'Meet me? Why? Is that … normal?' Alice felt a surge of panic. If she met this couple, then it would make everything that was happening very real.

'It's not usual, I'll admit,' replied Mrs Hartwell. 'But they are a young broad-minded couple, and I assume they want to get the measure of you.'

'A young couple? Why isn't he away fighting?'

'He's a doctor and working in a London hospital.'

'But it seems so soon.'

'I really think you should agree to meet them.' Mrs Hartwell glanced out of the window. 'Jack's coming back. I don't want to talk about it in front of him.'

Alice bit her bottom lip. She didn't know what to say. Part of her didn't want to meet them, because if she did, she would have to face up to everything. Since arriving at Telton Hall, she had pretended to herself that giving up the baby wasn't really happening. Her heart ached at just the thought. She hadn't wanted to acknowledge what lay ahead, as it was too painful to dwell on. But, on the other hand, would it be easier for her if she was confident the child was going to be well looked after and, most importantly, the child was going to be loved?

Alice fought back the tears that filled her eyes and blurred her vision as she mumbled a 'yes'.

'That's good. I think it's the right thing to do, dear. Now, don't let Jack see you crying.' Mrs Hartwell opened the back door to allow Jack through with his armful of logs.

'Have they got other children?' Alice asked once Jack was out of earshot.

'No. For some reason, they haven't been able to have any. Does it make a difference?'

Alice fiddled with the edge of the tea towel. 'Not really, but I'm glad they haven't. It means that they will really love my baby and won't have to spread their love around.'

Mrs Hartwell gave a sympathetic smile. 'I know it's hard, Alice, but try not to think of the baby as yours. I know my words sound cruel and harsh, but I have your best interests at heart. If you think of the baby just as a baby, and once you've met Mr and Mrs Eggars, if you can think of it as theirs, it will help you when you have to part with it.'

Alice knew Mrs Hartwell meant well, she truly did, but the whole idea hurt so much, it was a physical pain. It was the same sort of pain she'd experienced when her mother had died. A deep sharp stab to the heart that made her stomach turn and her legs weak, it hurt so badly she wanted to double up and collapse in a heap on the floor.

She held on to the side of the sink to steady herself as the realisation of what she had to do fully hit her. She had to prepare herself to give up … to give up the baby. Oh, how wicked and guilty she felt already at just the thought.

'Are you all right, Alice?' Mrs Hartwell's voice was full of concern.

'Yes. I'm fine,' said Alice quickly. 'I just need some fresh air.'

'You should sit down.'

'No. Honestly, I'd sooner go outside.'

Alice dropped the tea towel onto the counter and exited the kitchen before Mrs Hartwell could say anything else. She paused at the coal shed, leaning against the concrete bunker. After a few long slow breaths, the light-headedness passed. Alice made her way along the brick path, which ran a direct route from the back door of Telton Hall to the gate in the wall at the end of the garden. Several paths spurred off on the left and right, giving access to the raised beds.

Once she was on the other side of the gate, Alice gave way to the tears she had struggled to hold back. She slumped down against the brick wall and brought her knees up, burying her head in her arms.

'*Va tutto bene?*'

The voice startled Alice. She had thought she was alone. She looked up and one of the POWs was standing in front of her. He was brandishing a knife in his hand. Alice got to her feet, her back still pinned against the wall.

'Stay away,' she said. It sounded dramatic to her ears, but she was panicking.

'*Va tutto bene?*' the man repeated, and followed up in English, 'Are you all right?' He took a step closer, but then stopped.

Alice gestured to the knife. 'Stay away from me,' she repeated as she side-stepped towards the gate, her back still against the wall.

'*Non aver paura.*' Then he looked down and must have realised he was holding the knife. He threw the knife to the ground and held out his hands palms up. 'Do not be scared.' However, Alice wasn't taking any chances. She raced through the gate, crashing it shut behind her and ran down the path, stopping only when she saw Billy in the kitchen doorway, smoking a cigarette.

'Oh, you look a scared little bunny,' he said. 'What's the matter?'

'Nothing,' said Alice. 'I'm fine.'

Billy looked beyond her towards the end of the garden. 'Something happen with one of those Eyeties?'

Alice stiffened at the casual insult. 'You mean the Italians. And no, nothing's happened.' She was buggered if she was going to tell Billy anything. Besides, in the few seconds she had scurried down the path, she'd had time to register that the POW had dropped the knife as soon as he realised he was holding it. She had probably – almost certainly – overreacted.

Brushing past Billy, because he wouldn't move out of the way, Alice went back to the kitchen. She was pleased Mrs Hartwell wasn't there anymore; Alice didn't want to face her right now. Cook had arrived and was preparing something on the range.

'Hello, Alice, my dear.' She paused and gave Alice an old-fashioned look. 'You all right? You look like you've been crying.'

'I'm fine.' Alice forced a smile to her face.

'Hmm. You don't fool me, Miss Renshaw,' said Cook. 'It's probably your condition. Does things like that to you. Makes you a bit more emotional.' She gave Alice a warm smile.

Alice shouldn't have been surprised Cook knew about the pregnancy. It wasn't as if Alice was the first girl to come to Telton Hall. Still, Cook's casual – not judgemental – comment did come a little unexpectedly. 'I didn't realise you knew.'

'Well, you're not the first girl who's in trouble to come this way. Mrs Hartwell's a decent woman and likes to help other women, especially youngsters like yourself. You couldn't have come to a better place.'

'My dad arranged for me to come here,' said Alice. 'He works for Mrs Hartwell's sister. The father stood me up at the altar.'

'Again, you're not the first.' Cook tore the top sheet from a notepad. 'Now, I usually get one of the prisoners to do this, but today you get the honour. That way I can keep an eye on you.' She handed over a list. 'It's the veg I need for tonight's dinner.'

Alice took the list, grateful the conversation had moved on. She was on the verge of tears again, and this wasn't like her at all. Cook was right – it was all to do with being pregnant. All the same, Alice didn't like the overwhelming emotions that she had no control over.

'Will Mrs Hartwell mind me doing this?'

'Of course not. Besides, it's my kitchen. No one interferes with that.' She winked at Alice. 'Now, run along. Oh, no, don't run, best you just walk.'

Alice was glad there was no sign of Billy when she went back into the garden. She hated the way he appeared and disappeared like a spectre. It made her uneasy to think she could just turn around and he'd be there. He'd probably gone off to pester some other poor soul.

With the list in her hand, Alice headed for the vegetable part of the garden. Cook wanted new potatoes and spring cabbage. Alice had to admit, since being at Telton Hall her diet had very much improved. As she picked up the fork to turn up some potatoes, she thought of her dad and had an unexpected surge of sympathy for him. He was all on his own now, with no one to cook for him or wash his clothes, or to make him a cup of tea when he got in from work. She hoped he was all right and was looking after himself.

The ground was harder to dig than Alice had expected, and she gave a grunt as she tried to lift up one of the potato plants to get to the roots. The gate opened and in came the

Italian she'd run away from earlier, pushing a wheelbarrow of horse manure ahead of him.

He saw Alice and immediately put the wheelbarrow down. 'Sorry,' he said in English. 'I did not mean to frighten you.'

Alice nodded. 'It's fine.'

'My name is Paolo Sartori.' He held out his hand and then must have thought better of it, for he pulled it back quickly.

Alice gave a small laugh. She held out her hand, realising that even though the prisoners ate their meals with them, she knew none of their names. 'Alice Renshaw.'

The Italian looked surprised, but pleased, and accepted the gesture of the handshake. 'Pleased to make your acquaintance.'

It sounded very formal and funny to Alice's ears, especially with the Italian accent. 'Nice to meet you.'

They stood in an awkward silence for a moment before Paolo nodded towards the fork. 'I help you?'

Alice went to say no, but something stopped her. She felt he was trying to apologise and make up for scaring her. To say no to his offer would be like shunning his apology. She planted the fork into the soil and stepped back, holding one arm out in the direction of the fork.

'Be my guest.' He looked confused. She smiled. 'Please.'

The prisoner came over and swiftly dug up the plant, plucking the potatoes from the roots, shaking off the excess soil and dropping them into the basket Alice had brought with her.

'Hey! What's going on?'

Alice groaned inwardly at the sight of Billy limping his way up the path. 'He's helping me,' she called back.

Paolo stood up, pushing the fork into the freshly turned soil. He looked guardedly from Alice to Billy.

'He's got his own work to do,' said Billy, coming to a halt in front of them. He wagged his stick in the direction of the POW. 'Get back to what you're supposed to be doing – spreading this shit about.'

For a horrible moment, Alice thought Paolo was going to object.

'Thank you for your help,' she said. She wanted to apologise for Billy being so embarrassing, but it wouldn't help Billy's temper and ultimately wouldn't help Paolo. 'I asked him to help me.' Making her point again, she looked directly at Billy and stood as tall as she could. 'In fact, I *told* him to help me.'

Billy glared at the prisoner. 'He should know better. Go on. Clear off.' He jabbed his walking stick into the Italian's upper arm; the other man hesitated for the briefest of moments before going back to his wheelbarrow. Billy turned to Alice. 'If you want help, ask me. I'll always oblige. Stay away from these prisoners. I'll see he's punished for this.'

'What do you mean, punished?' Alice was horrified.

'They have to be kept in line. Especially these young ones who get to stay on the farm. If I had my way, they'd all go back to the camp and be locked up for the night. It's only because Louise is a soft touch that they're here at all. They should all be bloody shot, if you ask me.'

'They are human beings and deserve to be treated properly.'

'Huh. They are prisoners of war. They'd no sooner slit your throat if you didn't keep them in line. That one will be going without his lunch today. A little reminder who is in charge around here.'

'That's cruel. You can't do that. I'm sure there's a law against it.' Alice was horrified that she had got Paolo's rations cut. 'He was helping, which is what he's here for.'

'I didn't tell him to do that, though.' Billy sighed and his face softened. 'Maybe I've been a bit hasty. You don't know the rules, I suppose. And I wouldn't want you to think I'm an unreasonable man.' He moved closer to Alice. 'As a favour to you, I'll make sure he gets his lunch. I'll let him off this time. How does that sound?'

'Good. It sounds good,' said Alice, very much aware of how close Billy was standing. 'Right, well, I'd better get back to gathering the veg for Cook.'

Billy smiled. 'Yes, best do that. I'll see you later, Alice.'

Alice didn't reply or look up from the list she was making a big deal out of studying. She could hear the uneven plod of Billy's departing footsteps.

16
Nate

2022

Nate had wanted to kick himself by the time Rhoda's car had reached the end of the drive. He had overreacted and been pretty disingenuous, to the point of being pompous. What harm was she doing, looking at the photos? None, as it happened. He had just been angry that she hadn't asked him – he would have been quite happy for her to do so. He knew the remains up at the chapel had struck a chord with her, and it had bothered him that she was so upset about it. After looking through the Facebook page for her missing brother, it had given him an insight into just how important it was to her, and he appreciated how the discovery at the chapel must be making her feel.

He wanted to help her in some way, but didn't know how, and now he'd made a right dick of himself by sending her away with a flea in her ear.

The whole scenario had bothered him all the previous

night and all of Sunday – so much so that by the time it came to taking Isaac home to Siobhan, he'd decided the only way to resolve things was to contact Rhoda directly. He didn't have her personal number, but he had the number of the museum, and he would call her first thing in the morning to apologise.

'You look like you've lost a tenner and found a pound,' said Jack as Nate came downstairs with Isaac's bags to load up in the car.

'Was just thinking about all this business with the chapel.'

His dad gave a shrug. 'There's not much to think about, is there? The chapel is destined to be taken down and moved.'

'I meant the remains.'

'Nothing to worry about there, either. No case to investigate.'

'I thought they may at least try to find out a bit more,' admitted Nate. 'I know they haven't officially closed the case, but it's not one they're going to spend any significant time on – if any. Shepherd made that perfectly clear.'

'Why would they want to? They've got better things to think about.' His father took off his reading glasses. 'Anyway, I thought you weren't bothered about it. Having second thoughts? Nothing to do with a certain young lady from West Sussex, is it?'

Nate flicked his father a glance. 'Of course not.' He was blowed if he was going to admit anything like that to his father – he was having a hard time admitting it to himself. 'I need to get going.' He stepped out into the hallway and called up the stairs, 'Isaac! Time to go!'

The house phone in the hallway rang and Nate picked it up. 'Hello, Telton Hall.'

'Oh, hello, is that you, Nate? It's Aggie.'

'Hello, Aggie. Everything OK?'

His father had never promoted his phone to a cordless one, so Nate leaned as far as he could into his father's line of sight and with his hand over the speaker, informed him who was calling.

'Yes. Everything is fine. I didn't realise you were still there,' Aggie continued. 'I won't keep you. Tell your father to call me when he gets a moment.'

'I can put him on now, if you want?'

'No, no. It's fine. Goodbye, dear.'

Aggie abruptly hung up.

Nate went into his father. 'Aggie said can you call her when you get a moment. She didn't want to talk now, for some reason.'

'Hmm. Will do.'

Aggie and Nate's dad had always been close growing up and were more like brother and sister than cousins. Their great friendship had continued throughout their lives. Nate had often wondered what it would be like to have a sibling, and whether he'd missed out on something.

Once again, his thoughts landed right back at Rhoda and her relationship with her twin brother: how, despite what Nate imagined was a difficult and perhaps estranged upbringing, it mattered deeply to Rhoda that she knew what had happened to Dean.

Nate woke earlier than usual the following morning and had a moment of unexplained sensation that something important was happening that day. Then he remembered.

He needed to speak to Rhoda and apologise for the way he'd spoken to her. In the cold light of day and after a couple of nights' sleep, he felt even more ashamed of himself.

Once he'd showered, dressed and made himself a strong black coffee, Nate opened the Facebook app on his phone and went straight to Dean Sullivan's page. There had been no new information from the last time he looked.

Nate checked the last post Rhoda had made on the page. There was no profile picture, just a graphic of a white silhouette of a person's head and shoulders against a grey background – the standard avatar for someone who hadn't posted a profile picture. Nate entered Rhoda's name into the search bar.

It turned out there were rather more Rhoda Sullivans than he expected. The list went on for two pages. Nate scanned the profile pictures until he found the anonymous avatar and then clicked on it, whereupon he was taken to her Facebook page. There were no pictures, no contact details, and one solitary post which redirected people to the 'Dean Sullivan – Missing Person' page. He wasn't sure what he was expecting to find out about Rhoda, but he was intrigued by her and what made her tick. He wondered if she had a business page at all for her stained-glass work, but checking his watch, he knew he didn't have time to look.

He closed the app and slipped the phone into his pocket, at the same time scoffing at himself for acting like some sort of MI5 agent trying to discover the secret identity of a spy.

He got to the office at 8.15, like he always did. It was too early to call the museum – he assumed they wouldn't open until at least nine o'clock, or even ten – so there was no point trying to get hold of Rhoda just yet. His first call, as always, was to Isaac. It was a routine they had in the morning; in the five years they had been living apart, Nate hadn't forgotten once, no matter where he was in the world or what he was doing.

'Hi, Isaac. You OK?'

'Mum said we did my homework wrong.'

Well, that was a good start to the conversation.

'We did? I thought we did good. What was wrong?'

'It wasn't on her list of ideas.'

Isaac seemed unfazed by it, so Nate tried to adopt the same attitude. 'It's OK to have your own ideas. I expect your teacher will like it.'

He could hear Siobhan talking in the background.

'Mum wants to speak to you. I've got to go.'

'OK, mate. See you Wednesday after Chess Club.'

'Hello, Nate?'

'Siobhan.'

'Just wanted to clarify the conversation I had with Isaac about his project. All I said was, I was surprised to see what he'd done, as it wasn't what I was expecting.'

'That's cool. Don't worry.'

'I thought he might do something a little more academic,' she continued, 'but he seems happy with the photographs.'

Nate wasn't entirely sure where the conversation was heading, but it seemed a lot of fuss about a school project. 'Sometimes it's good to explore other mediums,' he settled for as an answer.

'Hmm.' Siobhan didn't sound especially convinced. 'He was talking a lot about someone called Rhoda. You took him to meet her and then she came back with you both to

Telton Hall. I'm not saying you can't have a girlfriend, or that Isaac can't meet them—'

'I'm pleased to hear that,' Nate interrupted, now fully aware of where the conversation was going. For nothing more than his own amusement, he allowed Siobhan to carry on.

'I'm just saying, I think you should have told me first so I could at least be prepared for Isaac talking about her. I was totally in the dark. He knew more than I did.' She was in full flow. 'If it's a new relationship, you might want to take things easy. I'm not sure Isaac should be meeting a new person in your life unless it's already on a stable footing. Nate. Nate? Are you listening to me? I'm not being unreasonable.'

'No. I completely agree with what you're saying.'

There was a small silence.

'Right. So, why didn't I know?'

'Because there's nothing to know. She works for the museum that is taking the chapel from the farm. She came over on a business visit. Isaac was interested in the museum, so I took him. There's nothing to tell.'

'Really?'

'Yes. Really. Now, I've got to go. Have a good day, Siobhan.'

He hung up without waiting for her to reply. It had been a bit of childish sport, but sometimes she was so intense, it reminded him of their married days – which wasn't a great way to start the working week.

Nate kept himself occupied for the next ninety minutes or so, going through a complex set of accounts for one of his clients, although he kept finding himself clock-watching.

At ten o'clock, he was on the phone to the museum, and was relieved when Rhoda accepted his call from the receptionist.

'Hi, Rhoda. It's me, Nate Hartwell.'

'Yes, they said. What can I do for you?'

She sounded very business-like, and Nate knew he probably had his work cut out. He didn't imagine Rhoda as the kind of person who would just roll over and accept an apology from someone who had been so rude.

'Firstly, I wanted to apologise,' he began, noting an unusual hesitancy to his voice. 'I was very rude on Saturday evening, and I regretted it almost instantly.'

'*Almost* instantly?'

'By the time you were in your car, I knew I'd been an—'

'Arsehole?'

'Err ... Well, that's not what I was going for, but I guess if the cap fits, I should wear it.' He pitched for humour, but the telling silence told him his attempt was wide of the mark. This was harder than he'd imagined. 'I am genuinely appalled by the way I spoke to you. I hope you can accept my apology. I won't try to make excuses, because it's inexcusable.'

'In that case, apology accepted.'

Nate sat up in his chair. 'It is?'

'Yes. I was going to phone you myself today and apologise for snooping around when I shouldn't have been. I deserved to be kicked out.'

'Kicked out? Yes, that doesn't sound good. Sorry.'

'You were right. I should have asked first. Can't say I appreciate the way you did kick me out and, yes, that's definitely what happened, but let's forget about it now, seeing as we are both sorry.'

Nate was momentarily stunned into silence. He hadn't expected the conversation to go quite like this, but he appreciated Rhoda's directness. 'That sounds good to me.'

'Perfect.' There was another silence and Rhoda spoke again. 'So, what was the other thing?'

'I wondered if there was anything I could do to help you find out who the body in the chapel was.'

It appeared it was Rhoda's turn to be momentarily stunned. 'You really want to help me?'

'Yes, I do.'

'Why?'

'Because I know it means a lot to you for more than one reason, and I have to admit, I'm quite curious, too.'

'It does mean a lot – you're right.' She paused. 'And thank you for wanting to help.'

'Good. That's that sorted. Maybe we could meet up to discuss a plan of action?'

'I'm due back down to Somerset on Wednesday. Are you about in the afternoon for a chat?'

'Ah, sorry, can't do Wednesday. I have Isaac mid-week. He has Chess Club, so I pick him up from school at four o'clock.'

'That's nice you get to see him mid-week, too.'

'Yeah. Every other weekend and every Wednesday, plus anything that crops up in between. I quite often do the after-school clubs and swimming, as it helps Siobhan out with her work.'

'What does she do?'

'Life guru.'

'What?'

'Yeah. It's probably not your thing, but apparently loads

of people, women especially, like to get help organising their lives. Every aspect, in fact – their health, work, parenting, mental health ... If you need any help, Siobhan's your woman.'

'You might need to work on your sales technique there. I get the feeling you don't quite buy into it.'

'That obvious, huh?'

'Totally.'

He could hear the amusement in her voice, which made him smile. 'I could meet you for lunch. I could drive over to the farm around midday.' He had a quick look at the digital diary as he spoke. 'In fact, I could make it a long lunch.'

He could shuffle a few things around, and if he came early, he could easily take the afternoon off work. That was the beauty of being his own boss.

'OK, that sounds good. I'll look forward to it.'

'Yeah. Me, too.'

Nate finished the call and sat back in his chair, realising he was grinning rather more broadly than necessary.

17
Rhoda

2022

Rhoda looked at her notebook. She'd written down a list of questions to which she wanted answers concerning the body in the chapel, as she was now referring to it in her mind, which in a self-deprecating way made her feel like a modern-day Miss Marple.

She went down the list:

Double-check names of people in photo.
Full names of the two girls in the photo.
Where are they now? Ask Jack. If he doesn't know, try to find family Bible at Telton Hall for details.
Try to talk in person to any who are still alive.
Try to find out if there was a record of POWs in Telton Hall. Try local sources first.
Speak to older people in Telton village. Does anyone remember someone going missing?

It would do for starters, anyway. It wasn't dissimilar from how she had gone about first trying to find Dean. It was a case of methodically going through all the possibilities, making notes, cross-referencing, following up leads – not that it had got her anywhere with Dean, but maybe she could do something for this man found in the chapel.

Rhoda had been surprised when Nate had called her, and also pleased. She knew she'd been snooping when she shouldn't have been, but the inherent distrust of people that had organically grown inside her since childhood had got in the way. She knew that. She knew it was one of her faults, but it was hard to break a habit that was there as protection. Crikey, a psychiatrist would have a field day with her. Rhoda was well aware of the impact of her childhood on her adult life but, if she was honest, she had no desire to change anything. She was who she was. She was comfortable and secure with her adult self. Most of the time, anyway.

And now, it was Wednesday and she had woken up with a belly full of butterflies at the excitement of heading down to Somerset later that morning to oversee the erection of the scaffolding in the chapel, so the removal of the window could start. And, secondly, she was looking forward to seeing Nate and discussing the body in the chapel.

Rhoda had to go into work first, just to pick up some paperwork from the office that she needed to get the scaffolders to sign. Her boss had been late organising it, so she hadn't been able to collect it the day before, but she didn't mind; she also wanted to nip over to her studio and grab her camera.

'Ah, morning, Rhoda.' Nancy, who worked on reception

at the museum, greeted her. 'Eric has left the paperwork with me.'

'Thanks very much, Nancy. I'm just shooting over to the studio.'

'Before you run off ...' said the receptionist, reaching over to the tray on her desk. 'Here's your post.'

'Ooh, post. I hope it's something nice. Not often I get post these days. It's all usually done electronically.'

'Yes, I thought that myself. Oh, there's the phone. Excuse me.'

With the paperwork and envelope in her hand, Rhoda headed through reception and along the gravel pathway towards her studio. She waved to Geoff, one of the stable lads, as she went – although, as he was well over sixty, it was a hard push calling him a lad. It made Rhoda smile nonetheless.

She popped the documents for the scaffolders into her bag, along with her camera and the letter, which she'd look at when she had more time.

Rhoda arrived at Telton Hall just before midday, the traffic being far heavier than it had been on her previous trips. The scaffolders were already in the car park.

'You didn't have to wait,' she said to the guy who had got out of the van to greet her.

'We would have got started, but the farmer has lost the key to the gate. Apparently, that's the only way up.'

'He's lost the key? Is that what he said?'

'Yep.'

'Wait there a minute. I'll go and speak to him.'

Rhoda knocked on the front door of Telton Hall and eventually Jack Hartwell opened the door to her. 'Ah, you made it.'

'Yep. So it appears.' Rhoda raised her eyebrows at Jack. 'Apparently, you've lost the key to the gate.'

'Hmm. It's my age. I'm getting forgetful.'

'Come on, Jack. You're as sharp as a pin. Look, there's no point holding things up, it won't make any difference. We need to get the scaffolding up so I can take the window out.'

Jack looked past her shoulder towards the scaffolders. 'I don't like it.'

'I know you don't, and I'm sorry you're having to go through this but, honestly, there's no point being difficult now.'

Jack let out a long sigh. 'Some days I think I'll be well rid of the place. Other days, I'm scared to leave it. Telton Hall is all I've ever known.'

His eyes glistened and he clenched his jaw as he pulled a handkerchief from his pocket and dabbed at his nose.

Rhoda instinctively rested her hand lightly on his arm. 'I know, Jack. I really do understand the mix of emotions you're feeling. It's only natural. It's not just what you're leaving behind – it's what's ahead of you, too, especially when it's the unknown.'

Jack rooted around in his pocket again and pulled out a key. He handed it to Rhoda. 'You'd better let them in before someone snitches on me to Nate.'

Rhoda gave a gentle smile. 'Thanks, Jack.'

She unlocked the gate and gave the scaffolders instructions how to get up to the chapel from the other side of the hill, where it was less steep. Then she went back to Telton Hall to speak to Jack.

'All sorted?' he asked.

'Yes. I'll have to go up there myself in a minute, but I wanted to have a quick word.'

'That sounds ominous. You'd better come through.'

Rhoda followed him into the living room, where he took his usual position in his armchair and she perched on the edge of the sofa.

'I don't mean to pry, and I know it's not my business, but I keep wondering what you're going to do for a home once Telton Hall is sold. Have you got somewhere to live yet?'

'Has Nate put you up to this?'

'No! Not at all. I am genuinely concerned.'

'Well, no, I don't as it happens. If it comes to it, I can stay with my cousin Aggie across the road, but it's not ideal. She's not allowed to have someone there long-term. There's a clause in her tenancy agreement preventing her having lodgers, which is what I'd be.'

Rhoda took a piece of paper from her bag and passed it over to Jack. 'Here's a list of some local housing associations that may be able to help find you somewhere. Also, there's the number for one of the housing officers – it's their direct line, and they've been given the heads-up you're going to call. They might be able to help you.'

Jack looked at the piece of paper. 'Friends in high places, eh?'

'Not by choice.' Rhoda got up from the sofa. 'I'd better go and see what those scaffolders are doing, especially as I'm going to be working off it.'

Rhoda left Jack and went up to the chapel. While she let

the scaffolders get on with the job, she took the opportunity to sit down with her laptop and check her emails. She found herself drawn to the end of the pew near to where the bones had been found.

As she checked her emails on her phone, a draught tickled the back of her neck and caught a stray wisp of hair, which brushed against her face. She gave a shiver and as she glanced around the chapel, she was grateful she wasn't alone. There was something about this place she didn't like – a similar sort of sensation to the one she'd got at Telton Hall the other day.

'Ah, there you are.'

A voice from behind made Rhoda spin around in her seat. It was Nate. 'Where else did you think I might be? Don't worry, I haven't been anywhere I shouldn't.'

The words came out a little more defensively than she'd planned, as images of her in the study looking at photos sprang immediately to her mind.

Nate shrugged. 'I didn't think for one minute you had. Anyway, I thought we were over all that.'

Rhoda closed her eyes for a moment as a bout of embarrassment washed over her. 'Sorry. Didn't mean to sound so touchy.'

'So, we're still OK for a spot of lunch in the village?'

Rhoda stood up. 'Absolutely.'

She gathered up her bag and, after checking with the scaffolders that they didn't need her, she left the chapel with Nate.

The cafe in Telton village overlooked the stream which ran through the village, and they bagged a table on the patio. It was warm enough to sit outside if you had a lightweight jacket on, which fortunately they both did. They ordered coffee and looked at the menus.

'I much prefer sitting outside,' said Nate. 'I spend enough time stuck indoors behind a desk.'

'What do you do?'

'I'm an accountant. Got my own firm in town.'

'So, if you grew up on a farm and prefer to be outside, what drew you to a life of numbers in an office?'

Nate fiddled with his sugar spoon. 'I was adamant I didn't want to be tied to the farm. I'd seen Dad struggle year after year to make ends meet, to balance the books, to get up at the crack of dawn. He worked early mornings and long nights during harvest time, and growing up, we all had to do our bit.'

'And that put you off?'

'Yeah. I've always been good with numbers, and it felt like the easy option, if I'm honest. Plus, it gave me a way out.'

'Did you ever feel guilty about not taking over at the farm?'

Nate eyed her steadily, saying nothing as the waiter came out onto the patio with their food. Nate had gone for scampi and chips while Rhoda had opted for a jacket potato.

'This looks good,' said Nate, picking up the salt.

'It does. Didn't realise how hungry I was.' Rhoda waited a moment before speaking again. 'You didn't answer my question.'

'Are you always this direct?'

'I try to be. That way there's no misunderstanding.'

'Does that stem from your childhood?' He popped a chip into his mouth.

'You're avoiding the question.'

Nate sighed. 'If you must know, then, yes. Not taking over the farm does make me feel guilty. But only because I know it's disappointed Dad. On the other hand, just as well I didn't – otherwise, what with this CPO, I'd be out of a job and a home, just like him.'

'I gave your dad a couple of phone numbers today,' said Rhoda. 'A local housing company and someone in the council who could help.'

'Someone in the council?'

'Yeah. I know a man who knows a man sort of thing.'

'Insider information.'

'Something like that.' Rhoda concentrated on her food, aware that Nate was studying her again.

'So ...' said Nate, breaking the silence. 'The body in the chapel.'

Rhoda was pleased with the turn of conversation. 'Yes. You want to help?'

'If I can.'

'I really need to see if anyone in the photos at Telton Hall are still alive, so I can speak to them. Or at least find out what happened to them, so they can be accounted for. Even the POWs, although that might not be so easy to do.'

'Didn't the police already do that? They spoke to Aggie. And, of course, Dad.'

'Yes, but there are the two other girls as well. I don't think the police even tried to trace them. Anyway, I'd like to speak to them myself. Sometimes people are wary of the police. They might be more open with me.'

Rhoda took her notebook from her bag and opened it

up to her list of questions and action plan, before turning it around so Nate could see it.

He took a moment to read it. 'You've thought about this.'

'Of course.'

'And you're going to do it regardless of any help I can give you?'

'Of course.'

'I'd better help you, then.'

Rhoda felt a smile break across her face. 'Thank you. I appreciate that.'

'I'll have to tell my dad.'

'I know. I'm fine with that. I wouldn't want to deceive him – that would be disrespectful. Is there a ledger at all, of the POWs and the people who came to Telton Hall?'

'There was mention of one, years ago. I think maybe my mother was the last one to talk about it, but I'm pretty certain it's here somewhere.'

'That would be amazing if you could find it,' said Rhoda.

'When we go back to Telton Hall, we can have a quick look up in the study.'

Rhoda had to try hard not to scoff her lunch down and appear overeager to get back to the house. She'd had an enjoyable hour or so and realised it had been a long time since she'd been out for a meal with anybody. In fact, as she finished her food and sipped her cup of tea, she was hard-pressed to remember when the last time was.

She'd had the grand total of three boyfriends in her lifetime, the most recent being some time ago, when she'd finally admitted to herself she wasn't good at relationships.

'Penny for your thoughts,' said Nate.

'They're really not worth even a penny.'

'You looked pretty far away there – I'd say it was a penny well invested.' Nate signalled the waiter for the bill.

Rhoda picked up her bag and fished out her purse. 'Dutch. We'll go Dutch.'

'No, we won't,' said Nate. 'I invited you out for lunch, so it's my shout. Put your purse away.'

'I insist,' said Rhoda.

'While you're in my home village, we'll do things my way.' Nate winked at her. 'Please, let me.'

'I'd rather just split the bill.'

Nate shook his head. 'Tell me what you were thinking just now and you've got yourself a deal.'

'That's unfair.'

'I'm a country boy, I work with numbers, I like to barter. What can I say?' Nate took the bill from the waiter before he'd had time to put it on the table.

'OK,' said Rhoda reluctantly.

Nate gave a satisfied smile.

Once they'd left the cafe and were walking back along the High Street, Nate prompted her. 'Come on, then. Let's hear it.'

'It wasn't very exciting,' said Rhoda reluctantly. 'I was just thinking it had been a long time since I'd been out for a meal with anyone.'

'That's it?'

'Pretty much.'

'And when was the last time?' persisted Nate.

'A long time ago,' Rhoda found herself confessing.

'With a boyfriend?'

'Yes, if you must know,' said Rhoda, feeling the burn of embarrassment hit her cheeks. 'I've not got a very good success rate when it comes to relationships. And just because I'm sure you're going to ask me, I'll save you the bother – I've come to the conclusion I'm better off on my own.'

'Wow. That sounds very harsh. Writing yourself off at twenty-eight.'

'I'm quite happy, actually.'

'Are you?'

'Yes. I am.' Rhoda met his gaze, irritated by the way the conversation had gone. 'What about you? You're on your own. Why haven't you got yourself a replacement?' There was a flicker of hurt on his face and for a split second, Rhoda was pleased. In the very next second, she was remorseful. 'I'm sorry. I shouldn't have said that.'

'It's OK. I'm getting used to your ways.'

'Which is far too outspoken, verging on rudeness,' said Rhoda. 'I'm quoting that directly from one of my social worker reports.'

'Yeah, well, they don't know everything, even if they think they do,' Nate replied simply. 'And just for the record, I haven't had the time or inclination to meet anyone else. I tried a couple of dates via a dating app, but my heart wasn't in it. My friends have given up trying to fit me up with their single girlfriends.'

'So, are you quite happy on your own, too?'

'For the moment, but I wouldn't like to think I'll spend the rest of my life alone.'

They walked on a little way in silence, but instead of carrying on to the end of the High Street, Nate stopped at a junction.

'We're going down here first.'

'We are?'

'There's someone you might like to meet.'

'Who's that?'

'Joyce Colburn. She's lived in Telton all her life. She used to run the post office when we had one. She might remember something.'

'Ooh, do you think she will? How old is she?' Rhoda couldn't deny the feeling of excitement.

'I'm not sure, but she's older than Dad. Maybe around Aggie's age.'

'Did the police speak to her, do you know?'

'I don't. But we'll soon find out.'

Nate headed down the side road and came to a halt outside a small stone cottage, with honeysuckle clambering over a wooden archway. The front garden was bordered by a wall and was filled to the brim with tubs and pots to display the glorious selection of plants and shrubs.

'Believe it or not, this actually used to be the post office itself, before it moved into the convenience shop about twenty-five years ago.'

'And you're going to tell me you could buy a bag full of sweets for ten bob, or something like that,' teased Rhoda.

'Hey, I'm not that old!' said Nate with mock indignation. 'But, yeah, I do remember when a bar of chocolate was about twenty pence.' He rang the bell to the cottage.

'How old are you?' Rhoda asked as they stood on the doorstep.

'Thirty-seven. Why's that?'

'No reason. Just wondering.'

The front door opened as far as the chain would allow

and an elderly lady with permed white hair and blue-rimmed glasses eyed them through the opening. 'What do you want?'

'Hello, Mrs Colburn. It's me – Nathan Hartwell. Jack Hartwell's son from Telton Hall.'

'Ah, so it is. Just a minute.'

The door closed and then reopened a few seconds later, minus the safety chain. Joyce looked Rhoda up and down.

Nate introduced her. 'This is Rhoda Sullivan. She works at the museum who are buying the chapel.'

'Oh yes. I heard all about that. Nasty business that. A body ... well, I never.'

'More of a skeleton,' said Rhoda. 'Human bones.'

'That's actually why we've come to see you,' said Nate. 'We're keen to try to find out the identity of the remains. The police haven't got the time or resources to look into it, so we thought we'd do a bit of sleuthing.'

Rhoda wasn't sure if she liked it described as 'sleuthing', but she let the comment pass.

'Nate – I mean, Nathan – tells me you've lived here all your life,' said Rhoda, wanting to get to the point.

'That's right.'

'You don't remember anyone going missing from Telton Hall around the time of the war, do you? Maybe one of the farm workers, or even a prisoner.'

'That's a long time ago.' Joyce frowned as she thought back. 'I don't remember anyone going missing. That's not to say they didn't ... I just can't recall. A lot's happened since then.' She gave a chuckle.

'Do you remember any of the people who lived at Telton

Hall around that time? Did you know any of them?' asked Nate.

'Well, there was Mrs Hartwell, your grandmother – she used to take in girls who needed somewhere to stay for a while,' said Joyce, lowering her voice. 'Girls who'd got into a bit of trouble. I was only a youngster myself. We didn't much mix with the girls from Telton Hall – it wasn't encouraged. I think our parents thought their ways would rub off on us. That's not to say we always did as we were told.'

Rhoda felt hope dip and rise almost simultaneously. 'Do you remember any girls by the name of Lily or Alice?'

Joyce directed her reply to Nate. 'You should be asking your aunt. She was up there a lot. She'd know.'

'We're going to speak to Aggie,' said Nate. 'We were in the village, so we thought we'd call by.'

That was news to Rhoda, but she was glad Nate had already thought about speaking to his aunt.

'You know, I think I do remember an Alice. She came to the post office one day, wanting a stamp for Italy – Italy, of all places. I remember now. My father was the postmaster and there was an argument. He called her a traitor. That's right. It's coming back to me. I didn't really know then what it was all about. I know she never came into the post office after that, and I remember my father saying "good riddance to bad rubbish".'

'Was this during the war or after?' asked Nate.

'I'm sorry, I don't really know, but it must be either the end of the war or later, when we still had Italian POWs.'

'What happened to Alice?' asked Rhoda. 'Did she move on from Telton Hall? I don't suppose you remember her surname, do you?'

'Well, funny you should ask, I do as it happens. It's just come back to me.' Joyce looked very proud of herself. 'Renshaw. Alice Renshaw.'

'Renshaw,' repeated Rhoda. 'That's wonderful. Thank you.'

'I can hear my father now, as clear as day, saying, "That Renshaw girl should go back to where she came from. Nothing but trouble, that one." Funny how things stick in your head. My father was a very patriotic man. Didn't much care for the prisoners.'

'I always got the impression most people in the village accepted them,' said Nate.

'I think most people did, but like I said, my father was very patriotic, and he always thought of them as the enemy, even when the war was over and they were still here. You should see if you can find the parish records. There might be something in there about them. I do remember a couple of them coming to church on Sundays. Apart from that, I don't really remember much else.'

'You've been really helpful,' said Rhoda. 'We've got a surname, which is more than we had before. Thank you so much.'

'Can I leave you my number in case anything else springs to mind?' asked Nate.

'Of course, but don't get your hopes up – it was a long time ago.'

Thanking Joyce, Rhoda and Nate left to return to Telton Hall.

'Thank you so much,' said Rhoda. 'That was genius of you. It might trigger some more memories. And we've got a surname. I can look Alice Renshaw up in the archives.'

'How do you think it will help to identify the remains, though?'

'I'm not sure, but we've got to start somewhere. What if she's still alive? She might be able to tell us something. She might know if the other girl, Lily, is still alive. Of course, your aunt may be able to shed some light, too. Basically, we need as much information from as many people as possible.'

Although Rhoda was excited at the thought, she knew from bitter experience not to get her hopes up; all the same, she was eager to try to find Alice Renshaw.

They arrived at Telton Hall as the scaffolders were pulling through the gate from the hill.

'I just need to have a quick word,' she said.

'Sure. I'll be up in the study having a look for those books,' said Nate, carrying on into the house.

'All done,' said one of the scaffolders. 'Let us know when you want it taken down. I was told you'd need about two weeks – is that right?'

'Yeah. Should be able to get it all done by then,' said Rhoda. 'After that, we'll need more scaffolding to take the building down, but I think my boss is going to arrange all that with you.'

'Okey-doke. We'll get off now.'

Rhoda watched the truck trundle down the driveway. Two weeks: that's all she had to find out about the remains in the chapel. After that, she'd have no legitimate reason to be here. She wasn't on the team for taking the chapel down and moving it to the museum. Once the windows were out and all marked up, her work here would be over.

She quickened her step as she crunched across the gravel up to the front door. Folding the paperwork the scaffolders had given her, she opened her bag and slipped it in. As she did so, she noticed the envelope that had been sent to her at the museum.

She'd better have a quick look in case it was important. She'd meant to open it earlier but had forgotten all about it.

Walking up the stairs to the first floor to the study, Rhoda slipped her thumb under the sealed edge and opened the envelope. Inside, there was a single sheet of paper folded in three. Rhoda read the typed message. She stopped dead in her tracks at the top of the staircase. She had to read it again, to make sure she wasn't mistaken.

> DON'T GO POKING YOUR NOSE IN WHERE IT'S NOT WANTED.
>
> LEAVE THE SECRETS OF TELTON HALL CHAPEL BURIED.
>
> YOU WILL REGRET IT IF YOU DON'T.

'What the hell?' Rhoda said out loud.

She turned over the envelope and looked at the postmark, but it was too smudged to read. Surely this had to be some sort of joke. Had she really just received a poison pen letter? It was unbelievable.

Nate appeared on the landing from the study.

'Everything OK?'

18
Alice

1945

Alice sat on the edge of her bed in her room at Telton Hall, a letter in her hand that Mrs Hartwell had just given her. She recognised Jess's handwriting. They had exchanged several letters since she'd been in Somerset, and she looked forward to hearing from her friend. Alice hadn't heard from her father at all, though, and was surprised at how disappointed she was. Since Mrs Hartwell had mentioned the couple who wanted to adopt the baby, Alice had half-hoped her father would contact her and tell her to keep the baby and come home – but she knew that wouldn't really happen.

She tore open the envelope and pulled out two sheets of writing paper.

Dear Alice,

How are you? God, I miss you! Do you think I can

come and visit you? I could save the train fare and maybe your Mrs Hartwell will let me stay for one night. Would you like that? Do you think it would be possible?

Have you been keeping well? I hope they're not making you do too much. I'm glad you have a friend there but don't forget I'm your BEST friend.

Alice smiled – she could imagine Jess saying that in a semi-serious tone. She missed Jess, too. She went back to the letter.

Look, I have some news for you, but it's not good. I didn't know whether I should tell you or not, but I thought it was best you knew and best that it came from me.

Please sit down if you're not already.

Howard came to see me at Rice's the other day. He caught me as I was coming out of the shop on my lunch break. I thought it was strange to see him there, and I could tell from the look on his face it wasn't a social visit. There was an officer waiting in a car parked over the road.

It was about Brett.

I'm so sorry, Alice, there's no other way to say this, but Brett was on a bombing mission and his plane was hit by enemy fire. It went down in the sea. There were no survivors. Brett's dead.

Alice's breath caught in her throat. Her hands began to shake as she absorbed the news. She read the letter again and her eyes filled with tears. Brett was dead; despite his standing her up at the altar and her being here at Telton Hall, somewhere in her heart, she'd had this tiny flicker of hope that he would turn up one day and declare his love for her. That he'd made a mistake and wanted to marry her. Then he would whisk her away with him, she would have the baby and they would live happily ever after. There was no happy ending now.

Alice flopped onto the bed, burying her face in the pillow and crumpling the letter in her hand. The knowledge that Brett was dead was more painful than she had ever imagined it could be.

Alice had no concept of time, but she was aware of Lily coming into the room and gasping.

'Oh my God, Alice! Whatever's the matter?' She rushed over and put her arm over Alice's back. 'Alice, please, what's happened?'

Alice sniffed and moved herself to a sitting position. She wiped away the tears from her face.

'I've just had a letter from home. The father of the baby has been killed in action.'

The words sounded hollow and distant – unreal, even. How could it be true?

'What? Oh, Alice, I'm so sorry.' Lily put both arms around Alice and pulled her in for a hug. After a while she sat up and, with her hands on Alice's shoulders, looked at her. 'Now, I know it's very sad. It really is. The death of a young man is tragic, but don't be crying over him anymore. Remember he abandoned you. He didn't shed any tears for you.'

Alice prickled at the harsh words. Lily may have been right, but they stung all the same.

'I know. He may not have loved me – or loved me enough – but I did love him. I really did.'

Alice flattened out the letter on her knees and read the rest of it.

I know this will be a shock to you, Alice, and I am sorry to be the one to tell you. I wish I was there to tell you in person.

You must look after yourself now. You and the baby. It's probably for the best the baby is being adopted, and I hope the meeting with the new parents goes well. Let me know, won't you?

Take care, my dear friend, and I hope to see you soon.

Love, Jess. x

She passed the letter to Lily to read.

'She sounds like a good friend,' replied Lily. 'Although I see I have competition for being your best friend.' She gave Alice a nudge with her shoulder. 'I suppose it's all right to have two best friends. One here and one there.'

Alice smiled and, taking the letter back, folded it up. 'I suppose so, too.'

'I'd better get back to work,' said Lily. 'Mrs Hartwell sent me up here to make sure you were all right. She thought you'd be down, but I'll explain why. She'll understand. Get some rest. You've had a nasty shock. I'll bring some tea up mid-morning.'

Alice didn't argue. She was overcome by a wave of tiredness and all she wanted to do was sleep.

*

As promised, Lily brought Alice up a cup of tea at eleven o'clock, together with a small slice of cake that Cook had somehow managed to make with no eggs.

'Mrs Hartwell said to have the rest of the day off,' said Lily. 'Cook said she can manage on her own.'

'That's kind of them.' Alice took a sip of her tea. 'I think I need to get some fresh air. I'm over the shock, just feel really, really sad. You know, like a deep sadness.' She looked up to the ceiling and gulped back fresh tears. 'I'm fed up of feeling sad and losing everything.'

'Hey, come on, now. No more crying. It won't do you or the baby any good.'

Alice broke the little sponge cake in two and offered one half to Lily. 'You have some.'

'No. You're eating for two. You eat it all.' She backed away. 'I've got to get back to work. I'll see you later.'

'Thanks, Lily. You really are my best friend here.'

'I should think so.'

Lily winked before opening the door and disappearing down the hallway.

Alice finished her tea and cake and forced herself to take her own advice and get some fresh air. She went through the kitchen, which fortunately was empty. She could see Cook at the end of the garden talking to one of the POWs. Alice nipped out of the door and hurried along the side of the house, through an archway cut in the hedge and out onto the back lawn of Telton Hall.

Somehow, Mrs Hartwell had managed to persuade whoever it was to allow her to keep her lawn, and not have it dug up for planting vegetables. The flower beds were full and very soon the opening blooms would be a riot of colour. The other side of the lawn mirrored this side, surrounded by a hedge with an archway through into another part of the grounds. Beyond that was more of a wooded area, where there was a bench tucked away under a willow tree.

Alice sat down on the bench and, with her eyes closed, breathed in the fresh air. There was only a gentle wind, but enough to allow the smell of the farm to drift her way. *One of the drawbacks of having pigs and chickens*, thought Alice.

The sound of someone whistling had Alice opening her eyes. She didn't recognise the tune, and it was getting closer. Then through the gap in the hedge came Paolo, the Italian prisoner, with his wheelbarrow full of horse manure.

Alice sat stock-still. He hadn't noticed her under the shade of the drooping willow branches. Should she say something? Cough? Sit still and hope he walked past?

He stopped a few feet away from her, alongside the rose bushes.

He must have felt her eyes on him, for he turned around and when he saw her there, he jumped in alarm, stumbling backwards into his wheelbarrow, right on top of the manure.

Alice leaped to her feet but couldn't stifle the small giggle that erupted from her throat.

'Sorry! I didn't mean to scare you,' she said, controlling her laughter. 'Are you all right?' She didn't know whether he understood her or not. She took a few steps towards him, emerging from the willow branches, and held out her hand. 'Here, let me help you.'

Paolo raised his eyebrows at her, but took her hand and

hauled himself, with the help of Alice, from the wheelbarrow. He brushed himself down. 'I smell like poo now.'

Alice tried to suppress her smile. 'I am sorry.'

'Do not worry.' He looked at her, his face filling with concern. 'You have been crying?'

Alice looked down at her feet. 'I'm all right.'

'Why are you sad all the time? Do you not want to be here?'

Alice wondered whether he'd seen young women like her come to Telton Hall before.

'I had some bad news today,' she found herself explaining.

'Oh. I am sorry. Please, you should sit.' He motioned towards the bench and Alice sat back down. 'Bad news is more bad when far away from home.' He spoke with the sentiment that only someone who had experienced it themselves could.

'Someone I used to know – a man – has died,' explained Alice.

'I am sorry. That is the worst news to receive. Was he someone special to you?'

Alice fiddled with her sleeve cuff. 'He was once but hadn't been for a while. He was ...' She stopped herself from speaking.

'The father of your baby.' Paolo finished the sentence for her.

Alice nodded. 'So, I suppose you know why I'm here.'

'I guessed. My sister has a child. Also my cousins. When they were pregnant, they looked the same as you.'

'I didn't think I was showing yet. Not properly.' Alice slid her hand across her stomach.

'No, but you have a look on your face. I cannot explain, but you look like they did.'

Alice gazed up at the sky and the plump white clouds drifting by. A bird darted across the hedge, landing briefly in a silver birch. It was a magpie. Another followed it, and then they both took off.

'One for sorrow, two for joy, three for a girl, four for a boy.'

Paolo looked confused. 'What?'

'Magpie superstition,' said Alice. 'So ... your sister. She has a child?'

'Yes, she has a son. His name is Luca, but I have not met him yet.'

'I hope it's not too long before you can see them again. Her husband must be very proud of his family.'

Paolo dropped his gaze and shook his head. 'Husband killed in the war.'

Ah, now Alice understood. She felt a wave of compassion for the Italian and for his sister, even though she didn't know her. 'I'm sorry,' she said. 'That's very sad.'

Paolo clenched his jaw and took an audible breath. 'Too many lives have been lost in this war. Too much hardship. Too much pain and sorrow.'

'And even when the war is over, the legacy will continue for a long time.' She held Paolo's gaze and an unspoken understanding passed between them. They may have been on opposing sides, according to their leaders, but there was no animosity between them.

'When the war is over, we must try to make the world better place to live,' he said solemnly. 'It is our duty as people.'

Alice nodded.

A shout from somewhere on the other side of the hedge, calling Alice's name, broke the spell. Alice took a hurried step away from Paolo. 'That's Mrs Hartwell. I'd better go.'

She nipped through the gap in the hedge, unsure what had just happened with her and Paolo, but certain that she no longer viewed him as a prisoner. He was another casualty of the war, just like her.

'Ah, there you are, Alice,' called Mrs Hartwell from the terrace, and then as Alice neared, 'I see you found the rose garden.'

Alice wrapped her cardigan around her body. 'Sorry, I was just having a few minutes to myself.'

'Of course.' Mrs Hartwell looked towards the garden. Alice followed her gaze and the figure of Paolo tending to the roses could just be made out. 'Lily told me your sad news. Come in and have some lunch.'

Alice was grateful Mrs Hartwell didn't mention Paolo. She wasn't quite sure what she would think of Alice talking to a prisoner. As they walked back towards the open French doors, Alice's relief dropped as Billy stood in the doorway, adopting his usual pose of cigarette in hand.

'Alice,' he said in acknowledgement. 'Sorry for your loss.'

Alice swallowed. She hated the thought that Billy knew about Brett. It was personal. 'Thank you,' she forced herself to say.

'If you need anyone to talk to …' He left the rest of the sentence hanging in the air.

'Thank you,' she said again, as she followed his stepmother through the French doors.

Billy stood back to let them through, but put his hand

out, resting it on Alice's arm. 'Don't be taken in by the prisoners,' he said in a low voice. Mrs Hartwell was occupied with Jack, telling him to wash his hands before lunch. Billy moved his head closer to Alice's. 'You can't trust them. We've had problems before when our guests have become too trusting of them. I wouldn't want anything to happen to you.'

'Thanks for the warning,' said Alice, relieved that Billy removed his hand. 'I'll bear that in mind.'

5 May 1945

Carissime Mamma e Sofia

I have heard on the radio that Berlin has fallen and Hitler is dead. This surely must be the end of the war. I am of course praying that it is. It cannot go on for much longer now the Allies have control of Europe. I hope the soldiers will be honourable and respectful to the civilians. Please write to me as soon as you can so I know you are safe.

I received your letters this week and I could hear the sadness in your words, Sofia. I can only imagine how much you are grieving for Franco. I am so very sorry.

It was good to hear how well Luca is doing. I bet now he is crawling you have to watch him all the time. Do you remember the story Mamma always tells of me when I was crawling? One day she left me on the rug in the living room and went to the kitchen to make some lunch. When she came back, I was nowhere to be seen. She thought I had been stolen! Eventually, she found me under the sofa.

And Mamma, I hope you are recovered from your cold and cough. It is indeed an unusual time of year to become ill, but we are in unusual times, so maybe we shouldn't be surprised. Keep taking the warm honey, that will help your throat. I remember how you used to make us drink it when we were ill. I also remember the boiled cabbage leaves you used to make us drink. I have to confess – it was the most disgusting thing I have ever had to consume in my entire life.

It really can't be much longer before the war ends and

I am able to return home. It is my dearest wish to see you both again and to meet Luca for the first time.

Il vostro amorevole figlio e fratello

Paolo

19
Nate

2022

Nate stared at the letter Rhoda had just shown him. 'What the fuck?' he muttered. 'Is this for real?'

'It appears so,' said Rhoda. 'It was sent to the museum. I picked it up this morning before I drove down here. Didn't have time to open it earlier.'

'It seems so ridiculous. Have you got the envelope?'

Rhoda handed it over. 'The postmark is smudged, but it would only be the area from where it was posted. My guess is it came from around here, though. I mean, who in West Sussex would know anything about the remains? It didn't make the national news.'

'It does seem weird. What's your gut feeling?'

'That if this is real, like a genuine threat, then it proves we're on to something. That there's someone who doesn't want us – or rather, me – to discover the identity of the remains.' She gave Nate a purposeful look. 'It also means that I'm more determined than ever to find out who he was.'

Nate glanced down the stairs, where he could see the door to the living room was open. 'Come into the study. I don't want Dad to overhear.' He closed the door behind them. 'Look, if this is for real, if we're treating this as a serious threat, we should tell the police. They're likely to take over the investigation then.'

'I doubt it. This letter isn't a direct threat. It's more like a warning. What can the police do? They can't do anything until whoever it is has broken the law.'

'Isn't threatening behaviour an offence?'

Rhoda read the letter out loud.

DON'T GO POKING YOUR NOSE IN WHERE IT'S NOT WANTED.

LEAVE THE SECRETS OF TELTON HALL CHAPEL BURIED.

YOU WILL REGRET IT IF YOU DON'T.

'It's not really a threat. They haven't threatened to do anything.'

Nate blew out a breath. She was right, of course. 'I don't like it. Let's just assume for a minute that it's an empty threat. We can carry on looking into it and no harm done. If it's a serious threat, then we can wait to see if the sender ups their game.'

'Yes. I don't think they're going to leap from sending a letter to cutting my brake cables without anything in between.' She grinned and shrugged.

'I guess you're right.' He looked around the study. 'So, let's see if we can find this Bible or ledger for the work carried out at the chapel. Preferably both. The Bible might throw up a name that we haven't considered, or someone Dad has forgotten about. Especially as Dad would only have been about ten at the time.' He walked over to the bookshelves on the left-hand side of the desk. 'They're more likely to be over here. This is where Dad keeps all the paperwork to do with Telton Hall. My grandmother was very organised, but I can't say Dad has inherited that trait.'

Nate began scanning the shelves, occasionally pulling out a book to check its contents. There were three rows of box files, and on the bottom shelf were two document storage boxes.

'Is the Bible likely to be over here?' asked Rhoda, looking at the other bookshelf. 'What does it look like? Is it big, small, colour?'

'In my mind, it's maybe A4 size. A mottled green sort of colour with gold lettering. I haven't seen it for years. I just remember it from when I was a kid.'

'I'll have a look over here.'

'Yeah, they look older books. My grandmother was a bit of a bookworm and in later life, used to collect special and limited editions. They're all along where you are.'

'It's like looking for a needle in a haystack,' said Rhoda after ten minutes of searching through all the books. 'Any luck with the ledgers?'

'Nope.' Nate pushed the first of the storage boxes back on the shelf. It had contained manila folders, dated throughout the mid-1930s to early 1940s, containing all the expenses, in and out, that went through Telton Hall. He pulled the second box out. 'Hopefully, this one will cover the dates we're looking for.'

'Ah, looks like I've found the Bible,' said Rhoda.

Nate looked up as she pulled out a book from the shelf. It looked smaller than he remembered. 'Is that it?'

Rhoda opened the cover and flicked through the pages. 'This can't be the right one.' She came over and handed it to him. 'There's nothing written inside.'

'No. That's not it.' He looked back at the shelf. 'What's next to it?'

'Nothing. It was on the end of a row.' Rhoda kneeled down beside him. 'Hopefully we'll have more luck with the box.'

Nate removed the lid. Another stack of manila folders occupied the space, and he began flicking through. 'September 1940. October, November ...' He took them out, placing them in order on the floor. 'See what I mean about my grandmother. A folder for every month.'

He removed the next batch of folders.

'1944,' said Rhoda, taking them from him and flicking through them. 'Yep. January through to December.'

'This batch must be 1945.' Nate lifted some more folders out. 'January, February, March, April ... July, August, September, October, November, December.' He paused and took out the remaining folders. 'That's odd. May and June 1945 are missing.'

'What about in this box?' Rhoda pulled the final box from the shelf.

A hurried search by Nate proved fruitless. 'Nope. These are 1947, 1948, '49, '50 and '51.'

'Are there any other boxes?'

'I don't know. I'll have to ask Dad. My grandmother was still alive in the fifties, so I assume she was still dealing with the paperwork. It makes sense that there are, but where?'

'When did your dad take over the farm?'

'Oh, couldn't tell you. I think it just happened over the years. He left school at fourteen and would have helped on the farm then. I assume my grandmother's stepson, Billy, was working on the farm at some point. Then he cleared off and Dad was left to run the farm on his own.'

There was a silence as each of them went over the detail.

'So, the missing files are for May and June 1945,' said Rhoda. 'That was when the war ended. Do you think in all the excitement they didn't keep the records up to date? Have a check through the folders for July in case they've all been merged into one.'

A thorough search of the July and August folders revealed nothing.

'They must have been misfiled somewhere,' said Nate. His eyes grazed the bookshelf and settled on one book in particular. 'Aha!' he said as he pulled out the book.

'What have you found?'

Nate opened the book and scanned the contents. 'This is my grandmother's diary of all the girls who came to stay at Telton Hall.'

'Oh, wow! Does it cover 1945?'

Rhoda was crouching next to him now and the faint smell of her perfume teased his senses.

Nate focused on the book. 'Here we go. Yep, 1945. And here is Alice Renshaw.'

He looked across the page where Alice's expected due

date was, but the following columns, where his grandmother had listed dates of birth of the babies, the gender and the names of the people who had adopted the baby, were all blank. Alice's name was the last entry in the book.

'What do you make of all that?' asked Nate.

'I've no idea. Do you think she left before she had the baby?'

'I suppose so. Or something might have happened to her.'

'What – like she died?'

'It's possible.'

'Maybe your aunt can shed some light on it,' suggested Rhoda. 'I know she would only have been about twelve herself, but she might know why your grandmother stopped taking in any girls.'

'It might be because the war ended,' said Nate. 'Perhaps there wasn't the need for it, or maybe she just wanted to stop doing it.' He looked at his watch. 'I've got to get Isaac soon, but I'll have a good look through this evening.'

He replaced the record book back on the shelf and lifted the ledger box onto the table in the centre of the room, next to the photographs, while Rhoda returned the Bible to its place on the shelf.

Nate watched her pause as she pushed the book into place. Her finger tapped the edge of the shelf.

'Look at this,' she said.

'What's that?'

Nate went over and looked at the shelf.

'Can't you see?'

'Nope.'

Rhoda ran her finger along the edge of the shelf, lifting it and holding it up in front of Nate's face. 'Look.'

'Yeah, the place is bloody dusty,' said Nate. 'I don't think it's high on Dad's list of priorities. Please don't write "Clean Me" in the dust, he'll never see it and it will be there forever. Well, until this place is ripped apart by the builders.'

'Never mind all that,' said Rhoda. 'You're missing the point. Look here, at the space next to the Bible. It's not dusty. There's a clear line where the dust came up to. There was another book here. You can see where the dust has been disrupted when the book was taken out.'

Nate looked closer. Rhoda was absolutely right.

'OK. So, a book was here but isn't anymore. Probably taken out recently, as there's no new dust where the book had stood.' He looked back at the other books on the shelf: two Bibles, a prayer book and several hymn books. 'This looks like the religious section of the collection.'

'And it looks like it could have been a reasonable sized book,' said Rhoda. 'Judging by the space, quite a thick book. Not dissimilar to how you'd imagine the size of an old Bible.' She looked expectantly at him.

'I don't know what to say,' he confessed. 'Who's moved the Bible – assuming that's what it is?'

'Maybe you could ask your father.'

'Yeah. Not right now, though. I haven't really got the time. I'll talk to him this evening after dinner.'

'I should head off, too,' said Rhoda. 'Let me know what your dad says, won't you?'

'Yeah, of course. I'd better just put those other boxes back.'

Rhoda paused at the table where the photographs and boxes were. 'I meant to have another look at these photos.'

'Did you want to stay for dinner?' Nate found himself asking. 'Although I appreciate you've had to share a meal with me once already today.'

Rhoda gave a laugh. 'I would say yes, but I really need to get back and catch up on some work I'm a bit behind on.'

'When are you next back here?' Nate tried to sound casual. He'd enjoyed Rhoda's company, and had to admit he was a bit disappointed she was heading off.

'Tomorrow. Now the scaffolding is up, there's nothing to stop me.'

'Well, come and have a look at the pictures then. I might have some news on the missing paperwork and Bible.'

'That will be good. It does seem odd that both things we are looking for are missing.'

'Yeah, it does seem strange none of it is here, but it doesn't mean Dad had anything to do with it,' replied Nate, although he couldn't really come up with a plausible alternative.

The telephone in the study rang out.

'Bloody hell! I didn't know those things still existed.' Rhoda eyed the vintage looking telephone on the desk. 'I thought it was for show.'

Nate grinned and picked up the receiver but stopped. He could hear his dad answer the phone downstairs.

'Hello. Telton Hall.'

'Jack? Is that you?' It was Aggie.

'Who do you think it is?' came his father's reply.

Nate replaced the receiver gently so as not to disturb the phone call. 'Dad beat me to it.'

'Does your dad not have a mobile?' asked Rhoda as they made their way out of the room.

'Yes, but he doesn't use it. Only switches it on if he's out in the field and needs to use it. Which, incidentally, is never.'

As they made their way down the staircase, Nate was aware of his father's raised voice.

'No. Now is not a good time ... Don't be so stupid, Aggie ... You know how I feel.'

There was no pretending neither Nate nor Rhoda couldn't hear his dad's side of the conversation. Rhoda pulled an 'eek' face.

'I'll just slip out,' she said softly.

'I can't talk now ...' Jack was saying. 'Yes, she is as a matter of fact.'

They were at the foot of the stairs and Nate felt obliged to cough loudly, which elicited a smothered giggle from Rhoda. 'Sorry,' she whispered.

Nate saw her to the door. 'Don't apologise. God knows what's going on in there. That was Aggie on the phone. They're probably standing at their respective windows looking along the driveway at each other. Funny old buggers they are at times.'

Nate waved Rhoda off and went back indoors. All was quiet. He popped his head around the living room door. 'You OK, Dad?'

'Yes. Fine.'

'Sounded like you and Aggie were having a bit of a set-to. I picked up the phone just after you did and heard her say hello,' Nate added by way of explanation.

His father's eyes narrowed. 'Nothing for you to worry about. Now, where's that young lady from the museum, Rhoda? What were you doing upstairs with her?'

Nate let out a laugh. 'It's all right, Dad, we were just in the study. We were trying to see if we could find the Bible.'

'What do you want that for? I thought all that business was going to be forgotten about.'

'Do you know where it is?' Nate asked again, choosing not to answer the question. 'It looks like it's been there, but recently moved. Also, we were looking for the ledgers for the work carried out here and oddly, the files for May and June 1945 are missing. You don't know anything about them, do you?'

'No! No, I don't. Can you just leave it all alone? I don't know what the fascination is.'

'We're just curious, that's all. Rhoda wants to do what she thinks is the right thing. It's not hurting anyone. If anything, it's helping someone know what happened to their loved one.'

'Or hated one,' said his father. 'Well, I think you should leave the past in the past. Things happened during the war that might not have happened any other time. You won't be doing anyone any favours digging up a load of trouble after all this time.'

'Currently, we're doing no harm,' said Nate.

'Are you sure that's the only reason you're helping her?'

Nate did an exaggerated eye-roll. 'I've got to get Isaac. See you in a while.'

Isaac chatted happily in the car about his chess game and Nate listened attentively. Isaac loved going. It suited his analytical mind, where there was order and set rules with no deviation. Nate tried as much as he could to provide that same level of stability in his son's home life and, despite their differences, he and Siobhan were still united in their ambition for Isaac to make the most of life and the opportunities which came his way.

'How was school?' Nate asked as Isaac finished a move-by-move account of the chess match that afternoon.

'It was OK. I showed Mr Barnden my Victorian project. He thought it was good. He liked the pictures of the school.'

'Ah, that's brilliant. I'm glad he approved.'

'He said it was good I actually got to go there, and not just look on the internet,' said Isaac, gazing out of the window.

'I think so, too. We should go there again another day.'

'Singlewood Open-Air Museum, Singlewood Hill, Dean Woods, West Sussex, PO19 7AA.'

Nate smiled at his son and reached out to ruffle his hair as Isaac then recited the grid reference from the Ordnance Survey Map.

'I won't need the satnav next time,' said Nate.

By now they had reached Telton Hall, and as Nate slowed the car to turn into the driveway, he looked over towards Telton Cottage.

'There's Aunt Aggie at the window,' he said, exchanging a wave with her.

As he drove up towards the house, he remembered the disagreement he'd inadvertently overheard between his father and aunt. Something about it was bothering him, but he couldn't quite put his finger on it. He pulled up into his usual parking spot and he and Isaac hopped out of the car.

'Nosey Parker,' said Isaac. 'N-O-S-E-Y-P-A-R-K-E-R. Noun. A person who is nosey.'

Nate laughed. 'Who's a Nosey Parker?' he asked as he followed Isaac in through the front door.

'Aunt Aggie said Rhoda was.'

'When did she say that?'

'On Sunday. On the telephone to Granddad.'

Nate eyed his son. 'Were you listening in on their telephone conversation on another phone? You know you're not to do that.'

'I wanted to say hello.'

'And did you?'

'No. They sounded cross, so I put the phone back down.'

'Right,' said Nate. 'Well, good lad for putting it down, but you really mustn't pick it up.'

'OK.'

Isaac broke into a run and raced down the hallway to the kitchen, where he was greeted by his grandfather. Jack always had a glass of milk and a chocolate biscuit waiting for Isaac's return from Chess Club.

Nate made his way down the hall, perturbed that his aunt had already formed an undeserved opinion of Rhoda.

20
Rhoda

2022

Rhoda went directly home, stopping only to grab a takeaway pizza. It would have been nice to stay to dinner with the Hartwells again – something which surprised her, as she wasn't given to striking up close friendships so easily. She paused mid-thought – she'd used the term friendship. Really, they were more like acquaintances – or they should be, given the little time she'd known them – but strangely, she felt at ease with Nate and Jack.

Anyway, dinner had been declined mostly because she was eager to try to find out what she could about Alice Renshaw. It was just a hunch, but Rhoda felt sure the remains at the chapel were connected with something that had happened around the end of the war. The ledgers were missing for that period of time, which she felt was significant. If the floor in the chapel was repaired at around that time, they might also show who carried out the repairs – which could also be significant. It was troubling that the meticulously filed documents were missing; it couldn't be a coincidence. By the time she reached home, Rhoda had made up her mind to focus on those two months.

As soon as she was in her flat, Rhoda changed out of her jeans and T-shirt and into her pyjamas. Sitting cross-legged on the sofa, the pizza box next to her and the laptop on her knees, she grabbed her bag to find her notebook. She saw the poison pen letter tucked inside and read it again. She still didn't really know what to make of it. Rather than dwelling on it, she set about scrolling the internet and genealogy sites for any information she could get about Alice Renshaw.

Half an hour later, she looked at the rather meagre offerings.

Alice Renshaw, DOB 3 March 1927.

Father: Thomas Renshaw. Occupation: Gardener.

Mother: Emily Louise Renshaw. Occupation: Housewife.

Rhoda had been able to track back and find the grandparents' names, but they weren't of any use to her. She needed to find more about Alice going forwards, but without dates, there was no way of knowing where to search for a marriage or death certificate.

If Alice was at Telton Hall around the end of the war, she would have been eighteen, so assuming she was there because she was pregnant, there was a child somewhere who would be seventy-seven now. It was likely they had been adopted, so whether finding them would throw any light on the mystery, Rhoda wasn't sure. If Alice was still alive, she'd be ninety-five. Rhoda was at a dead end unless she knew if Alice had married, and what her married name was.

Rhoda scrolled through her phone to the picture she'd taken of the group photo. Would any of them still be alive? If they were around Alice's age, then again it was a possibility, even if a remote one.

What a shame Joyce Colburn couldn't remember any more details. There was, of course, Nate's Aunt Aggie. Rhoda wondered whether she'd be able to talk to her tomorrow about it.

Rhoda flipped the lid of her pizza box closed. It was so frustrating. How on earth was she going to find anything out if everyone was dead? No wonder the police weren't interested in pursuing it.

For no particular reason – other than that she needed something to do, rather than dwell on what she couldn't do – Rhoda looked up Louise Hartwell, Nate's grandmother. An internet search of the name came back with numerous Louise Hartwells, all very much alive. Rhoda typed in 'Louise Hartwell Telton Hall'.

This search yielded more information than she'd anticipated. The first result was a small section on an obscure blog by a local history group, about adoptions during the Second World War. There was one account from someone whose mother had worked as a community midwife and had visited Telton Hall.

> 'During the war, my mother, Anne Roberts, worked as a community midwife in and around the Telton area. I would often go along on her visits rather than be left on my own. I always remember going to Telton Hall, where there were young unmarried women who were pregnant but unable to keep their children. It was sad as some

of the women were upset because they didn't want to give up their babies. One particular time that sticks in my mind was when my mother came out wiping tears from her face. I'd heard the pregnant woman crying in the room and my mother and Mrs Hartwell comforting her. No one wanted to give up their baby, but you didn't have a choice in those days. This particular day, a young couple were waiting outside in the hallway. They looked very anxious and asked my mother if everything was all right. I remember the man saying he was a doctor and asking if they needed his help. My mother just asked him if he was a heart surgeon because the young woman in the room had a broken heart.'

Rhoda jotted down the name of the woman giving the account – a Sylvia Roberts. She wasn't sure if it was an important piece of information or not.

It would be easier to trace the men in the photograph, as they hadn't changed their names when they got married. From another quick search of the internet, Rhoda learned that tracking down the names of the POWs in England wasn't that easy. Most of the records had been destroyed after the war, and she was more likely to get some, if any, information from the International Red Cross, British POW Camps local archives, and/or local history groups. She sighed as she acknowledged the lengthy process this would entail, potentially for no reward.

The only complete name she had of the POWs was that of Paolo Sartori, who had made the stained-glass window. She'd see if she could track him down on the international ancestry site. She typed his name into her internet browser, which only served to inform her it was not an uncommon name, with most of them being on Facebook and therefore unlikely to be her Paolo Sartori, even if he was still alive. She doubted a man in his nineties would bother with Facebook.

She found the Telton parish website, where there was a small section on the stained-glass window at the chapel. It didn't provide her with any new information, other than to say Paolo Sartori was twenty-one when he was brought to England, having spent time en route from the Middle East in South Africa, where he was treated for a broken leg. If he was still alive, he'd be ninety-eight.

The last paragraph added a further piece of information, stating that Paolo Sartori had come from a small village in Tuscany near Pisa, where his mother and sister lived. Rhoda made a note of this information, her mind already racing ahead that she may be able to contact the family. His mother, of course, wouldn't still be alive, but perhaps his sister would – or, more likely, some relatives, children even.

Rhoda considered it all. The only way to be sure if it was Paolo Sartori would be through DNA, which would mean tracking down his family in Italy. That was, of course, beyond her limits. She knew from past experience with trying to trace her brother, not to get blinkered and fixated on one theory. She needed to keep looking at other possibilities.

She turned her attention to Billy – Jack Hartwell's stepbrother. She'd see if she could tactfully ask Jack what Billy's surname was. He would be dead by now, but if she could trace any family he had, they might be able to tell her something. Maybe Billy had spoken to them about his time at Telton Hall.

It was all extremely frustrating, and Rhoda went to bed quite dejected. She tried to put all thoughts of Telton Hall from her mind. She needed to clear her head so she could think straight. Her brain was full of information that she couldn't quite put in order, or join up with any other information she had. It all felt very disjointed.

When Rhoda awoke the next morning, she felt slightly more optimistic. The weather wasn't as nice as it had been the previous week; as she picked her way over the pebbles to the sea, she hoped the invigorating cold water would perk her up a bit.

There was no sign of Shani yet, and Rhoda swam up and down parallel with the coastline in a bid to warm herself up. The waves were choppy that morning and kept trying to push her onto shore. A couple of times she caught a mouthful of salt water, which she spat out.

She didn't speak to Shani that morning, but they did exchange a wave as Rhoda was padding back to her flat and spotted Shani at the end of the road, heading for the beach. Rhoda liked the comfortable nature of their relationship, neither feeling they had to speak to each other or wait for each other on their morning swim, and both knew no offence would be given or taken. Rhoda liked this unpressurised rhythm of their friendship; it was uncomplicated and honest. She didn't think she'd ever had that type of relationship with anybody. It was easier to keep people at a distance, as there was less chance of getting hurt that way.

'Have fun in Somerset!' called Shani as she steered her bike onto Beech Drive.

'Thank you!' called back Rhoda.

Within half an hour after showering and getting her work bag together, Rhoda was in her car and driving down to the West Country. With each mile she clocked up, the clouds increased, and by the time she'd hit Somerset, they had turned from white to grey and the wind had picked up considerably.

Great. Perfect weather for taking out a stained-glass window and making sure the chapel was left weatherproof.

By the time she'd reached Telton, splodges of bulbous raindrops were splattering the windscreen. She slowed as she came to Telton Cottage, preparing to take the turn into Telton Hall. A movement in her peripheral vision made her look again at the cottage, and she saw someone hurrying out of the front door, pulling the hood of their jacket up over their head. At first, she thought it was Nate and went to wave, but the figure got into a BMW X5. Rhoda noted the little tug of disappointment that it wasn't Nate but forced herself not to overanalyse her reaction.

Under a dark grey sky and falling rain, Telton Hall looked particularly oppressive that morning. The windows looked like soulless black eyes, all fixated on the approach to the house, boring into her. Rhoda parked in what was becoming her usual spot, on the left near the gate that led up to the chapel.

Now that looked even more oppressive. Standing alone on the hill, the clouds appeared darker and threatening. Rhoda had to admit, the thought of trudging up the hill was unappealing in itself, but then to be working in the chapel alone on such a miserable day, next to the site where the skeleton was found, didn't exactly put a spring in her step.

As she was unloading the equipment she needed to lug up to the chapel, Jack came out of the house.

'Morning,' he said, tipping the peak of his flat cap. They exchanged niceties, enquiring after each other. 'Had a phone call from the local paper. They want to do a piece on the chapel being taken down and moved. Are you all right with that?'

'Yes, of course. More than happy.'

'Good. I hope you don't mind, but I gave them your number,' said Jack.

'No problem at all.'

'Do you need a hand with taking anything up to the chapel?'

'No, I'll be fine, thanks,' said Rhoda. 'I've got everything I need.'

She was sure Jack was only asking out of good manners. There was no way she'd expect him to carry anything up and, equally, there was no way she was going to get on the back of a quad bike with him. She'd already made her mind up about that, but fortunately he didn't offer.

'Shall I take the key?' she asked.

'Oh, yes,' said Jack. 'Here it is. It's the only one we've got, so mind you don't lose it.'

Rhoda took the long skeleton key from him. 'I'll keep it safe, don't worry.'

'Now, don't forget you can come down to the house to use the bathroom and make yourself a cup of tea. Come in through the kitchen garden and the kitchen, save walking all the way around.'

'Thanks, Jack. Much appreciated.'

'I know the museum are bringing one of those Portaloo

things down, but that's for the workmen. Don't want you having to share that with them.'

'You don't know how glad I am you said that.'

Rhoda managed to lug her equipment up in one trip and was just in time to miss the first cloudburst of rain. It hammered onto the church roof and streamed down the windows. The surveyor had assured the museum that the footings were safe and the chapel wasn't going anywhere soon, despite having moved at some point. Rhoda hoped his prediction was correct.

With her radio playing softly in the background, Rhoda set about tackling one of the smaller side windows. It would give her a chance to see how easy – or difficult, as the case might be – it would be to remove the stained-glass. From what her previous inspections had shown, the newer window – Paolo's window, as she had started calling it – had been installed in the traditional method of straight into the stone, rather than being set in a wooden frame.

Her first job was to set up her tables, where she'd be laying each panel of the stained-glass windows on a full-sized sheet of carbon paper. She'd then be able to make a rubbing of each panel to show the imprint of all the lead and copper-edged pieces to use as a reference point when the window was reassembled.

Once that was organised, Rhoda climbed up on the scaffolding tower to begin removing the ties which kept the glass attached to the rods. It was always higher than she'd anticipated at the top of any scaffolding tower, but the chapel certainly wasn't the biggest one she'd worked on, and she was comfortable enough not to let it bother her.

Rhoda worked happily away on the task, losing herself

in the job she had loved for so long. The first panel was always the hardest one, as you didn't know what to expect, which is why she had started with one of the smaller stained-glass windows.

It wasn't until her stomach started rumbling that she realised it must be getting on for lunchtime. She had already drunk the bottle of water and snacked on the fruit she had brought with her. She had removed the rods and ties holding the window in place, and with her tool had scraped away the old lead around the edge of the windowpane. Now the tricky bit was tilting the glass to just the right angle so she could lift it out of the clips which held it in place. As it was a small window, she was able to do this herself, removing the panel and placing it on the cloth beside her.

Getting it down from the scaffolding to the safety of ground level was her next task. With the window wrapped in cloth, Rhoda slipped it into a rucksack, which she put on before she made her descent. Once on terra firma, she removed the window from the rucksack and placed it on the workbench. The next step was to board up the opening of the window to make it weatherproof. Fortunately, the rain had stopped but the clouds were gathering overhead, grey and dark blue like a bruised sky. It was only a matter of time before it started pouring down again, and with the wind picking up, it would be driving it straight into the chapel.

From her earlier measurements, Rhoda had already prepared a piece of plywood that would fit exactly into the space the stained-glass window had previously occupied. It fitted perfectly, and she hammered in the tacks to keep it in place.

Now seemed a good time to make the journey down to Telton Hall to use the bathroom, have a cup of tea, and eat her sandwiches, which she had left in the cool box in the boot of her car.

It was slippery on the track going down, and a couple of times Rhoda nearly lost her footing, but she made the descent in one piece. As she reached her car, an idea sprung to mind. She checked her watch and, before she had time to think it through, Rhoda found herself driving into the village.

She pulled up outside Joyce Colburn's house and knocked at the door.

Joyce opened the door as before with the chain on. 'Oh, it's you,' she said when Rhoda introduced herself. 'What do you want?'

'I'm really sorry to bother you, but I wondered if you remembered the village midwife – or, more importantly, her daughter, Sylvia Roberts?'

'Sylvia Roberts. She was just a young girl when her mother was the midwife.'

'Is she still local, do you know? Did she marry?'

'Sylvia married the vicar, if you must know. Stephen Montgomery.' Joyce frowned and let out a sigh. 'Look, I shouldn't be telling you all this, really. People don't want to be bothered by the past and what went on here during the war.'

'I'm only trying to find out who that man was at the chapel, just so I can tell his family.'

'You seem a nice young girl,' said Joyce. 'Don't get mixed up in all that. As I said, no one wants to bring all that business up.'

'What business?'

Joyce went to close the door and Rhoda instinctively put her hand in the way; then, realising how intimidating that appeared, she removed it.

'I can't tell you anything else,' said Joyce. 'Now, please leave me alone and don't come back asking any more questions.'

With that, she shut the door and Rhoda heard the chain being slid back into place.

Rhoda was sorry for upsetting the old lady, but Joyce had given her Sylvia's married name. All Rhoda had to do now was to find out where Sylvia was, and she planned on doing that as soon as she got back to Telton Hall and her iPad.

As Jack had instructed, Rhoda made her way through the gate in the wall of the kitchen garden and followed the path which ran directly down the middle to the kitchen. She hesitated, not wishing to just bowl in as if she owned the place, so she knocked on the back door. After a moment, she knocked again, this time harder, but there was still no answer. Perhaps Jack had nodded off, or he was busy around the farm. Although there was no actual farming for Jack to do now the property was in the last stages of being sold, Rhoda knew he liked to keep busy.

She had a quick scan of the farm buildings but couldn't see Jack anywhere. Returning to the kitchen door, Rhoda tried the handle and the door opened without resistance. She called out his name. There was a stillness within the house that only came when a building was empty. Without going further than the kitchen, Rhoda was already certain that Jack was out. Nevertheless, she called his name again, just in case she was mistaken and he was asleep in the living room.

The room was empty, as were the dining room and a second reception room she hadn't been in before. Standing at the foot of the stairs, Rhoda called up into the cavernous stairwell.

She was convinced she was alone in the house. She wanted to use the bathroom and remembered Nate had told her to use the one upstairs. She nipped up to the first floor, hoping this would not be the point at which Jack returned home and jumped to the conclusion she was snooping around again.

It wasn't until she was back in the kitchen that her heart rate settled into a more normal pattern. She felt guilty, and she hadn't actually done anything this time. It was then she noticed a handwritten note propped up against the kettle. It was from Jack, saying he had nipped over to see his cousin Aggie, and Rhoda was to help herself to tea.

Rhoda felt a wave of relief. Jack obviously felt he could trust her to be in the house on her own. She set about making a cup of tea and while the kettle boiled, she went out to the car to fetch her sandwiches.

As she turned to head back to the house, she glanced up at the windows on the first floor and, for a moment, she thought she saw movement inside the house. It was so fleeting she couldn't be sure. Was it just a shadow from one of the trees being blown about in the wind? She watched the window for a moment, waiting for the shadow to fall across the glass again, but it didn't, even though the trees were swaying energetically behind her.

She had come out through the front door and left it ajar,

but it was now closed. Again, the rational part of her brain told her it was the wind. A perfectly logical explanation. But the irrational part of her brain told her it was a big oak door, and it would have needed a draught from somewhere within the house to make it close – and it would have slammed shut, surely. She didn't remember hearing it slam.

Rhoda went around to the back of the house and into the kitchen; this time her caution was tinted with a dash of fear. What if there was someone other than Jack in the house? He had, after all, left the back door unlocked – anyone could have simply walked in. She paused in the kitchen, listening attentively for the slightest groan of a floorboard, the tread of a foot on the stairs or the creak of a door – in fact, any tell-tale sign that she wasn't alone.

She was just being silly, she told herself. There was no one in the house. She was letting her imagination get the better of her. When did she start being afraid of nothing?

Despite the little talking-to she'd given herself, Rhoda kept an ear out to any strange sound while she made her cup of tea and sat down at the table to eat her sandwiches. Just as she had begun to relax and convince herself that there was no one in the house, she heard the unmistakable sound of a thud directly above her.

Rhoda froze.

21
Alice

1945

For some reason, Alice hated being upstairs in Telton Hall on her own. There was something about the high-ceilinged rooms with their long Georgian windows which should have an uplifting effect, but they made Alice think of all the young women, like her, who had been here: all with their growing bellies as new life formed inside them; all sent away from home to spend their confinement far from the prying eyes of their villages or towns; all with a sense of shame for what they had allowed to happen – for what they had willingly taken part in. They had all come here to have their babies in secret and to give up their flesh and blood for adoption. In Alice's mind, the rooms and the hallway echoed with their silent tears; the carpets absorbed their sorrow and the curtains soaked up their despair.

She was due to meet the couple who were going to adopt her baby – *the* baby, she corrected herself.

'Don't look so glum,' said Lily, coming into the room.

Alice was relieved to see her. 'I didn't realise I did,' she said, sitting down at the dressing table. She picked up her hairbrush.

'You don't want to put them off.' Lily came and stood behind her, taking the hairbrush from Alice's hand. She began brushing Alice's hair for her.

'Don't I?'

Lily stopped mid-brush. 'No. No, you don't.' She gave a sympathetic smile to Alice's reflection in the mirror. 'You want them to feel good about adopting the baby. This couple can give the baby everything you can't. I don't mean to be harsh, Alice, please don't get upset now. I'm just being honest.'

Alice plucked her handkerchief from out of her sleeve and dabbed at her eyes. 'I know, but I can't help it.'

'They are loaded. He's a doctor in London. This is the best thing you can do for the baby. It's the ultimate sacrifice a woman can make. You are giving the baby the best chance it is going to get in life.'

Alice nodded. She knew Lily was right – pragmatic as ever. Alice knew it made sense, but the yearning to keep the baby was overpowering. It was a physical ache that Alice didn't know was possible.

'Have you ever regretted giving up your baby?' asked Alice softly.

Lily brushed Alice's hair vigorously. 'No. I haven't.' She didn't meet Alice's gaze for a moment, but then looked up at her friend. 'I've wished I could have kept her. A beautiful little girl with a shock of red curls. She had the longest lashes possible. Tiny little fingers and tiny little fingernails. Her skin was so delicate and translucent. She was just perfect. I know they tell you not to name her, but in my mind, she was called Kathleen. Her dad was Irish. He worked on the travelling fair. He never even knew I was pregnant – had moved on to the next town and the next girl by the time I realised.' Lily sat down on the edge of the bed, her thumb flicking the bristles of the brush. 'I wish every day she was here, but I don't regret the decision I made. She's with good people. Wealthy people. They can give her the life I never had, and one I could never have given her.'

Alice turned to face Lily and held her hands in her own. 'I'm so sorry.'

Lily had never opened up to Alice about her baby – not properly. This revelation felt as if their friendship had moved to the next level.

'Don't be. I'm not sorry. It was the best thing that could have happened to Kathleen. What future did she have with me? She would have been taken off me, as I haven't got anywhere to live or a job or any money. I loved her so much, I knew I had to give her up. I would have been a selfish mother if I'd kept her. Love isn't always about keeping someone. Sometimes it's about letting them go.' Tears fell from Lily's eyes, landing on their hands.

'Oh, Lily, you're so brave. So very brave.' Alice pulled her friend towards her and hugged her tightly.

After a few moments, Lily pulled away and dried her face on the towel in the bedroom. 'Look at me, getting all upset. I promised myself I wouldn't do that. I don't want to torture myself for doing the right thing.' She brushed her dress down and stood up straight. 'And I've made you cry.

Mrs Hartwell will have my guts for garters. Come on, we need to get you presentable.'

At that point, there was the sound of the doorbell ringing.

'Oh, that's them,' said Alice, suddenly feeling panicked.

This was real. She was going to meet the couple who wanted to adopt her baby. She didn't correct herself this time. The baby, for now, was hers. And if she was only going to have another six or seven months with the baby, she was jolly well going to acknowledge it as hers. No one could take these precious months from her. They were hers, and hers alone.

Giving herself a final check over in the mirror, Alice deemed herself presentable. Her eyes were a little red from crying, but with a tiny touch of mascara that Lily had got from somewhere – Alice didn't ask questions; she knew Lily liked to barter, and Alice decided the least she knew, the better – and a dab of face powder, origin also unknown, disguised the fact she'd been upset.

Alice made her way downstairs, with Lily trailing behind. Lily herself wanted to get a glimpse of the couple and made sure she was walking down the hallway just as Alice opened the door to the sitting room.

The couple, Mr and Mrs Eggars, were introduced to Alice. They were younger than Alice had imagined, and Mrs Eggars had a warm and welcoming, if slightly nervous, smile. Mr Eggars was equally welcoming, if more formal.

'So good of you to meet us,' he said, as he shook Alice's hand.

'Yes, thank you, so much.' Mrs Eggars gave a discreet glance to Alice's stomach and when she realised Alice had noticed, she blushed. 'Please sit down here next to me.'

Alice perched awkwardly on the edge of the sofa and took the cup of tea Mrs Hartwell passed over to her.

'Alice has been a great help in the few weeks she's been here,' said Mrs Hartwell. 'She's been helping in the kitchen and around the house. Just light duties.'

'How have you been keeping?' asked Mr Eggars. 'Do you feel well in yourself? Are you being seen by a midwife?'

'Freddie, one question at a time,' said Mrs Eggars with a nervous laugh. 'Sorry, Alice, my husband sometimes forgets he's not in doctor mode.'

Alice returned the smile. 'I'm very well, thank you. I haven't seen a midwife yet.'

'The midwife is calling by in about three weeks' time,' put in Mrs Hartwell.

That was news to Alice, but she kept her expression neutral.

'Oh, that's good. And have you had much morning sickness?' asked Mrs Eggars.

'Not really. Just felt a little queasy. Been sick only a couple of times.'

'Ooh, it might mean you're carrying a boy, then,' said Mrs Eggars, glancing at her husband.

'That's an old wives' tale, darling,' replied Mr Eggars, and he squeezed his wife's hand.

It was at that moment Alice saw the love pass between the Eggars. A tiny moment, just a fleeting look, but she could tell they loved each other. It filled Alice with hope and confidence that this couple would love her baby, too.

'I expect you want to know about us,' said Mrs Eggars. 'I know it's not usual to meet prospective parents beforehand, but we firmly believe, or at least like to believe, that it sets everyone at ease, and this ultimately will be beneficial for you and the baby. Peace and love start before the child is born, and we want it born wrapped in positivity.'

Alice wasn't quite sure if she knew what Mrs Eggars meant, but she liked the sound of it.

'My wife is very holistic,' explained Mr Eggars, as if reading Alice's mind. 'I'm more pragmatic and scientific, but we celebrate our differences. We truly believe a rounded approach to bringing up children, where they are confident in their surroundings and have the love of their parents, will make for a happy, contented and confident child and adult.'

Alice nodded. 'Being loved is the most important thing.'

'Yes. I agree.' It was Mrs Eggars. 'We ... I ... can't have children of my own, and yet it is the only thing I have ever wanted. So, to have this opportunity is a blessing, and we give you our word – we will love the baby as if it were our own, and we will always be open and honest with them, so they know about you.'

'That's one of the reasons we wanted to meet you,' said Mr Eggars. 'We won't be keeping you a secret from them.'

Mrs Hartwell had been right when she'd said the Eggars were open-minded and progressive. Alice looked from wife to husband and back again. 'Thank you. It will be a great comfort to know that.'

They spent another hour talking together in the living room and by the time the Eggars left, Alice was certain they were the best choice and the best chance her child would have. They had talked of their plans to give the child a good education, to travel abroad, to give the child experiences that Alice could only ever dream of. She learned they lived in Bath in a big Regency house with a large back garden.

Mrs Eggars' parents lived nearby and would play an active part in the child's life. This both saddened and comforted Alice, as she thought of her own mum and how different her pregnancy might be if she were still alive.

Despite all the luxury on offer to the child, none of this meant anything if Alice wasn't sure of the love, and she was certain the Eggars would love the child.

'There, aren't you glad you met them now?' asked Mrs Hartwell as they waved the car off down the driveway. 'Has it put your mind at rest?'

'A bit,' admitted Alice.

In truth, she still felt torn at the idea of giving her baby to someone else. If only her circumstances had been different. If only Brett Cunningham hadn't stood her up. But that wouldn't have stopped him being killed on a bombing mission, would it? He had to go where he was ordered. It wasn't like he had a choice in the matter. She'd be a widow, but at least she'd still have her baby. Once she gave the child up, she'd have nothing.

'Are you all right, dear?' asked Mrs Hartwell, ushering Alice back into the house.

'Yes. I think I'll just have a few minutes to myself, if that's all right with you?'

Mrs Hartwell tipped her head to one side, considering her request. 'Yes. Of course. But, Alice, try not to think of how you feel. Try to focus on the future for the baby.'

Alice nodded, unable to form an answer as she felt a ball of emotion churn over in her stomach and a vice-like grip on her heart. She walked straight through the house to the kitchen and out of the back door. Fortunately, there was no sign of Billy, and initially she was going to head towards the willow tree, but changed her mind, just in case Billy was camped out there, expecting her to seek solitude after the meeting with the Eggars.

She'd outwit him, she decided, and changed direction, nipping through the gate and out into the farmyard.

She wasn't sure what drew her to the chapel. She certainly wasn't religious, and normally the place gave her the creeps, but, at the same time, she felt a pull. As she opened the oak door and stepped inside, she felt a calmness settle around her.

Her footsteps echoed on the stone floor, and she slipped into a pew halfway up on the left, sliding along into the shadows of the walls.

Alice thought she should pray, but she didn't know what to say. Her mother had taken her to church when she was younger, but once she became ill, those visits had stopped. Alice's father had turned his back on the Church at roughly the same time, blaming God for his wife's illness. Alice had gone along with the narrative; it was easier than trying to understand why God would want to take her mother from her.

Now, sitting in the pew, she somehow felt close to her mother. Alice clasped her hands together in her lap and, with her head bowed, she closed her eyes.

'God, if you're there, please make the Eggars be a nice couple and look after and love my baby. Please let me be making the right choice. And, Mum, if you're there, too, please know that I'm doing what I think is best for the baby. I wish you were here. You'd tell me what to do, I know you would. I miss you so much. Please forgive me for not being able to keep the baby. I love you.'

It was only then she realised she wasn't the only person in the chapel. Something made her look up, and in the front pew on the opposite side of the building, sitting in the far corner, like she was, she could see the bowed head of a man.

She gulped as she noted the red patch of cloth across the shoulder of the prisoner uniform. It was a patch to show he was a POW. It was hard to make out the colour of his hair in the dim light, so Alice wasn't sure if it was Paolo or Carlo. From the back they both looked the same, with their dark hair cut short.

He must know she'd come into the chapel. He couldn't have failed to hear her footsteps. Had he heard her talking to God and her mum?

The prisoner rose and crossed himself and, as he turned to walk to the aisle, she saw it was Paolo. He looked over at her as he made his way down the centre of the chapel and nodded his head in acknowledgement.

Alice nodded back at him. She wanted to say hello but suddenly felt shy and nervous. He stopped at the end of the pew. 'How are you?'

He smiled, and immediately Alice felt at ease. 'I'm sorry if I disturbed you,' she said.

'No. I should not be here. I am sorry.'

'Why shouldn't you be here?' Alice felt indignant on his part. 'Who said you shouldn't?'

'I do not think Billy will like it.'

'It's not up to him. Mrs Hartwell would say it was all right.' Even to Alice, she didn't sound convincing. They both knew that Billy would be an utter bastard about it. 'Don't worry, I won't say anything. We're all allowed to pray, you know.'

'I like to come to look at the windows,' explained Paolo. 'My father was a ... I try to think of the word ... erm, glazier. Yes, I think that is the word. He made glass. Coloured glass like this window. Since I was twelve, my father teach me to do the same.'

Alice had never really thought about what the Italian prisoners did before the war. She supposed they were no different from the young men from Britain, who had been farmhands, mechanics, postmen and bank clerks one day, and then the next day they were soldiers, risking their lives and often giving their lives in the name of war.

'I expect your father can't wait for you to come home.'

'My father, he died when I was sixteen.'

A look of sadness crossed Paolo's face and Alice immediately recognised it as grief.

'I'm sorry,' she said. 'My mum died when I was young, too. She used to be a dressmaker. I used to work in a department store, selling clothes. It's not quite the same thing but it makes me feel close to her.'

'And did you make that dress?' Paolo nodded towards the floral print dress of which Alice had let out the seams just the day before, to allow for her increasing waist.

'No. I bought this one from the department store. Staff discount.'

'You are dressed up today?'

'I had to meet someone earlier. Well, two people. A couple,' said Alice, then wondering how she was going to explain.

Paolo nodded. 'I understand. I am sorry.'

Unexpected tears filled Alice's eyes. She was so used to being told to keep a stiff upper lip that this little display of kindness from a stranger – an Italian POW, no less – touched her more deeply than she expected. 'Thank you,' she whispered.

Suddenly, the door to the chapel swung open and Lily came racing in. 'Oh, Alice, there you are. Come on, you need to get back to the house.'

'Why? What's the matter?' asked Alice.

Lily hurried over to her and, from the pew behind, urged her out. 'Billy was asking where you were.' She glanced at Paolo. 'And where he was.'

Alice exchanged a worried look with Paolo. 'You go,' she said urgently. 'Go quickly, before he finds you here.'

'I am not scared of him.'

'I know you're not, but don't make trouble for yourself,' said Alice. 'Now go, quickly. We won't say a word. If he asks, we haven't seen you.'

'Thank you,' said Paolo, and hurried out of the chapel.

'Now we'd better get ourselves down to the farm sharpish,' said Lily.

'What's up with him anyway? Why does he want to see me?' asked Alice.

'No idea but I thought I should warn you.'

7 May 1945

Carissime Mamma e Sofia

Is it possible to have feelings for someone when you hardly know them? How do you know if your feelings are real, or if they are distorted by your circumstances and where you are in that moment in time?

Can it be that the nationality of a person can be such a divide that they cannot be anything more than friends?

It is two o'clock in the morning and I cannot sleep. I have been thinking about this all night and I do not know what the answer is. I thought I'd write it down here in my letter in the hope that it would make things clearer, but I'm not sure that it has.

I know, Sofia, you say I think too deeply about things, and maybe you are right. Should I not worry and just live in the moment, or should I make a conscious decision not to pursue this any further?

I don't know if I will send this letter. Maybe I will wake in the morning and rip it up, but tonight I felt the need to write to you and ask the two wisest women I know.

Take care.

Il vostro amorevole figlio e fratello

Paolo

22
Nate

2022

Telton Hall looked particularly gloomy, Nate thought as he pulled into the driveway. The day had started off overcast and the threat of rain hovered overhead, blocking out any daylight – so much so, the sky seemed closer today. He could see Rhoda's car parked up near the gate and wondered how she was getting on with the window. He was intrigued to see the process for removing the glass – that's why he was here, of course. It was absolutely nothing to do with the person undertaking the work. No. Definitely not.

Before he went up to the chapel, Nate popped into the house to make sure his dad was OK. He let himself in through the kitchen so he didn't have to disturb his father. Nate usually had his key to the house with him, but he'd managed to leave that in his briefcase in the office.

As Nate went into the kitchen, he saw there was a half-drunk cup of tea on the table, together with a sandwich sitting on a sheet of tinfoil. He recognised Rhoda's iPad on the table, with its distinctive art deco styled case. No sign of Rhoda, though, who was probably in the bathroom.

He went over to the kettle and topped up the water to make them both a fresh cup of tea. There was no sign of Tink trotting down the hallway to greet him, and the living room was empty. Nate whistled as he set about sorting the cups out, so he didn't startle Rhoda when she came back in.

As he waited for the kettle to boil, Nate eyed the open notebook on the table. He was tempted to have a peek – not for any particular reason; he was just curious – but he employed his better judgement and ignored the urge.

By the time the kettle had boiled and he had made two teas, Nate thought Rhoda should be back from the bathroom by now, unless she was snooping around again, especially if she thought she was alone in the house. That thought annoyed him, even though he wanted to give her the benefit of the doubt. Surely she wouldn't do it twice; not after he'd assured her he wanted to help.

'Bollocks,' he muttered under his breath.

He pushed himself away from the worktop and went down the hall in search of her.

A quick recce of the ground floor told him it was empty, so that meant upstairs. He called out her name and listened.

'Up here!' The voice sounded muffled, but it was definitely Rhoda. 'Nate! I'm upstairs! I'm stuck! Help me!'

Nate took the stairs two at a time, reaching the landing in seconds. 'Rhoda? Where are you?'

'Here!' Rhoda was banging on the other side of the door that overlooked the back garden.

What the hell was she doing in there?

Nate turned the china doorknob – and then, because it had always been a bit difficult, he gave it an extra flick, which released the catch. He opened the door and the light from the hallway found its way into the darkened bedroom.

'What happened? What are you doing in here, and why are the curtains drawn? What happened to your head? Are you OK?'

'Which question would you like me to answer first?' Rhoda gave him a look that Nate always thought was reserved for teachers – mean teachers – when a pupil had clearly not been listening and couldn't answer a question.

'Sorry. Are you OK? Are you bleeding?'

There was an egg-shaped lump on the side of Rhoda's forehead.

She lifted her hand to it and touched it with her fingertips, wincing as she did so, before taking her hand away and examining her fingers. 'Nope. No blood. Just sore.'

'You need to get a cold compress on that. Here, sit down on the bed.'

Nate opened the curtains, allowing the meagre offering of overcast daylight into the room. He nipped out and reappeared a few moments later with a clean flannel from the airing cupboard, which he'd run under the cold tap from the sink in the corner of the room.

'Hold that on your head,' he instructed her.

'Thank you.' She screwed up her face as the flannel came into contact with the lump. She looked around her and took in her surroundings. 'Oh, no. Don't say I'm in your father's room.'

'Nope. It's my room. Well, my old room when I was a kid. You seem surprised you're here.'

'That's because I am surprised!' She took her hand down from her head.

Nate moved her hand back in place. 'Don't get all defensive. And keep that on there for a bit longer.'

She did an exaggerated eye-roll but complied with his instructions. 'I'm not getting defensive. I genuinely didn't know.'

'What are you actually doing in here?'

'I was downstairs, having my lunch, when I heard a thud from up here,' she explained. 'Your dad had left a note to say he'd gone out, but I thought maybe he'd come back and I didn't know. I was worried he'd fallen over. So I came up here.'

'OK. But why this room?'

'Because the noise was directly above me, and I guessed it was this room. It was dark. The curtains were drawn and as I stepped into the room, I tripped over something.' She looked back to the floor.

Nate followed her gaze, but there was nothing obvious that would cause her to trip. He didn't doubt that she had; no one in their right mind would whack their head on purpose to uphold their account of events.

'I don't know what you tripped on, but I guess you came down and caught your head on the ottoman at the foot of the bed.'

'I was stunned at first, and then the door closed behind me. When I got up and tried to open it, I couldn't.'

'Ah, yes. The lock does get stuck from time to time. Dad was always promising to fix it, but never got around to it.' He nodded towards the bank of wardrobes on the far wall. 'That end door isn't part of the wardrobe. It's just made to look like it is. It actually leads into the bathroom. It's a Jack and Jill bathroom. The amount of times I got stuck in here and had to make my exit via the loo.'

'You're joking! You mean I could have got out myself?'

'Yep. If you'd known.'

'Brilliant.'

'Strange the curtains were drawn, though,' said Nate. 'No one comes in here. I only use the room when I'm staying over. I wouldn't have closed them in the first place.'

'Does your dad have a cleaner?'

Nate gave a snort. 'You must be joking. I keep telling him he should get one, but he's a stubborn old sod and refuses to entertain the idea.'

'Well, they were closed.' Rhoda frowned and Nate could tell she was mulling something over. He waited for her to speak. 'I definitely heard a thud. I don't know what it was, but I didn't imagine it. And why would the door close on its own? It's not spring-loaded, is it?'

'No, it's not.' Nate contemplated Rhoda's story. 'Maybe you caught it with your foot when you went down, and pushed it shut.'

'I doubt it. My legs aren't that long.'

Nate met her gaze. 'What's your theory then, Miss Marple?'

'Don't take the piss.'

Nate held his hands palm-up. 'Sorry.'

Rhoda let out a frustrated sigh. 'I'm sorry, too. Just a bit touchy. Blame it on the bump on the head.' She offered him a weak smile. 'This may sound weird, but before the noise, I felt as if there was someone in the house. I can't explain it, but I felt twitchy. I dismissed the idea as nonsense and an overactive imagination, but I think actually I was right. There was someone in the house and they were up here. I disturbed them. They tripped me up and shut the door.'

'Wow. That's some theory,' said Nate. 'I'm not dismissing it, but it sounds quite …'

'Far-fetched?' finished Rhoda. 'Yes, I know. But I did get that note about not poking my nose into the chapel business. Seems a bit more than a coincidence, if you ask me.'

Nate couldn't argue with her. 'To be honest, both things sound far-fetched, but seeing as you've had a note and then are so sure of what's happened, I'm not ruling anything out. I just don't know who it could be.'

'I don't care who it is, this is just making me even more determined to find out the truth. I don't give up that easily.'

'I have no doubt about that,' said Nate. And he didn't. Rhoda was tenacious, if nothing else.

'Thank you for rescuing me, anyway.' She gave him a wry smile. 'I'd better get back to work.'

'I've just made a fresh cup of tea.'

'I'll pour it into my flask and take it up to the chapel with me, if that's OK?' She must have registered his disappointed look, which he didn't manage to hide. 'Why don't you come up with me?'

'Yeah. Great.' Why did that sound so sarcastic? He noted Rhoda attempting to hide a smile.

'You don't have to,' she said.

'No. Seriously, I mean it. I'd love to come up and see what you're doing.'

'I'll just need to grab my phone charger from my car on the way.'

While Rhoda went to collect her charger, Nate waited in the kitchen, having a quick square-up.

Rhoda returned within a few moments, and he smiled as she came into the room. 'All set?Excellent ...' His words faded away. The look on Rhoda's face told him everything was other than excellent. 'What's up?'

23
Rhoda

2022

'My car – that's what's up. It's been bloody well broken into!'

'You're joking?'

Rhoda resisted the urge to say of course she wasn't sodding well joking but managed to construct a more cordial reply.

'I wish I was.'

'How did they break in?' Nate was already walking past her and down the hallway.

Rhoda followed him out to the car, where the passenger window was shattered. 'Someone must have really wanted to get in to break the window. It's not exactly easy.'

Nate looked around the car. 'I'm so sorry, Rhoda. Look, don't touch anything. I'll call the police.'

'Oh, don't bother. They won't want to come out. It's not exactly crime of the century. I doubt they're going to dust for fingerprints and launch a full-scale enquiry. They'll tell me it's not a priority, they don't have the resources and it's not in the public interest.'

She knew she was being bitter about the response they had given to the body in the chapel, but it made her feel better anyway.

'You should still report it and get a crime reference number.'

'I don't know if it's worth the hassle. I don't want to claim on my insurance, it will only push the premium up. I'd sooner just get it fixed.' Rhoda sighed and opened the rear door, leaning in to look through her bag on the back seat. 'There doesn't appear to be anything missing.'

'Maybe they got disturbed,' suggested Nate.

Rhoda stood up and rubbed her face with her hands. 'I've just had a horrible thought.' She looked at Nate. 'Maybe there was someone upstairs in the house just now. Maybe they smashed the car window, too?'

Nate appeared to consider this for a moment. 'It's a possibility, but I don't know why. What purpose? To frighten you?'

Rhoda shrugged. 'That's all I can think of. I must be treading on toes.'

'But you've only spoken to Dad, Aggie and Joyce Colburn. They're hardly likely to wage a vendetta against you. I can't see Joyce Colburn hotfooting it into the house, locking you in the room and then running downstairs and smashing your window.'

'When you say it like that, it does sound ludicrous.' Rhoda looked back up at Telton Hall, her dislike for the place growing by the second. 'You don't think you should get the police out to check the premises? Make sure whoever it was isn't still here – hiding in the house somewhere.'

'I'll have a quick scope around.'

'No. Don't. Not on your own. I'll come with you.'

'Protection?' Nate raised his eyebrows.

'Yeah. Why not? I didn't spend time in a kids' home without learning how to look after myself.'

Rhoda fell into step with him as they went back across the drive and into Telton Hall. It was quite nice to have a look in all the rooms she wouldn't get to see under normal circumstances. There were six rooms on the first floor – all bedrooms, apart from the study – and in the attic there were two rooms, one each side of the landing.

'This is where the prisoners of war slept,' said Nate, opening a door on the landing which Rhoda had assumed was a cupboard. It revealed a steep narrow flight of stairs. She followed Nate up to the landing.

They stepped into the room on the right, which had dormer windows overlooking both the front and back of the house. The room was something of a store, with a couple of old chests of drawers, a wardrobe, several cardboard boxes, a dismantled cot, a wicker rocking chair – the seat of which was broken – and a couple of old wooden dining chairs. A thick layer of dust and countless spiderwebs clung to the furniture.

'When did anyone last come up here?' asked Rhoda.

'Years ago. I don't even know what's in those boxes.'

'You didn't come up here when you were a child?'

'No. Was always told to stay out of the attic – just full of junk.' Nate crossed the landing and opened the door to the second room. 'Nothing in here at all, except an old rolled-up carpet. Probably a nice warm space for mice.'

Rhoda pulled a face. 'Let's not disturb them.'

Five minutes later, after every room had been looked into, they were back in the kitchen.

'I'll tell Dad to keep the kitchen door locked in future. He and Aggie are buggers for not locking up,' said Nate, checking the handle. 'I don't even know where he is. He's been gone a long time.'

'Oh, he left me this note,' said Rhoda, pulling the crumpled sheet of paper from her pocket. 'Gone to see your aunt.'

She passed it over to Nate to read.

'I'd better go down there and let them both know at the same time. Might make Aggie take it seriously. Are you going to be all right on your own, or do you want to come with me?'

Admittedly, Rhoda didn't fancy being in Telton Hall on her own now. 'I should get back to work, really.'

'Can you just wait until I can come up with you? For my own peace of mind, so I know you're OK up there.'

'Yeah, sure.'

Rhoda appreciated Nate was making it sound as if he was concerned and allowing her to give in without losing dignity. Truth be told, the prospect of being in the chapel alone wasn't exactly appealing.

'Then I'll get your car window fixed, so you can at least drive home safely.'

Rhoda wasn't used to anyone looking after her, but

she stopped herself from protesting. She appreciated the gesture.

Aggie and Jack made all the appropriate sounds of being shocked at what had happened, but neither seemed overly concerned.

'I can't imagine why anyone would do that to your car. Must be kids,' concluded Aggie. 'Anyway, I'm glad you're here. I need a word with you two.'

Rhoda exchanged a look with Nate, who appeared equally bemused.

'What's that?' he asked.

'I've had Joyce Colburn on the phone. Apparently, you ...' She pointed her finger towards Rhoda. 'You've been round there pestering her about Sylvia Montgomery.'

Rhoda was aware of the sideways look Nate gave her, but she avoided eye contact with him. Instead, she addressed Aggie. 'I was just asking her if she knew who Sylvia Roberts was. I wanted to find out if she remembered anything that could help discover the identity of the remains in the chapel. I didn't mean to upset her.'

'There's not many of us oldens left,' said Aggie. 'We don't want to feel hounded just because you've got some fanciful idea about those old bones.'

Rhoda was just about to protest at Aggie's description, but Nate beat her to it.

'Aggie, it's not just old bones, it's someone. A man. He deserves to be laid to rest properly, and the only way to do that is to find out who he was. That's all Rhoda wants to do.'

'But if he was murdered, as is claimed, then someone is

going to be upset,' said Aggie. 'They'll want to know who did it. Then that could be a proper can of worms opened. Mark my words, no good will come of this. You're both best leaving well alone.'

'I can't promise that,' said Rhoda. 'But I really must get back to the chapel now, otherwise I'll get in trouble for holding up the work, and they'll send someone else down to do the job.'

She said her goodbyes and left Telton Cottage with Nate alongside her.

'Sorry about Aggie,' said Nate. 'She speaks her mind.'

'I don't have a problem with that.'

'No. I don't suppose you do.'

Nate grinned at her and Rhoda couldn't help breaking into a smile herself.

'Does Sylvia Montgomery still live in the village?' she asked.

'She does, as it happens, and I know what you're going to ask me next.'

'No time like the present.'

'Hmm. I thought you had work to do?' said Nate, coming to a stop at the beginning of the drive to Telton Hall.

'I can go and see her while my car gets fixed. After I've done my work, that is.'

'You've got it all figured out, haven't you?'

'I like a plan. Now, can you see if Sylvia Montgomery will speak to me? Please?'

'All right, I'll see what I can do.'

They made their way up the driveway, stopping at Rhoda's car to have another look at the damage.

'I don't think it was kids – do you?' she asked.

'Probably not. I'll get on to the garage once I've checked the chapel for you.'

They made their way up the hill.

'You know all this is connected to the letter I received,' said Rhoda, zipping up her jacket as the wind cut through her sweatshirt. 'Someone doesn't want me finding out the truth. Or some people.'

'Yeah, I did realise. But I also know why this is important to you.'

They came to a halt outside the chapel door.

'You do?'

'Of course.' Nate reached out his hand and rubbed Rhoda's upper arm. 'If you can't find peace for your own family, then you want to find it for this man's.'

Rhoda nodded. 'I hate feeling helpless. Trying to find Dean makes me feel that way. I don't know how much longer I can go on. Every day, waking up with hope there's been a breakthrough, a sighting – a message from Dean, even. And every morning, I look at Facebook and my phone and there's nothing. It's demoralising, not to mention painful. I feel a failure. I've let him down.'

'Hey, you're not a failure at all,' insisted Nate. 'I know you might not like to hear this, but Dean has failed you. Walking away like that, not even letting you know he was OK. He must have known how upset you'd be. It's not fair what he's putting you through.'

Rhoda bristled at the criticism levelled towards her brother. A flare of indignation rose within her, and she shrugged off Nate's hand. 'He hasn't let me down. What if he was suffering with mental health issues? That's the logical explanation. He wasn't thinking straight. Going off like that was out of character. Don't you dare say he's let me down.'

She could see the alarm in Nate's eyes, swiftly followed by hurt, but she was angry and she didn't know how to handle what was essentially the truth. Dean's lack of contact – anything to say he was OK – hurt her deeply; it was something she could only acknowledge privately to herself. She didn't need anyone pointing it out to her. Admitting that Dean had let her down would be disloyal, and if she was disloyal, she'd be forever punished by never knowing what had happened to him.

Rhoda opened the door to the chapel and went in, not waiting for Nate to check it out first. Everything looked as she'd left it, which was a relief.

'All OK?' Nate went over to the confessional box and looked inside.

'Yes. Everything is fine.'

Nate turned and looked at her. She met his gaze but couldn't bring herself to say she was sorry for snapping at him. She wasn't good at apologising – she knew that – but you didn't survive the care system by being a soft touch. It was a habit she found hard to shake off.

Nate blew out a breath. 'Right. Well, I'll leave you to it.' He placed the skeleton key to the chapel door on the pew. 'You might want to lock the door after I've gone. If I need you, I'll phone or text.'

'Yes. That's fine.'

Rhoda picked up the key. The apology was on the tip of her tongue, and she was just about to force the word out when Nate spoke again. 'Do you want to give me your car key so I can get the window sorted?'

Rhoda pulled the key from her trouser pocket and chucked it over to him. 'Thanks.'

'Catch you later.'

With that, Nate was gone.

'Damn it!' said Rhoda out loud. No wonder she didn't have many friends. She was pretty crap at friendships.

24
Alice

1945

'Careful, don't be running now,' said Lily as she and Alice sped out of the chapel. 'Don't want you falling over and hurting yourself.'

'Is Billy angry about something?' asked Alice, watching where she walked.

'He had a face like thunder. I've no idea what it's all about, though. Just said he wants you and me in the study.'

'I don't like the sound of this. Is Mrs Hartwell there?'

'No. She's gone into town. It's Cook's day off.'

'Where are Jack and Aggie?'

'Waiting in the kitchen for us.'

They reached the house and collected the cousins on their way through. Like nervous schoolchildren sent before the head teacher, they gathered outside the study door. Alice took a deep breath and knocked on the door.

'Come!' came Billy's voice from the other side.

Alice gave Jack a reassuring smile. 'It will be all right. Don't worry. Just Billy playing lord of the manor.'

Jack and Aggie followed Alice in, with Lily bringing up the rear.

'Ah, good, all four of you here together. Perfect.' Billy was standing in front of the window which overlooked the driveway. His hands were clasped behind his back and his walking stick was propped up against the bookcase. 'Right. I wanted to do this while Louise is out, to save her the embarrassment of having to ask you all something. Trouble is, she has a soft spot for you all, so it makes things like this even more difficult for her.'

Alice gave Lily a sideways look. What on earth was Billy going on about?

He carried on. 'So, I've been looking through the ledgers and noticed that we've been getting through quite a lot of food recently. Does anyone want to comment on that before I continue?'

After a moment's uncomfortable silence, Alice spoke up. 'Have you asked Cook?'

Billy sighed. 'Yes. That was my first port of call. Unfortunately, Cook can't shed any light on it. Seems she hasn't been paying close enough attention. And just so you know, I'm deadly serious about this – I've told Cook she's on a warning. She'll be looking for a new job if she can't keep track of the provisions.'

'It's not her fault!' protested Alice. She hated the thought of Cook being made an example of.

'Which leads me nicely on to my next question.' There was a thinly disguised smirk on Billy's face. 'Whose fault is it? Who is stealing from the pantry? Who is taking food that Louise has provided?' He reached for his stick and walked around the desk. His stick tapped on the wooden flooring as he took up a new position in front of the desk, looking directly at the four of them. 'Which one of you is the thief?'

'None of us,' said Lily indignantly. 'Why would we steal from the kitchen?'

'That's what I would like to know.' Billy tapped his stick on the floor impatiently. 'Wouldn't be taking any extra food up to the prisoners, would you?' He was looking directly at Alice.

'No, we haven't,' said Alice, feeling her patience grow thin with this pointless questioning.

'What about you, Jack? You're being very quiet.' Billy hit the floorboards hard with his walking stick, making Jack flinch.

Alice put her arm around the boy. 'Jack hasn't either.'

'Right, it must be one of the prisoners, then. I would ask them, but they're all lying, cheating bastards. They wouldn't know truth and honour if it slapped them in the face,' said Billy, his words curdled with disgust. 'They can go on half rations for the rest of the week. That will teach them.'

'You can't do that!' Alice found herself saying, before she'd had time to think about it.

Billy gave a snort. 'Sorry? What did you say? I can't do that?' He tutted and shook his head. 'I think you'll find I can. Especially that young one. Paolo. He's particularly untrustworthy. I don't know what Louise was thinking, letting them stay here in the house.'

Alice knew better than to say anything else. It was her fault Paolo had been singled out. She knew Billy didn't like him but putting him on half rations was just the sort of despicable thing Billy got enjoyment out of.

The sound of someone calling excitedly outside caught their attention. Billy turned around to look out of the window.

'What the blazes? That's Louise!'

Alice stood on tiptoe to look out. Sure enough, Mrs Hartwell was running, no less, up the driveway, waving her hands in the air with an excited look on her face.

'My word,' said Lily. 'I don't think I've ever seen Mrs Hartwell run.'

'Mind out of the way,' commanded Billy, before limping his way across the room.

'Come on,' said Alice, taking Jack's hand.

They hurried out of the study. By the time they reached the top of the stairs, Mrs Hartwell was bursting through the front door.

'It's over!' she cried. 'The war is over!'

'What?' Billy stood looking down from the top stair.

'I just heard it in the post office. It was on the wireless. There's going to be an announcement tomorrow. It's going to be all official tomorrow! The Germans have surrendered!'

Alice and Lily squealed at the same time. Alice caught Lily's hands and they jumped up and down before hugging each other. Alice swept Jack up into an embrace as well.

'Oh, did you hear that, Jack? It's going to be over.' She pulled Aggie in for a hug, too.

Even Billy was smiling. 'Thank God for that!' he said. 'I knew those Germans were bloody cowards. Yes!'

Then, without warning, he caught hold of Alice's arm, yanking her away from the children, and spun her around to face him. Somehow, amid the cheering, he pulled her close to him and kissed her, before letting her go.

It all happened so fast that Alice could barely register it. Had Billy really just done that? She didn't have time to think about it, as Mrs Hartwell was calling them all down to celebrate with a glass of sherry.

Alice shuddered at the lingering feeling of his lips on hers, and the touch of his hand around her waist.

'Here, Alice, have a sherry,' said Billy, holding out a glass to her.

Alice shook her head. 'No, thanks. I'd rather not.'

'Oh, don't be a stick-in-the-mud.'

'Leave Alice alone, Billy,' said Mrs Hartwell sternly. 'If she doesn't want a drink, then she doesn't have to have one.'

'One won't hurt. Not every day we celebrate victory over the Jerries.' Billy pushed the glass into Alice's hand.

Alice took the glass but had no intention of drinking it.

Billy made an official toast and, as he gulped the sherry down, Alice was very aware of his watchful eyes on her.

Alice had politely stayed for one drink and then made her excuses about not feeling too well, before going up to her room. She could hear the laughter and celebrations carrying on below her. Billy had downed his sherry and then moved on to a bottle of whisky he had produced from the cellar. With any luck, he'd be flat out soon, snoring on the sofa.

She lay down on her bed and looked up at the ceiling. It was then that it struck her: no one had told the POWs.

Making sure she wasn't spotted, Alice crept down the stairs, the sound of the gramophone playing and chatter coming from the living room covering any sound she made. The door was slightly ajar, and she could see Aggie's mother, Marjorie, sitting on the sofa laughing with another woman Alice didn't recognise. She must be a friend Mrs Hartwell had invited over to celebrate. Aggie was dancing with Lily in the centre of the room. Fortunately, Billy had his back to the door and Alice was able to nip past unnoticed. She hurried down the hallway, through the kitchen and out into the garden, leaving the sounds of laughter and music behind her.

Alice found Paolo in the rose garden.

'Alice.' He smiled as she went through the archway.

'Have you heard the news?' She couldn't keep the smile from her face.

Paolo looked confused. 'What news?'

'The war is over.'

Paolo's face remained impassive. Alice wondered if he hadn't understood her.

'The war is over,' she repeated more slowly. 'Germany has surrendered. No more war. End of war.' She didn't know what else to say.

'The war is over?' His eyes filled with tears.

'Yes, Paolo. It's over.'

He flung the rake to one side and clasped his hands together, saying something in Italian which Alice could only guess was akin to thanking God. Then he launched himself at her, enveloping her in an embrace. Alice flung her arms around him and hugged him back. They did some sort of jig, still holding on to each other and laughing. It didn't feel awkward or uncomfortable with Paolo, as it had when Billy had grabbed her. This felt joyously natural and exhilarating.

Then Paolo let go and took a step back. 'I am sorry.'

'No. Don't be sorry,' said Alice. 'It's good we are happy. We're not enemies anymore. Not that we were before, but we're certainly not now.' She grinned madly at him. 'You'll be free to go home soon. You'll be able to see your mother and sister again. You'll be able to hug your nephew.'

Paolo wiped fresh tears from his eyes. 'I cannot believe it.'

'There's going to be an official announcement by Winston Churchill tomorrow. It's going to be Victory in Europe Day, or something like that.' Alice stopped talking, noting the sadness on Paolo's face. She took his hand again. 'Don't be sad.'

'I am just thinking of all the people who have died during this last five years. Not just men doing their jobs, but civilians trying to get by.'

'I understand. But it's the right outcome.'

Paolo looked at her. 'Yes. It is the right outcome.'

They stood in silence for a moment, Alice suddenly feeling self-conscious. 'Will you tell Carlo?'

'Of course. I should tell him now.' Paolo gave her a brief nod of his head. 'Thank you for finding me with the news.'

'Oh, Paolo, before you go, there's one more thing,' said Alice, suddenly remembering the grilling Billy had given them. 'Just to warn you, Billy is on the warpath. He thinks someone has been stealing food from the kitchens and giving it to you and Carlo.'

'That is crazy.'

'I know. I think he's lying, but he said he was going to punish you.'

'Me?'

'Yes,' said Alice. 'He's got it into his head that you've been receiving the food. I'm sure he thinks I've been giving it to you. He's going to put you on half rations as a punishment. Sorry, but I wanted to warn you.'

There was something about the look on Paolo's face that brought Alice up sharp. Was that a guilty look he'd tried to disguise? 'Paolo,' she said slowly, 'have you had extra food from the kitchen? Is there any truth in what Billy's saying?'

He wouldn't meet her eye. 'I must go,' he said, and walked straight past her.

'Paolo! Wait!'

But he strode away without looking back.

Alice couldn't quite believe it, but the more she thought about the look on his face, the more she realised he was guilty. It didn't seem possible. Not Paolo. Had she really misjudged him that much? The thought that she had been deceived hung around her shoulders like a heavy blanket – uncomfortable and dirty.

10 May 1945

Carissime Mamma e Sofia

The war is over! THE WAR IS OVER!

I have longed to write these words for so many months and I cannot believe I am actually saying them now. There has been much celebrating here in England. Everyone was cheering and dancing in the streets when they heard the news. I wanted to join in, but I didn't think that would be appropriate. Instead, me and Carlo celebrated in our own quiet way in our room.

Honestly, Mamma, I am so happy.

I hope you are both all right, and baby Luca is, too. I cannot wait to be home. I hope it will not be long before we are repatriated. I don't know what will happen to us in the meantime. We will still be prisoners for the foreseeable future, but I am keeping my spirits up because I know it is one step closer to coming home. Day by day, I am closer to you.

Il vostro amorevole figlio e fratello

Paolo

25
Nate

2022

Nate took Rhoda's car into town, to the garage where his car was regularly serviced.

'Won't be able to get a new window for a few days,' said Jim, the owner. 'Not the sort of thing we have much call for, so don't keep it in stock.'

Nate had agreed to leave the car with the garage and hired a courtesy car from Jim.

'I'll give you a call with all Miss Sullivan's details,' he said. 'Then you can swap the insurance into her name.'

'No problem. Don't let her forget to email me a copy of her licence.'

The Ford Ka probably wasn't exactly what Rhoda would have chosen, Nate mused as he pulled into the drive of Telton Hall, but at least she'd be mobile and could commute back and forth between Somerset and Sussex as needed. He didn't envy her the long drive each day.

Next on his list of promises was to see if Sylvia Montgomery wouldn't mind talking to Rhoda. Despite his aunt warning them off, Nate wasn't going to be put off that easily. He found himself wanting to do this, as much for himself as for Rhoda. Discovering the identity of the body in the chapel had become important to him. Last night he'd looked at the 'Dean Sullivan – Missing Person' Facebook page and followed some links Rhoda had put up, taking him to the Missing Persons Register. He'd ended up losing a couple of hours reading other people's stories and plights, the good outcomes and not so good ones – it really had touched him as he tried to imagine what it would be like if he was ever in the unenviable position of not knowing what had happened to a loved one. He could only imagine the pain and anguish he'd feel, though; he knew whatever emotions it stirred in him, they were nothing compared to the agony Rhoda experienced, day in and day out. She was certainly a strong woman, to be able to carry on like she did and to try to find her brother.

It went a long way to explain why she had this tough exterior – a little bit edgy, outspoken, and at times uncompromising. Resilient. That's how he'd sum her up. She was one of life's fighters.

Nate's father was at the house when he got back to Telton Hall.

'How did you get on with the car?' Jack asked from his chair in the living room, with Tink snuggled up on his lap. Tink pricked up one ear and gave a couple of wags of her tail in greeting to Nate before snuggling back down. She was far too comfortable for any overly exuberant welcome – much like her owner, Nate had often thought.

'Going to take a few days before Jim can get hold of a new window.'

Nate went over to the sideboard and opened the first drawer, which was stuffed with old Christmas cards, pens, bits of string, and a whole load of other rubbish his father shoved in there when he didn't know what else to do with it.

'What are you looking for?' asked Jack.

'The old name and address book. The black leather one that Mum used to keep by the telephone.'

'What do you want that old thing for?'

'I'm looking for Sylvia Montgomery's phone number,' replied Nate, now rummaging through the second drawer.

His father gave a huff – one Nate recognised with the benefit of a well-trained ear, having heard that huff many times over the years. It was his dad's unspoken signal that he was upset about something. Nate waited for his father to speak – which he did, of course.

'You two are obsessed with that bloody chapel. I wish I'd just got the thing bulldozed. Shouldn't have bothered getting that museum to buy it. More trouble than it's worth. And as for questioning Sylvia Montgomery – you're taking it all too far now.'

'Aha! Here it is,' said Nate, ignoring his father's little rant.

He pulled out the name and address book and flicked to the M's. Sylvia's name was at the bottom of the page. Nate took out his phone and snapped a picture of it. He certainly wasn't going to call her while in the same room as his dad, whom Nate wouldn't put past trying to heckle him.

'Haven't you got anything better to do?' asked a very disgruntled Jack. 'Shouldn't you be at work?'

'Yes, and yes,' replied Nate. 'But I have the luxury of being the boss, so I can take some time off if I need to. Right, I'll see you before I go.'

'Where are you going now?'

'To find a bit of peace and quiet,' Nate called good-humouredly as he went out of the door, leaving his father muttering curses under his breath.

Ten minutes later, Nate was outside the chapel. He knocked on the door and called out Rhoda's name. He could hear the radio playing inside and wondered if she would be able to hear him. When the door didn't open after a couple more knocks, he took out his phone and called her.

Rhoda opened the door a few moments later.

'I'm sorry for upsetting you,' said Nate, taking Rhoda's lead at getting straight to the point. 'That wasn't my intention. I was clumsy.'

She eyed him for a couple of seconds before speaking. 'Apology accepted.' She paused and Nate sensed there was more to come. 'I might be a bit sensitive when it comes to my brother, but I'm not going to apologise for that. Just wanted to explain, that's all.'

'Fair enough. I get that.' He smiled. 'Is the air clear?'

'Yeah. Don't see why not.' She returned the smile.

'Excellent. Now, I've got some good news.'

'You do?'

'Yep. Sylvia Montgomery has agreed to see you. If you can come now, that is?' Nate glanced over towards the workbench, where a large sheet of paper was laid out and two small stained-glass windows were lying on top.

'That's brilliant. Give me two minutes.'

Rhoda rushed around the chapel, putting a few things away, before climbing up the scaffolding to secure the board on the second window.

Nate watched as she athletically negotiated the tower, without any hesitation, her ponytail swinging as she ducked under a bar to start her descent.

'You've done that a few times,' he remarked.

'I used to be really nervous being on a tower. Couldn't stand up without holding on to the rail; preferred to be sat down whenever I could,' said Rhoda, picking up her bag and jacket. 'But these days I barely notice.'

'I can't imagine you being nervous about anything.' Nate locked the chapel door behind them.

'Oh, you'd be surprised.' Rhoda zipped her coat up and fell into step alongside Nate as they made their way down the hill.

He resisted the urge to say he suspected that it wasn't the physical things that scared her, but he was aware that they'd already fallen out once about her feelings and emotions, and he didn't want to upset her again.

As they were leaving, Rhoda's phone rang. She answered it as they continued down the hill.

'Yes. Tomorrow will be fine,' Rhoda was saying. 'OK … Yes … Right, see you then. Ten o'clock.' She ended the call. 'That was the local paper. They're coming over tomorrow. I also had a call from a Vince Taylor – he's a local historian. He asked if he could have a look at the window and write an article for the historical society he runs. He's coming over tomorrow, too. I checked with your dad and he said it was OK.'

'You're popular.'

'I don't think it's me,' she replied with a laugh. 'It's the window everyone's interested in.'

Nate wanted to argue the point but decided against it.

Sylvia Montgomery welcomed them into the retirement flat she lived in on the west side of the village – a new development to cater for the elderly Telton villagers.

'Now, what can I do for you?' she asked once they were seated. 'Are you sure you wouldn't like a cup of tea?'

'No, we're fine, thank you,' said Nate. 'Erm ... As I mentioned on the phone, we're trying to research some of the residents who lived in the village during 1945. Rhoda found an article online where you spoke about your mother being a midwife.'

'Yes, that's right! Oh, I didn't realise you could get that on the computer. I did it a few years ago now.' She smiled at Rhoda. 'How can I help you, dear?'

Nate sat back and let Rhoda take the lead, asking Sylvia questions about her mother. Sylvia seemed more than happy to share what she knew, obviously enjoying the company and the chance to have a chat.

'Yes, I did go with Mother to Telton Hall,' she was saying. 'You probably know that Louise Hartwell, Nate's grandmother, was very good to young women who found themselves pregnant and on their own. She organised the adoptions. Poor children, they wouldn't have had a very good start in life if it hadn't been for Louise Hartwell. I know it sounds harsh, but a lot of those young mothers weren't very old and had nothing to offer a newborn baby.'

'Were these adoptions done through official channels?' asked Rhoda. 'Are there records of who adopted whose baby? I mean, what if the babies grew up and wanted to contact their birth mothers – where would they look for records? Did your mother keep any notes?'

'Oh, erm ... I think they were legally adopted. Louise didn't do it for money, though, she did it for the good of the child.'

Nate shifted in his seat, aware they were treading on dangerous ground here. He knew Rhoda well enough to spot the tension rising in her voice. Her attitude towards the system dealing with children in care had been soured by her own experiences, and she obviously still had issues with it. He got in first, to try to defuse the potential bomb.

'Did your mother keep any notes about the babies she delivered?'

'She did, actually. She kept a diary. A personal diary, but she always liked to keep a note of the babies she'd delivered. She delivered more than twenty babies in Telton alone over the years. She would have delivered your father.'

'Have you got the diary?' asked Rhoda.

'Yes. It's in the cupboard over here. I have a box with all her midwifery things – her brooch, her belt buckle, the watch she used.' Sylvia rose from her chair and retrieved a black doctor's bag from the cupboard. 'It's all here, and this is her diary.' She passed it over to Rhoda. 'You can't take it, though, but you can look at it.'

'Of course,' said Rhoda. 'Is it all right to take some photos of the relevant pages?'

'I suppose so, but you can't go around showing every Tom, Dick and Harry what's written in there. It's private and confidential. Some of the villagers might not like it, especially if they're in the book.'

'Oh, it's OK,' said Nate. 'We will be very discreet. We promise.'

'How long was your mother a midwife for?' asked Rhoda.

'Here, in Telton? She finished in 1946. My father came home from the war and nine months later I had a sister. Mother stopped working then.' Sylvia gave a laugh. 'Baby Boomer – isn't that what they're called?'

Nate took a photo from his pocket. It was of the group stood outside Telton Hall.

'Do you recognise either of these two young women in the photograph? That's my Aunt Aggie and my grandmother, but these two – did your mother deliver their babies?'

It was a bit of a long shot, but no harm in asking. He gave the photograph to Sylvia.

Sylvia picked up a magnifying glass from the table and held it to the black and white image. 'That must have been taken at the end of the war, or thereabouts.'

'That's right. Here's another, of some POWs, which we think was taken around the same time.'

'A couple of them – Italian, I think – stayed on at the farm for another year or so after the war,' said Sylvia. 'The girls, I'm not sure about.' She peered more closely at the photograph. 'It's hard to remember everything all those years ago. Especially the war. When all the men came home, it was an unwritten rule we weren't to ask them about the war. They didn't want to talk about it either. Some of them had witnessed terrible things, been through awful times, they just wanted to come home and have a settled life. My father never once mentioned the war.'

'It's understandable, I suppose.' Rhoda handed the book

back to Sylvia. 'Thank you for letting me look at this. It's so interesting, seeing all those births and the comments your mother made. It's really something special to treasure, knowing your mother helped all these babies into the world.'

'You know, I've just remembered something,' said Sylvia. 'I'm sure one of those girls in the photograph got married that year. Erm ... Let me think ... Oh, I don't know ... I'm not sure which one it was.'

'Why does that stand out in your mind?' asked Rhoda.

'I'm not sure. As I say, I was young then, and at my age, you don't remember everything.' Sylvia frowned. 'Maybe because she'd had a baby and wasn't marrying the father? I don't know, but more than likely something like that. Of course, back then, things like that mattered. These days, it's all the rage, isn't it – you know, to have babies and not be married. Poor kids. Back in the day they were better off getting adopted, if you ask me.'

'If you do remember, perhaps you could phone me,' said Nate, not wishing to be accused for the second time of harassing an old lady. Neither did he want Rhoda to bristle at Sylvia Montgomery's somewhat tactless, albeit ignorant, comments about adoption.

'You should ask your aunt,' said Sylvia. 'I'm sure she was a bridesmaid.'

Nate and Rhoda exchanged a surprised look.

'Aunt Aggie?' clarified Nate.

'At least I think she was. Sorry, I might be getting muddled up again.'

Nate thanked Sylvia and he and Rhoda said their goodbyes.

'What do you make of that?' asked Rhoda as they walked back towards Telton Hall.

'I'm not sure. Funny Aggie never mentioned being a bridesmaid. There's always the possibility Sylvia has got it wrong.'

Rhoda opened her phone. 'I took lots of photos of the diary, I'll go through them all later and try to gather as much information as I can. I don't know what I'm looking for, or if it will be of any help, but you never know. It might be we just need to join up some dots. We might have more information than we realise. I'll put it all together in a dossier.'

'You're very thorough, aren't you?'

'Yes, and I make no apology for it.'

'Wasn't asking for one.'

There was her defence. The thing she fell back on to keep her going. Prickly determination. Nate couldn't help but admire her for it; he just wished she wasn't so defensive.

26
Rhoda

2022

After speaking to Sylvia Montgomery, Rhoda went back to the chapel. She had taken out three of the smaller stained-glass windows now and laid them out on the carbon paper, before taking a rubbing of the lead work, and finally marking up the outline so she knew which pieces of glass went where. Once she got the fourth window out, she'd do the same. Then it was a case of removing the glass from the lead, marking each individual piece of glass, and then cleaning them up ready for packaging and transporting. It was important she got this bit right, as it made life so much easier when putting the window back together. The side windows had fortunately not been damaged by the movement of the chapel, so it would be a relatively straightforward task. The main window, however, would prove more of a challenge, not just because of its size, but also because of the damage. Rhoda liked a challenge so she wasn't particularly daunted by it.

The rest of the afternoon went by in a flash, and it was with some reluctance that Rhoda downed tools at six o'clock. She still had to contend with the drive back to West Sussex.

When Nate had texted her to let her know he'd arranged a hire car, she was, of course, grateful, but the thought of travelling back in a small car designed more for nipping around town than motorway driving had left her more than a little disappointed. Not that she had a lot of choice, and it was thoughtful of Nate, so she couldn't complain.

Nate had left the key with his dad, and once Rhoda had collected it, she was on her way home. She had never been more grateful to see her little flat than she was over three hours later. Roadworks on the M27 around Southampton, together with an accident, had made progress slow that evening. Tea consisted of an uninspiring microwave meal she'd had in the freezer, and by the time she'd eaten, all she wanted to do was flop into bed. She wanted to see if she could follow up on any of the information she'd got from Sylvia Montgomery, but she was too tired. Rhoda knew if she started, she'd end up losing several hours on the internet, and it would be midnight before she even considered going to bed – none of which was conducive to an early start the following morning.

'How long have you got to keep this commute up for?' Shani asked Rhoda the following morning, as they undertook their daily swim.

The water was calmer today and looked almost blue. The early morning sun was already reflecting warmly on the surface.

'Two, maybe three weeks,' replied Rhoda. 'I should get the smaller windows finished by the end of the week, maybe beginning of next week. Then it's on to the main window, which is going to take a lot longer.'

'Wouldn't you be better off staying down there?'

'I was wondering that myself. Even if it's just for this week, while I've got that little hire car. It's not ideal for motorway driving.'

'There's bound to be plenty of B & Bs down there.' Shani twisted over and floated on her back.

'I'll have a look into it. There might be a guest house in Telton itself. Depends how expensive it is, really.'

'You'll be saving on petrol.'

'True.'

'And you might have a decent meal for a change, instead of the microwave rubbish you seem to love so much.'

'"Love" is a bit of a stretch,' replied Rhoda. '"Like" is perhaps more appropriate, but they're convenient, if nothing else.'

'And unhealthy.'

It wasn't unusual for Shani to turn up on Rhoda's doorstep with what she claimed were leftovers, when Rhoda was certain the meal had been cooked especially for her. At first, Rhoda had objected but Shani had been persistent, and Rhoda knew the gesture came from the right place. Sometimes, it was nice to be looked after.

Rhoda couldn't fault Shani's logic of staying down in Somerset while she worked on the chapel; it would also free up several hours each night which she could use researching the identity of the chapel remains.

Before she set off for Somerset that morning, she sent Nate a quick text message asking if he could recommend any accommodation in Telton or nearby. As an afterthought, she added she didn't want anything fancy, just somewhere to put her head at night. Nate had texted back immediately.

Sure. No problem. Leave it with me.

The drive back down to Somerset that morning did nothing other than convince her that finding accommodation close to Telton Hall was the best idea. What were all these people doing on the road this early in the morning? The radio travel information service piping up with a warning of extra delays around the New Forest area, due to a broken-down lorry blocking one of the carriageways, was the deciding factor. Rhoda was glad she'd packed a bag and wouldn't have to make the return journey that day.

It was a brighter day in Somerset and, having been given the key to the chapel to hold on to, Rhoda made her way up the hill as soon as she arrived. She didn't want to be pestering Jack all the time.

It was amazing how different the chapel looked when the sun was out, and as Rhoda went over recent events, including the poison pen letter, she didn't have the same sense of foreboding. However, she did check all the pews and the confessional box just to be certain she was alone in the chapel, before locking the door and getting on with the next side window.

When it came to lunch, Rhoda went back down to the house, where she could make use of all the mod cons. She tapped on the kitchen door, hoping Jack would hear her, and as she looked through the pane of glass, she was surprised to see Nate in the kitchen. He opened the door for her.

'I've popped in on my lunch break. Was hoping to catch you,' he said before she had a chance to ask. 'I've just made the tea. Come on in.'

'Thanks. I'll nip to the bathroom first.'

'Dad's in the living room,' said Nate over his shoulder.

Rhoda poked her head around the door and exchanged pleasantries with Jack. She couldn't help noticing he seemed a little on edge. 'Everything OK?' she asked.

'Hmm. As good as it will get, I suppose.' He picked up a letter from the side table. 'The developers won't budge on the sale date. I've got three months and that's that.'

'Oh no. I thought they'd let you have a bit more time in light of everything.' Rhoda stepped into the room. 'Have you been in touch with any of the housing contacts I left you?'

'I haven't had time.'

Rhoda reined in a smile. He sounded like a sulky schoolboy. She was in no doubt he hadn't rung because he didn't want to. 'Would you like me to call them?'

'No. It's all right. I'll do it this week.'

'I'll check up on you.'

'I'm sure you will.'

This time, Rhoda didn't withhold the smile. She couldn't help warming to Jack Hartwell, despite his reluctance to conform to what society expected of him. She got that. 'Erm … Actually, Jack, can I ask you a quick question?'

'You can ask. Doesn't mean I'll answer.' There was a twinkle in his eye, despite the grumpiness of his tone.

'It's about one of the girls in the photo that was hanging in the hall. Do you remember one of them getting married? Aggie was bridesmaid?'

'You're not still going on about that, are you? I thought you were going to forget all that.'

Rhoda perched on the edge of the sofa adjacent to Jack, so she didn't seem overbearing – not that she thought he'd be easily intimidated, but it felt the polite thing to do.

'I can't. I really can't. I feel compelled to find out who those remains were. Someone somewhere will have missed him. Someone would have cared, I'm sure of it.'

'And if they didn't?' Jack held her gaze.

'If they didn't, then maybe we should.'

Jack made a huffing sound, his fingers drumming on the arm of the wing back chair. 'I was only a lad. I can't remember, to be honest. If there was a wedding, it would only have been a small affair. Not like weddings these days. You're better off asking Aggie.'

'One last thing. I promise,' said Rhoda. 'Billy, your sort of stepbrother. What was his surname?'

Jack looked at her for a moment before finally answering. 'Stoker. Now, is that all?'

'Yes. Thank you, Jack. I'd better get on. Nate's threatening me with a cup of tea.'

Jack held up his hand. 'Oh, before you go. Nate told me you were looking for some digs for the next couple of weeks.'

'That's right. The commute is longer than I anticipated,

especially with that little hire car. It makes sense to be somewhere more local during the week.'

'Right. That's solved, then. You can stay here.'

For a moment Rhoda was dumbfounded. 'Oh, that's very kind, but honestly, I wasn't angling for an invite. I was genuinely looking for a B & B.'

'We know that.' Nate came into the room. 'It makes sense to stay here. In fact, it was Dad's suggestion when I mentioned it to him. It's not like we're short of space.'

'Oh, I don't know,' said Rhoda warily. 'I feel like I'm imposing myself on you.'

'Stop being so silly,' said Jack. 'Nate's going to make one of the rooms up for you. Now, don't be arguing, even though I know you'd like to.'

There was that twinkle in his eye again and Rhoda felt the fight going out of her. She had somehow been ambushed by the Hartwell duo and, much as her instinct was to decline the offer, she couldn't think of a sensible or logical reason to do so. She pushed aside her reservations about Telton Hall itself; the oppressive and maleficent feeling she sometimes experienced was just her imagination – a leftover from her institutional childhood, when a big house like this had often meant unhappy children and unhappy memories.

'Thank you. That's very kind. Much appreciated,' she said eventually. 'I'll stay on one condition.'

'Of course, there had to be a condition,' muttered Jack.

'You let me cook for you in the evenings. It's the least I can do.'

A short while later, when she went back to the kitchen, Nate was waiting for her with a sandwich and a cup of tea. 'Glad to see you didn't let him have it all his own way.'

'Where would the fun be if I did?' Rhoda pulled out the chair and sat at the table. 'This looks very nice. Thank you.'

'Did you get a chance to look at any of the info from Sylvia Montgomery?' asked Nate, taking the seat adjacent to her.

'I was too tired last night,' Rhoda confessed. 'The drive home was a complete pain, and I knew once I started on the research train, there would be no getting off it until well past my bedtime.'

Nate laughed. 'I don't blame you. Hopefully, that's one problem out of the way now. I'll sort the room out in a minute. It's the one at the end of the landing. It overlooks the back garden.'

'Has it always been a guest room?' asked Rhoda, thinking back to when Telton Hall housed the young women.

'Yeah, as far as I know. Being an only child, it was always the spare room.' Nate took a bite of his sandwich.

'Haven't you ever thought about all the people who have lived in the house before you, and imagined what they did?'

Nate finished his mouthful of sandwich before answering. 'Not especially. It's just always been my family home. The history is just part of the house.' He paused, putting his sandwich down. 'Sorry, I didn't mean to sound insensitive. I didn't mean to flaunt my privilege to you.'

Rhoda waved the apology away. 'Honestly, I'm not that sensitive about it. I've never had what you describe. I don't have roots or a sense of belonging. I'm not bitter and twisted about it. Not at all. I've never known any different.'

'Doesn't mean you can't wish for it, though,' said Nate gently.

'No, you're right, it doesn't. And when I was younger,

I did wish I was more like the other kids at school, but it wasn't a deep burning desire. Not enough that it made me sad – just wistful at times, that's all. The one stable thing in my life was my brother – and look how that's turned out.'

She gave a self-deprecating laugh to mask the pain. The lack of home life, lack of permanent friendships, lack of stability didn't bother her; she could cope with all that, but having Dean disappear from her life was another matter.

'What about your parents?' asked Nate.

Rhoda shrugged. 'Not much to tell. I've no idea who my father is. Mum always claimed it was a one-night stand at a festival.'

'And your mum?'

Rhoda ran her finger around the edge of her cup. She rarely spoke about her mum; it was a habit she'd adopted soon after she went into care. Somehow, though, she felt compelled to open up to Nate.

'My mum was a drug addict. That's how me and Dean ended up in the care system. They tried to let us stay with her, but she was too hooked on heroin. Eventually, they took us away for our own safety. She couldn't look after us. Even when she tried to get clean, she was a complete train wreck.'

Nate reached over and took her hand. 'I'm sorry, I had no idea.'

Instead of pulling her hand away, Rhoda held on to Nate's, anchoring herself as she spoke again. 'She did love us, but she was ill. Addiction is an illness. That's why she couldn't look after us.'

'Where is she now?'

Rhoda pressed her lips together and looked up at the

ceiling, blinking back the tears. 'She's dead. An overdose when we were thirteen.'

'Christ. I'm so sorry.'

Rhoda shook her head and swallowed hard. 'It's fine. I can't deal with sympathy, though.' She took her hand away and plastered a smile on her face. 'I really need to get back to work. Thanks so much for the sandwich.' She got up from the table, aware she was leaving Nate rather shell-shocked. 'Will I see you later?'

'Ah, not tonight. Sorry. Got to catch up on all this work I keep missing.' Then he added, 'I can come back though – if you need me to.' He gave her a meaningful look.

She appreciated his thoughtfulness. 'I'm OK. Honest. But thank you.'

'I'll pop in again tomorrow, though. Make sure you're all right and Dad hasn't driven you to distraction.'

'Or the other way around,' said Rhoda, wanting to upgrade the mood from downright miserable to something rather more cheerful.

'No danger of annoying Dad. He likes you really.'

As Rhoda glanced back from the doorway, the wink and grin Nate threw her way sent a flurry of butterflies in her stomach.

After a productive afternoon and a pleasant tea with Jack, where he stuck to his side of the bargain and allowed her to make an evening meal for them both, Rhoda retired to her room early. She didn't want to get under Jack's feet, and she also had some research she wanted to do in private.

She'd already been up to her room to wash and freshen

up after a day's work. It was a square room with a fireplace on the interior wall, which she assumed backed onto the bedroom wall next door to her. Apparently, that was Isaac's room. Nate's room was on the opposite side of the hallway – not that it was of any interest to her.

Rhoda sat on the bed and began looking through the photographs she'd taken of the midwifery diary belonging to Sylvia's mother. Anne Roberts had indeed delivered a lot of babies. There was a page for each birth, where she had noted the parents' names and any siblings they had, together with their addresses. She flicked through the pages, looking for Alice Renshaw's name, but found nothing. A second, more careful look was equally fruitless.

That was annoying and a little strange. Why wasn't Alice's name in the book? Had she had the baby somewhere else? Maybe she didn't stay at Telton Hall, or maybe the babies of unmarried mothers weren't recorded. Or was it because the baby was adopted? Something didn't sit right, but Rhoda had no idea what. It struck her that a search of the parish records might tell her if any of the babies had been christened. She wasn't sure of the protocol for children who were to be adopted, but it was worth looking into. There was a christening font up at the chapel; maybe the babies had been christened there – out of sight of the disapproving congregation? It was all conjecture, and without the blasted records for Telton Hall, Rhoda was at yet another dead end.

Her thoughts turned to Dean. Although she had never given up hope that he would turn up one day, Rhoda was also very pragmatic, and she knew there was the god-awful possibility that Dean would die, and she wouldn't know.

Her fingers hovered over the keyboard. It wouldn't be

the first time she'd searched for a death certificate for her brother. It wasn't something she did often, but once or twice a year, she needed to reassure herself that he was still alive. It wasn't a failproof determination, but it was the only thing she had available to her.

She swallowed and tapped in his name and the year 2022. All she had to do now was press Enter and, in a few moments, she'd know if a death certificate had been issued in the last ... She thought back to when she last did this – eight months.

She closed her eyes and pressed the Enter key before she could talk herself out of it.

It was a good thirty seconds before she opened her eyes, and the screen of the laptop came into focus.

NO RESULTS MATCHED YOUR SEARCH.

Rhoda blew out a breath.

'You're still out there, Dean,' she whispered. 'I'm still looking for you.'

27
Rhoda

2022

The interview with the newspaper went well. It was made up of the standard sort of questions Rhoda was usually asked about the conservation of the buildings, and in particular stained-glass windows. She always made sure the museum was credited properly, as it was good publicity, and she knew her boss would appreciate it. For the most part, Rhoda tried to stay out of the limelight and declined having her photo taken.

'The interest is in the window, not me,' she insisted.

Her afternoon meeting with Vince Taylor, the local historian, was rather less formal and less intense. Fortunately, Nate had just got back from school with Isaac, and had met the historian down at the house before bringing him up to the chapel.

'Thank you for seeing me,' said Vince enthusiastically,

resting his weight on his walking stick. 'It's a bit of a trek up here, though. I wasn't expecting that.'

'I did offer to bring Mr Taylor up on the quad,' said Nate.

'The exercise is good for me,' smiled Mr Taylor. 'And please, call me Vince.'

'Well, you're here in one piece, that's the main thing,' said Rhoda with a smile.

She liked talking to historians; they were often most enthusiastic, and had a wealth of knowledge themselves. They spent a good twenty minutes talking about the window and how it was going to be restored – the process Rhoda would undertake to remove it, repair it and restore it.

'The three R's of conservation,' she said.

At that point, Nate had to take a phone call and went out of the chapel.

'Are you interested in history?' Vince asked Isaac, who had been following them around the chapel as Rhoda explained her work.

'Some of it. We're doing a project on the Victorians at school. V-I-C-T-O-R-I-A-N-S.'

'Good spelling,' said Vince. 'And a good era, too. Lots of things happened in Victorian times. The Industrial Revolution changed so much. You know the viaduct at Telverton was built in Victorian times?'

'Have you always lived in the area?' asked Rhoda.

'Yes. Bristol born and bred. What about you? You haven't got a Somerset accent.'

'Neither have you,' replied Rhoda.

'Ah, I spent a lot of my time in Oxford, teaching. I lost the local burr somewhere along the line. Where did you say you were from? West Sussex, is it? Where the museum is?'

'I moved around a bit, but essentially I'm from West Sussex,' said Rhoda.

'Rhoda lives by the seaside,' said Isaac. 'Elmer Sands.'

'Don't worry,' Rhoda said, 'it's not as glamorous as it sounds. It's just home.'

'Doesn't matter where it is,' said Vince, 'if it feels like home, then it's home. Especially if you've got family connections. Family is very important, don't you think?'

'Rhoda has a brother who is missing,' said Isaac.

'Oh, I'm sorry to hear that,' said Vince.

'It's OK.' Rhoda wasn't cross that Isaac had mentioned Dean, but if she was honest, she didn't want her personal life discussed with a stranger. 'Anyway, is there anything else you wanted to know about the window?'

'No, I won't take up any more of your precious time,' replied Vince. 'I've got enough to be getting on with.'

'If you need any more info, just give me a call. Here's my business card. The number on the card is the museum, you can leave a message there.' She passed him one of the cards she kept in her work bag. 'Do you have the address for your website? The museum would love to be able to mention the write-up.'

Vince flipped over a fresh sheet of paper in his notebook and jotted down the web address. He ripped the page out and handed it to Rhoda. 'There you go. I'll let you know when it's up.'

'Sorry about that,' said Nate, coming back into the chapel. 'Was rather more complex than I expected.'

'I'm just on my way now,' said Vince. 'Miss Sullivan has been most helpful.' He turned to Rhoda. 'Thank you, my dear. And I hope one day your brother gets in touch.'

'Me, too,' said Rhoda, folding the sheet of paper over and slipping it into her bag.

They said their goodbyes and Nate, together with Isaac, accompanied Vince down the hill, leaving Rhoda on her own in the chapel. It was nice talking to people about her work, but she was aware she was a bit behind schedule now. Not that Jack would mind – he'd be happy if it took her all year – but she knew there'd be penalties, and she didn't want to give the developers the slightest chance to reduce their price.

Putting on her music, Rhoda had a quick look at Vince's website. It was just a landing page, with basic information about the historical society: a photograph of Vince and an elderly woman standing in front of the Tower of Pisa, and another of him standing underneath a Victorian-looking viaduct. If anything, it looked like it was either a work in progress or a rather neglected site.

Aware she was wasting even more time, Rhoda got to work and was soon immersed in recording all the glass pieces on the paper.

She didn't hear the door to the chapel open, and when Nate tapped her on the shoulder, she nearly jumped out of her skin.

'Sorry!' said Nate.

Isaac appeared alongside his father.

'It's OK, I was in a world of my own,' said Rhoda, switching off the music. She looked at her watch. 'Oh, goodness, I didn't realise it was as late as that.'

'We were just coming up to see if you wanted to come out for a pizza,' said Nate. 'Dad's over at Aggie's and I don't fancy cooking.'

'That's really kind, but I couldn't intrude.'

Nate rolled his eyes. 'Not that again. Come on, come for a pizza. There's nothing in the fridge, I checked. You'll be starving.'

'Please come,' said Isaac. 'I like Margherita, stuffed crust with chicken. M-A-R-G-H-E-R-I-T-A. A common pizza made with tomatoes, cheese, basil, salt and olive oil.'

Normally, Rhoda would have stuck to her guns, but how could she refuse Isaac? He wouldn't understand, and she didn't want him to feel she'd rejected him. Besides, what was wrong with sharing a pizza with the Hartwells?

'OK. I'll come. Don't want to starve.'

'What's this?' asked Isaac, looking at Rhoda's laptop, which she'd left on the side.

'Hey, you shouldn't be looking at other people's things,' reprimanded Nate, and then to Rhoda, 'Sorry.'

'Oh, it's OK.' She went over to where Isaac was standing. 'That's just the website of the guy who came to look at the window earlier. Vince Taylor. The historian.'

'How did it go?' asked Nate. 'I missed most of it while I was on the phone.'

'Seemed a nice enough bloke. He's going to put a write-up on his blog.' Isaac had wondered off now, so Rhoda closed her laptop. 'Right, let's get that pizza.'

Pizza turned out to be a great idea, and Rhoda enjoyed the company. Isaac spent most of the time quizzing Rhoda about living by the beach, and was fascinated to find out she went swimming every day in the sea.

'Do you want some ice cream?' asked Nate, interrupting Isaac's interrogation about what seaweed was like to eat, and if it made her feel sick when she swallowed sea water.

'I'm sorry about all the questions,' said Nate, when Isaac was at the ice cream machine.

'It's fine,' said Rhoda, taking a sip of her water. 'It's nice he's interested. I like that he asks questions. Kids should always be asking how, when, why, what.'

'I appreciate your patience with him. Not everyone is … comfortable talking to him.'

'He's got character. I like that a lot. He'll be OK. You shouldn't worry about him so much.'

'Is it that obvious?'

'Just a bit.' She smiled. 'Which is perfectly OK. It's also obvious you love him very much.'

'I do. He's a good kid.'

'Sorry, that's my phone vibrating,' said Rhoda, as her phone buzzed on the table from where she'd been showing Isaac some pictures of the sea. 'Oh, it's Shani. I'd better take this.'

'Sure. I'll pay the bill and meet you outside,' said Nate, signalling to the waiter.

Rhoda answered the call as she headed out of the door of the restaurant. 'Hi, Shani. You OK?'

'I'm so sorry to bother you,' said Shani. 'I went around to your flat this evening to water the plants, like you asked, and the front door was wide open.'

'What? How did that happen? Had you left it open, by mistake?'

It would be most unlike Shani to forget to close Rhoda's front door, but that must be the logical explanation.

'I definitely locked it, I always double-check,' replied Shani. 'It looks like there was a break-in.'

'Oh no! Is it bad?' Rhoda's stomach churned at the

thought of someone in her flat – her home, her sanctuary, that was all hers and no one else's.

'No. It all looked tidy. It was only because I noticed your desk drawer wasn't closed properly that I realised someone had been in. And the door to your bedroom was open. I called the police as soon as I realised, and didn't go in.'

'What did the police say?'

'They came out, eventually. Asked me if anything was missing. Gave me a crime reference number. And that was that.'

'Have they been all through the flat?'

Nate came out of the restaurant and must have registered the distress on her face. He gave a slight nod as he mouthed *you OK?* at her. Rhoda moved the phone away from her mouth.

'My flat's been broken into,' she whispered, before going back to what Shani was saying as Nate muttered an expletive.

'I'm assuming they did,' said Shani. 'It wasn't ransacked, as I say, it was only a couple of things that caught my attention. It was more like a methodical search. As if they had time, because they knew they wouldn't be disturbed.'

'Someone who knew I was away,' said Rhoda. 'Not an opportunist, but a premeditated break-in.'

'I'm really sorry, sweetheart,' said Shani. 'I've had the lock changed for you and the door frame fixed. They used a crowbar, by the looks of it.'

'Bastards,' said Rhoda. 'Thank you for doing what you did. Let me know how much I owe you. Do the police want to speak to me?'

'Don't worry about the money. And, no, I don't think

they do. I'm sorry, it's like a formality. I've asked around in the road, but no one saw anything or anyone.'

'OK. Thanks, Shani. I do appreciate all that.' They said their goodbyes and Rhoda ended the call. She turned to Nate. 'Some fu— I mean, horrible person.' She corrected herself, remembering Isaac was there. 'Some horrible person has been in my flat. Nothing taken, from what Shani can see, and only a drawer and a door left open.' She felt the anger burn in her stomach, rising through her chest. Tears stung her eyes. 'I feel … I feel so exposed. I feel dirty, even though I'm not even there. Bastards.'

'Hey, come here.' Nate put his arm around her shoulders. She stiffened and resisted the sympathy for a moment, but he put his other arm around her and she allowed herself to relax and soak up the comfort.

'Bastard,' said Isaac, breaking the silence as he looked at his phone. 'B-A-S-T-A-R-D. An unpleasant or despicable person. Or a person born whose parents were not married when he or she was born.'

'Hey, enough of that,' said Nate.

'Sorry, that's my fault,' said Rhoda, grimacing at Nate, but she was relieved to see he was trying to hide a smile.

'Do you need to go back to your flat?' he said. 'I can come with you.'

'You don't have to do that.' Rhoda wiped at the tears on her face.

'I know.'

'I can manage on my own.'

'I know that, too.'

She looked up at him. 'You know a lot.'

'I know.' He grinned at her. 'Come on, don't be so

independent all your life. A bit of moral support never did any harm.'

He was right, and she knew she was being churlish. 'I'm not very good at accepting help.' She held up her hand. 'And don't say you know.'

'I'll make this easy for you,' said Nate. 'I'll drop Isaac at school in the morning and then I'll drive you back to Sussex. We'll leave at nine, so we'll miss the worst of the traffic. You can put your mind at rest and check the flat over while I busy myself in the car with my laptop and some work files. Then we grab some lunch and drive back. How does that sound?'

'Tempting.'

'Right, that's good enough. It's a deal.' He held out his hand.

Rhoda shook solemnly on the deal. 'Thank you.'

It felt strange to be accepting help, but at the same time, she knew it came from a genuine place and she very much appreciated it. She also appreciated that Nate had made a point of saying he'd stay in the car, so she didn't feel he was intruding on her personal space. Not that it felt very personal or private now someone had broken in, but all the same, Nate's thoughtfulness and care touched her.

The drive to Sussex was stress-free and by late morning, they were pulling up outside Rhoda's flat.

'Shani lives a bit further down the road,' said Rhoda. 'I'll call in to hers to get the key. Are you all right here? There is a cafe back in the village if you want somewhere a bit more comfortable.'

'I'm good here,' said Nate. 'Just shout if you need me.'

Shani gave Rhoda a big hug when she opened the door.

'Oh, bless you for coming back,' she said. 'Do you want a cup of tea first? You must be tired from all that driving.'

'I… err … I didn't come on my own,' Rhoda admitted. 'Nate Hartwell drove me.' She laughed at the eyebrow-raise her friend gave her. 'He's just being kind, that's all.'

'Yes. Sounds like it. Well, here's the key. Let me know if you need anything. Oh – and take this, too.' She pressed something small and hard, wrapped in tissue, into Rhoda's hand. 'It's a crystal. A healing one. Leave it in the flat and it will cleanse the place for you. I bought it this morning. I was going to put it in there before you came, but you beat me to it.'

'Ah, thanks, Shani. That's really kind.'

Rhoda walked back to her flat with the stone in her pocket. She didn't believe in crystals and things like that, but Shani did, and there was no reason or need to be disrespectful to her friend's beliefs. It was a nice thought, even if Rhoda didn't believe a polished pink stone was anything more than a polished pink stone. She waved the key at Nate, who gave her the thumbs up sign from the driver's seat.

Rhoda nipped up the steps to the front door of her apartment. Up here, she could see the sea and smell the salty air. She took a deep breath, realising how much she'd missed her home ground. Just breathing in the air and letting the breeze ruffle wisps of hair and tickle the back of her neck made her feel a million times better. She took a moment to steel herself before unlocking the door. The new door frame would need painting to match the rest of the woodwork, and she made a mental note to pick up some paint when she could.

Rhoda pushed open the front door, hesitating before going in. She looked back at the car, where Nate was watching her. He gave her a nod of encouragement. Rhoda's hand found the crystal Shani had given her and, for all her scepticism, she squeezed it tightly as she stepped across the threshold.

Her flat looked exactly how she'd left it. If it wasn't for the new door frame, she might not even have realised someone had been in the flat. And that was the bit that didn't make sense. She walked down the hallway, passing the bathroom and kitchen on her left, which looked out onto the road, and her bedroom on the right, which was the beach side. The living room stretched across the width of the flat at the end of the hallway.

Rhoda went over to her desk, checking the first drawer. Everything was as she'd expected to find it. The same for the second drawer. When she opened the bottom drawer, it was then she saw the folder, where she kept everything to do with Dean's disappearance, was the wrong way up.

She pulled the file out and went through the contents. There wasn't anything missing, as far as she could tell, and it all appeared to be in the order she kept it. Nothing looked out of place. She put the file back.

Rhoda closed the drawer and looked around the room. Everything was as it should be. She went back down the hall to the bedroom. Her door was closed, as she liked it to be – an old habit from her days in care, when privacy was at a premium and a closed door was both a physical and emotional boundary, not to be crossed unless invited.

Shani had said her bedroom door was open, so whoever had broken in must have gone into her room.

It felt even more intrusive to think someone had been in her bedroom. Her jewellery box with its meagre offerings was sitting in the middle of her dressing table. A quick look inside told her nothing was missing. Perhaps the intruder was an expert in jewels and could tell at a glance that everything in there were fake gems. She checked the drawer and her chest of drawers before taking a final look at her bedside table. In the cupboard, she kept a box which had things like her passport, NI details, her birth certificate and a couple of letters Dean had written to her before they had phones and could text each other.

She didn't look in this box often. It was also where she kept her papers from her time in care. Rhoda picked up one of Dean's letters from the top of the pile and eased it from the envelope.

Hi Rhodes

You OK? They said you were back in St Wilfred's. I was hoping you wouldn't go back to the home. I take it the foster place didn't work out well. Hope you're all right. If you give me the number, I can ring from a payphone.

Did they tell you I'm in Wales? It's a home for the naughty boys. Fucking hate it here. Will tell you about it when I speak to you because you know they read our letters. Yes, you CARERS I'm talking about you lot who are reading this now!

Rhoda pressed her lips together. Dean had always hated

being in Wales. She remembered him phoning her and saying it was only because he was one of the older lads that he got left alone. He'd had a fight with one of them and 'knocked seven bales of shit out of him'. The kid had left Dean alone after that. Dean had said you had to pretend to be a nutter – that made you unpredictable, and the others scared of you. It was the only way to survive. She returned to the letter.

I'm getting out of here the day we're 18 and I'm going to come and get you. We'll be OK. Me and you. Fuck the rest of them.

Let me know your phone number and I'll ring you.

Love Deano.

Rhoda tucked the letter back in its envelope and returned it to the drawer. He hadn't come for her. Whatever had happened that drove him to run away a few weeks before their eighteenth birthday, she didn't know. She put the box away and left the flat, double-checking it was locked.

'You OK?' asked Nate as she climbed into his car.

'Yeah.'

She couldn't look at him – could barely speak, because she knew she was on the brink of tears. From her peripheral vision, she could see Nate turn to face her in the car. God, he was going to talk to her. He knew she wasn't OK. She grabbed at the door handle and jumped out of the car. Breaking into a run, she headed down the footpath. She could hear Nate calling her, but she ran faster, hitting the stony beach a few seconds later.

Her feet sank and buckled over the pebbles, but she

carried on, charging towards the sea, her vision blinded by the tears. The stones tumbled after her, and she raced down the pebble embankment before reaching the sand and then the sea.

A hand grabbed her shoulder.

'Rhoda! Stop! Stop!'

Her legs suddenly felt weak, all energy zapped from them. She stopped running and turned to Nate. The water was lapping at their shins; their trousers were soaked.

'He didn't come back for me,' she sobbed. 'He promised me he would. But he left me. He's left me in a living hell. He should never have said he'd come for me. I hate him for leaving me.'

She threw her head back and screamed at the clouds above her. All the pain and anguish came pouring from her. Thoughts she'd kept pent up in her mind, sharing them with no one – the anger, the hurt, the despair – came rushing out, unable to be held back.

'Hey, hey, hey. It's OK.' Nate held on to her hands.

Rhoda's legs finally gave way as a wave broke against her. She sank to her knees, pulling away from Nate and burying her face in her hands. All she could do was sob.

At some point, Nate helped her to her feet and, supporting her, took her back up the beach and to the door of her flat.

'You'd better get some dry clothes on,' he said.

'Oh God, I'm sorry,' said Rhoda. 'I'm so embarrassed.'

What on earth had happened to her? She'd had some sort of mini breakdown. And the things she'd said – make that screamed – about Dean … she could barely believe it.

'No need to apologise. Go on, get yourself sorted.'

Rhoda took the key from her pocket as Nate started

back down the steps. 'Nate! Don't go.' She swallowed as he halted on the second step. 'You're soaking wet, too.'

He gave a shrug. 'It's only water. It will dry.'

'That's not what you just said to me.' She pushed the key in the lock. 'Come inside. I haven't got any clothes you can borrow.' She gave a half-hearted smile at her attempted humour. 'But I've got a tumble dryer.'

Twenty minutes later, Rhoda had showered and was dressed in dry clothes. Nate, on the other hand, was sitting on her sofa with a towel wrapped at his waist while his jeans whirled around in the dryer.

Rhoda put a cup down on the coffee table. 'Black coffee, I'm afraid. No milk.' She sat down next to him. 'I am sorry for that outburst.'

'Please stop saying sorry.' He shifted position slightly to face her; reaching out with his hand, he gave her shoulder a gentle rub. 'Are you OK? Do you want to talk about it?'

'Not really, but I think you deserve an explanation.'

'Only if you want to.' His hand was still on her shoulder. Comfort and reassurance oozed from just his touch. She tipped her head and briefly rested her face against his fingertips.

'I'm angry with Dean.' She took a moment. She'd actually said the words out loud to someone else. 'I'm angry he disappeared and never thought to let me know he was all right or what he was doing. What he had planned. Even if something has happened to him since then, I just feel I'll never know. And not knowing is the hardest thing.' Her voice was soft, but she could feel the injustice stirring within her again. 'I've spent all my adult life not knowing. I've been saddled with this void, this emptiness, this black hole in my life that just grows and grows. It's consuming. I want it to end.' Her voice wavered. 'I just want it to be over.'

Nate's hand moved slowly up and down her shoulder. 'Do you think there's any way you could just accept that you'll never know? Or compartmentalise it so you can move on with your life?'

'I don't know.' It was an honest answer. 'I've thought about it, but I feel disloyal leaving him behind.'

'Maybe not leaving him behind, then. Take him with you, but not as a burden. Not as this all-consuming riddle that you can't make sense of. Have you thought about speaking to other families? I don't mean to try to find Dean, but to try to find ways to cope.'

'I don't know.' She looked away from Nate. She knew he was challenging her thought process, asking her to look at it in a different way, but she didn't know if she could.

'You won't be abandoning him or anything. It's not being disloyal, but you've done everything possible and you can't punish yourself forever.' There was no accusation in his tone, just concern. 'And trying to identify the bloke in the chapel isn't the answer either.'

'I know that, but if I can save another family from this living hell, then at least I will feel as if I've done something.'

'Like atonement?'

Rhoda considered this before answering. She met Nate's gaze. 'Yeah. Exactly that.'

'You don't need to atone for anything,' said Nate gently. 'None of what's happened to you as a child, as a teenager and as an adult is your fault. You didn't have control over your past, but you do have control over your future. You just need to draw that line and then step across.'

'As easy as that?'

'I didn't say it would be easy.' He stroked her hair. 'Just start by imagining the line. Like you've drawn it in the sand. You can practise stepping across. Just in your mind. Then when you're ready, you can do it in real life.'

'That sounds like some psychobabble a social worker would say.'

'It worked for me.'

Rhoda sat up a little straighter. 'It did?'

'When they told me about Isaac. I found it hard to accept. I didn't understand. I blamed myself. I blamed Siobhan. I even blamed the school.' He rubbed his chin with his other hand. 'To my shame, I even thought it was Isaac's fault.'

'Oh, Nate.'

'It's OK. Don't feel sorry for me. I was a dick. I know that now. But it took me a while to accept I couldn't change anything. I couldn't change Isaac. And why would I want to change my son? He's unique. He's special. He's Isaac, and I really wouldn't have him any other way. I accepted him for who he is. I drew that line. I crossed it. And I have never looked back.'

'Thank you for being so understanding,' said Rhoda. 'It means a lot.'

'It means a lot that you let me.' Nate leaned over and dropped a kiss on top of her head. 'I know it's not easy for you to take advice.'

The small kiss from Nate felt as intimate as if he'd kissed her soul. How could one simple gesture of kindness make her feel so exposed? Not in the way she'd felt about her flat being broken into, but she'd told Nate things she'd never voiced out loud – things she'd kept buried; she'd shown her raw emotions, her true emotions. It should have frightened her, but somehow it made her feel safe.

They returned to Telton Hall later that day, and Rhoda was disappointed when Nate left to go home.

'I'll give you a call tomorrow,' he promised.

This time, he kissed her cheek when he left. The tingle of his lips against her skin stayed with her for a long time afterwards.

Rhoda lay awake for what felt like hours when she went to bed. She thought about what Nate had said about drawing a line in the sand. He'd made it sound so simple. Could it be as easy as that? She wasn't sure. She closed her eyes and imagined the line, but that's as far as she got. Stepping over it might take a little while to achieve, but she was patient, if nothing else.

The spell of unsettled weather across the south-west wasn't showing any sign of easing, and the rain was splattering against the windows as the wind picked up. As the rhythmic sound of the raindrops pulled her into sleep, her thoughts drifted to images of the chapel standing atop the hill against the backdrop of a shadowy, darkened sky.

28
Alice

1945

'I hate this bloody place,' said Alice as she pushed open the door to the chapel.

'It's always given me the creeps, too,' said Lily.

As they entered the chapel, the cold air was a welcome greeting in contrast to the June sun, which had been particularly warm for the past few days. Today it felt hot and muggy.

'Oh, it's nice in here,' said Alice, puffing a strand of hair from her face.

She placed the cleaning bucket on the stone floor. Mrs Hartwell had tasked the girls with freshening up the interior in preparation for the vicar coming over to perform a blessing. Now the war was over, Mrs Hartwell wanted to start making more use of the chapel, and to her mind, a blessing and a small service of thanks was ideal.

There was no running water at the chapel, so Alice and

Lily had carried a bucket each up the hill. Paolo had seen them, and had left what he was doing to come over and take the buckets from them.

'You must let me help you,' he said to Alice. 'You should not be carrying heavy things.'

Alice had been grateful, even though she felt she was capable; she didn't want to offend Paolo and refuse his help. Carlo had appeared a few moments later, and had insisted on taking Lily's bucket for her.

'Thank you so much,' said Alice as Paolo set the bucket of water down near the altar.

'You are welcome,' he replied.

There was a shy smile to his mouth and Alice found herself returning the smile, except rather more broadly.

They stood awkwardly looking at each other.

'Oh … err … would you like a sip of water?' Alice held out the flask she'd shoved in her pocket earlier.

'No. I am fine, thank you,' said Paolo. 'You must drink plenty of water. And eat. And rest, too.'

Alice laughed. 'You sound like a fussing mother hen.'

Paolo frowned. 'A mother hen?'

'Clucking around making sure everyone is all right,' explained Alice.

At this remark, Lily made a scoffing sort of noise. 'I think it's a bit more than that.' She raised her eyebrows innocently at the look Alice gave her.

'We must go back to work,' said Carlo, having placed Lily's bucket on the ground. 'Please, when you have finished, if you need us, come and get us.'

'Oh, we will,' Lily assured him.

Alice rolled her eyes and she and Paolo laughed again at the not so subtle flirting.

'How are you?' asked Paolo as they walked to the door.

'Not so bad.' Alice smoothed her hand over her stomach. 'I'm supposed to be blooming, according to Cook.'

'Blooming?'

'Be at my best and enjoying being pregnant,' explained Alice, with little conviction.

'But you are not?' Paolo's voice was full of concern.

'The couple who are adopting the baby are visiting next week.'

'And that makes you sad?'

'A bit.' Alice looked away for a second. 'I didn't think it would be this hard – you know, giving up the baby. I have to stop myself from thinking about it, but sometimes I can't help it.'

'I think it is a very hard thing that you are doing. It must be the hardest thing you have to do as a mother.'

He went to touch her arm, but withdrew his hand before he did so.

For no reason that Alice could fathom, she reached out and caught Paolo's hand. 'It is the right thing to do, isn't it?'

She didn't know why she was asking an Italian soldier, but Paolo seemed wise beyond his years, and she didn't think he judged her.

He considered her carefully and was just about to say something when Carlo called to him.

'Come, Paolo. We will be missed and then that idiot Billy will be after us.'

'It's all right. You go on,' said Alice when she saw Paolo

hesitate. 'I don't want Billy getting on at you. He's in a bad mood today. I heard Mrs Hartwell telling him to stop being so miserable and that now the war was over he should look to broaden his horizons.'

'In other words, she wishes he'd clear off,' said Lily. 'Just like the rest of us wish.'

'I wish he would go too,' said Paolo. And then to Alice, 'We will speak later.'

He and Carlo jogged off down the hill towards the field they were working in.

'Ooh, he likes you,' said Lily, nudging Alice.

'He is just being friendly. Anyway, you're the one flirting with Carlo.'

'Oh, I'm not judging you. In fact, I think they're both very nice, despite being Italian POWs.'

Alice chose not to challenge the 'despite' bit. 'As far as I'm concerned, they are just young men, stuck here until they can go home again.'

'Better not let Billy hear you say that.' They went back inside the chapel. 'He was looking daggers at Paolo this morning, after you said good morning to him.'

'Billy is ridiculously childish.'

They spent the morning cleaning the chapel, and by lunchtime it was certainly looking and smelling a lot fresher.

'We can manage the buckets now they're empty,' said Alice as she sloshed the last of the grey water out onto the fields.

The weather had changed in the space of a few hours, from a hot summer's day to one more used to showing up in winter. The sky had clouded over and the wind had picked up, causing Alice's dress to flap around, the hem whacking at her knees. Lily was wearing trousers, but Alice could no longer fit into hers.

'We're in for some rain by the look of it,' said Lily.

As Alice turned back to the chapel, she saw Aggie heading up the hill towards them, with little Jack alongside her. Alice waved at the cousins.

'Cook sent us up,' Aggie puffed as she reached them, with Jack trailing behind, his cap pulled down low and his gaze trained on the ground. Aggie glanced back at him briefly, before addressing Alice and Lily again. 'Billy's in a bad mood.'

Alice rolled her eyes. 'What's new?'

'I've brought lunch.' Aggie held up a basket with a tea towel over it. 'Cook filled it up.'

Alice exchanged a look with Lily. They both understood the unspoken message from Cook – to stay out of Billy's way.

'We'd better go back into the chapel. It's going to rain any minute now,' said Alice.

The quartet took themselves inside. Alice and Lily sat in one pew with Aggie and Jack in the pew in front. Aggie passed over a ham sandwich to each of them; her hand shook a little as she did so.

'Is everything all right?' asked Alice, taking the food from the twelve-year-old.

Aggie avoided eye contact but nodded her head. 'Yes. Fine.'

'No, it's not,' retorted Jack, not turning to look at Alice or Lily.

'Shh, Jack.' Aggie's voice was low and urgent.

'What's going on?' asked Alice. 'One of you needs to tell

me or I'm going down to the house right this minute to find out.'

'Billy is going to knock that bloody Eyetie's head off,' said Jack.

Alice took a sharp intake of breath. 'Paolo?' Jack looked around and nodded. It was then Alice noticed that he had a black eye. She took another intake of breath. 'What happened to you?'

'You're not supposed to say,' scolded Aggie. She turned to Alice. 'You can't make him tell you.'

'I can and I will,' said Alice, putting her sandwich down. She reached over the pew and, with her hand cupping Jack's chin, she turned him around to face her and took off his cap. 'Someone's hit you, haven't they?' Jack was trying desperately to hold back the tears. 'You can tell me, Jack. You won't be in trouble, and it will save me asking at the house. What happened?'

'Billy hit me.' Anguish filled Jack's voice. 'I hate him.'

'Why did he hit you?' asked Alice, looking once again at Lily, who had an equally shocked expression on her face.

'Jack was sticking up for you,' said Aggie.

'Me? I don't understand. Please, someone just tell me what happened.'

'He saw Paolo up here with you earlier. Carrying the bucket,' explained Aggie. 'When Paolo came back down, Billy went looking for him. Punched him. Yelled at him to stay away from you.'

Alice let out a cry. 'Punched Paolo?'

Aggie nodded. 'Aunt Louise came rushing out. Shouting at Billy, she was.'

Alice felt sick at the thought. 'What happened to Jack?'

'Billy came back in the kitchen in such a bad temper, he just lashed out at Jack for being in the way,' explained Aggie. 'Swore at him and everything. Jack caught his face on the kitchen table as he fell.'

'I hate him,' said Jack again.

Alice ran her hand over his head. 'Poor you, Jack. What did your mum say?'

'She doesn't know,' admitted Aggie. 'Cook said best not to say anything. It would only cause more trouble. That's why she's sent us up here with the picnic. When we go back down, we will have to say Jack caught his face on a tree or something.'

They sat in silence for a few moments. The ham sandwich suddenly didn't taste as nice as it had a minute ago.

'I don't know why Billy would behave like that,' said Alice after a while.

'Are you stupid?' scoffed Lily. 'Haven't you seen the way he looks at you?'

Alice glanced in the direction of the younger ones and gave a shake of her head towards Lily, with an expression which said, 'not now.'

'Lily is right,' said Aggie. 'He watches you all the time.'

Alice shivered at the thought and was decidedly uncomfortable that a twelve-year-old girl had noticed. 'I've no idea why he'd be interested in me.' Her hand automatically stroked her stomach.

'He's waiting.' Aggie looked at Lily as if asking permission to continue. 'He was like that before, with the other girl who was here. Waiting until she'd had her baby and then … you know.'

Alice shook her head. 'What?'

'I heard Cook saying Billy thinks the girls who come to Telton Hall are fair game once they've had their babies,' said Aggie.

'That's enough now,' said Lily. 'Eat your sandwiches. We'll have no more talk of Billy.'

The idea of Billy making advances to poor young women who'd just had a baby made Alice feel physically sick. Billy disgusted her. There was no way on this earth he was going to do that to her. Over her dead body.

She turned her thoughts to Paolo and hoped he was all right. She'd try to speak to him later in the day. Billy had no right to do that to him – and as for Jack ... the poor little lad must be terrified. The more she stewed about Billy and what he'd done, the angrier and more outraged she became. She wished she could teach that bullying git a lesson.

When teatime came and Paolo didn't appear at the table, Alice's heart dropped. Billy came in and stood there for a moment, looking around at the faces. His gaze paused on the empty chair. 'Oh, where's the Eyetie tonight? Not eating with us?'

Carlo shifted in his chair, looking at Billy, but said nothing. Alice could feel the tension oozing from Carlo. If anyone personified the expression of looks killing, then he had perfected it.

'Paolo is having tea in his room tonight,' said Cook, as she placed a pot of stew in the centre of the table.

'Best place for him,' snarled Billy. 'You didn't want to stay with your mate, then?'

Carlo lifted his chin and whatever he was about to say was cut off by Mrs Hartwell.

'Did you hear that Margaret Hemmings had her baby? I

saw Anne Roberts, the midwife, in the shop this morning. She'd just come from Margaret. A healthy baby boy. Now isn't that good news?'

Mrs Hartwell was in full swing, going into as much detail as she could, in a bid to divert the conversation. It had the desired effect, and Billy sat down at the table opposite Alice.

Throughout the meal, Alice kept her eyes down, looking at her food. She was hyper-alert to Billy after what the girls had said in the chapel earlier that day. She could feel his gaze on her, and when he tried to engage her in conversation, she still refused to look at him.

Making her excuses, Alice left the table first. She didn't wait for pudding, even though she was still hungry; she just wanted to get away from Billy.

Out in the garden, where dusk was drawing in, the wind was whipping up a frenzy now. She really should go back inside, but Alice needed the fresh air. It was poisonous, stale and evil inside the house – Billy was the carbon dioxide to her oxygen, and she didn't want to be anywhere near him.

Pulling her cardigan around her, Alice headed over to the rose garden behind the tall hedge. She liked it in there, and if she stood underneath the willow tree, she could see who was approaching from the house. If it was Billy, it would give her time to nip out through the back of the garden and around the side of the house.

It wasn't until she reached the hanging boughs of the tree that she realised she wasn't alone. She gave a small yelp.

Paolo stepped out from under the branches. 'It's only me. Don't be scared.'

'You made me jump.'

'Sorry.'

As Alice neared him, she noticed he had his head turned to one side. She came to a halt in front of him and lifted her hand to his cheek, turning his face towards her, just as she had done to Jack earlier.

His eye was black and swollen, almost closed, and his lip was split. He'd clearly been hit more than once.

'Oh, Paolo, I'm so sorry,' she whispered.

Paolo turned away from her and stepped back under the shelter of the willow tree. 'Do not feel sorry for me.'

Alice followed him, her anger towards Billy fuelled yet again. She didn't know what to say. What could she say? Standing in front of him again, her hands sought his. 'You should have fought back. He deserves a good thumping himself.'

'That is not my way,' replied Paolo softly. 'Besides, if I had, then he would have me sent back to the camp. I do not want that. Not now.' He paused, lifting her hand and brushing her knuckles with his lips. 'I would miss you.'

Alice nodded and swallowed. She could feel her body tense with nerves, but she managed to speak. 'I would miss you, too.'

Paolo pulled her towards him, embracing her in his arms. Alice resisted for a fraction of a second, before slipping her arms around him. They stood together for a long moment, holding each other. His body warmed her to her soul, and her heart contracted at the sensation.

It was only the howl of the wind and the deluge of rain exploding from the sky that made them pull apart.

'You should go inside. You will get wet and cold. I do not want you to get ill,' said Paolo.

'What about you?'

'I will be in soon.'

'You must be starving.'

'Cook gave me some food. Now, please, Alice, go inside.'

Alice rose on tiptoes and gave Paolo the briefest of kisses, before running back to the house.

The rain still managed to soak through her clothes, such was the downpour.

'My goodness, look at you!' cried Cook. 'You're soaked! You'll catch your death of cold. Now go upstairs and put some dry clothes on. Light that fire in your room and dry yourself off good and proper.'

Alice didn't argue. It might be the middle of summer, but she was cold and wet and the thought of a fire to warm her up was too appealing to dismiss. As she darted past the living room, she could hear Lily talking to Mrs Hartwell. Billy was no doubt in there, too, and Alice was glad she had a legitimate excuse not to join them that evening.

Up in her room, she lit the fire, then slipped out of her dress and dried herself, putting on her nightdress, by which time the fire was burning well. She wrapped a blanket around herself and huddled in front of the hearth, thinking of Paolo. She closed her eyes and let her mind replay those few moments with him under the willow tree.

29
Rhoda

2022

Rhoda stirred from her sleep and rolled over. She could taste something strange in the back of her throat. It was making her choke. She coughed, and was aware she was throwing her head from side to side. Something was covering her mouth. Smoke! There was a fire, but she was trapped.

As she clawed at her mouth, she came around from her sleep properly and realised she'd been having some awful dream about being trapped in the chapel by a fire. She shivered and a cold sensation travelled from her head to her toes.

It was dark – the night-time kind of dark. She felt as if she'd been asleep for ages and that it should be the morning. The wind was blowing hard outside, and she could hear the rain splattering against the window. She leaned over to the bedside table and switched on the lamp so she could see the time. It was just gone midnight. She was at Telton Hall, Nate having brought her back earlier that day. He had been so kind and comforting at her flat, it had made her feel cared for. It had also made her feel vulnerable, but for some inexplicable reason, it didn't scare her as it usually did. In fact, Nate had also made her feel safe – she wasn't sure anyone other than Dean had ever made her feel like that.

Rhoda's throat was parched, and she wished she'd thought to bring a glass of water up with her. Did she really want to get out of bed and pad down to the kitchen in the middle of the night? The answer was no, but she really needed a drink.

'Sod it,' she huffed, throwing back the duvet and pulling on her fleece over her pyjamas. She found her socks and pulled them on, making a mental note to bring her slippers when she came back the next week. Telton Hall was a draughty old house, where the cold snatched at your feet and ankles if you sat still for too long.

Using her phone as a torch, Rhoda slipped out into the hallway. The floorboard creaked under her foot, and she hoped she wouldn't disturb Jack. There wasn't any light coming from under his bedroom door, and she assumed he must be in bed, fast asleep. She didn't want to risk putting the hall light on in case it shone through under his door – besides the fact she didn't know where the light switch was, and couldn't be bothered fumbling around trying to find it.

The stair carpet muffled her footsteps, and she made her way around and down to the ground floor. It was then she noticed the living room door was open, and an orangey glow was flickering from within the room.

For some reason – she didn't know why – Rhoda slid her

phone into her pocket to hide the torchlight. She paused at the doorway; through the crack at the hinged side of the door, she could see Jack sitting in his chair. In front of him was some sort of box, and he was taking what looked like folded reams of paper and tossing them onto the fire.

Up to this point, Tink had been happily snoozing in her basket, but her ears pricked up and she lifted her head. She was looking straight at the door.

Rhoda shot back out of view, holding her breath as she pressed herself up against the wall. She could hear the silence expand in the room, pushing against the walls and seeping out around the door. She knew with absolute certainty Jack was looking towards the hallway. She could feel his eyes boring through the wall and into the back of her head. She wanted to swallow, but was scared even that would be too loud and he would hear her.

'Good girl,' she heard Jack say.

And then there was the sound of the lid being put on the box. Jack gave a small grunt and shuffled across the wooden parquet floor. Rhoda stayed perfectly still, not daring to look, as she tried to imagine what he was doing. There was the sound of a cupboard door being opened, accompanied by another couple of grunts as the box must have been put inside. She heard the click of a lock, and then the distinctive tinkling sound of something metal, probably the key, being dropped into something ceramic – possibly a cup or a vase. This was followed by a small clonk, and Rhoda guessed the vessel was being put on a shelf somewhere.

'Right, you ready for bed?' Jack was talking to the little dog.

Rhoda closed her eyes for a second. The last thing she

wanted was to be caught now. How was she going to explain herself? Quickly, she nipped back to the staircase and took her phone from her pocket.

Tink gave a couple of barks.

'What's up, girl?' she could hear Jack saying. 'Is that you, Rhoda?' he called out.

'Sorry, I didn't mean to disturb you,' she called back, trying to keep her breathing calm.

Tink trotted out of the living room, with Jack following. He shut the door behind him. 'You all right?' He eyed her closely.

Rhoda forced a smile. 'Yes. Fine. Just needed a glass of water.'

'Help yourself, you know where it is. I'm just heading up to bed. Everything's locked up.'

'OK. Night, Jack. See you in the morning.'

Rhoda went down to the kitchen. Her heart was certainly getting a workout. Even her legs felt wobbly. It was like being in the middle of a spinning class at the gym!

She ran herself a glass of water and drank it down in one go, before refilling it to take back upstairs.

Rhoda waited several minutes. She wanted to be sure Jack was tucked up in bed and not planning on coming down.

Satisfied she wouldn't be disturbed, Rhoda hurried along the hallway to the living room. Jack had left the lamp on at the foot of the stairs, so she tucked her phone into her pocket. Very carefully and slowly, she clasped the doorknob with one hand and rested the palm of her other hand against the door itself.

Please don't let it be a squeaky door.

Rhoda turned the handle and eased the door open. There was a small squeak, but fortunately no other sound. The fire had died out, but there was just enough light from the glow of the hall lamp to enable her to see what she was doing.

There in the fireplace were the cinders of the burned reams of paper, still holding their shape. At the back of them was a half-burned envelope. Even in the dim light, Rhoda recognised it as the same type of off-white ledger envelope she and Nate had found in the study. She reached in and plucked it from the ashes. It was stuffed with papers and must have been too thick to catch light properly. Rhoda blew on the singed edges to make sure they weren't still smouldering, and pushed the wodge into her pocket.

She stood up and looked around the living room, wondering where Jack had put the box. Along the back wall were two bookcases with cupboards underneath. Her eyes travelled upwards. An art deco style vase was on top of the bookcase. She knew without having to look that it was where Jack had popped the key.

She was just about to reach up for the vase when she heard Tink yap. *How the hell did that bloody dog know Rhoda was poking around in the living room?*

Rhoda decided not to push her luck. She'd have to look the next day, when Jack was out of the house.

Taking care to close the door quietly behind her, Rhoda went up the stairs, remembering to pick up the glass of water she'd left on the telephone table while she was snooping around.

As she reached the top stair and went to turn right to her bedroom, she practically walked into something – make that someone. She let out a scream and jumped back, her water slopping from the glass.

'Sorry,' said Jack, stepping out of the shadows. 'Think Tink needs to go out.'

'It's OK. Don't worry,' Rhoda managed to say through ragged breaths. 'Got my glass of water.' She held up the glass as proof. She was flustered and was certain Jack knew it. 'Goodnight.'

She sidestepped her host and headed for her room.

As soon as she was inside with the door closed, Rhoda took a deep stabilising breath, in and out. She listened with her ear against the door to Jack's footsteps on the stairs as he made his way to the ground floor to let Tink out.

She eyed the skeleton key in the lock of her door for a moment, before turning it – the gentle click of the deadbolt falling into place a reassuring sound.

Feeling wide awake now, Rhoda flicked on the main light and sat on her bed with the charred remains of the envelope, the handwritten number 1945 still legible. Very carefully she teased the papers out, unfolding them and spreading them out on her bed, keeping them in the same order.

They had all been meticulously folded, exactly the same way up, so Rhoda was only able to read what was on the right-hand side of each page. Most of them were invoices and receipts. The description of the works these related to were clearer on some than others; Rhoda had to guess what might have been on the left-hand side of the page.

She stopped when she came to one for 28 June 1945. The first part of the description had been burned away, but the words 'paving slabs × 3' were still visible. There was a price in the figure column. There were also some more figures below, but the description must only have been short.

Rhoda's stomach gave a little tumble of excitement. These could logically be the new paving stones used at the chapel, and this document would tie in to when the body was buried there.

She scanned the papers strewn across the bed, snatching up the one which had the words ME SHEET still visible. She guessed it was a time sheet, where Louise Hartwell had kept a log of who was doing what on the farm.

She swore out loud. The names had all been destroyed from the fire, and all that was left were the locations of the workers and what days they were working. She could see someone had been assigned to work at the chapel, but it didn't say who.

Before putting everything away, Rhoda took photographs of what she considered to be the important information. More pieces of a puzzle: she had a rough idea where they went, but couldn't quite match them up with any of the other pieces yet. It was like trying to do a jigsaw without the lid of the box.

Rhoda had finally drifted off to sleep, listening to the relaxation app she had on her phone. She hadn't used it in a while, but that night she knew her brain was in danger of going into overdrive. She had sleepless episodes from time to time – something that had been with her since childhood, and often occurred when there was a lot of uncertainty in her life. She didn't like it, and couldn't stop it, but these days she had coping strategies she could fall back on.

Jack was in the kitchen making a pot of tea when Rhoda went down at eight o'clock.

'Ah, that's good timing,' he said. 'Just made a fresh brew.'

Tink trotted over to her from her place in front of the Aga and Rhoda crouched down to make a fuss of the dog. 'Have you been up long?' she asked Jack.

'Up with the dawn. Not that I've got anything to get up for these days, but old habits die hard.'

'I usually get up early for a morning swim in the sea,' said Rhoda, standing up. Tink went straight back to her blanket. 'I think I'll have a walk instead, before I start work.'

After a quick cup of tea with Jack, Rhoda set off for a brisk walk. As she reached the end of the drive, she could see the light on in Aggie's cottage. There was the X5 parked at the side of the cottage again. She wondered if Aggie had some sort of home help in the mornings, although the man she'd seen the other day didn't look like a home carer. Not that she should stereotype, of course.

The village was slowly waking up, getting ready for the day. The little cafe that she and Nate had visited for lunch was open, and Rhoda nipped in to grab a takeaway latte.

'Morning,' said the woman behind the counter. 'Nice to see you again.'

Rhoda was surprised the woman had remembered her. 'Hello.'

'You're here early. Staying at Telton Hall, are you?' The woman smiled. 'Belinda Marshall. What can I get you?'

'Rhoda Sullivan. Latte, please. And yes, I'm staying here while I work on the stained-glass window of the chapel.'

She suspected Belinda knew this already.

'It's being taken away to some museum, isn't it?' said Belinda.

'That's right. Singlewood Open-Air Museum. They specialise in conserving old buildings. I work for them.'

'I think the village will be pleased to see it go, although not so pleased to see a load of new housing going up. Poor old Jack, didn't have any choice in it.' Belinda spoke over the noise of the coffee machine gushing hot milk into the cup.

'Pleased to see it go?' queried Rhoda.

'Well, apart from finding those old bones up at the chapel, the place itself hasn't had a happy history. Jack Hartwell's father died in a nasty machinery accident. All those poor young pregnant girls who had to give their babies up. Those prisoners of war, where one was killed. Jack Hartwell's wife going off and leaving him.' Belinda put the latte on the counter and tapped at the electronic till. 'It's all bad luck up there.'

Rhoda nearly missed the line Belinda had slipped in about the death of a POW. 'Sorry ... When you say a POW was killed, do you know any more about that?'

'Before my time, dear. I may look old enough to have been around in the forties, but that's what working every day in a cafe does for you.' Belinda gave a laugh and held out the card machine for Rhoda to wave her bank card over. 'No, that's just something that everyone knows about.'

'Everyone?' Rhoda tucked her card back into her pocket. *Why hadn't the Hartwells mentioned the POW death to her or the police?* 'How did the POW die, do you know?'

'Fell from the hayloft and broke his neck. Freak accident.

I don't know the details. I'm not sure anyone really does. You know what these stories are like when they get passed around and down.'

Rhoda thanked Belinda for the latte and headed back to Telton Hall. All the time, the same question was going around her head – why hadn't anyone mentioned the POW death? Was it the glazier, Paolo Sartori, who had fallen and died? Or another prisoner?

By the time she reached the driveway to Telton Hall, she knew she had to find out what had happened to Paolo Sartori. There must be Italian army records for him, and she might be able to find him on the Italian ancestry database. What she needed to do was to find out if he was still alive, or if he had died at Telton Hall.

Rhoda looked over at Telton Cottage; the driveway stood empty of any sign of Aggie's early morning visitor. Despite the warnings Nate's aunt had dished out to them, Rhoda was unperturbed. She was just going to ask her outright.

Before she had a chance to change her mind, Rhoda was knocking on the front door. She felt it too forward to go around to the back, as Nate had. A sharp tap on the living room window had Rhoda stepping back. Aggie was at the window, which she pushed open.

'What do you want?' Aggie clearly wasn't pretending she was pleased to see Rhoda.

'Hello, Aggie. I wanted to ask you something, if I may?' Rhoda began.

'If it's about the chapel, then you're wasting your breath.'

'It's about the POWs that were at Telton Hall.' Rhoda spoke quickly before Aggie had a chance to interrupt. 'One of them fell from the hayloft and broke his neck. Is that right? Do you know where Paolo Sartori is now? Was he the one who died?'

Aggie's eyes narrowed and eyed the takeaway coffee cup in Rhoda's hand. 'Where have you been hearing all that nonsense? Don't tell me – Belinda Marshall. Village gossip. What she doesn't know, she makes up.'

'I was also told there was a wedding between one of the POWs and one of the girls who stayed at Telton Hall – Alice Renshaw. You were bridesmaid, apparently.'

Aggie's face paled and she swallowed hard. 'I don't know who you heard that from, but it wasn't me.'

'Sylvia Montgomery seemed to think it was.'

'Well, she's wrong. I think I'd know if I was bridesmaid or not. Now, like I've said before, leave well alone. You're only stirring up unnecessary trouble and upset for people who were around at the time. And that includes me.'

With that, she pulled the window shut and, with one quick movement, yanked the curtain across.

Conversation well and truly ended.

Rhoda headed back across the road, feeling frustrated. It was becoming a familiar feeling where the Hartwell family were concerned. She needed to grab her phone and the chapel key from her room.

As she came around the back of Telton Hall, she looked in through the kitchen window but there was no sign of Jack. She tried the handle, half-expecting it to be locked as Nate had instructed, but the door opened freely. She didn't know whether to be pleased or not.

Rhoda nipped up the stairs to her room and grabbed her phone from the bedside table and the key from the drawer, slipping them both into the side pockets of her utility trousers.

The ringing sound of the old-fashioned telephones dotted around the house made Rhoda jump. It was a wonder there weren't more heart attacks back in the day, when these things rang so violently and loudly.

The phone was being particularly demanding, and with no answerphone to cut in, the shrill ringing was grating on Rhoda's nerves. She was debating whether to answer the damn thing herself when it stopped.

Thank goodness for that.

Rhoda jogged down the sweeping staircase. She could hear Jack's voice – it was low and insistent. For some unexplained reason, Rhoda stopped outside the door. Once again, she felt compelled to spy on Jack Hartwell.

'You're going to take it too far,' he was saying. 'You need to stop.'

Rhoda's heart gave an extra beat. She wiped her damp palms together. There was a pause for several seconds before Jack spoke again.

'I'm not happy about this … Yes. I know that! … It will all blow over, just be patient … What do you mean, it's too late?' There was another long pause and when Jack spoke again, his voice was heavy with defeat. 'OK, but I still don't like it.'

Rhoda was determined not to be caught hanging around outside the living room again. The previous night she was sure Jack had been suspicious of her, and she really didn't want to add fuel to the fire. She didn't know what he was talking about, or who he was talking to, but she didn't like the idea, and felt sure she wasn't a million miles away from the topic of conversation.

Rhoda hurried out of the house and up the hill to the chapel. She couldn't wait to be inside, where she could lock the door and feel safe. Weirdly, for all its ominous atmosphere, the building was also a safe haven. Even so, Rhoda checked the chapel as she had previously and, satisfied she was alone, locked the door.

She had one last small window to do. This one was the highest, being over the main entrance door. The scaffolders had erected a fixed tower in advance of this job, as the tower would be too high for her to move it around, as she had for the lower side windows.

With her bag on her shoulder, Rhoda pulled herself up the ladder and onto the first level. It wobbled a fraction and Rhoda paused, looking down to check the feet were firmly in place and the stabilising feet were all out. It wasn't unusual for scaffolding to feel unsteady, but it was something she'd got used to and it was strange that she had hesitated. She continued her ascent up the side, reaching the middle platform, which was level with the top of the oak door. Just a few more feet and she'd be up on the third platform, where she'd be working from.

She hoisted her bag higher on her shoulder and climbed the remaining side rungs to the third level. Rhoda pushed her bag onto the walk-boards and then climbed on, using the bottom guard rail to pull herself up. The window was circular, with a simple design of a white dove and a rainbow behind it. Rhoda wondered if this was what had given Paolo Sartori the inspiration for the main window. She rested her hand on the top guard rail to take a closer look at the fixtures. As she leaned forwards, the guard rail suddenly gave way at one end.

Rhoda screamed as she lost her balance and felt herself pitching forwards.

She managed to throw her weight to one side to stop herself going through the small gap between the scaffolding tower and the interior wall of the chapel. With a thud, she landed on the walk-boards – her left side taking the impact. The metal guard rail clattered against the wall at the same time.

Rhoda lay perfectly still as her heart raced. She could feel her pulse throbbing in her neck.

After several seconds, her brain kicked into gear. Without moving her head, she looked at the guard rail. It was still clipped into place at one end and the other end was resting on the walk-board next to her. Logically, she would be right to assume it was just that one piece of scaffolding that had somehow come loose.

Gingerly, Rhoda rolled onto her back. She groaned at the pain in her hip as she shuffled her body over. She was probably going to have a nasty bruise there.

Her next move was to get herself into a sitting position. Again, she managed this, and the scaffolding tower stood steady. All she had to do now was to get herself down from there in one piece. Her eyes sought out the ground fifteen feet beneath her – concrete slabs directly below, and hard wooden pews on the flanks. Neither was an inviting landing.

With her bag back on her shoulder, Rhoda made a tentative and cautious descent, her confidence in the tower improving with every step down on the ladder rungs. It was just the top guard rail that hadn't been fixed properly.

By the time she reached the floor of the chapel, her fear had been overtaken by anger. *Those bloody scaffolders, not doing their job properly*. There could have been a very different ending had it been the guard rail on the opposite side. It was just good fortune it was on the side against the wall. Where was their number? She was going to get on the phone to them right that second and give them a piece of her mind. Amateurs!

As she waited for the call to be answered, she paced the central aisle up to the altar and back to the tower. Her phone bleeped to tell her there was an incoming call from an unknown number.

Rhoda never ignored unknown numbers. There was always the possibility it would be someone phoning about Dean. Without hesitation, she ended the call to the scaffolders and answered the new caller.

'Hello, Rhoda Sullivan speaking.'

There was a small silence. Then a raspy whispered voice came through the phone.

'Mind your own business. Wouldn't want a nasty accident to happen.'

Rhoda had heard the expression of blood running cold but up until that point, she'd never experienced it.

'Who is this?' she demanded.

'This is your last warning.'

With that, the line went dead.

30
Alice

1945

That night, the storm raged without letting up. From her bedroom window, Alice could see the trees being whipped back and forth by the howling wind. The kitchen garden, although protected by the brick wall, was still taking a battering. Canes were blown over, the buckets stacked in the corner had tumbled across the path, and the glass in the greenhouse was rattling so much, Alice was certain not all the panes would survive the night.

Somewhere beyond the garden wall, she could hear the constant sound of metal flapping around. She suspected it was a piece of corrugated iron roof on the stables. She hoped Pegasus, the horse, would be all right in there.

'Why don't you get back to bed,' said a sleepy Lily, pulling the blanket higher up over her shoulder.

Alice climbed back into her bed, but it was a long time before she finally fell asleep.

When she awoke in the morning, the first thing she did was look out of the window. Although the wind was still apparent, the worst of the storm had blown itself out. The kitchen garden looked wrecked, with bits of wood and canes scattered across the raised beds. As she'd suspected, one of the windows in the greenhouse was cracked where the watering can had been blown into it.

She looked up towards the chapel. Something didn't look right, but it took a while for her to realise what it was.

'The tree's gone over up on the hill,' she said in alarm, suddenly realising what looked different.

'What?' came the bleary response from Lily. She pushed the blankets back and came to stand at the window with Alice. 'Oh, crikey!'

'Sadly, it doesn't look like it's brought the awful place down, though,' said Alice. 'The other tree's still standing, by the look of it.'

They got dressed and went down for breakfast, where talk of the storm was on the menu, and of how much damage had been done to the chapel. Alice was pleased when Paolo appeared at the table, but upset that the side of his face looked worse than yesterday. She kept trying to catch his eye, but he avoided looking at her – probably because Billy was there and, as usual, was monitoring her constantly.

'Paolo and Carlo went up there first thing this morning,' Mrs Hartwell was saying. 'The tree has smashed the main window.'

'How bad is it?' Billy asked. 'That's going to cost a fair bit to fix.'

'Paolo thinks most of it will need replacing,' replied Mrs Hartwell.

'What does he know?' snorted Billy.

'Actually, it's his trade,' explained Mrs Hartwell. 'Paolo's father was a glass maker back in Italy. Had his own business and taught Paolo the trade.'

Billy chose not to comment.

'Maybe Paolo could fix it, then,' suggested Alice.

This comment earned her a look from everyone at the table.

'I was thinking that myself.' Mrs Hartwell looked to Paolo. 'Do you think you could repair the window, or make some new glass for it?'

'It will not be easy,' said Paolo, 'but I can do it.'

'Really, Louise, are you going to let some Eyetie loose on the window?' Billy's tone was nothing short of derisory. 'I'm sure there are some English glaziers who can do just as good, if not better, job.'

'I would like Paolo to do it,' said Mrs Hartwell firmly.

'It will be my pleasure,' said Paolo.

'We can get Ted from the chandlers to look at it,' said Billy.

'No. I said I want Paolo to do it,' insisted Mrs Hartwell, and when Billy went to protest, she cut him off. 'It is up to me, you know.'

Billy shoved the last spoonful of porridge into his mouth, followed by a swig of his tea, before standing up, holding on to his stick and kicking the chair away behind him.

'Who am I to argue with the owner?' With that, he stomped as best he could out of the kitchen.

With Billy gone, the atmosphere in the kitchen changed immediately – as if not just the occupants, but also the building itself, gave a sigh of relief.

'Someone's in a bad mood,' muttered Lily.

'I'm sure he was born in a bad mood,' said Mrs Hartwell.

It was the first time Alice had heard Mrs Hartwell speak ill of anyone, but she could quite see how Billy would drive even the most patient of people to distraction. Poor Mrs Hartwell, she must be so sick of hearing Billy moan and groan about everything.

After breakfast was over, Mrs Hartwell spoke at some length with Paolo about the chapel, while Alice and Lily cleared up the kitchen to get it ready for when Cook arrived later that morning.

'We need to cut the tree into logs to get it out of the window,' Paolo was saying. 'We will need ropes, saws, and the tractor or Pegasus to pull the tree away from the chapel.'

'Use the tractor, it will be easier. We have enough fuel for it,' Mrs Hartwell instructed. 'Make a list of tools and materials you will need to fix the window. I'll go into the village to get everything organised.'

It turned out to be a couple of days before all the equipment Paolo had requested was delivered to Telton Hall.

Alice went out to the fields to find Paolo. His eye wasn't looking so bad, and Alice was glad there seemed to be no permanent damage. She had taken to seeking him out at the end of the day, just to talk to him and spend a little time in his company.

'I've been sent to fetch you,' she said. 'There's a delivery in the yard. All the things you need for the chapel window.'

Paolo's eyes lit up. 'That is good. I am looking forward to repairing the window. It will remind me of days before the war, when life was kind and I worked with my father.' He gave a wistful sigh.

'You miss your home and family a lot, don't you?'

'Very much. I have not seen them for so long.'

'Hopefully it won't be too long before you can go home.' As Alice said the words, she felt a pang of sadness. She'd miss Paolo when he left – if she was still here, that was. 'I wonder which one of us will leave Telton Hall first?'

Paolo raised his eyebrows, a small look of amusement on his face. 'I think it will be you. I do not think I will be going home before Christmas.'

'I don't know if I want to go home,' admitted Alice. 'There's nothing to go home for.'

'But your father?'

She shook her head. 'I don't know if I can. It's not that I don't love him and he doesn't love me, but there is so much pain involved in being at home. We remind each other of who we have lost – my mother. Without her, we're broken pieces of the Renshaw puzzle.'

'Puzzle?'

'Oh, ignore me. I'm getting all deep and emotional.' Alice forced a smile to her face and swiftly changed the subject. 'Here, I nearly forgot.' From her pocket she took out a rock cake Cook had made that afternoon. It was still warm and she pushed it into Paolo's hand. 'Eat it quickly, before anyone sees.'

'I should not …' began Paolo.

'You jolly well should. Cook gave that to me and if I want to give it to you, then I can.'

'In that case, I do not want to offend you and I shall eat it.'

Paolo broke it in half and popped one piece in his mouth, offering the other to Alice, who declined.

'I've already had one. Cook gave me two, but she said I wasn't to tell anyone.'

'You are very kind to me.'

'And you are to me,' replied Alice.

They walked so close their shoulders touched and their hands brushed against each other's. At some point, by unspoken mutual agreement, their fingers entwined, and they walked hand in hand in a warm and comfortable silence. It felt so natural to hold Paolo's hand, but at the same time ripples of excitement reverberated through Alice's whole body.

As they neared the outbuildings, Paolo stopped before they reached the corner of the stable. He turned to Alice and, without saying a word, dipped his head and kissed her. This time it wasn't a fleeting brush of the lips. Alice found herself responding. It was exciting and scary all at the same time. Eventually, she pulled away and nestled her head against his chest.

'I have something for you.' From his pocket, Paolo produced a ring. 'I made it. From a penny.'

'Oh, Paolo, that's amazing,' said Alice, looking at the penny ring. 'You made this? How?'

Paolo lifted Alice's hand and slipped the ring on to the third finger of her right hand. 'With a hammer. I shaped it around the bar of the hay feeder.'

'You're so clever. Thank you so much.' Alice's heart swelled with happiness. To think Paolo had made this with his own hands, just for her. She wasn't sure she'd ever been given such a wonderful present. She hugged Paolo tightly, which wasn't so easy now her stomach was starting to get in the way.

Pegasus whinnied from his stable, alerting Alice and Paolo that someone was approaching. Alice jumped away from Paolo just as Billy's voice rang out in the yard.

'Oi! Sartori! Get here now!'

Alice wasn't one for being intimidated, but she knew Billy wouldn't like it if he saw her and Paolo together. 'You go,' she whispered. 'I'll go around the other way.'

She gave Paolo a gentle shove as he stood his ground. He was a proud man, but Alice knew standing up to Billy was not the most sensible thing to do. She hurried off around the back of the stables, glancing back at Paolo, who then disappeared around the corner and into the yard.

Alice could hear Billy berating Paolo – telling him to get a move on. She wasn't one for hating people – it was a wasted emotion – but she was sure she hated Billy.

Alice didn't see Paolo for the rest of the day, as he was busy up at the chapel and Mrs Hartwell had her in the house, sorting out the airing cupboard. Alice wasn't sure the cupboard needed much tidying, but appreciated the opportunity to work quietly indoors. Mrs Hartwell had the radiogram playing some classical music, and the gentle melodies drifted up from the room below. From time to time, Alice could hear Mrs Hartwell humming along to the tunes and it reminded her of her own mother, who used to do the same.

Alice had been so busy settling into life at Telton Hall, and so exhausted in the evenings, that she realised she hadn't thought about her mother as much as usual. However, her conversation with Paolo had triggered her emotions, and she wished she could tell her mother all about him. She was sure that she'd understand, and that it wouldn't worry her he was Italian. Alice wasn't so sure her father would approve but, to be honest, he would probably never know. She should really enquire after her father, and considered either writing to him or asking Mrs Hartwell if she could speak with her sister, Mrs Armitage from the Big House back home, to find out how he was.

Lost in thought about her parents, Alice didn't hear the tread on the staircase behind her until the last moment. She turned around just as Billy reached the landing.

Deciding to ignore him, Alice carried on with what she was doing and pushed the pillowcases she had just folded onto the shelf. She wasn't quite tall enough and they fell down.

'You look like you need some help there,' said Billy, openly admiring Alice's legs.

'No. I'm fine. I'll get a chair.'

The last thing she wanted was help from that slimy git.

'No need.' Billy was next to her. He slipped his hand around her back, resting it on her waist as he guided her out of the way. Alice wanted to vomit at the mere sensation of his touch. 'There, that was easy. Pass me the others.'

Reluctantly, Alice obliged. 'Thank you.' It was a begrudging thanks on her part. She wished he'd just clear off. The music was still playing downstairs, but it didn't give Alice the same feeling of enjoyment anymore.

Billy put the last of the pillowcases on the shelf. 'What's that?' he said.

'What?' Alice wondered if he'd found something in the airing cupboard.

'That thing on your hand – on your finger.'

Alice had forgotten all about the ring Paolo had given her. Automatically, she covered her right hand with her left. 'Just a ring.'

It angered her that she had felt the need to hide it. Somehow, it felt disloyal to Paolo but, at the same time, she didn't want Billy to see it.

'Show me. You haven't had a ring on before.' He tapped his cane on the wooden floorboards. 'Show me.'

Alice held out her hand, which Billy grabbed.

'Where did you get that from?' he demanded.

'I found it.' Alice knew better than to say it was from Paolo. 'It was in the field.'

'Liar!' Billy hooked his cane onto his arm and grabbed hold of Alice's wrist. Before she realised what he was doing, he had yanked the ring from her finger.

'That's mine! You can't do that!' she cried.

'Actually, I can. This was made by a POW from a British coin. That would be classed as theft, which is punishable by imprisonment, or even death. I need to confiscate that and turn it in to the authorities.'

Alice had no idea if Billy was telling the truth or not. 'You can't prove any of that.'

'No, but I can take measures to ensure this sort of thing does not happen again. Anyway, why are you so upset if you just found it, as you claim. You don't want me to start accusing anyone, do you?'

Alice wanted to think it was an empty threat, but she knew better than to put it to the test where Billy was concerned. She gave a nonchalant shrug. 'Keep it, if you want. Doesn't make any odds to me. Like I said, I just found it in the field.'

The sound of Cook ringing out the dinner bell brought the confrontation to a halt.

When they were all sitting at the table, with Paolo opposite her, Alice saw him glance towards her hand.

'Now, look what Alice found in the field this afternoon,' said Billy. He placed the penny ring on the table in front of him. Alice forced herself not to look at Paolo. 'Old piece of junk jewellery,' Billy carried on. 'You know, I was going to turn it into the authorities on the premise of theft but, for now, I think I'll keep on to it, even though, as Alice so rightly said, it's a worthless piece of tat.'

Billy returned to his meal, leaving the ring in full view, as if taunting her and Paolo.

At the end of the meal, when Billy reached over and picked up the ring, Alice had to tamp down the desire to stab his rotten hand with her fork. She resolved herself to thinking of all the horrible things she'd like to do to Billy. When she got the chance, she'd have to explain to Paolo how Billy had ended up with the ring – she hoped he'd understand.

It was about an hour after dinner, when Alice was in her room with Lily, that they heard a commotion from the attic room above them. It was angry shouting – all in Italian.

'That's Paolo and Carlo,' said Lily, sitting up and dropping the book she was reading onto the blanket. 'Whatever's going on? They're going to have the whole house up here in a minute.'

'They don't sound very happy,' said Alice needlessly.

Next, there was the thundering of feet on the floorboards, followed by a more heated exchange of words. The footsteps – or rather, foot-thumps – were stomping around, before Alice heard the door being flung open and hitting the wall.

'That doesn't sound good,' said Lily. 'They're coming downstairs now.'

The distinctive sound of boots on bare treads grew louder as whoever it was made their way down. Alice and Lily jumped up and went to the door, opening it a fraction.

The door to the attic staircase flew open, and Paolo stormed out with his bed sheets in his hand.

'Paolo!' called Alice in alarm, but he didn't appear to hear her.

He was already going down the main staircase.

A couple of seconds later, Carlo appeared on the landing.

'What's happened?' asked Lily.

Carlo looked down the staircase and back to Lily. He took a deep breath. 'Someone has pissed on Paolo's bed.'

Under any other circumstances it would have been laughable to hear an Italian use British swear words, but it was clearly not funny at that moment.

'Someone did what?' Alice could barely believe her ears.

'His bed has piss all over it,' said Carlo. 'He is going to wash it now, but it will not be dry and his mattress stinks.'

'Oh my God, that's terrible. Who did that?' As soon as she asked, Alice knew it was a ridiculous question.

Still, Carlo took the trouble to make it clear. 'It was not me and it was not Paolo. I do not think it was any of you ladies.'

Alice was seething. She could feel the anger bubbling up

inside her. 'This is because of the ring. It's my fault. I should have taken it off. I'm going to help Paolo.'

'No. Do not help him. He will be …' Carlo searched for the word. 'Ashamed.'

'But …' began Alice.

Lily put her hand on Alice's arm. 'He's right. Leave Paolo tonight. Speak to him in the morning.'

'At least let me give you clean sheets,' said Alice, going down the hallway and opening the airing cupboard door. She fished out the best bed sheet and top sheet she could find. Sod what anyone would say. Paolo didn't deserve that kind of humiliation. 'Here's a clean flannel. Wait there while I fetch some white vinegar to clean the mattress with. You can turn it over tonight and, in the morning, stand it up with the windows open to dry it.'

Alice went downstairs to the kitchen. The door to the scullery was half open and she could see Paolo standing over the enamel sink, scrubbing at his bed sheet. He must have sensed her looking and turned around. There was a mix of anger and sadness in his eyes. Alice went to say something, but Paolo reached out to push the door, pausing for a moment.

'It is not you, Alice,' he said, before closing the door.

Alice felt the burn of tears in her eyes as she grabbed the white vinegar from the cupboard under the sink. She didn't know what she was going to do, but she was going to make Billy pay for what he had done. One way or another, she'd get revenge on him for humiliating dear, sweet Paolo like that. Billy was nothing but a disgusting pig.

10 June 1945

Carissime Mamma e Sofia

I received your most recent letter, and I am glad you are all well even though it is so difficult for you to find enough food.

There is still no news when I can come home. Although, I must admit, I will be sad to leave Alice. We have become very good friends in recent weeks, and I enjoy her company very much. She is to have a baby soon and will be passing it up for adoption. I cannot imagine having to make that decision. It is very cruel. I wish there was something I could do to help but I have no idea what, even if I could.

We had a terrible storm. A tree came through the roof of the chapel and smashed the stained-glass window. Half of the wall was smashed, too. We are in the middle of rebuilding it and I have been asked to make a new stained-glass window.

There is not much to say. Life on the farm goes on and nothing much has changed since the end of the war. Billy continues to be his usual loathsome self. In fact, he has been particularly bad since Germany surrendered. He sometimes comes up to our rooms at night when he has had a drink and taunts us. He calls us names and tries to provoke us, but we are not as stupid as he thinks. He will get his comeuppance sooner or later and if I am there to witness it, then it shall be a very sweet moment. But don't worry, I'm not going to do anything rash. I am a patient man, perhaps more so than you remember, and I shall bide my time.

Il vostro amorevole figlio e fratello

Paolo

31
Nate

2022

Nate wasn't quite sure what had happened between him and Rhoda at her flat the previous day, but whatever it was, he had been left with a sense of closeness. It was as if their … He struggled to think of the right word, but settled on 'friendship' – it was as if their friendship was on the verge of being something more, teetering at some sort of tipping point, not knowing whether to fall back or rush forwards.

He liked Rhoda – liked her a lot – and he wanted to get to know her better, but wasn't entirely sure now was the perfect moment, if indeed there was such a thing. He didn't want to scare her off by coming on too strong and too fast, but he didn't want to be so laid-back that she didn't think he was interested.

Damn. When did dating get so convoluted? It was so much easier when you were younger and didn't have any complications. Rhoda was complicated. He was fully aware of that and, therefore, it was essential to get this just right.

Nate leaned back in his chair. He'd been in the office since 7.30, hunched over a pile of accounts in a bid to clear his desk so he was free for the weekend. He stretched his arms and rolled his shoulders. What he really needed was fresh air and a bit of exercise. He'd take a walk to grab some lunch from the deli on the High Street.

It was a really nice day now he was out. The weather had been so unsettled recently for the time of year; it was nice not to have to wear his jacket. He popped his sunglasses on and was soon waiting in the queue outside the deli. It was only a small place, takeaway only, and once you had two customers inside, it was full.

He was flicking absently through his phone when the sound of a car horn made him look up. A silver Fiesta had cut up a black BMW. There was a minor exchange of hand gestures and another blare of the horn before the Fiesta shot off. The BMW pulled in on the other side of the road, and as Nate moved along in the queue, he gave the vehicle another glance. To his surprise, he saw Vince Taylor getting out, except this Vince Taylor looked decidedly younger than before. Nate took a closer look, just to be sure he wasn't mistaken, but the Romanesque side profile convinced him it was the same man who had been to see Rhoda at the chapel. His blond hair wasn't scraped back on his head today, and he wasn't wearing the thick-rimmed glasses he had previously donned. Most surprisingly, the local historian was very steady on his feet – capable, even – with no need for a walking stick.

Nate watched the man open the rear door and pull out

the stick but, instead of leaning on it as he had done when he'd visited the chapel, he merely held it in his hand and strode around the back of the car to the pavement, where he then marched into the local council offices.

Well, there certainly wasn't anything wrong with his legs. Vince Taylor looked at least ten years younger. Why on earth would he feign frailty? Did he think it would curry more favour with Rhoda if he went for the sympathy vote?

As Nate ordered his sandwich and made his way back to the office, he continued to brood over what he'd just witnessed. The more he thought about it, the more it bothered him. By the time he'd reached his office, he'd made up his mind what he was going to do. He dropped the sandwich bag onto his desk as he sat down and then took his phone from his pocket and called his ex-wife.

'Nate? Is everything all right?' Siobhan asked immediately.

'Yes. Everything is fine.' Nate hesitated, reminding himself this wasn't for his benefit, and swallowing a bit of pride was in order. 'I need a favour.'

'A favour?'

'Yeah. I need ... I mean, I wondered if Harrison would do a background check on someone for me, please?'

Siobhan gave a laugh. 'A background check? You can't just ring up and order a check on someone.'

'It's important,' insisted Nate. 'There's some bloke snooping around at my dad's, and I don't one hundred per cent trust him.' He was aware he had made it sound more sinister than it was on the face of it.

'And you want Harrison to put his job on the line just because you don't like someone? Do you realise what you're asking?'

'I know. Can you just ask him, though?'

'No, I won't,' Siobhan replied.

He could hear Harrison's voice in the background as a quick exchange between husband and wife took place, before Harrison came to the phone.

'Nate. What's the problem? Siobhan said you've got someone hanging about at your dad's.'

'More or less. I just want to make sure he's genuine.'

Nate took a breath and gave his former best friend a rundown on the miraculous recovery Vince Taylor appeared to have made.

'Text me his details,' said Harrison. 'If you can get his car reg, too, that would help. I'll see what I can do.'

'Thanks.' Nate just managed to stop himself from adding 'mate'. It had been a long time since either of them had used that term to the other.

By mid-afternoon, Nate knew he would end up working late for the second day running. It was all right taking time off when he liked, but he knew he'd have to pay for it later. Sure, he could have got one of the junior accountants to undertake some of the mundane work, but it didn't sit easy with him. Delegating was one thing, but palming your work off on another member of staff because you were behind wasn't on – it wasn't the sort of ethos he liked to encourage at work. Nate was a great believer in never asking his employees to do anything he wouldn't do himself.

Damn it. He hated having morals sometimes.

It didn't help that the client he was currently preparing end-of-year accounts for was hopeless at paperwork and refused to move over to digital uploading of the finances and linking his banking automatically through the electronic systems his firm provided. It was like going back to the Dark Ages with physical paperwork, and wading through it all to marry up invoices and receipts.

Nate was glad of the excuse to stop work when his phone rang. He picked it up and looked at the screen.

Rhoda Sullivan

That cheered him up. He answered the phone on the second ring, leaning back in his leather chair. 'Hi, Rhoda. How's it going? Everything OK?'

He'd already made up his mind he wouldn't mention seeing Vince just yet. He'd wait to see what Harrison came back with. Rhoda had enough on her plate without him adding to it.

'Nate.'

He could tell instantly by the tone of her voice that she was anything but OK. He sat upright. 'What's up?' He listened while Rhoda filled him in on what had happened with the scaffolding. 'And you had a threatening phone call?' He didn't like the sound of this.

'Yep. Couldn't tell if it was male or female – it was too low and whispery. You know, like someone who's been a heavy smoker all their life,' replied Rhoda.

'Bloody hell. Are you OK? I mean, like, really OK?'

'Shaken up, if I'm honest, but in one piece. As for the call, I've had nicer ones.'

'We should go to the police.'

'And say what?'

'Show them the note. And tell them about this call. They might be able to trace it.'

'Unknown number, and if the caller had any sense, they would have made it from one of those ten-pound throwaway phones that are untraceable.'

'But the guard rail collapsing …' Nate was on his feet, looking out of his office window. 'That's basically sabotage. And your car window. All that, coupled with the break-in at your flat … It needs reporting.'

'I don't think they will be able to do anything. They can't prove the scaffolding was sabotaged. The scaffolding guys are here now, and they are so apologetic. I don't want them to get into trouble for something they haven't done.'

'I still think we should report it. Just for the record.'

'You can.'

'For fuck's sake, Rhoda!' Nate regretted his frustrated outburst instantly. He could feel Rhoda bristle on the other end of the line. She went to say something – a reprimand, no doubt – but he spoke over her. 'I'm sorry, I just … I just don't want you to get hurt.'

There was a moment's silence on the phone before Rhoda spoke. 'Erm … I don't either, as it happens. Thank you for your concern.'

'Look, I'm going to wrap things up here at the office and come over.'

'Oh, Nate, there's really no need. I'm fine. Honest. Plus, you've got a heap of work to do.'

Nate glared at the files on his desk with intense annoyance. 'OK, but I'm going to call the police. They probably won't even want to come out, but at least I'll have reported it. I'll come over later this evening once I've finished at work. How does that sound?'

'It sounds like a compromise.'

'It is. For both of us.' He exhaled slowly. 'Are you off back to Sussex today?'

'I was debating whether to bother. I wouldn't mind staying, but I don't want to get in your dad's way.'

'He won't mind at all. Stay the weekend. You could even have a day off and I could show you around the area.' Nate realised he sounded far more enthusiastic than he should and tried to tone his voice down. 'That's if you want to, of course. If you want to get on with the work at the chapel, then don't let me get in the way.'

He really needed to shut up. He was babbling like a fool.

'Sure. A bit of sightseeing would be nice.' There was a touch of amusement in her voice.

'Oh, that will be great. I mean, yeah. Good.' He cringed at his ineptitude at trying to sound casual, and at Rhoda's obvious entertainment.

'Look forward to seeing you later. Bye.'

'Bye.' Nate looked at his phone for a long moment. Rhoda had said she was looking forward to seeing him. Why did that idea make his stomach feel warm and glowing? It was a casual remark. Wasn't it?

He made the call to the police and, as Rhoda had predicted, they didn't seem that interested. The civilian who took the call said they'd get DS Shepherd to call Nate back, but added that he was off duty until Monday. Nate had no choice but to agree to wait.

He'd only just settled back down to his work when he received a text message. It was from Rhoda.

Does your Aunt Aggie have a carer come to her in the mornings?

Nate frowned at the somewhat left-field question. He tapped back a reply.

> You must be joking. She's worse than my Dad for being independent. Why?

He waited for a reply, but after twenty minutes of silence from his phone, he assumed he wasn't getting one. He'd ask her later; he really needed to get on.

Nate ploughed on through his work that day, eating at his desk and getting the receptionist to shield his calls and take messages for him. Usually, he liked to have his work up to date by Friday, so he could head into the weekend without the thought of anything urgent hanging over his head. He didn't have Isaac with him this weekend; Siobhan was taking him up to London to visit her mother. Usually when Isaac wasn't about, Nate's weekends felt empty and insignificant, but he certainly had that Friday feeling.

As it turned out, he was the last to leave the office that night, but he did so with a clear desk. Nate flicked off his office light, leaving the main light on in reception, before setting the security alarms and locking up the offices.

He rented office space in a larger building from where a firm of solicitors, a call centre and an insurance company also worked. It was a sure sign it was Friday – his was the only car left in the underground car park.

Nate headed for his Alfa Romeo across the parking bays, his footsteps echoing against the concrete. His phone buzzed a text message in his pocket. As he went to fish it out, he heard the rev of an engine, but it took a few seconds for him to register the vehicle was heading in his direction at an alarming and increasing speed. He looked towards the sound of the car; the headlights dazzled him, and he put his arm up to shield his eyes. Surely they'd seen him. He was right in their path, for God's sake! The engine revved louder. Nate swore and dived out of the way, just in the nick of time. He could feel the rush of air as the car whizzed past him. He rolled over in a rather inept James Bond fashion and tried to get a look at the number plate, but the soft amber lighting of the car park made it impossible. The car reached the end of the strip and made a U-turn, its tyres squealing on the concrete floor. Nate jumped to his feet. For a moment he stood there, as if they were about to duel, but the car revved several times and accelerated hard towards him. Nate wasn't taking any chances. He sprinted towards his own car. His initial instinct was to take cover behind it, but then it occurred to him if the other car rammed his, he would be squashed against the wall. Instead, he kept himself flat against the driver's door, looking over the roof, ready to make a sudden escape at the last second if he needed to.

The car tore down the centre of the car park, its horn blaring out. Nate fumbled for his phone, hoping to grab a picture of the car, but his phone wasn't in his pocket. It was too late anyway; the car had disappeared up the ramp and out into the street. It was then that he noticed his phone – or what was left of it – in the middle of the car park.

With rather shaky legs, he retrieved the device. The screen was smashed and the back was cracked. It was dead. Better the phone was dead than him.

In the safety of his car, Nate took a deep breath as he rested his head back and closed his eyes. What the hell had just happened?

32
Rhoda

2022

Rhoda had decided not to make a big deal of the scaffolding to Jack. She didn't want to worry him, but as it happened, by the time she had gone back down to the farm for lunch, he knew all about it.

'The scaffolders told me,' he said, as Rhoda sat at the kitchen table. 'You were bloody lucky. Those idiots should be sacked.'

'It was just an accident,' said Rhoda, playing it down. 'I'm all right, and they've fixed it and been around the whole tower double-checking everything.'

Jack had muttered to himself some more about how useless they were, but had let the matter drop, for which Rhoda was grateful. She didn't want to tell him about the phone call. It was unnecessary. Instead, she had moved the conversation on to housing for him. He had been characteristically reluctant to commit to even phoning the council; in the end, he had left her to take Tink for a walk.

Now, it was early evening and Rhoda was clock-watching, waiting for Nate to arrive. She had found herself thinking about him often that afternoon, and she didn't really know why. It was almost as if she was missing him. How ludicrous was that? She'd keep that thought well and truly to herself.

The house phone burst into life, making Rhoda jump. *Bloody thing* – it would be the death of her at this rate. Jack answered it, but he was obviously doing a lot of listening, just interjecting with a few grunts here and there, before finally finishing with: 'OK. I'll tell her. Bye.'

Rhoda looked up as he replaced the receiver.

'That was Nate,' he said. 'He's going to phone you himself, or text you or whatever it is. He's gone straight home tonight. Got some work to do. He'll explain, anyway. He's got a temporary phone or something, so expect a different number, he said.'

'Oh, OK.' Rhoda looked back at her laptop, hoping she was disguising the distinct feeling of disappointment that had pitched up at this news.

'He works too hard,' commented Jack. 'Mind you, darn sight easier than working the farm.'

Rhoda closed the lid to her laptop. 'I know he didn't take on the farm as you wanted, but he does feel guilty about it.'

Jack nodded. 'I know he does. He shouldn't. I was disappointed for a long time, but what with all this compulsory purchase order, I'm glad he didn't. He'd be stuck now, with no job to fall back on. Besides, he's made a much better living as an accountant than he could ever have expected running the farm.'

'You should be proud of him.'

Jack eyed her for a moment. 'I am. Very proud.'

'Maybe you should tell Nate that. He'd appreciate it.'

'Probably should. Just in case I snuff it before I get the chance.' Jack gave her a wink.

Although Jack was making light of it, Rhoda was sure he was serious. 'You don't want to regret not saying things … just in case.'

Jack shifted in his chair. 'Nate told me about your brother. I'm sorry.'

'Thanks. I haven't given up on him, though, and I hope I'll get the chance to tell him all the things I should have when we were younger.'

Rhoda's phone buzzed with a text message.

Hi. It's Nate. This is my new number. Phone's buggered. Can I give you a call in a minute? When my dad's not about. Also had to pick up Isaac for the night. His trip to his grandmother's been cancelled as she's not well. Might have a third wheel sightseeing tomorrow. Or we can do it another day.

Rhoda messaged straight back.

Hey, don't worry. More than happy to spend the day with two Hartwells. Entirely up to you, though.

She liked that Nate put his son first – it was how it should be. Besides, she liked Isaac. She recognised a lot of herself in him. The loner; the kid who was a bit different; the kid who struggled to fit in: she could relate to all that.

Nate replied.

Great. Two for the price of one it is!

Rhoda sent a final text saying she was looking forward to it, and she really was. It would be nice to do something different, and even nicer was the company.

'All sorted?' asked Jack as she put her phone back on the arm of the sofa.

'Yes. I'm being taken out by Nate and Isaac tomorrow.' Then a thought struck her. 'Why don't you come?'

Jack chuckled. 'Now that's being greedy. Three of us.'

'It would be nice.'

'I'm supposed to be going to Aggie's for lunch tomorrow.'

'That's nice. Does she cook?'

'No. We get fish and chips. OAP special on a Saturday lunchtime.' Jack rose from his chair. 'Anyway, I'm going to take Tink for a quick walk around the garden and then I'm off to my bed. Goodnight, Rhoda.'

Rhoda went back to her laptop. She was trying to find out what had happened to Paolo Sartori and had filled out a form for the Italian military website, but with very little information to input, she wasn't holding out much hope of a reply.

She heard Jack come in from his walk a short while later, and he called out another goodnight as he passed the living room door. Rhoda was itching to find out what was in the box he'd locked away in the cupboard, but she needed to make certain he was in bed and asleep this time. She didn't need any more surprises on a darkened staircase.

She allowed an hour to pass, and was just about to get

up from the sofa to look for the key when her phone rang. She grabbed it quickly to avoid it disturbing Jack. 'Hello?'

'Hey, it's me. Sorry to ring so late.' It was Nate on the other end of the line.

'That's OK. What's up?'

'Nothing. Just wanted to tell you something that I might not get the chance to tomorrow, with Isaac about.'

Rhoda sat back on the sofa. 'I'm all ears.'

'I had a bit of a fright this evening ...'

Rhoda listened as Nate explained the incident with the car in the underground car park.

'Oh, my God, Nate. Are you all right?' Rhoda sat forward on her seat.

'Yeah. I'm fine. A bit shaken, but that's all.'

'And you've no idea who it was or why they did it?'

'I don't think it was a disgruntled client,' replied Nate dryly. 'Would like to say it was kids messing about, but it was a four-wheel drive type of car. Didn't get a proper look at it. Just that it was black or dark blue.'

'Are you going to report it?'

'Isn't that my line?' He gave a laugh to defuse the situation, but Rhoda wasn't being fobbed off that easily.

'Maybe you should, especially in light of the scaffolding incident.'

'Probably should.'

'Do you think they're related?'

She could hear Nate blow out a breath before he spoke. 'Could be. Or it could be a coincidence.'

'I wasn't going to say anything to your dad, but the scaffolders let slip about the guard rail. I just played it down. Didn't want to worry him.'

'Thanks, appreciate that,' replied Nate. 'He gave me that list you provided him with. You know, with the housing people.'

'That's good, I thought he might throw it on the fire along with the—' Rhoda stopped in mid-sentence. She hadn't meant to blurt that out.

'Along with what?' asked Nate slowly.

'I haven't had a chance to tell you yet.' She glanced towards the door, which was closed, and lowered her voice. 'I came down for a glass of water last night and your dad was burning some papers.'

'He's always burning something,' said Nate. 'Doesn't believe in shredding anything.'

Rhoda hesitated, mulling over her choice of words, but ultimately deciding just to say it straight. 'They were the missing ledger envelopes from upstairs.'

'What? Are you sure? How do you know?'

'Not everything burned. I found some bits in the fireplace. I took some pictures. I'll send them to you.'

'I don't know what to make of that,' confessed Nate. 'Why would he be burning the ledgers and what's he doing with them anyway?'

'He obviously doesn't want us to find something out.'

'Like what work was carried out at the chapel.'

Rhoda could hear the confusion in Nate's voice. 'He must know something. I'm really sorry, Nate, but that can be the only reason.'

'I don't get it.' There was a long silence before Nate spoke again. 'Look, do me a favour, Rhoda. Don't say anything to anyone yet. I need time to think about it all. I should speak to Dad, really. There might be a perfectly reasonable explanation.'

'Of course.'

Rhoda eyed the cupboard on the other side of the room. She didn't want to add to Nate's distress by mentioning the box. There might, after all, be nothing in there. She'd look first, and only tell him if she found anything useful. In the background, Rhoda could hear a voice saying something to Nate.

'Sorry, I've to go,' said Nate. 'Isaac's up. See you in the morning. About eleven o'clock, after Isaac's swimming lesson.'

'Sure. Night.'

Rhoda sat there for several minutes, deliberating about looking in the box. It had seemed like a really good idea until now. Was she going to unleash a heap of pain on to Nate if she did? Would she be throwing suspicion on Jack?

How would she feel if at any time, someone out there had found Dean's remains – she winced at the thought – and they'd decided not to do anything about it? Rhoda acknowledged that, at this point in time, all she wanted to know was if he was alive and safe, or if he was dead. She needed to move out of this state of limbo; it wasn't a healthy place to be. With that overriding thought, she knew she had to push on with trying to find out who the man was who had been buried in the chapel. It wasn't about upsetting Nate – sure, that came into it, but it wasn't the basis of all decisions. The body in the chapel deserved to be acknowledged, their identity known, their family informed and, possibly, the victim given a proper burial.

With a new-found sense of purpose, Rhoda went over to the cabinet and, stretching on tiptoe, she was able to reach the vase at the top. She could hear the key tinkle inside it as she brought the vase down. She tipped the key into her hand.

'Right, let's see what Jack is hiding,' she whispered.

The box wasn't as heavy as she'd imagined, and she lifted it out onto the floor before removing the lid. There were several bottle green folders, the type that usually hung in a filing cabinet. Inside were papers which, as far as Rhoda could tell, were bills and invoices for the farm. Each hanging file was labelled with a year; these dated back to the 1970s. Nate had been right when he said his dad wasn't such a meticulous record-keeper as Louise Hartwell had been.

Rhoda lifted the files out, giving the contents a quick flick through as she did, to make sure it wasn't anything important. The last folder had a brown A4 envelope inside. Rhoda's pulse rate quickened for no particular reason, other than she sensed she had found something important.

As she took the folder out, underneath that she saw something that made her gasp.

A dark green leather-bound book with gold lettering embossed on the cover.

HOLY BIBLE

HARTWELL FAMILY

Rhoda pulled the Bible out and, with shaking hands, opened the front cover. Inside, as Nate had said, was a list of names and dates stretching back to 1901.

She took a moment to absorb the fact that this book had been handed down through the Hartwell family for all those years. The ink was black and a little faded, but still clearly legible. She swept her hand across the page, imagining all Nate's ancestors who had held this Bible and written the births, marriages and deaths of family members inside the cover.

The clock on the mantelpiece chimed eleven, jolting Rhoda from her thoughts, reminding her of what she was looking for.

She ran her finger down the page until she got to the mid-1930s, where it showed the marriage of George Hartwell to Louise Charlotte Morris in 1933 – they must have been Jack's parents. Louise Morris had become Louise Hartwell when she married. Rhoda moved down to the next line.

John Charles Hartwell, born 1936.

Rhoda knew from the museum's paperwork on the sale of the chapel, that Jack's real name was John, the name Jack being a common nickname for the latter, so that was obviously his birth recorded in the Bible. After that, the records had stopped. No other names were listed. Rhoda wondered why Jack's wife hadn't carried on the tradition. It troubled her far more than it should that Nate wasn't mentioned. It was almost as if he didn't exist. There was no entry for Louise Hartwell's death, either, or for Jack's father's death. The page looked unfinished and forgotten – an incomplete family history.

Carefully, Rhoda repacked the box, ensuring all the documents went back in the same order she'd found them, before returning the box to the cupboard and locking it up. She dropped the key back into the vase.

Rhoda couldn't help thinking of Dean. Would his life only be marked by his birth, and never his death? Would she be forever in this state of limbo, like the unfinished records in the Bible? She wasn't sure she could carry on like this – always wondering, always hoping, never knowing. Perhaps she needed to accept she'd just never know what had happened to her brother. The idea pained her, but she also acknowledged the pain that always looking for him had brought her. Which was the lesser of the two evils? She thought of Nate, and for the first time she realised she might have some sort of future beyond Dean's disappearance. She just had to be brave enough to cross that line.

33
Alice

1945

The morning after the awful incident of Billy urinating on Paolo's bed, Paolo was very quiet at the breakfast table. Alice could sense the tension in his body the moment he walked into the room. Billy was sitting at the head of the table and bade Paolo a cheery good morning.

'Did you sleep well?' he asked, clearly enjoying himself.

Paolo chose not to answer, and Alice spoke to avoid an awkward silence. 'Glad we didn't have any rain last night. I think the weather is going to be nice today.'

It was banal conversation, but it was better than listening to Billy bait Paolo.

'Oh, yes, let's hope so,' said Mrs Hartwell. 'I've got a long journey ahead of me today.'

Mrs Hartwell was going to spend a few days with her sister, Mrs Armitage, and was travelling by train that morning. She'd already asked Alice if she wanted to write her father a letter, but after consideration, Alice had decided against it. What was there to say, really? He certainly wouldn't want to hear about her pregnancy or anything to do with it.

'Can you just pass on my regards and tell him I was asking after him,' she'd said instead.

Mrs Hartwell was now questioning Paolo about the repairs to the window. This was a subject he was usually only too happy to talk about, but even this didn't lighten his mood or elicit any more than the bare minimum of words from him. If Mrs Hartwell noticed, she didn't say anything. She was suitably encouraging and grateful for the hard work Paolo was putting into fixing the window.

'Now, do let me know if you need any more materials,' she said. 'I know they're a bit hard to come by at the moment, but not impossible.'

'I have everything I need,' replied Paolo. 'Thank you.'

'I should bloody well hope so,' snipped Billy. 'Costs us enough money as it is.'

'It will be worth it,' said Mrs Hartwell. 'Now, everyone, I must love you and leave you. Billy, can you get the car ready? I'll be needing to leave in thirty minutes. I'd like Paolo to drive me to the station.'

'What?' Billy put down his fork. 'He can't drive you. That's ridiculous.'

'He most certainly can if I ask him to,' replied Mrs Hartwell.

'He needs a chaperone if he leaves the farm.'

'Then he will have one. Alice, be a dear and come along in the car with me this morning and chaperone Paolo back.'

Alice had to stop herself from grinning. 'Yes, of course,' she replied. *Ha!* That would put a stop to Billy's gallop.

'Now, don't argue,' Mrs Hartwell said firmly to Billy. 'I've made up my mind. I want you here to take the vicar up to the chapel. He's going to bless it for me.' And then she added, 'You might get him to bless you at the same time.'

Alice had to stop herself from laughing out loud at that one. Billy didn't disguise his feelings, though. Huffing and puffing, muttering under his breath about the 'bloody vicar' and the 'bloody chapel', he pushed his chair back and left the room with as much strop as he could muster.

Alice sat in the back of the car alongside Mrs Hartwell as Paolo expertly drove them to the station to catch the 9.30 to London, where Mrs Hartwell was changing trains for her second leg of the journey to the Suffolk countryside.

'Now, Alice, I'll be back at the end of the week,' she explained. 'On Friday we have the Eggars coming to see you.'

'Again?' They were nice people, but Alice really didn't want to see them. It was a harsh reminder of why she was at Telton Hall and what she'd have to give up in a few months' time. She just couldn't bear thinking about it.

'Well, they couldn't come last time because of the storm, so they asked to come on Friday. I couldn't very well say no. Besides, we don't want to put them off now, do we?'

Alice forced herself to agree with Mrs Hartwell. She gazed out of the window, not taking in the scenery, but instead imagining life beyond her due date without her baby. She knew she'd spend the rest of her life wondering about her child and what had happened to them, how their life was working out. She knew that every year on her child's birthday, she would think of them – not that she wouldn't be thinking of them every day for the rest of her life – but she knew the birthdays would be poignant and difficult. And what about the child? Would they ever wonder about their real mother? Or would they think badly of her for giving them up? She'd probably never know, and not knowing would torture her every single day.

'Mrs Hartwell,' she said, turning in her seat to look at the older woman. 'Will I be able to leave a letter for the baby … you know, for when it's older?'

'A letter? Saying what?'

'Saying I'm sorry.' Alice swallowed a lump that had appeared in her throat. 'Explaining I had no choice.'

Mrs Hartwell gave Alice a sympathetic smile. 'We can certainly ask the Eggars if that's possible.'

'What if they say no?' The fear was clawing at her heart and punching her stomach. 'How will the child ever know?'

'Don't upset yourself now, dear. It's for the best the child's life is as uncomplicated as possible.'

Alice felt a tear spill from her eye. She swiped it away. 'What if the child wants to find me? How will they know where I am?'

'Not all children want to find their real mothers,' said Mrs Hartwell. 'I don't mean to upset you, but it's best if I'm honest. Some of them are very happy with their adoptive parents, but if they ever did wonder about their real mothers, they would only need to contact me. Of course, it's all done legally, so the child may wish to contact the authorities who might be able to help them. I keep a record of the mothers who come to stay with me, along with details of their child and details of who adopted them. It's unofficial, but I like to create a social history that will be here long after I'm gone.'

More tears fell from Alice's eyes. 'And have many children come back to find their real mothers?'

'I can't answer that, I'm afraid. I've only been doing this for the past few years, since my husband died. So, you see, none of the children are old enough to know or to find out yet.'

Alice sat back in her seat, trying to make sense of the morass of emotions that were spinning around and around inside her.

Having dropped Mrs Hartwell off at the station, Alice was in the front seat next to Paolo as they drove back towards Telton. 'I'm sorry about the ring,' she said. 'I forgot to take it off and Billy saw it. He practically yanked it from my hand. I'm sure he would happily have cut my finger off to get it.'

'I understand. Do not worry. I will make you a new one.'

'No! Don't. If he finds it, he'll report you for theft of the coin.'

Paolo frowned. 'I do not think that is a crime.'

'I don't know, but I don't want to put it to the test.'

Alice put her head back against the seat and closed her eyes. It was nice, just the two of them being somewhere different on their own. Alice tried to push away thoughts of the fate of her baby, as she imagined what it would be like if there had been no war and Paolo wasn't a POW. Instead of lifting her spirits, it only served to dampen them.

'You look sad,' commented Paolo. 'What is wrong?'

So much for trying to pretend she was anything but all right. She sat up and opened her eyes. 'I'm scared,' she said finally.

Paolo pulled the car over to the side of the road and twisted around so he was facing her, one hand across the back of her seat. 'Scared?'

'I'm scared I'm going to regret giving up the baby,' admitted Alice. 'I'm scared I'll never know what happens to it. I'm scared the Eggars won't look after the baby properly.' An unexpected sob escaped her throat.

Paolo pulled her towards him, holding her with both arms around her, his chin resting gently on top of her head. Alice cried her heart out. All the pent-up emotion came pouring out at once. She clung to Paolo as if he were a lifebelt and she were being tossed around in a force 9 gale in the middle of the ocean. She didn't want to ever let him go.

'It's all right,' comforted Paolo after a while. 'Cry. It is good for the soul sometimes.'

Alice was unaware of time and felt she'd sobbed for an age. Finally, she pulled away from Paolo, her breath still catching as the tears subsided. Paolo passed her a handkerchief, and she blew her nose. 'I'm sorry.'

'Do not apologise.' He brushed away a strand of hair from the side of her face. 'Is there no other answer?'

'I can't keep the baby. How can I? A single mother. It would be different if I had been married before Brett died – a widow would be all right but a single mother is different. I think I could withstand it, but the stigma attached to the baby as it grew up would be unbearable.' She wiped her nose again. 'It's not just that, it's the practical side. How can I ever hope to give the child all the things it deserves in life? I would be penniless.'

'You could give the child love. There is nothing more important for a child than the love of their parents.'

'But love doesn't buy shoes for their feet, clothes for their back or put food on the table.' The words came out more harshly than she meant them to, and she saw the look of hurt flit across Paolo's face. 'Sorry. I'm not cross at you. I'm cross at myself for not being able to provide the basic things a child needs.'

Paolo stroked her face. 'I understand. I wish I could offer you some hope, or an answer.'

'It's not your problem, but thank you, it's kind of you to be so concerned.' Alice took a deep, steadying breath. 'We'd better get back. I dare say Billy is clock-watching, and if we're late it will just give him something else to moan about.'

When they arrived back at Telton Hall, after putting the car away in the garage, Paolo went up to the chapel and Alice went to the kitchen. Lily was peeling potatoes and Cook was kneading dough.

Alice could see from the look on Lily's face something was wrong, but she gave a small shake of her head and Alice knew not to ask.

'Ah, there you are,' said Cook. 'Mrs H get off all right, did she?'

'Yes. No problems. Can I do anything to help?'

'Can you just see where Jack and Aggie are?' asked

Cook. 'I haven't seen them all morning, and I want Jack to get some elderflower so I can make a cordial. Whilst you're at it, can you collect the eggs, too?'

Alice did a quick search of the house before heading out into the garden. With still no sign of the youngsters, she widened her search to the outbuildings. As she was just about to open the gate at the rear of the kitchen garden, it swung open and Paolo stormed through. His face was contorted with rage. His hand was gripping a piece of stained glass.

'Paolo! Whatever's wrong?'

'Mind out of my way, Alice.'

'Not until you tell me what's happened?' There was no way she was going to let Paolo march into the house. He clearly wasn't in control of his temper. She put both hands on his chest to physically stop him. 'Tell me – what's happened?'

Paolo breathed heavily through his nose as his jaw clenched. Finally, he was composed enough to speak. 'The window at the chapel has been broken. On purpose. Someone has smashed the glass I made.'

'Oh no! You're sure it was on purpose? Could it have fallen?' Alice's mind raced through the possibilities.

'It is all in place on the table, as I set it out, but someone has broken five pieces of glass. They are all cracked. It has not fallen on the floor, and nothing has fallen from above. The hammer was placed on the glass as a sign to show it was done on purpose.'

'Who did it?' Alice was sure she didn't really need to ask.

'Who do you think?' Paolo went to sidestep her, but Alice stood firm.

'I don't know what you're going to do, but whatever it is, you mustn't. You can't go accusing him. He will only deny it. He's trying to get you to do something stupid so he can have you arrested or sent back to the camp. You must not play his game. Do you hear me?' She gripped the tops of his arms and felt the muscles contract.

'I do not care.'

'I do! I care very much.' She looked him straight in the eye. 'I don't want anything to happen to you. Please, don't do this. Please. I couldn't bear being here without you.'

Alice surprised herself with the emotion in her voice. She hadn't even realised up until that point that she felt so strongly about Paolo, but now she'd made it clear to both of them. He looked down at her and she could feel the tension lessen in his biceps.

'You mean that?' he asked.

'Yes.'

He nodded an understanding and the rage in his face dissolved. 'I will go and find Carlo. We start again on the glass.'

The sound of the gate opening behind Paolo made them both look around.

'Oh, Jack, Aggie,' said Alice. 'I've just been looking for you. Glad you've appeared – that saves me hunting around in the barns and stables.'

The two youngsters exchanged a furtive look. Jack's gaze immediately went to his feet, while Aggie stood taller and jutted out her chin. 'We were up at the chapel, weren't we, Jack?'

'Yeah,' mumbled Jack.

'The chapel?' Paolo looked confused. 'I was there, but I did not see you.'

'We went to the woods after,' said Aggie quickly. She gave Jack a nudge.

'Yeah. The woods.'

Alice looked suspiciously from one child to the other. 'Did you see anything at the chapel? Was anyone else in there?'

'We didn't go in,' said Aggie quickly. 'Just went to look at the fallen tree. Anyway, why did you want us?'

'Cook's looking for you,' said Alice. 'She wants you to pick some elderflower.'

'All right. Come on, Jack. Let's go.' Aggie took hold of Jack's wrist and trailed him past Paolo and Alice as she hurried down the path and into the kitchen.

'Before you say anything,' said Paolo. 'No. I do not believe either of them would damage the glass. Jack has been interested in what I am doing. Neither of them would do it.'

'I know. That only leaves one person, and he would definitely do it.'

'Exactly. Now, I must go and find Carlo.'

'I'll come with you. I need to get the eggs.'

'Do you need to get the basket?'

'I'll use one of the buckets from the stables.'

Alice was relieved Paolo's temper had died down now. She was desperately sorry for him. She knew how much he loved working on the window and how much comfort he got from it. To have it sabotaged was outrageous, and it made it all the more frustrating that there wasn't a single thing either of them could do about it.

Paolo pushed the door to the barn open and called out to his friend. 'Carlo! Carlo!'

He stopped mid-stride; said something in Italian before quickly turning around to try to stop Alice from entering the barn. It was too late; she was already at his side.

Alice let out a scream at the sight before her, before burying her face in Paolo's chest.

24 June 1945

Carissime Mamma e Sofia

I received your letter yesterday and am relieved to hear you are well.

I still don't know when I will be repatriated but I have been thinking very carefully about this.

I have become very fond of Alice, who lives here at Telton Hall. The one who is expecting a baby very soon. She is in turmoil about whether to put it up for adoption or not. I think I know how to solve her dilemma, if she will listen to me, that is. I won't say any more until I have spoken to her, but as soon as I have news, I will let you know.

I have to admit I will be glad to get away from this place. My dear friend and comrade Carlo met with a tragic death last week. I still cannot believe it's happened. He fell from the hayloft in the stable. Or so they say. I must confess, I find it hard to accept this version of events. The police have not bothered looking into it properly. They don't care about another POW who has died. One less for them to worry about, as far as they are concerned. I KNOW who is behind his death. I do not believe it was an accident. It just wouldn't happen that way. There are too many coincidences. I don't know what I'm going to do yet, but I am going to make sure there is justice for Carlo. Don't worry about me, I am not stupid and won't do anything rash, but I will not let the matter just be swept away.

Until we see each other again, which I hope will be soon.

Il vostro amorevole figlio e fratello

Paolo

34
Rhoda

2022

It was a struggle to get out of bed the next morning. Rhoda had replaced the box in the living room and popped the key back in the vase, but even then, once she had gone to bed, her mind was wide awake, thinking about her brother and the crossroads she now found herself at. Could she really leave Dean behind? Even her relaxation app had been of little use and eventually she had drifted off into a disturbed sleep. She woke several times from dreams of trying to reach Dean but coming up against closed doors and obstacles constantly in her way.

Sitting on the edge of the bed, she reached for her phone to check Facebook for any alerts. There was a message on Dean's missing page. Rhoda had long since stopped getting excited about these messages; they were usually just someone who wanted to share a memory of her brother privately, or who was in the same boat as her and looking for a loved one. She opened the message and read it. This one was neither.

James Smith

I have information about your brother Dean.

There was no profile picture – just the standard Facebook white silhouette graphic of an anonymous head and shoulders. Rhoda clicked on the profile. There was absolutely no personal information whatsoever. No friends. No photos. No posts. Nothing.

It was probably some crank. She'd had this a couple of times. Someone who thought it was funny to try to get her hopes up. A sick individual who enjoyed making more misery for someone else. Preying on their fears.

Despite this knowledge, Rhoda also knew she couldn't ignore it. Her earlier thoughts of not actively pursuing her brother were instantly dismissed. What if this was genuine and she deleted it? What if this was the one lead she had to finding Dean? She wouldn't be able to live without knowing.

She sent a reply.

Hello. Can you give me some more information so I know this is genuine? Sorry, but I have to ask. Thanks. Rhoda Sullivan.

Leaving her phone on the bedside table, she went for a shower. It was better than sitting there staring at her mobile, waiting for a reply which may or may not arrive.

Twenty minutes later, she was dressed and had dried her hair with a hairdryer Nate had bought from the shop. He was thoughtful like that, and she appreciated it. She wasn't used to being considered by anyone else – but it was quite nice, she had to admit.

Rhoda picked up her phone. She had a reply already.

I've spoken to him. We lodged at the same B & B. He said he had a sister called Rhodes.

Rhoda's mouth dried instantly. Dean called her Rhodes sometimes. No one else did, just her brother. This James Smith wouldn't know that unless he'd spoken to Dean himself.

Her hand shook as she typed the reply.

I believe you. What can you tell me?

She watched the three dots pulsate as her reply was read, and then they disappeared. He'd gone.

'No!' Rhoda cried out loud.

She closed the app and reopened it, in case it was some technical issue, but James Smith remained offline. She updated the message three times in the hope that his reply was drifting in cyberspace, waiting to hit her message box. But nothing appeared.

She sat there for another frustrating five minutes before finally resigning herself to having to exercise patience. Maybe James Smith had to attend to something important, or had been interrupted, or was at work – there could be a multitude of reasons why he hadn't replied.

Rhoda pushed her phone into her back pocket and headed downstairs to grab a bite to eat. By the time she'd reached the kitchen, her phone had beeped through two text messages. One was from Nate, just saying good morning and that he'd be over at lunchtime after Isaac's swimming lesson. Rhoda sent a reply saying she was looking forward to seeing him. She didn't mention the little tingle of excitement that zipped through her at the prospect.

The other message wasn't anywhere as exciting. It was from Vince Taylor.

Hello dear can I come and see the window this morning? I am busy next week and cannot come over. Sorry to be a nuisance but I'd love to see how you are getting on.

Rhoda couldn't think of a logical reason why not. It wasn't as if she had any plans that morning. Over the course of a few messages, they agreed he would call by at 9.30, about an hour later. It would give her a good distraction, she decided.

'Good morning.' Jack came into the kitchen. 'Did you sleep well?'

'Morning,' said Rhoda. 'Yes. Fine, thanks. Tea?'

'Silly question.' Jack winked at her and took his seat at the table.

'There you go.'

'Lovely. Looks a nice strong brew.'

Rhoda sat down opposite him with her tea. 'Vince Taylor from the local historical society is coming over again this morning.'

'Is he?' Jack didn't sound very impressed by the idea.

'That's if you don't mind,' said Rhoda quickly. 'Do you want me to see if I can cancel him?'

'Bit late now, I suppose.'

Rhoda picked up her phone, feeling embarrassed that she'd assumed Jack would be all right with the visit. The number just rang out. 'He's not picking up.' She tried a couple of more times without success. 'Sorry, Jack.'

'Don't worry about it now.'

Rhoda took a sip of her tea, eyeing her host over the rim of the cup. She put the cup down. 'Jack, what is it about Vince Taylor you don't like? He seems pretty harmless to me, if I'm honest. He's just taken a keen interest in the chapel window, that's all.' When he didn't answer, she continued. 'We get visitors like that all the time at the museum. It's lovely really, to find like-minded people who are genuinely interested in the history and the craft. I think Vince is simply an enthusiast.'

'I need to get on,' said Jack abruptly, getting up from his chair. 'Going to take Tink for a walk and pop over to see Aggie.'

Wow, she'd really upset him today. Rhoda could kick herself for being so presumptuous. The chapel was a very sensitive subject for Jack, and she should have realised.

An incoming text message from Nate, instantly cheered her up.

Looking forward to seeing you too.

It really shouldn't be that big a deal, but there was that tingle of excitement again.

Vince Taylor arrived at 9.30 on the dot in his 4 × 4. Rhoda watched from the living room window as he got out of the vehicle and went to make his way over to the door, but after a few strides, he returned to his car to fetch his walking stick. She gave her phone one last check for a message from James Smith, before going out to greet Vince.

She already had her jacket and boots on. If they went straight up to the chapel, rather than hanging around chatting, then he would be gone sooner – hopefully before Jack returned.

'Lovely morning,' remarked Vince as they made their way up the hill. When they reached the chapel, he stood looking out across the vista. 'What a view. Shame to think all this is going to be smothered in houses in the not too distant future.'

'Yes, it really is a shame,' agreed Rhoda, unlocking the chapel door.

'How's the research going on the body?' asked Vince in a conspiratorial way. 'Know who it is yet?'

Rhoda wasn't sure she liked the patronising way he'd loaded the question, but she let it go. 'Not yet.'

'Who's been shortlisted as prime suspect?'

'No comment,' said Rhoda, trying to make light of it.

They walked into the chapel.

'Very intriguing. You sound like quite the detective.' Vince gave a small laugh.

'I don't know about that.' Rhoda's thoughts automatically went to Dean, and she found herself checking her phone while Vince took a closer look at the work she'd been doing that week. There was still no message from James Smith.

'Is everything all right?' asked Vince. 'You seem a little preoccupied this morning.'

'I'm fine,' Rhoda replied, smiling probably wider than

necessary. She slipped her phone back in her pocket. 'Just waiting on a message from someone.'

Vince looked at the glass for a moment, before looking back at Rhoda. 'This business with the body – do you think it's worth all the trouble you're going to? I mean, even if you find out who the body is, what good will that do?'

'Justice. That's what good it will do,' said Rhoda, trying to keep the defensive tone from her voice. She was sick of having to explain this to people all the time. 'People can't get away with murder. Why should they? Why should this poor man have no justice? Why can't his family know he's been found, so their agony of not knowing can be stopped and they can put their loved one to rest?'

'But the murderer is probably dead themselves, or at least in their nineties,' Vince pushed on. 'You'd take a ninety-year-old to court for murder?'

'Yes. Yes, I would. There's no time limit on justice. Just because you're old, it doesn't make you less culpable.'

'You sound very determined.'

'That's because I am,' retorted Rhoda.

He nodded and turned his attention back to the glass. 'This is amazing ... to see the craftsmanship in this window up close. To think no one had touched this before now – only the POW. Have you been in contact with the Italian who made this?'

'I haven't been able to find out much about him,' confessed Rhoda. 'The records were destroyed soon after they were all repatriated.' She glanced over towards the shallow grave where the bones had been found. 'I've put an enquiry in to the Italian military records office, but I'm not holding out much luck.'

'Do you think he could be your mystery man?'

'It's possible. I've no firm evidence. Most of it is just notions in my head with no proof to back it up.'

'But you have a theory?'

'Not really.' Rhoda needed to divert the conversation. 'So, this is the last of the smaller windows. I'm going to start on the main one next.'

She let Vince browse for a few more minutes. He was nice, but he wasn't in any hurry to leave, and Rhoda was aware Jack didn't really like him being there.

Vince looked around the chapel, his gaze resting on the main window. 'I don't suppose I could have a look up there, could I? Would you show me how you take it out of the walls?'

'Up there? On the scaffolding?' Rhoda tried not to sound too surprised. 'It's not that easy to get up.'

'Oh, I'm more agile than you think.' Vince was walking towards the end of the chapel. 'Just for a few minutes.'

'I don't know if you should.' How was she going to dissuade him? 'The insurance doesn't cover you. I could get into trouble.'

'Nonsense. The world has gone crazy with insurance. All that health and safety nonsense.' Vince was at the foot of the scaffolding. 'Come on, just a quick look.'

'Honestly, I'd rather we didn't.'

If Vince had heard her, he'd decided to ignore her. Discarding his walking stick, which Rhoda was beginning to suspect was purely for aesthetic purposes, he began his ascent up the side of the scaffolding.

'See, I'm quite capable,' he called as he reached the first platform.

Rhoda groaned and followed him up the tower. If she quickly showed him how the glass was held in, then the quicker they could get down again. To be fair, Vince was very capable of climbing to the top of the tower. Rhoda was surprised.

'You've done that before,' she said, coming to stand next to him.

'Once or twice. It's rather nice up here in the gods. Wouldn't want to fall.' He looked over the edge of the guard rail.

Rhoda's stomach did a little somersault, not just at the glib comment, but also at the memory of the warning note she'd received. All of a sudden, it was a really bad idea being up here. 'We should get down.'

'But we haven't had a look at the fixings yet,' protested Vince.

'We shouldn't be up here.' Rhoda went to turn, but felt Vince grab her elbow. His fingers dug into her flesh. She gave a small cry of pain and twisted around. 'What are you doing?'

Vince's gaze locked with hers; his lip curled as he went to speak, and his hand gripped her a little harder, pulling her nearer the edge.

The sound of the door opening, and Jack's voice calling out, had Vince letting go and moving away. He grabbed the guard rail with both hands. 'I'm so sorry. I got dizzy then.'

'We really need to get you down. Do you think you can manage it?'

'Hey!' shouted Jack. 'What on earth are you doing up there?'

'We're just coming down,' called back Rhoda.

Great, just what she needed – a witness to Vince's reckless act and her inability to stop him.

They clambered down the scaffolding and Rhoda was relieved once Vince's feet were firmly on the ground again.

'Probably time you were on your way,' said Jack stiffly.

'Yes,' said Vince. 'Of course. Sorry to have taken up so much of your time.'

'It's fine,' replied Rhoda. 'No problem.' That wasn't strictly true, but it was the easiest thing to say. 'I'll walk you back.'

Ten minutes later, Vince Taylor was driving away from Telton Hall.

'Good riddance to that,' said Jack. 'Bloody dangerous, going up that scaffolding. What did you think you were doing?'

'Sorry. I tried to stop him, but he was climbing up before I knew what was happening. I thought I'd better get up there with him, at least to make sure he was safe.' Rhoda rubbed her face with her hand. 'Sorry. I shouldn't have agreed to him coming in the first place.'

'You can say that again.'

Feeling fully chastised, Rhoda went back to the house and up to her room, making an excuse that she needed to make a few phone calls and check her emails. The truth was, she was embarrassed, and didn't want to have to face Jack for a while.

In the safety of her room, Rhoda lay down on her bed and closed her eyes. Her anxiety was having a field day. She hadn't felt this way for a long time. The anticipation of a reply from James Smith was making her heart race and her legs fidgety. Nervous energy was building up inside her, with no outlet. She sat up on the edge of the bed. This was no good. She'd have to get some fresh air and try to calm herself that way.

Rhoda's phone pinged out an alert into the silent room and her body flinched in response.

She grabbed her phone. It was a message from James Smith.

I have someone who wants to see you. Meet me at Telverton Viaduct. Be there at 12.

Rhoda stared at the screen. Her stomach lurched and she thought for a moment she was going to be sick.

She read it again before springing into action.

Where the hell was Telverton in relation to where she was now? Did she have enough time to get there? Someone wanted to see her? *Could it be Dean? Oh God, please let it be Dean. Please.*

35
Alice

1945

The sight of Carlo's body lying on the floor of the barn – his leg twisted back at an agonising angle, his head to one side further than a neck should stretch, and his eyes wide open, staring up to the heavens – shook Alice to the core. She could not get the image out of her mind; it haunted her for days and days.

In the aftermath of Carlo's death, Alice had been ordered to take bed rest by the midwife, whom Cook had called out. Mrs Hartwell returned early from her visit to her sister's, and the local police descended on Telton Hall as they tried to work out the sequence of events.

Paolo had been devastated by the death of his friend and Alice longed to comfort him, but being confined to her bed, it wasn't possible. It was made worse by the knowledge that he was just above her in the attic room. At night, she stared up at the ceiling, hoping in some way Paolo would know she was thinking of him.

She listened for movement on the floor above and tracked him as he got up in the mornings, dressed and went downstairs. That morning he had paused on the landing near her bedroom, and she wondered if he was looking towards her door. It had been four days since the incident. Alice had seen no one except for Lily, Mrs Hartwell and the midwife. The latter was coming to see her again today, and Alice hoped to convince her that she was well enough to be allowed to leave her room.

The Eggars had been on the phone every day, asking how she was. In the light of recent events, their visit had been postponed yet again. The further along she got in her pregnancy, the more upsetting the idea was that she would have to give up her baby.

Around mid-morning, Alice heard the wheels of a vehicle pulling up on the driveway and the sound of two car doors slamming almost simultaneously. The bell rang, and shortly after, she could hear a deep voice talking to Cook.

It sounded like two men, and Alice assumed they were the police. When Mrs Hartwell's voice could be heard – 'Good morning, Officer' – this confirmed it. No doubt it was about Carlo. Alice hoped that they were here to arrest Billy. She had absolutely no proof of Billy's involvement whatsoever, but she felt sure he was responsible in some way. Carlo wouldn't have simply fallen from the hayloft.

A short while after the policemen left, Lily appeared in the room. 'Mrs Hartwell said I was to come and see you,' she said. 'The police are treating Carlo's death as an accident.'

'What? That's so wrong!'

'Now, now, Alice. Don't go getting yourself all worked up, especially not with the midwife coming to see you today. She won't let you get up if your blood pressure is sky-high.'

Alice gritted her teeth. Of course, Lily was right, but still the injustice was agonising. 'I can't believe they're not even going to investigate it properly.'

'Apparently, they have. They've questioned everyone who was here. They gave Paolo a good grilling. Billy kept saying Paolo was the one who found Carlo, he was also the last person to see Carlo alive, and all that sort of stuff.'

'He's a bastard,' snapped Alice. She didn't care she was swearing, and she certainly wasn't going to apologise for the fact. 'Why didn't they question Billy properly. He was the one with a grudge against Carlo and Paolo. He's the one who's remotely strong enough to push Carlo from the hayloft.'

'Yes, but he's claiming he can't get up there with his dodgy leg.'

'I'm bloody sure he can.'

'Yes. So am I.' Lily gave her a sympathetic smile. 'Anyway, the police said Carlo died from a broken neck which was consistent with falling from a height. They are going to advise it to be treated as an accident.'

'What did Paolo say?'

'He hasn't said much.'

'How are you?'

Alice knew Lily had become good friends with Carlo. Their relationship may have only been one of friendship, but she knew Lily would be upset.

Lily shrugged. 'I'm really sad. I liked Carlo a lot. Not in the way you like Paolo, but ... you know what I mean.'

'Of course I know what you mean. Come here.' Alice put her arms around her friend and hugged her. She wished she could comfort Paolo in the same way.

Lily sat back. 'Do you really think Billy did it? You know – pushed Carlo.'

'Look, I've had a lot of time to think about it,' said Alice. 'You know about the glass in the window being broken – the one Paolo was restoring.'

'No. What's that?'

'It must have got forgotten in all the commotion about Carlo,' said Alice, frowning. 'When we got back from dropping Mrs Hartwell at the station, Paolo went up to the chapel.' Alice went on to explain how she'd intercepted Paolo in the kitchen garden. 'And I'll tell you something else, I'm sure Aggie and Jack know more than they're letting on. They looked petrified when they came in the garden. Made up some flimsy excuse about where they'd been. I didn't believe them, but I was too busy calming Paolo down to ask them. I intended to speak to them later, but then all hell broke loose when me and Paolo found Carlo's body.'

She shivered as the image of Carlo lying on the stable floor came back to mind.

'So what are you saying?' asked Lily. 'That Billy killed Carlo by pushing him?'

'Basically, yes. Maybe Carlo caught him up at the chapel, breaking the glass. Maybe they had a big argument and somehow Billy lured Carlo up to the loft and then pushed him. Or maybe they just got into a fight up there and it was an accident.'

'But you can't prove any of this.'

'No. But what if Jack and Aggie saw him up at the chapel, and are now too scared to say anything?'

'It doesn't prove anything, though,' replied Lily. 'I know what you're saying, and I agree, it sounds plausible – probable, even – but without any proof. Even if the kids do say Billy was at the chapel, there are still no witnesses or proof that he pushed Carlo.'

'I'm going to speak to Aggie and Jack as soon as I'm allowed out of this bloody bed,' said Alice, feeling the frustration building up inside her. 'Where's the midwife? I wish she'd hurry up.'

'As I said, don't go getting yourself all worked up. She'll be here soon. Look, I'd better go. See you later.'

Lily gave Alice a hug and then left the room.

The midwife came and finally gave Alice the all-clear to get up, as long as she was especially careful for a few days. Alice had duly promised, and as soon as the midwife left, she was up out of bed, getting dressed. She wanted to find Paolo. She knew he must be hurting after the loss of his friend, and that he would feel there had been a great injustice – as, indeed, she felt herself. All she wanted to do was to put her arms around him and offer him some sort of comfort, much the same as he had offered her over the past few weeks.

Alice slipped out of the front door without being noticed and made her way around the side of the house, taking the long route, avoiding going through the kitchen garden so Cook didn't spot her.

Just to be extra careful, she took the circuitous route up

to the chapel, to again be out of sight, but also it was less steep, if a little longer. Finally, she reached the chapel.

The door gave a small groan of protest as she eased it open, the sound giving her presence away to Paolo, who had stopped work in anticipation of the visitor.

His eyes grew wide, and for a fleeting moment there was happiness on his face. 'Alice!' Then his expression clouded over. 'What are you doing here? You're supposed to be in bed, resting.'

'The midwife came and said I could get up.' Suddenly Alice felt shy and apprehensive. 'I wanted to see you.'

There was a pensive silence as they looked at each other. Paolo placed his chisel on the workbench and approached her. 'I have been very worried about you.'

'I've been worried about you, too,' said Alice.

'I'm glad you came.' He held her hands at arm's length and surveyed her. 'Are you sure you should be out of bed?'

'Positive.' Alice couldn't help herself; she flung her arms around Paolo's neck and hugged him tightly. 'I'm so sorry about Carlo,' she whispered in his ear. 'So very sorry.'

Paolo held on to Alice for a long time. She wasn't sure if he was crying, but if he needed to let out his emotions, then she wasn't going to stop him. Even men cried. She knew that, despite what they liked to have you believe.

Eventually, Paolo composed himself and they sat down in one of the pews. 'I do not believe it was an accident,' he said.

'Neither do I,' Alice reassured him.

'I don't know how or why, but I am sure Billy is involved in some way.'

They spent several minutes discussing the various theories. Both agreed that they suspected Carlo had witnessed Billy's sabotage of the window and confronted Billy, which had ended in some sort of ruck and Carlo's fall.

'Billy must have lured Carlo up to the loft somehow,' said Alice.

'Billy is strong,' said Paolo. 'His leg might be damaged, but he has upper body strength. He could easily have got himself up there. Whether he meant to kill Carlo or not, I do not know. Maybe he just meant to injure him, but whatever, I do believe it was intentional.'

'It's just so awful.'

'It is. They buried Carlo yesterday. I attended the ceremony.'

'I'm so sorry, Paolo. I really am.'

The next few days passed gently by. Alice kept out of Billy's way as much as possible. She couldn't bear being in the same room as he was for more than a few minutes, and was glad no one questioned her when she used the excuse she was tired and needed to have a rest. Mrs Hartwell was very understanding, and insisted Alice didn't undertake any household duties for the time being.

By the time Alice had been up and about for a week after getting the all-clear from the midwife, Mrs Hartwell was reassured enough to rebook her visit to her sister.

'She's not been too well, and I would really like to see her,' Mrs Hartwell had explained. 'I won't be long. Just five days, like before. Now, you promise you will be careful, won't you, Alice? The Eggars are going to come and see you once I'm back. They've been very patient and, of course, concerned.'

Alice smiled and promised she'd be extra vigilant, as well as making the right noises about looking forward to seeing the Eggars, when in actual fact it was the last thing she wanted to do. However, she didn't want to upset Mrs Hartwell – not after the couple of weeks she'd had.

'Billy is driving me to the station today,' Mrs Hartwell continued. 'I think he needs something to do. He's been in an awfully bad mood recently. I think he's restless. He was talking about going to visit some of his old army chaps. It will probably do him some good.' She let out a sigh. 'I still have hopes that he will meet a nice girl one day and it will lift his spirits, but he's got to stop going around so bad-tempered to get a girl in the first place.' She tutted and gave a shake of her head.

Alice hoped that no woman would willingly get involved with Billy. He was rotten to the core and it would be a crying shame if some innocent girl got saddled with him.

Once Mrs Hartwell was on her way, Alice quickly prepared the vegetables for dinner. Cook was unwell and had had to take the day off. It was most unusual for Cook to be ill, and just bad luck it happened to be when Mrs Hartwell was going away. Alice and Lily had reassured Mrs Hartwell they could easily manage a couple of days and they were more than capable of looking after Jack. Besides, Aggie's mother was just over the road at the cottage should they need anything. Alice really didn't want Mrs Hartwell to miss out on the opportunity to visit her sister for a second time.

Somewhat reluctantly, but also gratefully, Mrs Hartwell had agreed.

'Right, that's that done,' said Alice, popping the lid on the saucepan of peeled potatoes. 'I'm going to nip up and see Paolo before Billy gets back.'

'Good idea,' said Lily. 'Mind how you go.'

Paolo greeted her warmly when she arrived at the chapel. 'I have missed you very much,' he said, echoing her own thoughts.

Alice was pleased he sounded more upbeat. He was still grieving for Carlo, but each day she noticed the chink of light in his eyes grow bigger.

'How are you getting on with the window?' she asked, walking around the workbench to admire his craftsmanship. 'This is so beautiful, Paolo. I wish I could see more of your work.'

He came to stand beside her. 'Maybe you can, one day.'

'Oh, I'd love that.'

Paolo rested his arm around her shoulder and went to say something, but before he could speak, the door to the chapel burst open and in raced Lily, with Aggie and Jack.

Instantly, Alice was on high alert. 'What's the matter?'

'It's Billy,' said Lily. The pupils of her eyes were dilated and Alice could see her body shaking. 'He's come back in a terrible temper. He's after Jack. I've brought him up here to hide him. I didn't know what else to do.'

'Why is he after Jack?' asked Paolo.

Alice was about to ask the same question, but, all of a sudden, she had a moment of clarity. She knew why.

36
Nate

2022

Nate was sitting poolside, sweating from the humidity in the leisure centre despite already stripping off his jumper. The cacophony of noise echoing around the building was at just the pitch that was torture to his ears. Still, Isaac was doing well, and every time he completed a length of the pool, he looked to check Nate had seen and was suitably impressed.

Nate's mobile phone vibrated in his pocket. It could only be Siobhan or Rhoda – they were the only one's he'd passed on his temporary number to. He'd ordered a new phone which would be available to pick up on Monday. Until then, he had one of Isaac's old phones which his own SIM card didn't fit.

It was Siobhan's number.

'Hi.'

He was surprised to hear Harrison speak.

'It's me – Harrison,' he said needlessly. 'Sorry to bother you, Nate, I can hear you're at the pool, but I wanted to check you'd got my message yesterday. Siobhan said your phone's broken or something.'

'Yeah, managed to get it run over.' Nate had a vague recollection of his phone ringing just as he was diving out of the way of the car. He hadn't told Siobhan about the car park incident. He didn't want to worry her, or for her to start thinking Isaac wasn't safe with him. Nate would be the judge of that. 'I didn't get your voicemail, if that's what you're asking.'

'No. It's about that Vince Taylor you asked me to check out.'

'OK,' said Nate, warily. He held his hand over his other ear to block out the noise of the swimming club.

'This is entirely off the record and I'm only doing it … Well, you know—'

'Out of guilt?' Nate couldn't help himself, and then regretted it as soon as the words were out of his mouth. 'Old times' sake.'

'Yeah, something like that.'

'So, off the record, what did you find out?' Nate gave Isaac a thumbs-up at his dive into the water and replaced his hand over his ear.

'Vincent Taylor is a retired secondary school teacher. Lives in Bristol. Married. Two children. No criminal record. Not known to the police in any way. Just a normal bloke.'

'Is that it? Is that what after nearly twenty years in the police force your detective skills amount to?' Nate was relieved on the one hand, but on the other, he still was uncertain. He needed more convincing.

'There's nothing else to say.'

'OK. Thanks.'

Nate ended the call and flopped back in the plastic seat, dropping his phone into the duffel bag at his feet.

Twenty minutes later, Nate was in the car with Isaac, heading towards Telton, when he heard the faint sound of a phone ringing.

'Is that your new phone?' asked Isaac as he scoffed a packet of crisps.

'Oh God. Yes. I'm still not used to the ringtone. It's in that bag on the back seat. Reach around and get it, can you, mate?'

Isaac didn't exactly rush, and by the time he'd got the bag and located the phone, it had stopped ringing. Nate hadn't set up voicemail on it yet. A message bleeped in.

'It's from Rhoda. Do you want me to read it to you?' asked Isaac, holding the phone flat in the palm of his hand.

'Yes, please.'

Sorry. Tried to call. Got a lead on Dean. Am going to the viaduct at Telverton.

'Wow. A lead on Dean.' Nate was surprised. Of course, it was good, but it was out of the blue and odd that she should be going to the viaduct. He presumed Rhoda didn't know about the viaduct, so he could only assume whoever she was meeting had suggested it. The idea was unsettling.

'What does she mean, she has a lead on Dean?' asked Isaac. 'He's not a dog.'

Nate smiled at his son. 'It's an expression. She doesn't

mean a dog lead, but a clue that will lead her to something. She's trying to find her brother.'

Nate wanted to keep things simple for Isaac, so he had a chance to process the basics before adding extra information.

'Is he still lost?' asked Isaac.

'Rhoda doesn't know where he is,' replied Nate, stopping at a set of lights. 'But someone else might. I thought she was seeing Vince Taylor this morning.'

'Vince Taylor? He's the old man from the history club.' Isaac peered inside his crisp packet and gave it a small shake. 'Taylor. T-A-Y-L-O-R. An occupational surname from the French word *tailleur*, meaning cutter.'

'Lots of surnames came from the occupation someone did.'

'I thought he was Italian.' Isaac tipped the crisp packet up to his mouth to catch the crumbs.

'Not with a name like Taylor,' said Nate.

Isaac wiped his mouth on the cuff of his sleeve, which earned him a disapproving look from Nate. 'There's a photograph of him standing by the Leaning Tower of Pisa, with a woman,' Isaac carried on.

'Probably went there on holiday. It's a famous tourist attraction. Where did you see this photograph, anyway?'

'On his website. It's in the background of his welcome page. He's sitting at his desk and it's behind him. Rhoda had it open on her laptop. She said I could look. It's not a very good website. Just got one page. Doesn't show anything to do with history stuff.' Isaac tapped at the screen of his phone and held it up to show Nate, and then zoomed in on the photograph. 'There. But he must live in Somerset now. Here's another one of him. He's standing on the viaduct. Is that the one Rhoda has gone to?'

Nate glanced over at the phone screen and caught a glimpse of the photo Isaac was showing him, before turning his attention back to the road. Telverton Viaduct was well known for its historic railway line. It wasn't that unusual that a local historian would have his photo taken standing underneath it.

They travelled on for a few minutes in silence. Nate's mind was whirring. He was missing something – something important, but he didn't know what. His conversation with Isaac was setting his nerves inexplicably on edge. What was he missing?

And then it dawned on him.

Nate hit the brakes, sending Isaac lurching forward, the seat belt stopping him crashing into the dashboard.

'Dad!'

'Sorry, mate. Let me see that webpage again.'

Isaac found it on his phone and passed it over. Nate studied it closely, zooming in on both images.

'Shit.' Nate grabbed his own phone and punched at the keys. He could hear it ringing at the other end. 'Come on. Come on. Pick up.'

'Nate? You OK?' came Siobhan's voice.

'I need to speak to Harrison. It's urgent.'

'Now? We're just about to go out for lunch—'

'Yes. Now. Please.'

'OK.'

A few seconds later Harrison was on the phone. 'What's up?'

'That Vince Taylor. How old is he?' Nate didn't bother to hide his impatience.

'Er ... Not sure. Let me have a look.'

Nate waited an agonising minute while Harrison located the information he'd found out on Taylor. 'Right, date of birth ... 3 September 1945.'

'What about his parents? Who were they?'

'For God's sake, Nate, I'm CID, not MI5. How the hell would I know that?'

'Can you find out?'

'Probably, but it won't be today.'

'Has he ever been known by any other name?' pushed Nate, his fingers drumming wildly on the top of the steering wheel.

'Again, I don't know without digging deeper. What's going on?'

'Is Vincent his full name?'

'Bloody hell, Nate. What is this?'

'Can you look?'

'Hang on.' The sound of the keys clicking on the keyboard filled the next few seconds before Harrison spoke. 'His full name is Vincent Thomas Taylor. Are you in some kind of trouble, Nate?'

'No. Not me. Thanks.' Nate hung up. He turned to his son. 'Google the meaning of the surname Sartori.'

Isaac peered at his phone and typed in the Italian surname. Nate tried not to lean over and exercised patience like he'd never done before. Finally, Isaac had a result.

'That's funny. It means "tailor". Like Mr Taylor, but spelled T-A-I-L-O-R.'

'Fu— I mean, bother,' Nate said, correcting himself quickly. He immediately called Rhoda's number but it went to voicemail. 'Rhoda, it's me – Nate. Don't go to the viaduct. Something funny's going on. I need to speak to you first.

Taylor hasn't been honest with us. He's something to do with the body in the chapel, I'm sure. He knows the viaduct. It's all connected somehow. I need to work it out, but I don't want you going there. Call me as soon as you get this.'

He was aware it was a rather convoluted and confusing message. His mind was frantically trying to put all the pieces together, but he needed to know Rhoda was safe before he could think about it properly. All he knew was his gut was telling him she was in danger.

37
Alice

1945

'We've got to hide Jack,' Alice said, rushing over to the little lad. 'What about you, Aggie? Are you safe?' Aggie hesitated for a moment, her eyes darting between the adults. Alice was keen to reassure her. 'It's all right. I know. Or at least, I can guess. Tell me, Aggie, does Billy know you know?'

'What are you talking about?' It was Lily's turn to be confused.

Another tense moment passed before Aggie finally spoke. 'He might guess.' Her bottom lip trembled ever so slightly.

'Can someone please tell me what's going on?' insisted Lily.

'Jack and Aggie know how Carlo fell,' said Alice, her gaze fixed on Aggie. 'I'm right, aren't I?'

The twelve-year-old nodded her head, taking hold of Jack's hand at the same time. 'We were hiding in the barn – we'd taken some apples from the store. We were hungry but we knew we wouldn't be allowed to eat anything. Not with rationing still in place and all that. Cook wouldn't let us.'

'It's all right, you don't have to explain,' said Alice reassuringly. 'What did you see happen in the barn?'

Aggie scuffed at the floor with her shoe. 'Billy told Carlo there was a dead rat in the hayloft. Said Carlo was to go up there and get it.'

'Then what?' prompted Alice, when Aggie ground to a halt.

'Carlo couldn't find it.'

'Did he see you?'

Aggie nodded. 'He looked at us and saw us with the apples. He put his finger to his lips and pushed some straw over us.'

'So Billy wouldn't know you were there,' said Lily. 'Dear Carlo. He was such a kind man.'

Alice squeezed Lily's hand. She gave Aggie a small encouraging smile. 'What happened after that?'

'Carlo said there weren't any rats. Billy told him he was blind and climbed up the ladder. We stayed where we were. We were too scared to move. Next thing, Billy was saying how sick he was of the Eyeties being there. Carlo told Billy he was a bitter man who couldn't accept he was discharged from the army. Carlo said he knew it was Billy who broke Paolo's stained glass.' Aggie glanced over at Paolo's workbench. 'Next thing, they were fighting. Billy grabbed Carlo in a headlock … Carlo couldn't move. Billy was too strong … He twisted Carlo's head.' Aggie's voice broke.

Jack took up the story. 'There was a big crack like a stick

being broken. Carlo went all limp, like a dead rabbit, and Billy threw him down from the loft.'

Alice and Lily both gasped, and Paolo muttered something which Alice assumed was a curse in his native tongue.

'He broke Carlo's neck before he fell.' Paolo gave a roar and thumped his hand hard on the workbench, narrowly missing the glass.

'And how does Billy know you saw this?' asked Alice.

'I don't know,' said Aggie. 'We stayed hidden. When he left, we climbed out of the back window of the barn and slid down the pulley rope. We ran around the barn and made it look like we were coming from the chapel. Billy was standing outside smoking. He stopped us and pulled a strand of straw from Jack's hair and asked where Jack had been.'

'What did you say?' asked Lily, wiping a tear from her face.

'We just said it was from earlier,' explained Aggie.

'Did he believe you?' Lily blinked more tears away.

'He just looked at us for a long time before telling us to clear off,' replied Aggie. 'We came through the gate and that's when we saw Alice.'

'Have you told anyone else?' asked Alice. 'Did you say anything to your mother?' She directed the question at Jack.

'No,' said Jack, 'but I keep having bad dreams. She said I was talking in my sleep about Carlo being pushed. She said I was saying a lot last night. I can't help it. I don't know what I say when I'm asleep.'

'It's all right,' said Alice. 'You're not in trouble. It's not your fault. I wonder if your mother mentioned it to Billy this morning and that's why he's come back in a rage.'

The door flew open, making everyone jump and turn. Billy stepped into the chapel, his beady rat-like eyes taking in the scene before him. Alice automatically pulled Jack and Aggie behind her, while Lily stood next to her and Paolo moved in front of them.

'Well, well, well, look what we have here,' mused Billy, a smirk on his face. 'Looks like a mothers' meeting. Might have known Paolo would be gossiping with the women and children.' He moved into the building, pushing the door closed with his walking stick. 'So, has my dear little stepbrother been telling tales out of school? Or is it his cocky cousin?'

Jack flinched at the words and Alice squeezed his hand. 'Leave the kids alone,' she said, trying to sound braver than she felt.

'Or you'll do what?' Billy was clearly in his element. 'You'll get your cowardly friend here to protect you? I wouldn't count on him being any use. He'll end up like his mate.'

Alice managed to grab Paolo before he'd had time to translate what Billy was saying. 'Don't, Paolo! He's baiting you. He wants you to get angry.'

Paolo shrugged off her arm and planted his feet firmly on the ground, his legs astride. He fixed his gaze on Billy. 'I am not scared of you.'

'You should be, mate,' said Billy. 'Anyway, I'm saving you for another day. In the meantime, I need to speak to Jack and Aggie. Come on, you two. Back to the house now.'

'You stay where you are,' Lily ordered to the children.

'Oh dear, girls, please don't be tiresome,' sighed Billy. He moved closer to them.

'Leave them alone,' said Paolo.

His voice was firm and strong, unlike Alice had ever heard before. He may have been smaller in stature than Billy, but he was stronger, she was sure. She'd felt his hard biceps and firm chest. Alice had no doubt Paolo would win if it came to a fight. Sadly, though, he would win only the battle, and not the war. Billy would make him pay in other ways. He'd have Paolo transferred back to the POW camp in a flash.

'Get out of my way,' snarled Billy. Paolo stepped in front of Billy and pushed him backwards. It caught the Englishman off balance and he staggered back a few paces, only saved by his stick to keep him upright. 'You idiot!'

Billy was breathing hard, and from his pocket he pulled out a pistol. Alice had seen the weapon before, when Billy had been cleaning it one evening in front of the fire. It was his service pistol – he'd never handed it back in and somehow it had slipped through the net. What she didn't know was whether it was loaded.

'Don't do anything stupid now, Billy,' warned Alice. 'Put the gun away.'

'I don't think you're in any position to tell me what to do.' Billy waved the gun at her. 'Now, be a good girl, and stand back.'

Before Alice realised what was happening, Paolo had launched himself at Billy, grabbing the muzzle of the gun and grappling for control. Chaos ensued and then, all of a sudden, the gun went off.

Alice didn't know who had screamed the loudest but they dived for cover among the pews. Fortunately, the bullet implanted itself in the chapel wall.

The two men struggled with each other as they tried to

gain control of the gun. Every now and then, Alice had to duck behind the pew when the pistol was waved in their direction. She poked her head back up over the wooden bench. From behind Billy, she could see Jack. He must have sneaked around when she wasn't watching him.

Alice jumped to her feet. 'Jack!'

If he'd heard her, he ignored her. It was then that she realised he was brandishing a solid brass candlestick that usually sat at the side of the church, near the baptism font. It was at least a foot long, and Jack was holding it in the air behind his shoulder. Paolo and Billy were bent double in a tangle of limbs as they wrestled for the gun.

'Jack!' Alice yelled at him again. 'Stop!'

It was too late.

There was a sickening thud as the candlestick came into contact with bone, and the men collapsed in a heap. The gun went flying across the flagstones.

There was a second or two of silence before Alice sprang into action, rushing out from the pew to grab the pistol. She picked it up, her hands shaking wildly as she tried to keep her aim steady towards the men on the ground.

There was a groan – she didn't know who from – followed by another. Paolo rolled on to his back and got to his feet. Then Billy, swearing like mad, pushed himself on to his hands and knees, swaying slightly. He put his hand to his head, and when he took it away, his fingers were red with blood.

'You stupid fucking kid,' he mumbled.

'Alice, give me the gun,' said Paolo steadily.

Alice shook her head. 'No.'

'Please, Alice. Just give him the gun,' pleaded Lily.

'I can't. If he has the gun, then he will be charged with attempted murder or trying to escape, or something like that.'

She didn't take her eyes off Billy, who was now pulling on his stick to get to his feet.

It took a moment for him to focus properly. 'Alice, what are you doing with that gun? Give it to me.'

'NO!' She gripped it with both hands to keep her aim steady. 'Stay away.'

Alice had no idea how she was going to get out of this; all she knew was that she had to protect everyone in the chapel, including Paolo, despite what he thought. Her head felt fuzzy. Her legs were jiggling with fear, and she wasn't sure how much longer she'd be able to stay on her feet.

'You have to give me the gun,' said Paolo. 'I can end this.'

Alice looked at him. 'I won't let you do that.' Tears blurred her eyes.

Without warning, Billy launched himself at her. Paolo reacted instantly, with Lily just a split second behind as they all tried to grab the gun. It was a complete blur. Alice could hear everyone shouting.

'Give it to me!'

'Let go!'

'Get back!'

She didn't know who was shouting what. The words were reverberating around the chapel, bouncing off the walls, clashing and clattering like crockery being smashed.

BANG!

Immediately after the gun discharged, there was silence. The huddle of Alice, Paolo, Lily, Billy – and somehow Aggie had got herself in the ruck – all stopped still, looking at one another in shock.

Alice looked from one shocked and ashen face to the other, each covered with blood. Her gaze travelled to Billy, to Paolo, and then back to Billy again.

They all stepped back, in an unconscious synchronised movement. The gun dropped from the group of hands. Blood spurted from Billy's throat. His hand instinctively went to his neck to try to stem the bleeding, but it was futile. Within seconds it was streaming out between his fingers. He dropped to his knees. He swayed. His eyes were glazed and unfocused. Then he keeled over. He was dead before his face hit the stone floor.

Alice grabbed the edge of the pew as her body reacted to the sight of the dead body in front of her. Lily grabbed her arm and made her sit down.

'Is he dead?' came the small voice of Aggie.

'Yes, he's dead,' said Lily. 'Don't look. Come and sit over here. You too, Jack.'

Alice fought to calm her breathing. She needed to think. Needed to work out what they must do now. She looked across at Paolo. He had sunk to the ground and was leaning back against the end of the pew on the opposite aisle, his arms folded over his drawn knees and his head bowed.

'Are you all right, Paolo?' she asked.

It took a moment, but then he looked up at her and gave a swift nod. 'Are you?'

'I think so.'

'Is everyone all right?' Paolo got to his feet and dragged a hand down his face as he surveyed the dead body in front of him.

'What are we going to do?' ventured Lily.

'We have to tell the police,' said Paolo. 'We need to explain exactly what happened.'

Alice jumped to her feet. 'No.' She went over to Paolo. 'We're not calling the police.'

'What?' Lily shifted closer to Aggie and put her arm around the girl. 'We've got to. We can't just leave him here.'

Alice clasped her hands together, raising them to her mouth as if in prayer. 'If we call the police, they will want to know who killed Billy.'

'Naturally,' said Lily, albeit unnecessarily.

Alice continued, 'Well, who did kill Billy?' She purposely avoided looking at the dead man. She needed to keep a clear head, and watching the blood pool around his body wasn't helping. 'Which one of us killed him?'

'I had hold of the gun,' said Lily.

'So did I,' said Paolo.

'And I did as well,' said Alice. 'Not to mention Aggie … So which one of us pulled the trigger?'

The question hung in the air.

'I don't know,' said Lily at last.

'Exactly,' said Alice. 'It could even have been Billy himself. And what if Jack hitting him on the head was enough to kill him? You don't always die straight away from a head injury. I don't know about you, but I saw blood trickle from his nose. He could have been bleeding on the brain.'

'Oh, don't say that.' Lily bit her lip. 'Jack couldn't have killed him.'

'Alice is right,' said Paolo at last. 'Any one of us could be responsible for his death. So, what we do now is very important.' He took a deep breath. 'We call the police. I will confess to killing Billy. I alone struggled with him. That way, none of you will be suspected. They will accept it was me – a prisoner. Of course I cannot be trusted. I am a killer.'

'NO!' Alice didn't mean to shout as loud as she did, and her voice echoed around the chapel. 'No. I won't let you do that. If you confess, then I will confess, too. They won't believe you – like you said, you're not to be trusted. They will believe an English girl over an Italian POW.'

She didn't mean to hurt his feelings by being so blunt, but now wasn't the time to worry about that. There was no way she was going to let Paolo take the blame.

'What are we going to do, then?' asked Lily. 'We can't all confess to killing him. They will ultimately make their own minds up, and I'm sure they will be happy for Paolo to take the blame. And what about Mrs Hartwell? I know Billy wasn't her son, but she won't want us here anymore. We'll be homeless – and you in your condition, as well. She won't be able to let us stay.' Lily was on her feet as the panic set in.

'I know exactly what we're going to do,' said Alice. 'Now, listen to me, everyone.'

38
Rhoda

2022

It was only when Rhoda was driving over to the viaduct that she questioned how much of a coincidence it was that James Smith should have chosen a meeting point within half an hour's drive of Telton Hall. He hadn't asked her where she was based, or even if it was convenient. For all he knew, she could still be in West Sussex. It bothered her, but she didn't have time to question it. Maybe he'd heard she was working on the chapel windows. After all, it had been reported in the paper recently. That would be the logical explanation, wouldn't it?

Her phone rang, but it was in her bag in the footwell and she didn't want to pull over to answer it – she didn't have time. All she could think about was meeting this James Smith. If he had information about Dean, then she wasn't about to give up that opportunity. She was sure it was more than a wild goose chase; after all, he'd given her the nickname that Dean had used for her. He'd said 'Rhodes' in his message; only Dean had called her that. It must be him.

The traffic was insufferably busy and slow-moving. Rhoda was checking her watch constantly. It didn't help that she had to rely on the satnav to get her there; she wasn't familiar with the area and didn't know any possible short cuts or traffic hotspots to avoid.

Finally, she reached Telverton Viaduct. The brick-built Victorian engineering feat dominated the landscape, curling its way through the valley, spanning the river with over twenty arches as it loomed a good fifteen metres above the countryside.

Once a railway line, it was now part of a local walk. Rhoda parked the hire car in the parking area and followed the signs for access to the structure. Hers was the only vehicle in the car park. The wet and windy weather had put off any sightseers or walkers.

She climbed stone steps, which ran up the side of the viaduct. The steps were wet and a little slippery underfoot. The only barrier to falling to the concrete below was a single handrail. By the time she reached the top, her legs were aching, and she was breathing heavily. On a better day, the view must be wonderful, but Rhoda had no mind for stopping and taking in the scenery around her. It was eerily quiet at the top, with just the wind buffeting her hair around her face. She pulled it back and, fishing a bobble from her pocket, secured it in a ponytail.

Rhoda looked along the walkway of the viaduct. It was empty. She had a sudden fear: she'd come to the wrong place. Was there more than one viaduct? Was there another part to it? She looked back down at the car park, which was still empty.

She took out her phone to check the message she'd received. She was definitely in the right place. She saw she had a missed call from Nate, and a voicemail. Rhoda clicked to listen to it.

'Rhoda, it's me – Nate. Don't go—'

She didn't hear the rest of the message. Her hand dropped away as a figure stepped out on to the viaduct walkway further ahead of her. He was dressed in dark clothing, with a beany hat pulled down over his ears. He was too far away for her to see his features.

Rhoda could hear Nate's voice message playing out on her phone. It sounded distant and thin. She didn't know what he was saying; all she could focus on was the figure in front of her. Was it Dean? Could it be her brother? Her twin. She realised she had no idea what he looked like now. The man standing there was roughly the right height, but of his build she had no idea.

Her throat was dry, and her tongue wanted to cling to the roof of her mouth. She slipped her phone back into her pocket and began to walk towards the man.

'Please let it be Dean. Please let it be Dean.'

She repeated the whispered sentence over and over. Surely, he'd know it was her. It's not like he'd be expecting anyone else. Why wasn't he waving at her? Calling her name? Moving towards her?

It was raining hard, and the droplets stung her face as they hit her skin. The sky had turned a dirty shade of grey and the wind had upped its aggressiveness.

She was about thirty metres away. The man turned and

moved to the side of the viaduct, resting his hands on the wall, looking down at the river below. Rhoda hesitated. This didn't feel right. She closed her eyes for a moment. No … whatever she felt, it was her nerves, her anticipation, her excitement. It was just adrenalin surging through her. If she carried on walking, she'd know soon enough whether it was Dean or not.

Rhoda forced her feet forwards, one in front of the other. If this wasn't Dean, then it must be James Smith, who could tell her where Dean was. She didn't care what he was doing, where he was living – she just needed to know he was alive and happy.

The rain was lashing her face, stinging like tiny kitten claws. She slowed as she got nearer, still unable to make out the man's features. He was looking down, his face obscured by his shoulder and arm.

'Dean? Dean, is that you?' Her voice was whisked away on the wind. 'Dean Sullivan!'

The man didn't look up. She moved forwards. She was just a few metres away from the man. He pushed himself away from the wall and, with his feet planted slightly apart, his arms tense at his sides, he looked up at her.

The rain impaired her vision and Rhoda swiped at a strand of hair that had blown across her face. A flash of lightning lit up the sky, illuminating the figure who was now just a few steps away. Rhoda screamed at the black balaclava hiding the man's face. His eyes stared out at her.

Rhoda froze as she tried to make sense of what she was seeing.

'Dean?' she said, her voice a whisper. She tried again, this time louder. 'Dean? Is that you?'

Thunder rumbled in the sky. She peered harder at the eyes staring back at her. It was impossible to see the colour in this light, but her instincts told her it wasn't her brother. There was something about the eyes – something maleficent. They weren't the kind eyes of Dean.

'I know where your brother is.' The man's voice sounded unnaturally deep and husky. 'I've been in touch with him.'

'You have? You've spoken to him?' Rhoda could hear the tremble in her voice.

'Spoken to a friend of a friend.'

'Where is he? Why isn't he here?' She spun around to check if Dean was maybe standing in the shadows somewhere, waiting to come out.

'You've got to go to him,' said the man. 'He's in Ireland.'

'Ireland? Where? How long has he been there?'

'You've got to get over to Cork. Once you're there, I can set up the meeting.'

Rhoda frowned. 'I've to go to Ireland and wait for instructions? It sounds like a spy movie. It's ridiculous. I need to speak to Dean first.'

'No. You can't. These are the terms. I don't care one way or the other. I can just walk away.'

This didn't sound right at all. Alarm bells were ringing loudly in Rhoda's head. She needed to stop and just think about it for a moment.

'Who are you?' she asked, looking at the man. 'Why the balaclava?'

'It doesn't matter. I'm just the go-between.'

'No. I don't buy it. This is weird.' She wanted to believe this man knew where Dean was, but her gut instinct was telling her something was wrong. 'Take your balaclava off and let me see your face.'

'Look, this isn't part of the deal. You want your brother. You get yourself on a ferry or a plane to Cork in the next two days.'

There was a note of desperation in his voice – and something else. As he spoke, his voice had broken a little and it sounded familiar, but she couldn't place it. She stood her ground for a moment, weighing up what she should do. All her life she'd relied on her gut instinct, and it had never let her down.

'I don't believe you,' she said finally.

Although she could only see his eyes, and despite it being dark, with the rain still lashing down, the anger was undeniable. A sense of danger swamped her. She couldn't explain it, but she knew she couldn't trust this man and had to make her escape. She spun around to run as fast as she could back towards the steps. She wasn't quick enough. Firm fingers caught the back of her hood and yanked at her; the zip dug into her neck, almost choking her as she stumbled backwards.

'Don't go!' the man shouted.

His hand grabbed the top of her arm, his fingers vice-like in their grip.

Rhoda tried to fight him off, but he had managed to grab her wrist and twist it around behind her back into an armlock. She tried to kick him, but he pushed her arm higher up her back, causing her to cry out in pain.

Still holding on to her, the man forced Rhoda over to the wall, shoving her face flat against the cold wet stone. She could feel him lean over her, so his mouth was close to her ear.

'Now, I don't want to hurt you,' he whispered. 'But you've got to stop poking your nose in where it doesn't belong. Stop trying to find out who the body in the chapel is. Do you understand me?'

Rhoda didn't. The chapel? The body? Why was he talking about that when she was here to find Dean?

'Where's my brother?' She attempted to shout, to sound less scared than she was, but the tremble in her voice betrayed her. 'You said you had information.'

She heard the man sigh. 'There is no news on your brother. I just needed to get you on your own.'

Rhoda wanted to cry. No news on Dean. It had all been a hoax. A cruel lie. Her heart plummeted at the realisation, and she felt the fight leach from her.

'Please, just let me go.' A sob rose from her throat.

'You've got to stop with your meddling,' said the man. 'I don't want to have to really hurt you. Do you understand?' He gave her arm a jerk, causing Rhoda to cry out in pain.

'Yes. Yes, I understand.'

'Your obsession with finding who the body at the chapel is has landed you in a lot of trouble. You're good at your job. You should have stuck to restoring windows.'

The rain continued to lash down and thunder roared in the air, the storm showing no sign of letting up. Rhoda's instinct to stay alive kicked in. She knew she was in terrible danger, and she was up here alone. She felt the pressure of the man's hand on her head ease a little. She blinked the raindrops from her eyelids as she looked along the viaduct wall. At first, she thought she was imagining it, but she blinked harder and squinted through the rain. There was someone coming towards them. Running. They were running.

The figure was getting closer. It was Nate! Rhoda's hopes lifted and fell simultaneously. What if Nate couldn't help her? What if she'd put him in danger, too? If she died, probably by being tossed over the edge of the viaduct, it wouldn't matter. She didn't have any family. Not really. Dean was a ghost from her past. She realised that now. He wasn't her present and, if she had a future, he wasn't that either. Whatever had happened to him, whatever decision he'd made, he'd done that knowing he was leaving her behind. What she didn't want now was to drag Nate into this. Nate had so much to live for. He had his father and his son. He didn't deserve this.

The man must have seen Nate, too. He cursed out loud and then shouted towards Nate, 'Stop there! Don't come any closer!'

Nate ground to a halt, his hands outstretched, palms up. 'It's OK. Don't do anything stupid. Just stay calm.'

Rhoda lifted her head to shake the rain from her eyes. Something made her look the other way – a movement. It was Isaac. He was up on the wall, running full pelt towards her. He was holding something above his head.

Rhoda screamed at exactly the same time as she heard Nate cry out his son's name. The man went to turn, but by now Isaac was right behind him. Isaac let out an almighty roar like nothing Rhoda had heard before. She realised he was holding a lump of wood. There was a thud and the man cried out in pain.

Rhoda screamed as the momentum sent Isaac falling forwards. He threw his weight backwards to counterbalance himself. For an awful second, he was at the perfect point of balance. Before she had time to react, the man launched himself towards Isaac, catching him waist-high in a rugby tackle. Nate cried out his son's name. He was too far away to reach him. By some miracle, the man managed to throw himself to the right and fell backwards onto the viaduct walkway.

Pain ripped through Rhoda's arm as she dropped to her knees to grab Isaac from the man's hold. Nate raced towards them, almost sliding in like a baseball player as he enveloped his son, and Rhoda, in his arms.

'Oh, my God. Please tell me you're all right?' Nate gasped.

After the initial flurry of relief, Nate turned his attention to the man. Rhoda had to hold him back from attacking him, despite the white-hot pain searing through her shoulder.

'Nate! No! Stop!'

Nate hurled some obscenities at the man, who had managed to get himself into a sitting position. There was no threat in his body language, just dejection.

Holding her shoulder, Rhoda moved over to him, despite Nate's protests.

'Who the hell are you?' she demanded before pulling off the balaclava. She let out a gasp. 'Vince!' She looked back at Nate as if she needed confirmation.

'What the …?' Nate was equally shocked.

The sound of sirens screaming and wailing in the distance, getting louder with every passing few seconds, filled the air.

'I'm sorry,' said Vince. 'So sorry.' He dropped his head and rubbed at his eyes with his fingertips. 'I was just trying to protect her. That was all.'

'I don't understand,' said Rhoda, not for the first time that night.

'Come here,' said Nate, beckoning Rhoda back to him. 'We'll let the police sort this out.'

39
Rhoda

2022

Rhoda tried to wriggle into a more comfortable position. A night in a hospital bed didn't make for a restful sleep, especially when you had a fractured collarbone. In the previous night's struggle, she had landed heavily on her shoulder and headbutted the ground, leaving a nasty cut to her head which had been glued back together and Steri-Strips applied. The doctor had insisted on a night in the hospital for concussion.

It didn't help that it reminded her of being in care, where there was always something going on in the background: people moving around in the night, talking in hushed tones, doors opening and closing; sometimes, raised voices. Just the whole being somewhere she didn't want to be and having no say in the matter. She didn't like it one bit.

She was in a private room, which Nate had insisted

on, according to the nurse that morning. Rhoda was both grateful and uncomfortable with the idea that he was probably footing the bill for it. She'd have to sort that out with him later.

She rested her head back against the pillow and reflected on the night before. She still wasn't entirely sure about how Vince Taylor was connected to the body in the chapel. Nate had texted that he'd be over as soon as he could, and would explain everything.

As if just thinking about him could conjure him up, the door to her room opened and Nate appeared.

'Hey,' he said, stepping into the room. 'You're awake. How are you?'

'I'm OK.' She couldn't deny the rush of relief that he was there. 'A bit sore but the painkillers are helping. I've got to keep this sling on for about four weeks.' She rolled her eyes.

'How's the head?' Nate asked, inspecting the wound.

'That's sore, too. Might end up with a Harry Potter scar.'

'Good after-dinner story, though.' He gave her a smile and then looked more serious

'Is Isaac OK?'

'He's fine. Taking it all in his stride.'

'What's happened to Vince?' she asked

'He's nursing a sore but otherwise intact head. He was discharged late last night. The police picked him up.'

'He was arrested?'

'Yeah. Common assault.'

Rhoda's eyes widened. 'Are they charging him?'

'Don't know yet.'

'I'm still confused about last night. Why were you there? Who called the police?'

Nate pulled up the chair from the corner of the room, so he was alongside the bed. 'When I was out getting my lunch, I saw Vince Taylor across the road, hopping out of a black X5. I had to do a double take, as he didn't have his walking stick and looked pretty nimble on his feet. It was odd, but I didn't give it a great deal of thought other than maybe he didn't always need it. You know, if he had a back problem or something and only needed it from time to time. I don't know. I was going to tell you about it, but that was the same day I nearly got run over in the car park and, to be honest, I forgot all about it.'

'A black X5?' Rhoda looked at Nate for confirmation, and he nodded. 'I saw one parked outside your aunt's house a couple of times. At first I thought maybe it was a carer. It wouldn't have been Vince, would it?'

'Probably,' said Nate. 'Anyway, when I picked Isaac up earlier, he was chatting away like he does and, out of the blue, asked me if Vince was Italian. He'd seen a picture of Vince at the Tower of Pisa on his website, standing with a woman. I had a look, and he was right. It was definitely Vince.'

'That's right. I remember seeing it when I looked at the website. That was when you told Isaac off for looking at my laptop.'

'Well, that woman … I couldn't be sure, but she really reminded me of Alice Renshaw.' Nate paused as he waited for Rhoda to catch up.

She couldn't. 'Sorry, I am nursing a sore head. I don't understand what you're saying.'

'That the woman in the picture with Vince is his mother. Alice Renshaw is Vince's mother.'

'Bloody hell.'

'I don't know exactly what happened back in 1945 but I had a hunch. I know some of the POWs stayed in England. They married local girls.'

'You think Paolo married Alice?'

'It's possible, I haven't had time to check, or to speak to Vince, but some of them changed their surnames to English names so they could fit in better. The name Sartori means "tailor".'

'Tailor! Vince Taylor. They just changed the spelling. Oh my God.' Another piece of the puzzle fell into place. 'So, the body in the chapel isn't Paolo Sartori, but it's possible that Paolo and/or Alice had something to do with it – otherwise why would their son be trying to stop me finding out the truth?'

'Yep. Although Vince isn't Paolo's son. Vince was born in 1945; Alice arrived at Telton Hall then, presumably pregnant. Paolo and Alice must have got married and brought Vince up as their own. The adoption of the baby couldn't have gone ahead.'

'They might not even have got married,' said Rhoda. 'Alice might have just taken Paolo's name and they lived as a married couple. People did that back then, despite what we think about it being a modern thing to live together. Which would explain why I couldn't find any of them on the ancestry database.'

'I spoke to Dad last night. I told him what happened and what I knew.'

'And?'

'He went white as a sheet. Never seen him look so shocked. It was like he aged ten years in the space of one minute.'

'What did your dad say?'

'Nothing. Eventually, he got up, mumbled something about needing to speak to Aggie, and that was it. He went over there late last night. He came back about midnight. Refused to say anything and went straight to bed. Silent treatment about it this morning. I don't get it.'

'He hasn't said a word?'

'Nope. Not about Vince, anyway. I think he knows what happened at the chapel all those years ago, and if he knows, I'm sure Aggie knows as well.'

Rhoda reached out for Nate's hand. 'I'm sorry.' She could see the anguish in his eyes. 'It's probably why he never wanted to sell the farm. He knew the body would be discovered.'

Nate blew out a long and tired breath. 'I can't believe it.'

They sat in silence for a few minutes. Rhoda's head was beginning to pound as she tried to put everything into order. 'You should try speaking to Aggie.'

'I don't know if she'll be any more forthcoming than Dad. They've closed ranks pretty tightly.'

Another small silence rested between them. It was Rhoda who spoke first.

'If Vince was trying to stop me, it must be because he was trying to protect someone. He would have no reason to protect your dad or Aggie. His vested interest isn't in your family – it's in his.'

Nate slowly raised his head to meet Rhoda's gaze. She could see the significance of her words dawn on him. He sat up straighter. 'Which means Vince must be trying to protect either his mother or Paolo.'

'Exactly.'

'Who do you think the body in the chapel was?' asked Nate.

'It seems pretty obvious to me. It must be Billy – the one who everyone says went off ... sort of disappeared.'

'I need to speak to Dad,' said Nate, getting to his feet. 'I need to speak to him before the police do. They want to take a statement from you. What are you going to say?'

'I'm not sure. If I tell them everything, then that's going to open a whole can of worms. I need to speak to Vince.'

'What – the bloke who tried to kill you? Are you mad?'

'He wasn't trying to kill me. Just frighten me. He was trying to protect his mum or his dad, that's all and it got out of hand.'

'I admire your faith in human nature, but I don't agree.'

'I don't want them to press charges. I want to know what happened up at the chapel all those years ago before I speak to the police.'

'Then maybe I can help,' said a voice from behind them.

'Vince!' Rhoda and Nate said at the same time.

'You need to fuck off, mate,' said Nate, squaring up.

'Nate. Stop.' Rhoda grabbed at his arm. 'Let him talk.'

'You've got one minute,' said Nate, nodding towards the clock on the opposite wall.

Vince gave a small dip of his head before speaking. 'First of all, I want to say how very sorry I am for what I did last night. I never intended to hurt you. I just wanted to scare you off, that's all.'

'You didn't need to try to push her over the edge of the viaduct,' snapped Nate.

Vince bowed his head again. 'I would never have done that. As I said, I was just trying to scare her.'

'I suppose you're going to say that about the scaffolding, too.' Nate scowled at the older man.

Vince looked confused. 'I don't know what you mean.'

Rhoda could see the anger flare in Nate's eyes, and spoke first. 'The handrail was loose. Was that you?'

'No. That wasn't me,' Vince said hurriedly.

'And when we went up the scaffolding and you grappled with me?' asked Rhoda. 'Was that premeditated?'

'I am sorry. I was just trying to unnerve you, but it backfired,' replied Vince, looking suitably embarrassed. 'I was genuinely dizzy. That's why I stumbled.'

'My son nearly went over the edge of that viaduct because of you,' snapped Nate, who wasn't ready to forgive as willingly as Rhoda.

She could see the veins in Nate's temple pulsate. He did, of course, have every right to be angry at Vince for that.

'I cannot apologise enough,' said Vince.

'No shit,' muttered Nate. 'Forty seconds, by the way.'

'Were you acting on your own?' asked Rhoda. 'Or did someone put you up to this?'

Vince looked down at his shoes. 'I'd rather not say.'

'Well, I'd rather you did,' snapped Nate.

Rhoda inwardly winced. Knowing already the answer was only going to upset Nate more, she decided to soften the blow. 'You had been in contact with Aggie, hadn't you? Or maybe she was the one who made contact.'

Nate looked from one to the other. 'What do you mean?'

Vince cleared his throat. 'When my mother heard about the discovery, she was frightened. Aggie had contacted her. I hated to see my mother so scared. I wanted to protect her like she had protected me. She had stood by me before I was even born. How could I not get involved? Ultimately, it was a joint decision by us all.'

Nate's eyes widened. 'They were in on it? My father, too? No, that can't be right.'

'Your father wasn't so keen, but he did know.'

'Was it your car I saw at Aggie's house?' asked Rhoda. 'The X5?'

Vince nodded. 'I used my wife's car when I came to see you. The X5 is mine.' He turned to Nate again. 'If it's any consolation, your father wasn't so keen on me getting involved. It was more me and Aggie.'

'Did you also send the letter, telling me to stay away?' asked Rhoda.

'I apologise.'

'Ten seconds,' said Nate tersely, the anger clearly simmering just below the surface. 'I won't even bother asking if it was you who nearly ran me over in the car park.'

'You never had contact with my brother, did you?' Rhoda knew that, deep down, she just needed to hear Vince say it out loud.

He shook his head. 'I think for that I am most sorry.'

'You had no right to do that,' said Nate.

Rhoda reached for Nate's hand. 'It's OK. Honestly.'

Nate raised his eyebrows but said nothing. Rhoda realised the sadness she felt was for the unexpected acknowledgement that trying to find Dean was a futile quest. Something that probably wasn't going to happen. She parked the thought to one side. She needed more time to process this.

'Time's up,' said Nate.

'There is just one more thing,' said Vince. 'My mother, Alice, would like to talk to you. She wants to explain in her own words.'

40
Alice

2022

Alice had lived in fear of this day ever since that fateful night at Telton Hall chapel. She always knew that one day she'd have to answer for what she'd done. The only consolation now was that her beloved Paolo wasn't here. She'd lost him nearly twelve years ago, and she missed him every single day. She owed him a huge debt of gratitude for what he'd done for her – for loving her and her son. She was determined to stand by him, even in death. No one would hold him responsible for what happened. Alice wouldn't allow it.

Despite this knowledge, she had never envisaged today would come about quite as it had. She should never have asked her son to get involved. Her darling Vincent, the baby she'd so very nearly given up. If it hadn't been for Paolo and his proposal in the days that followed Billy's death, then her baby would have been adopted by the Eggars.

She remembered how kind Mrs Hartwell had been about it, and how guilty Alice had felt betraying her trust and lying to her about Billy's supposed disappearance. It had been an easy lie, though. Billy had often let it be known he hated being at Telton Hall. No one had been surprised – and, dare she say, even sad – to think he'd moved on. It would have been in typical Billy style, too, not to say a word, to just up and leave with no consideration for others.

And now, today, she was having to pay for her sins.

In front of her, in her house in Bristol, now sat Vincent, Jack, Aggie, Nate Hartwell and a young woman who had been the driving force behind unearthing the secrets of the chapel. They were all sitting expectantly, waiting for her to speak.

Alice looked to her son. Her darling boy, whom she'd put in an untenable position. Vincent had read about the body in the chapel and, of course, knew her connection to Telton Hall – his adoption by Paolo had never been kept a secret. Vincent had heard her soon afterwards on the phone to Aggie. Alice had been lackadaisical in what she said, not realising Vincent had called in to see her. He'd heard her discussing the possible repercussions with Aggie, and when she'd finished the call, she'd allowed herself to indulge in tears. Vincent had been so alarmed at her crying; he'd insisted she tell him the truth. In a moment of weakness, Alice had found herself confessing. How selfish she'd been to share that burden with her son. She should have known he would try to protect her. And it had all got out of hand.

'Mum?' said Vincent, breaking her thoughts.

*

'We're never going to get away with this,' whispered Lily as she and Alice climbed down from the horse and cart, in the builder's yard.

'We will. Trust me,' insisted Alice, trying to remain patient. Lily had fussed the whole way down from Telton Hall to the village. 'Let me do the talking.'

The bell jingled as they entered the shop front of the yard.

'Good afternoon, ladies.' Mr Michaels greeted them from behind the counter. 'What can I do for you?'

Alice smiled and cleared her throat, trying to act as casual as possible. 'We need three paving slabs. Mrs Hartwell meant to organise them, but she forgot.'

'Mrs Hartwell?' Mr Michaels frowned. 'It's usually Billy who sorts materials out for Telton Hall. Where's he?'

From the corner of her eye Alice was aware Lily had shot her a look. Alice kept her gaze and voice steady. 'Billy's asked us to come down.'

Mr Michaels' frown deepened as he eyed Alice's bump. 'Really?'

'You know what he's like,' said Alice. 'Please, could you help us? I don't want to upset him.'

Mr Michaels' face softened. 'No. Of course not. Right, I'll get one of the boys to load the cart. Then I'll sort out a ticket for you to take back for Mrs Hartwell to settle at the end of the month.'

'Oh ... err ... Billy's given us cash,' said Alice hastily.

'Cash? That's not like him. He likes to take full advantage of the twenty-eight days.'

Alice pulled the notes from her purse. They had taken the money from the petty cash tin Billy kept in the bureau. 'He insisted we give you cash today.'

She gave a shrug and Mr Michaels accepted the payment, before writing out a receipt and shouting through to the yard hand to load up the cart with the slabs.

Soon they were back at Telton Hall, driving the cart around to the west side of the hill where the track wasn't so steep and would allow Pegasus to pull the cart to the top.

Aggie and Jack were sitting on the remains of the uprooted tree, looking very solemn.

'I don't want to go back in there,' said Lily. 'I don't think I can face looking at Billy again.'

'Wait there with them,' said Alice, nodding towards the youngsters. She climbed down from the cart. A sharp pain shot through her stomach, making her wince and hold on to the wheel for support.

'Alice! Are you all right?' Lily jumped down.

Alice took a couple of deep breaths. 'Yes. I'm fine. Just the baby kicking, that's all.'

She pushed open the door and peered around. Where Billy's body had been, there was now just a pool of blood.

Paolo was over by the side of the chapel. He looked up as she came in. 'It is all right. I have moved him. You do not have to look at him now.'

Despite this, Alice went over to stand next to Paolo, looking down at their former tormentor. 'I need to see for myself,' she said.

Paolo held out the ring he'd made to her. 'It was in his pocket.'

Alice took it. 'I don't want it. Not now he's touched it.' She threw it into the shallow grave next to Billy.

'I will give you another ring one day.' Paolo pulled something from his top pocket and held it out to show

Alice. 'It is the two bullets from when the gun was fired. I dug one out of the wall. The other went straight through his neck. I found it over the other side. I will get rid of them somewhere else.'

'Give them to me,' said Alice, taking the bullets from him. 'I'll drop it in one of the ditches up by the top field.'

Paolo picked up the shovel and began scooping up the earth and throwing it onto the body. 'It is good there is an earth floor.'

'Me and Lily will go back to the house now and do what we said.'

'Yes. Go. I can do this on my own. Take the children with you.'

Alice paused and then hugged Paolo, holding him tightly. It was so surreal what they were doing – the conversation they'd all had – but at the same time it was all too real, and she couldn't think of any alternative. Not one that wouldn't see at least her, Lily and Paolo tried for murder.

'It will be all right,' she whispered into Paolo's shirt collar.

'We stay together. We trust each other. We will be strong together.' He kissed the top of her head. 'Now, go.'

Alice hurried down to the house with Lily, Aggie and Jack in tow. They bustled in through the kitchen.

'Right, you two, stay here,' instructed Lily. 'Jack, if you see anyone coming, you let us know straight away and, Aggie, you keep whoever it is talking. You understand?'

The two youngsters nodded.

'It will only be Cook, if anyone at all,' said Lily.

Alice and Lily hurried up to Billy's room.

'There's his case on top of the wardrobe,' said Alice.

'Let me get that.' Lily used the stool from the bathroom to lift the suitcase down.

Alice set about emptying Billy's drawers of clothing, while Lily saw to the wardrobe.

'Just get as much as you can,' said Alice. 'It doesn't matter if we leave a few things. If he was going, he'd only take what he could fit in the case. Don't worry about his work stuff.'

It didn't take long to ram the case full of Billy's clothes and the few possessions he had.

Out at the end of the garden, Lily dropped the case onto the bonfire and Alice doused it with some petrol from a can Paolo had found in the shed. Alice struck a match and threw it onto the suitcase. The fuel ignited immediately and Lily had to yank Alice back from the whoosh of flames.

They stood there in the garden, watching the case and its contents burn. Black smoke billowed into the air, before being blown over the wall and away from the garden.

Alice looked up at the faces sitting around her, bringing her back to the present day.

'We thought we were doing the right thing,' she said.

'What happened after Paolo buried the body?' asked Rhoda.

'We stuck to our story,' replied Alice. 'When Cook came in the next day, we made out we didn't know where Billy was. We acted all surprised that he didn't come down for breakfast.'

'And what about Mrs Hartwell?' Rhoda probed. 'What did you tell her?'

'The same. We didn't know where he was.' Jack dipped his head and clasped his hands together. 'All his clothes were gone. His money was gone. It was logical he'd just left. My mother was relieved, I think. Billy wasn't very nice to live with.'

'He was horrid,' said Alice. 'If Lily was still alive, she'd tell you that as well. Anyone that knew him knew what a cruel, horrible man he was.'

'Does that make what you did right, though?' asked Rhoda.

'No. Of course it doesn't.' It was Jack again. 'It wasn't right, but we were all kids. We were frightened. We didn't know what we were doing.' He looked around at the others in the room. 'You have to remember we were all very young when it happened, and the decisions we took then were without the benefit of age and wisdom.'

'Don't think over the years we haven't wished we'd handled it differently,' said Aggie.

'You see,' said Jack, 'I believe it was me who killed Billy.' He clasped his hands together and hunched forwards, not able to meet anyone's gaze.

'Don't say that, Jack,' said Alice, looking at him and seeing the boy of ten sitting there. He had carried this burden of belief and guilt for so many years.

'I delivered the blow that would have killed him,' he continued, 'regardless of what happened with the gun. I know everyone struggled with the gun and think it could have been them, but I could never get over what I had done. It has haunted me all my life. When I was a boy, I had nightmares about it. I would dream of being arrested and charged with murder, of swinging from the gallows. It got so bad, I think these days, they would say it impacted on my mental health.'

'Oh, Jack,' sighed Rhoda. 'That's a terrible burden.'

'Ultimately, the blame has to lie with me,' said Aggie, a look of compassion for her cousin sweeping her face. 'You can't blame Jack. I got in touch with Alice when I realised you weren't going to give up trying to identify the body.'

'And I asked Vincent to help,' said Alice. 'We were all still looking out for ourselves and each other. I'm sorry.'

'There's something I don't understand.' Rhoda looked at Vincent. 'Why did you make me go to the viaduct?'

Alice let out a sigh. She wished she hadn't asked her son to help. She hated the thought of the consequences. She'd been able to live with what had happened to Billy, but she had protected her son all his life and after all that, she'd dragged him into it at the last moment.

'I wish I'd never asked Vincent to help,' she said.

'It's all right, Mum,' said Vincent. 'It's not your fault. I could have said no.' He looked at Rhoda. 'I tried to talk to you. Tried to persuade you not to keep looking, but you were adamant. You kept saying you wanted justice for the dead man. There was no reasoning with you.'

'So, why the viaduct?'

'Originally, I thought if I could distract you and send you off on a wild goose chase about your brother, you'd lose interest in the chapel business. The viaduct seemed like a good place to get you on your own. At night, in the dark and with a balaclava, you wouldn't recognise me. I wanted to make you think about finding your brother and stop you thinking about the chapel.'

'How did you know to call me Rhodes? In the message, you used the name that Dean used to use. How did you know about that?'

Vince dropped his gaze. 'I'm sorry—'

Rhoda cut him off. 'Oh, God, it was you at my flat, wasn't it?' She threw her arms up. 'You broke into my flat. You found those letters from Dean. That's how you knew!'

'I'm sorry,' said Vince again.

'How did you know where I lived?'

'I followed you home,' said Vince. 'It was after one of the first visits.'

Rhoda jumped to her feet and pushed her hand through her hair. Nate was at her side, his arm around her. He glared back over his shoulder at the others in the room.

Alice could see the anger in his eyes, and he had every right to feel that way. What they had all done was unforgivable. She looked over at Jack, whose head was in his hands.

'We should have just come clean and none of this would be happening,' he said. 'We should have taken our punishment there and then.' He began to cry.

Alice felt tears come to her eyes as she looked at him. All she could see was the dear little ten-year-old boy she remembered from Telton Hall. She reached over and put her hand on his arm. 'Darling Jack, you were just a little lad. You had no say in it. It was my idea. I'm responsible. We may not know who actually pulled the trigger, but we adults … we made the decision to do what we did. And I am so sorry you and Aggie were both given the burden to bear for all your lives.'

Jack rose from his chair and went over to Alice. He took her hand. 'You don't have to be sorry.'

'What happens now?' she asked. 'Are the police going to arrest me? What's going to happen to Vincent?'

There was a long silence. It was Rhoda who spoke first. 'Nothing happens now.' She turned to face the room. 'I don't want to press charges against Vince. I haven't told the police anything. They're not interested.'

'But I thought ...' began Nate.

Alice watched as Nate and Rhoda held a long gaze. The young woman spoke first.

'I wanted to find out who the body in the chapel was in case there were family out there, wondering what had happened to their son or brother or uncle. As it turns out, his family knew all along. That's all I wanted to know. What happens now is not up to me. It's up to you.' She indicated to Alice, Aggie and Jack.

'You can't confess now,' said Jack, still holding Alice's hand. 'Not after all this time. You're ninety-five years old.'

'I haven't got much time left,' said Alice. 'I need to make my peace.'

'No. You can't.' Aggie picked up her bag and took out a letter. 'This is Paolo's confession to killing Billy.'

Alice felt her heart throw in an extra beat. 'What do you mean?'

'Before you left, Paolo came to me with this letter,' explained Aggie. 'He said in it, he has confessed to killing Billy and burying his body in the chapel. It says he acted alone. Out of jealousy. He got into a fight and shot Billy with his own gun.'

'Why didn't you ever say?' asked Jack.

'Because he made me promise I was only to use this letter if one of us, Alice especially, decided to go to the police after he'd died. He didn't know when or if he'd see me again, but he made me promise to keep the letter. And I have. I've kept it all these years.'

'You must burn that at once,' said Alice. 'He can't take the blame.'

'I'm not burning it,' said Aggie. 'Paolo loved you. He would do anything to keep you safe. He took on your child. He changed his name and married you.' She paused and turned to Rhoda. 'Yes, I was bridesmaid. I know I told you I wasn't, but now you know why I couldn't tell you the truth.'

'You don't have to explain,' replied Rhoda.

Aggie now looked back at Alice. 'Paolo stayed here in England when he could have gone home. He did all that because he loved you. I'm not going to disrespect his wishes. You can say what you like, but I have a signed confession.'

'I don't want his name dragged through the mud,' said Alice. Her darling Paolo. The only man she'd ever really loved. Aggie was right; he'd given up so much for her, there was no way she was going to let his name be tarnished.

'What good will come of confessing now?' asked Jack. 'We've lived this long with our guilt. It's a lifetime's punishment. If you go to the police, then I'll go, too, and say it was me.'

'And I'll go as well and say it was me,' said Aggie.

'We're back to where we were all those years ago,' said Alice eventually. 'Except with two more accomplices.'

She looked up at Jack's son and the young woman, Rhoda, who met her gaze for several moments before speaking.

'All I hear is three elderly people reminiscing over rumours and speculation as to what happened back in 1945,' said Rhoda. 'What about you, Nate?'

Nate looked at Alice, his father and aunt, before turning to Rhoda. He gave a shrug. 'Just old folk talking about nothing. You know what it's like at their age – they get facts and fiction muddled up.'

41
Rhoda

2022

'Dad rang the number of that housing officer you gave him,' said Nate, as he helped Rhoda into the car.

'Yes. He told me just now.' Rhoda sat back so Nate could lean across and pull the seat belt over for her. With her arm still in a sling, she was limited as to what she could do. A week on from all the antics at the viaduct, Nate was taking her back to hospital for a check-up. 'I'm so glad he did.'

'He's got two places to go and look at next week,' said Nate, clipping the seat belt in place. 'Thanks to you.'

'Are you and your dad OK?' asked Rhoda. She knew Nate had been shocked by the revelations.

'We're good,' replied Nate. 'I just keep thinking of him as a ten-year-old kid who was frightened and haunted by what happened. I keep thinking of Isaac, and imagining how awful it would be if it were him. I hate the thought that Dad suffered mentally, you know … was tortured by it all.'

Rhoda smiled. 'You're a good man, Nate Hartwell.'

She watched him as he walked around the front of the car and got in the driver's seat. Nate had been so good to her this past week. Both he and Jack had insisted she stay at Telton Hall, as not only did she need looking after while she was one-handed, but she couldn't possibly drive back to West Sussex, and Nate had no intention of driving her himself. She'd made a half-hearted protest and bandied about words like 'hostage', 'free will' and 'independence', but she was happy to stay with the Hartwells, especially Nate.

'And there's more good news,' she said as Nate took his seat behind the wheel. 'The council and the developers have agreed to extend the completion of the sale by another month. That will definitely give your dad time to move, and me time to finish the window. I really don't want anyone else brought in to do it, not now after all that's happened. Not just the last few weeks, but what happened all those years ago.'

'That is good news. Also, it means I'll see a lot more of you.' Nate smiled at her and put the car into gear before pulling away.

The consultation with the hospital went well and on the way home, they stopped at a pub for lunch.

'How are you feeling about the disappointment of not finding Dean?' asked Nate.

Rhoda picked at the edge of the sling. 'I was upset when I realised what Vince had done,' she said at last. 'How he'd tricked me. But all this has made me realise I can't put my life on hold. I may never know what's happened to Dean, but I'm going to try to live with that. I've done everything I can to try to find him, and after ten years I need to move on with my life. I need to let myself live – if that makes sense?'

'It does.' Nate reached across and squeezed her hand.

'In my head I've drawn that line, and now I'm ready to cross it because I have something to cross it for. I've only ever had my past, but now I think I might have a future.' She gave Nate a poignant look and hurried on, speaking before he could say anything. 'I'm going to close the Facebook page down. My private profile is on there. I'll just update it with a few details, so if Dean ever does try to find me, he won't have to look too hard.' It had been a difficult decision, but Rhoda knew it was the right thing to do. 'I have to accept, like you said, that maybe he doesn't want to be found. Let's face it, who wants to reconnect with a shit childhood like we had?'

'You're very brave. I admire you for that.' Nate drew her hand up and kissed her knuckles, sending a tingle up Rhoda's arm.

They stayed at the pub for another drink before finally heading back to Telton Hall.

'Honestly, I'm fine,' insisted Rhoda, as Nate helped her from the car. 'The doctor is very happy with everything. You don't need to fuss.'

'The doctor also said you're to go home and rest. And you're to be looked after.'

'I've fractured my collarbone, that's all.'

'You're still in a sling.' Nate reached out and took her

hand. 'Stop being so stubborn, not to mention independent, and let me look after you.'

Rhoda wanted to say yes. Every fibre in her body was screaming yes, she wanted to be looked after – but vocalising it just wasn't happening. She squeezed his hand and nodded.

'I'm going to take that as a yes,' said Nate.

'Is your dad always this bossy?' Rhoda asked Isaac, who had appeared on the driveway to greet them.

'He likes you,' said Isaac, his nose in his phone as he walked towards Telton Hall. 'He likes you a lot.'

Rhoda raised her eyebrows. 'Is that so?'

'Err … It is so, as it happens,' said Nate. 'Just didn't plan on letting you know quite so soon. Was going for the stealth approach, where I'd make you like me a lot, too. So much so, that you'd find some excuse to keep coming back down to Somerset once the window was finished.'

'A plan to like you a lot, huh?' said Rhoda, coming to a halt facing Nate.

'Yeah. A lot a lot.'

Rhoda leaned over and kissed him. 'Don't think you need to worry about a plan for that. You can tick that off as already achieved.'

'I can?' He kissed her this time.

'Yeah.'

'I need to level up.'

'Next level sounds good to me,' said Rhoda. 'Does this next level have a name?'

Before Nate could answer, Isaac's voice called out.

'Love! L-O-V-E Noun. An intense feeling of deep affection.'

Rhoda and Nate both laughed.

'He's way ahead of us,' grinned Nate.

'Oh, I don't know. I think it's more like he has the measure of us,' said Rhoda, before kissing Nate again.

About the Author

SUZANNE FORTIN also writes as Sue Fortin, a USA Today and Amazon UK & USA best-selling author, with *The Girl Who Lied* and *Sister Sister* both reaching #1 in the Amazon UK Kindle chart in 2016 and 2017 respectively. Her books have sold over a million copies and translation rights for her novels have been sold worldwide. She was born in Hertfordshire but had a nomadic childhood, moving often with her family, before eventually settling in West Sussex where she now lives with her husband and family.

Find her online at www.suefortin.com

Acknowledgements

As with getting any book to publication, there is a whole team of people behind the author helping to make that happen and I have been fortunate enough to have the fabulous team at Aria working on this book. Many thanks to my editors Hannah Todd and Martina Arzu for all their feedback and insight into making this story the best it can be.

I also want to thank my ace agent, Hattie Grünewald, who has been with me every step of the way with this book and offered many words of wisdom and encouragement.

Lastly, I'd like to acknowledge the Somerset village of East Chinnock and Anton Günther, the latter a German prisoner of war, held at a camp in Yeoville, whose story and connection with the village church inspired this book.